The Wolf Pack

THE WOLF PACK

Book 1 of The Wolves of Vimar

V. M. Sang

Copyright (C) 2013 V. M. Sang
Layout Copyright (C) 2016 Creativia

Published 2016 by Creativia
Book design by Creativia (www.creativia.org)
Cover art by http://www.thecovercollection.com/
Edited by Deanna Turner, Past Tense Books
This book is a work of fiction. Names, characters, places, and incidents are the product of the author's imagination or are used fictitiously. Any resemblance to actual events, locales, or persons, living or dead, is purely coincidental.
All rights reserved. No part of this book may be reproduced or transmitted in any form or by any means, electronic or mechanical, including photocopying, recording, or by any information storage and retrieval system, without the author's permission.

To my Children

Diane and Richard

The Continent of Khalram

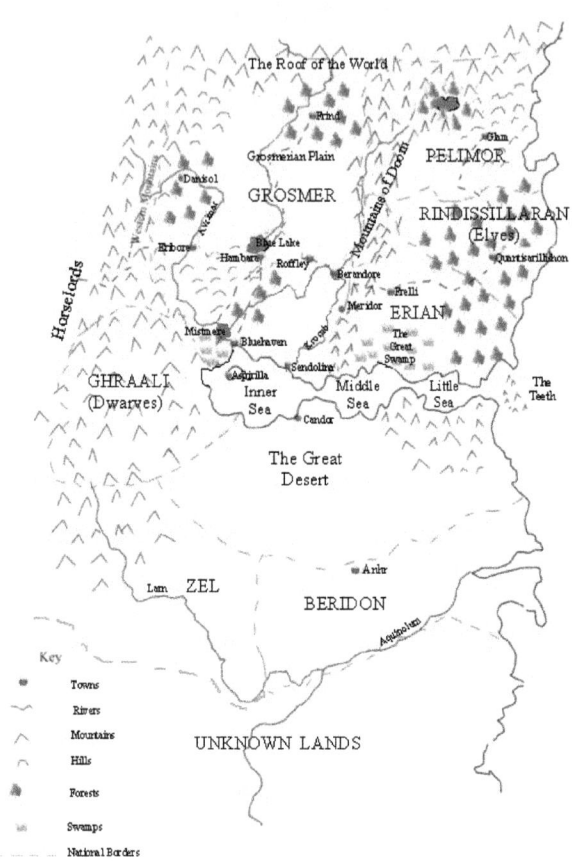

Contents

Prologue   1

Chapter 1: The Duke   5

Chapter 2: Thad   15

Chapter 3: Asphodel   22

Chapter 4: Job-Hunting   37

Chapter 5: Yssalithissandra   46

Chapter 6: Quest   54

Chapter 7: Research   68

Chapter 8: Translation   84

Chapter 9: Decisions   99

Interlude   110

Part 2: The Journey   112

Chapter 10: Followed   113

Chapter 11: Attack	131
Chapter 12: Roffley	138
Chapter 13: Wolf	160
Chapter 14: Mountains	171
Chapter 15: Yeti	179
Chapter 16: Valley	194
Chapter 17: Tomb	209
Interlude	230
Part 3: Homeward	**234**
Chapter 18: Hobgoblins	235
Chapter 19: Shepherd	246
Chapter 20: Quantissarillishon	256
Chapter 21: Bandits	271
Chapter 22: Home	291
Chapter 23: Nandala	313
Chapter 24: Yssa	329
Epilogue	337

Prologue

The Most High of Kalhera looked at his visitor.

'This is most irregular. What you propose is possible, but forbidden.'

The magister replied, 'I realise that, Your Holiness. That's why I've come to see you. I need your permission to perform the rite and to provide a cleric who can do it.'

'You would deny Kalhera some souls. She doesn't like that, you know. If you deny her these, she will demand some others in recompense. That is the way.'

The magister looked the Most High in the eye. He held the gaze of the other as he told him, 'It will not be for all time.'

He held up his hand as the Most High opened his mouth to speak. 'I cannot say for how long these souls will be denied to Kalhera,' he went on. 'It may be a few years, or it may be millennia. Your Holiness, I have had a dream. Sometime in the future, these souls will be returned. Please, grant me permission to perform the rite.'

The Most High looked at the magister and then he rose. 'I will go and commune with the goddess. If she permits it, I will grant you both your requests, permission to perform the rite, and a cleric to perform it. I believe it requires both a Cleric of Death and a mage?'

With that, the Most High of Kalhera, Goddess of Death and the Underworld left the room through a door obscured by a black curtain.

They carried the body of their king across the land and over the mountains until they reached the place he had asked to be his final resting-place.

High mountains surrounded a deep, forested valley with a steaming lake in the bottom. Warm water fed the lake from deep within the volcanic mountains. It had been the king's favourite place in the entire world, albeit not in his own lands. Here, he had met his true love. She was not mortal, but his love had been reciprocated and he wished to be near her in death.

They buried their king in a burial mound that they prepared and then they built two others, one on each side. They interred their king with due ceremony even though only fourteen of them came to the funeral. The magister had half-expected a fifteenth, but then she may have been watching from hiding. The king had loved this shy nymph above all others and had decreed he should be buried near her. Then, he looked at the others.

'Are you all ready?' the elven magister asked the assembled young warriors.

'Yes!' they chorused.

He looked round the group of twelve. They were so young. He had asked for volunteers, and they were all more than eager. At least at the beginning. Now, one or two of them seemed more than a little afraid. Not that he could blame them. He had asked a very frightening thing of them.

He noticed trembling in the youngest of them. A lad of only sixteen turns of the sun, and yet he had volunteered readily enough when asked. The old elf sighed. Better give them one last chance to change their minds. He hoped that not too many did or maybe there would not be sufficient for the task. Certainly, the tome in which he had found the ceremony recommended twelve, but maybe fewer would suffice.

'There is no censure to any who wish to change their minds. It is a fearsome thing you are volunteering to do.'

One member of the group looked at the youngest. 'Are you all right, Bry?' he said. 'No one will think you a coward if you withdraw.'

'Maybe not, but I would,' replied the young man. 'I said I'd do it, and do it I will.'

'So be it,' the mage said. 'Form the circle.'

The twelve young men formed a circle around the mage and the cleric of Kalhera, who had also accompanied them on their journey. They drew their weapons and knelt, sword tips on the ground and hands clasped over the hilts. They bowed their heads.

The young man known as Bry closed his eyes. He did not know what to expect, only the outcome. The mage could almost feel his fear. The others felt it too, but they were all warriors and none of them, not even Bry, allowed it to affect their determination to go through with it.

Bry heard the cleric begin his chant in the centre of the circle, and then the mage joined with his own. The two psalms seemed to weave around each other, in and out until the two men seemed to be singing one hymn.

'*A bit like a choir singing in harmony,*' Bry thought.

He felt a little strange, light-headed almost, and then came a sudden wrenching pain that seemed to be accompanied by a crack.

It went almost as soon as he felt it and he wondered if the spell had failed. He dared to open his eyes. Yes, something had gone wrong for there were his companions still kneeling in place. He glanced down at himself. Yes, there were his hands grasping his sword. But just a moment! What lay in front of him?

With horror, he realised his own body lay on the ground where he was looking. The spell had worked after all. He had truly died but the spell had tied his soul to Vimar. He would remain here to guard the body of his King until the prophesied time came.

The group of twelve warriors looked at their bodies. A little sadly, thought Bry. He himself thought of all the things he had not done in his sixteen years. He would never now marry and have the love and companionship of a woman, never hear his children and grandchildren laughing and playing. Never again eat a good meal or get drunk with his companions. For centuries to come, he would patrol this lake and the hidden tomb in the caves below, protecting them from harm until the eight came. The Wolves.

Chapter 1
The Duke

The Duke of Hambara looked at the four people that his butler, Daramissillo, had shown into his study. They were an odd-looking bunch—an apprentice mage, a novice cleric of Sylissa, the goddess of healing, a fierce-looking dwarf, and a tall man who, judging from his appearance, came from a land far to the south.

'Now, tell me who you are and why you are here,' he told them, steepling his fingers and resting his elbows on the desk. He looked from one to the other.

The young elven novice spoke.

'My name is Aspholessaria, Your Grace,' she said, looking into his blue eyes with her clear, grey ones, 'but people in the human lands call me Asphodel. The others are Carthinal,' she indicated the apprentice mage, 'Basalt and Fero.' She pointed to the dwarf and the tall, dark foreigner.

The man she had introduced as Carthinal handed the duke a letter.

'This is from Duke Danu of Bluehaven for you, Your Grace.'

The duke looked at the address and seal before he turned over the letter. It was Danu's seal all right and addressed to Duke Rollo of Hambara with the little flourish that Danu always put on his addresses. He smiled to himself at his friend's little eccentricities. Danu still dabbled in magic too, although he had to give it up before taking his tests due to the death of his elder brother in an epidemic. Unfortunately for him, he had to begin training to be a duke, not a mage.

Rollo looked up from the letter before picking up a knife and slitting the seal. He read it, looked up at the four companions, and then read it again. After the second reading, he put it down on his desk and turned to them.

'This letter tells me that a man called Mabryl would be bringing it to me and that he would have a token to prove it's from Duke Danu. You need to tell me where Mabryl is and why he hasn't brought it himself. Also, where is the token?'

The Duke looked severely at the four. This seemed highly suspicious to him. A letter from Danu saying some very odd things about a prophecy and that a mage, one man not four people, would deliver the letter.

'Mabryl was my master, Your Grace,' Carthinal said, 'and my adoptive father. We were on our way here for me to perform my tests. Just as we crossed the Brundella River, a flash flood swept down on us.'

Carthinal's voice broke as he said this and Rollo thought there may be some truth in what they were saying. The young half-elf was clearly upset. He decided to hear them out and ask a few more questions before having the guards throw them out.

'I heard nothing about a flood,' snapped the duke. 'Tell me about it.'

Asphodel began to speak, as it seemed that emotion overcame Carthinal for a moment.

'We were crossing the Brundella when a wall of water swept down on the caravan. It swept away everything and everyone.' Here she swallowed before carrying on.

'Men, women and children—it spared no one except three of us, no four because at that time Mabryl was still alive.' She dropped her voice to almost a whisper.

'I still hear the screams of the children in my sleep. The horses, too. Blood filled the water from where shafts had penetrated the poor beasts' sides.' Her eyes filled with tears and the dwarf, Basalt, patted her arm to comfort her.

Basalt then took up the story.

'Your Grace, the flood swept me downstream, but thanks to the goodness of Roth,' he mentioned the god of mining and metalworking, 'It washed me ashore a little downstream. I caught up with Asphodel, Carthinal and Mabryl. Carthinal had built what he calls a travois to pull Mabryl on. We continued together after that. Fero met us later when Mabryl had died.'

The duke rang the bell on his desk. The door opened and Daramissillo entered.

'Have you heard anything about the caravan from Hambara?' Duke Rollo asked him.

'No, Your Grace. Nothing really, except that it seems to be very late. That sometimes happens, of course, so no one is worried, yet.'

'Thank you, Daramissillo. You may go,' The duke turned from his butler back to the four standing before him. 'Well, so far there is nothing to say your story isn't true. I'll ask around about the caravan. Now, tell me why you haven't got the token from Duke Danu.'

Carthinal swallowed. They'd lost it due to his carelessness. He looked into the duke's eyes with his deep blue ones.

'After Mabryl died, Your Grace, I took his pack. I knew he had a letter for you with a figurine. He told me that it would reassure you that he was a genuine messenger.'

Carthinal did not tell him that Mabryl had also said that Duke Danu thought that Duke Rollo tended towards suspicion and would want confirmation as to the genuineness of the letter.

He continued. 'I had it in my pouch when we were on our way here, but a pickpocket managed to cut my pouch and with it went the figurine.'

'Hmm. Can you tell me what the figurine is?'

'Yes, Your Grace. A trotting horse about three inches long and two high and made of gold.'

The duke made no reply to this, preferring to keep his own counsel until he knew a bit more about these people. The letter worried him, if true, but the messengers were not the same as the letter led him to expect. This worried him more than the contents. He had to be certain of the veracity of this message if he were to act on it.

'There was something else in this letter. Something about a prophecy that was in a book that Mabryl had found. One that he thought dated back to before the Forbidding. Danu thinks he might be right and that it is truly a lost spellbook. What do you know about that?'

Asphodel, Basalt and Fero looked blankly at the duke, but Carthinal spoke up.

'Your Grace,' he said, 'I found a piece of paper in the book. It claimed to be a prophecy from The Oracle but wasn't dated. I can tell you what it said if you wish.'

'Do so.'

'*When Kalhera descends from the mountains and orcs once more walk the land,*'

'*When impossible beasts occur and the Never-Dying Man is once more at hand*'

'*Then the sword that was lost must once more be found*'

'*Only it can destroy the threat*'

And kill the immortal mortal to balance out his debt.'

The Duke said nothing to this but once more picked up the letter, then ringing his bell again, he called Daramissillo. back into the room.

'Escort these people to the door, please, and send one of the guards to escort them off the premises. When you've done that, come back here.'

A few minutes later, Daramissillo entered Duke Rollo's study.

'Those young people,' Rollo began, 'I want you to find out as much as you can about them. Where they go, what they do, whom they see. Make sure they don't leave the city just yet. The mage will be going to the mage Tower for his tests I expect, and the novice to the Temple of Syllissa. Ask Magister Robiam and the Great Father to come to see me as soon as they are able.'

Daramissillo bowed and quietly left as Duke Rollo leaned back in his chair to reread the letter and think.

Once they left the gates of the Ducal Palace in Hambara, the four stopped in the square. Many market stalls graced the open area in the very centre of the city. Carthinal ran his hands through his shoulder-length, auburn hair.

'That didn't go very well,' he exclaimed. 'I don't think the Duke believed us. Oh, what a pity I let my guard down and lost that figurine.'

'He might still not have believed us,' pointed out Basalt. 'We could easily have killed Mabryl and stolen the thing.'

Asphodel looked pensive. 'But, why would we do that and then come to give him the note? Surely thieves would just have sold the valuables and thrown the note away.'

Carthinal looked down at her. She seemed innocent. He supposed that a cleric, even a novice, would not have met much in the way of the real world. He smiled.

'There is a thing called "casing the joint,"' he told her. 'Thieves look at ways to get into a place and what they can steal once in there. The Duke of Hambara is a rich man and it would be worth a heist.'

Asphodel looked sceptical. 'Are you suggesting the Duke thought we were thieves? I'm a cleric of Sylissa. Why would he think I'm a thief?'

'Thieves can disguise themselves as many things, Asphodel,' Carthinal told her. 'Even clerics.'

She looked disgusted at the thought and looking at all three of them she said, 'I must be off to the temple. You aren't the only one to have a letter, Carthinal. I have one for the Great Father, although I don't suppose he knows about it yet.'

Carthinal watched her go through the crowds towards the area of the city where the temples were built. He sighed. He thought her very beautiful with her long, black hair and her grey eyes that held a steely determination. He remembered her anger at him when he tried to give her orders on their journey. His temper did not faze her at all. He would probably never see her again; a thought that made him sad.

He roused himself from his reverie and turned to his two companions, noticing that Basalt had been watching him closely.

'I must go, too,' he told them. 'I need to report to the tower. I'll come back to the inn later. The tests don't start for a couple more days.' He held out his hand and shook the hands of Fero and Basalt and set off for his destination.

He soon arrived at the Tower, situated at the edge of the Temple District. A high wall surrounded it. Inside the wall, he saw a green area with shady paths and pavilions. At the gate, a young apprentice met him.

'Hello, I'm Dabbock. You must be Carthinal,' he said. 'You're the last one for the tests. Follow me and I'll show you where to go.'

Dabbock led Carthinal through the grounds to the Tower. They entered through highly-carved double-doors.

As soon as they got inside, Carthinal stopped and looked about him.

The Tower seemed too small for the large, round room. Stairs wound up the wall on the opposite side and stairs went down too. The room had chairs and low tables scattered around, some of which were occupied.

Dabbock laughed at Carthinal's disorientation. 'Yes, it gets everyone like that at first. This room really is bigger than the outside.'

Carthinal's eyes widened as he turned to Dabbock.

'How is that possible?' he asked.

'Well, as I understand it, it's something to do with a node of mana. This node here can be used to manipulate space. The old mages, before The Forbidding, used it so they could have much more room than they were allocated to build the Tower. I don't really understand it. I don't think anyone now does either.'

'Well, I certainly don't. It's weird. Look, Dabbock, I have something here for Archmage Yssilithisandra. Where would I find her?'

'She's probably in the library. She's researching lost spells so spends a lot of time in there. Go up the stairs to the second floor. That's the library.'

'I've never met the archmage, Dabbock. How will I know who she is?'

Dabbock laughed. 'That's easy. Just look for a beautiful, golden-haired elf poring over books like there's no one else in the world. That'll be her.'

Carthinal mounted the stairs to the second floor. He looked around the bookshelves and quickly saw the archmage. Dabbock had spoken truly. She had a lovely face. Her work obviously engrossed her. She had her head bent over a large book and seemed to see little else. He crossed between the shelves until he found himself standing in front of her.

'Archmage?' he began.

She looked up, frowning. 'What is it? I'm rather busy.'

'I have something for you. My master, Mabryl, bought it in Bluehaven and thought it may interest you.'

'Really?' She looked up. 'Where is Mabryl? Why hasn't he brought it to me himself? And who are you?'

Carthinal looked down at his feet. 'I'm Carthinal, ma'am, Mabryl's apprentice and adopted son. I'm afraid he couldn't bring it himself, Archmage. He died on the way here. A flash flood swept down on the Brundella, and although I managed to pull him out, he'd hit his head rather hard. That and being so long in the water…'

The Archmage looked at the book that Carthinal handed to her.

'This is most important, Carthinal,' she said, hardly able to contain herself. 'I do believe it's a spell book from before The Forbidding.'

Many centuries before, there had been a war between rival groups of mages. The populace suffered the most and when it ended, the king of the time banned the use of magic on pain of death. He also ordered all books of magic to be burned, although a few were hidden and occasionally came to light.

In spite of the fact that a later king had lifted the ban on the use of magic, mages were still often held in suspicion. Since many spells had been lost during this time, mages like Yssalithisandra had decided to devote their time to researching them.

Carthinal smiled at the elf's enthusiasm. She seemed like a little kid with a new toy. She clutched the book to her chest as if she thought Carthinal would take it back. *As if I would know what to do with it if I did,* he thought.

Then, she became serious. 'I must study this in depth, Carthinal, so if you'll excuse me…' She sat down once more at the desk and opened the book very carefully.

Carthinal left her to her studies and descended the stairs to the ground floor for a briefing about the tests.

Once more in the impossibly large room, Carthinal met the other five apprentices due to take their tests this time. Six apprentices at a time took the tests as people considered six a lucky number.

Carthinal particularly liked a young man called Grimmaldo. Grimmaldo had a wicked twinkle in his eyes and he came out with amusing comments. He had blue eyes and brown hair and his face, while not particularly good looking, showed his personality quite plainly.

One of his companions he could not like. Hammevaro had long, blonde hair that he kept on tossing to draw attention to it. He knew just how attractive others found his face, but not how unattractive they found his personality. He let it be known that he would certainly pass the tests and to do better than all the others.

The others were a rather plain girl called Olepeca, a tall, lanky, young man called Laurre, and a black-haired elf that reminded Carthinal superficially of Asphodel, but she had muddy-brown eyes instead of clear, grey ones, and she also had the attitude that humans were beneath her. As for half-elves like Carthinal, well…

After the briefing by an archmage called Tharron, Grimmaldo suggested they all go out to explore the town. This they readily agreed to, except for Ebressaria, the elf. She said she would stay in and study.

After visiting a few inns and taverns, Grimmaldo suddenly said, 'Hey, isn't this The Warren? The place where the thieves hang out?'

Sure enough, the little group had wandered into that area. They did not call it The Warren for nothing. A maze of little streets wound around, crossing and re-crossing. The smells made the apprentices wrinkle their noses and hurry to get out of the place.

As they wandered round trying to find the way out, Carthinal suddenly began to chant. Grimmaldo recognised the spell. Why would Carthinal want to put someone to sleep? Then, the young mage released the spell and a red-haired boy at the end of the street yawned and lay down in the road, fast asleep.

'What the…' spluttered Grimmaldo.

Carthinal turned as he sped away towards where the boy lay.

'He stole something of mine this morning,' he explained, 'I'm going to get it back.'

Chapter 2
Thad

Carthinal lifted the young thief over his shoulder. The boy weighed little, so he found it easy to carry the lad. Shortly after they had left the Warren, he felt the boy stirring.

'Hey! Put me down, you bastard!' he cried.

Carthinal did so but did not release his grip on the boy's arm. The boy struggled but Carthinal was stronger, and his efforts availed him nothing.

'If you don't struggle, you won't get hurt,' Carthinal said. 'You'll come with me to the inn. I'll let go of you, but if you run, remember I am a mage. I may forget I said I wouldn't hurt you.'

'OK, I'll not run,' the boy replied, pouting.

The pair walked along side by side, each watchful and distrustful of the other until they came to the square where the Golden Dragon stood. This square was very important in Hambara. It housed the main market of the city. Now, stalls selling hot food graced the space that in other seasons would have had fresh produce.

On the south side of the square stood a building decorated with garish colours. Outside was a sign that said, *Madame Dopari's Emporium* and the letter L inscribed in a circle. Madame Dopari's was the official brothel of the city. The letter L indicated a licensed establishment, and that the priests of Sylissa inspected the girls' health every month.

The inn occupied the north side of the square. A veranda ran along the front, covered by the overhang of the upper story. In the summer, tables and chairs graced it, but now, in the cold of the winter air nothing stood there. A large sign depicting a Golden Dragon hung over the door in the centre of the veranda

'They'll not let me in there!' the boy exclaimed.

'Leave it to me,' Carthinal said. 'I think I can get you in. I'm good at talking my way out of situations, so I think I can talk my way into the inn with you.'

As luck would have it, there were few people about so Carthinal did not have any problems entering the inn with the young thief. As he passed through the public room, Basalt and Fero waved at him to come over to sit by the fire. He walked over with the boy in tow.

'What have you got there... and why?' Basalt queried while Fero raised an eyebrow at the boy's dirty and unkempt look.

'The thief who robbed me this morning. I spotted his red hair as he ran away after he'd picked my pocket and saw him again a few minutes ago,' Carthinal told them. 'I want to get my goods back. I'm taking him upstairs and I intend to find out what he has done with his ill-gotten gains.'

'I hope you don't intend to hurt him,' Fero said with an anxious look at the boy.

'Gods! What do people think I am? Of course, I won't hurt him,' Carthinal snapped.

'I apologise, Carthinal,' Fero sounded truly contrite, 'but I fail to see how just talking to him will make him give up his secrets.'

'I have my little ways,' Carthinal smiled, tapping the side of his nose, and with that he took the boy's arm and went up the stairs, leaving the others looking after him with bemused expressions on their faces. Fero shrugged and returned to his drink then after a few more seconds, Basalt did the same.

Once in the room, Carthinal surprised the boy by speaking to him in the language of the underworld, developed by the underclasses so that the Guard and others could not understand them when messages were passed.

'I want my goods back. You cut my pouch this morning. You ran. You are very good, but not good enough. I saw. I recognise you now.'

'How do you know cant?' the thief replied, with a look of amazement in his green eyes. 'You don't look like one of us.'

'No matter,' Carthinal replied. 'You get my pouch back and return it to me. But I don't trust you out in the streets. You'll run and hide. Then you'll stay low until I leave. I'll come with you to get it.'

'You must be one of us if you speak cant, even if you look like one of the grollin.' The boy used the disparaging word the thieves used for the honest population of Grosmer. 'I'll return your pouch. We don't steal from our own. You come with me now.' The boy stood and started to walk towards the door.

After a second's hesitation, Carthinal followed.

I should be studying for tomorrow, but this will probably be my only chance to get the figurine back. I must take it.

With that thought, he followed the boy out and down the stairs, quickly catching up with him.

'Going to get my stolen things,' he called to Bas and Fero, leaving them gaping after him, and wondering how he persuaded the lad to return them.

The pair of them walked through the Market Square.

'What's your name, boy?' Carthinal asked.

After a second's hesitation, the boy replied, 'Thad, sir.

'There's no need to call me "sir". I'm just another punter who has been stupid enough to be caught by a very good "dip." My name's Carthinal.'

'That's twice you said I were real good, s... er, Carthinal. D'you really think so? That's so cool.' The boy seemed to glow in the slight praise.

'Yes, I do. You have some things to learn yet, though. Like not getting caught. One thing you could do is hide your red hair with a hood, you know. You are not very old, are you? Thirteen? Fourteen?' asked the half-elf.

'Fifteen, Carthinal. Sixteen just after the Equinox.'

'You're rather small for your age. Still, there are plenty of folks who are small at your age and grow quickly after that to overtake their taller friends. You may be a giant yet!'

The boy laughed at that idea but seemed to be warming to his captor.

Soon, they arrived at the edge of the Warren.

'We're now on my patch. We talk cant from here or we'll be so bloody suspect,' Thad advised. 'There's always people sussing out guards in disguise. Everyone speaks cant on the streets in the Warren.'

'Done!' replied Carthinal, and the pair relapsed into the language of thieves, assassins, and other undesirable characters.

Eventually, they entered a dark, dismal and rather smelly back street. Carthinal entered with no hesitation, a fact that gained him an admiring glance from Thad.

Towards the end of the street, Thad bent down and lifted a grating in the middle of the road. 'Down 'ere,' he said, and Carthinal could see his grin in the dim light.

'Down here being, I presume, the sewers.' Carthinal peered down into the depths. 'Smells rather, but if your hiding place is down here, who would go looking? What are we waiting for?'

Thad looked rather taken aback by the fact that Carthinal willingly descended into the sewers. If he had any ideas of escaping through the sewer system while Carthinal rather fastidiously waited on the surface, he had to shelve them.

The pair climbed down into the depths. Water came up to Carthinal's knees, and he tucked the skirts of his robe up into his belt, leaving his legs bare. The water would not be so difficult to walk through then, and his robes would keep some semblance of cleanliness. He did not care to think what flowed past his legs. Wrinkling his nose at the overpowering, foul smell, Carthinal sighed. He winced as he felt solid things bump against his legs as he walked through the noisome fluid. He followed Thad's figure, which appeared to glow a deep red to his infra-vision. Again, if Thad intended to escape in the dark, he found it was impossible. Carthinal could easily track him, as elvenkind could see into the infrared part of the spectrum.

The young thief had no need of a light, as he could find his way through the sewers as well as he could the upper streets. They twisted, turned, and took many side branches until he had Carthinal completely disorientated. He half-wished he had invited Basalt to come along. Dwarves were used to being in caves and mines, and could not easily get lost underground.

Eventually, Thad stopped. He felt up to a ledge and pulled out a torch and a flint. Quickly lighting the torch, he pulled out a brick from the sewer wall. Reaching in, he rummaged around for a few seconds, and then pulled out a pouch.

'This it?' he asked Carthinal.

'Too right it is,' replied the other, opening it. He emptied out the coins onto his palm and counted them.

Thad quickly said, 'I spent a few crowns on some eats at the six-hour meal-time.'

'That's OK, Thad, but where's the figurine?'

The boy's face fell. 'The figurine? You mean that gold horse thingy? Yeah, well. I'm sorry, but I've fenced it already.'

'What? Already?'

'It's always good to get stuff changed to money real quick, right? Chances of being traced and all that. You know!'

'Yes, yes, of course. But, that really was quick.'

'I have a good fence, like,' said the boy dismissively. 'Was it important?'

'Someone I know thinks it is,' Carthinal sighed. 'Oh well. That's that then.'

'Maybe I c'd get it back for you. My fence'll do me favours if I ask, right? 'E's so into boys, see, (if you know what I mean) and 'e thinks if 'e does me favours, like, I'll do him one sometime. It's summat I don't try very 'ard to change. It's useful.'

'Yes, I'm sure it is. I just hope you know what you are doing with him that's all. That sort of game is dangerous.'

'Don't worry, Carthinal,' the boy replied, cheerfully. 'I have a dagger and am bloody good wi' throwing knives.'

'Just be careful, that's all, Thad. Don't go relying on weapons. That way lies the end of a rope.'

Thad looked up at Carthinal and grinned. 'I ain't scared of no old rope. Anyways, they'd 'ave to bloody catch me first.'

'Anyway, if you do manage to get the figurine, you can bring it to the Golden Dragon and give it to me. Now, are you going to show me the way out of here, or abandon me to wander forever through the dark and dismal sewers, never to see the light of day again?' This last said in a sepulchral tone.

Thad grinned and said, 'Don't tempt me! That'd be real cool, you comin' up at night to scare the bleedin' punters. All but me, o' course. We'd be partners an' all. You'd scare 'em away and I'd "acquire" their things. But come on, or you may end up as a zombie scaring the honest folk of 'Ambara for real, comin' from the sewers at night to prey on the innocent townsfolk.' He imitated Carthinal's tone.

The pair laughed and set off back through the sewers. Carthinal found he liked the young lad and wondered why had he ended up a thief in the Warren and not one of the honest poor.

The grating that Thad returned him to was near the edge of the Warren, in a place he recognised.

'You don't think I'd, like, take you straight to me bleedin' hidin' place, do you? Or bring you straight back? That would be so not sensible,' grinned Thad. 'Don't worry, I'll get that statue thingy.' With that, the young thief slipped back down the sewer grating and disappeared.

'Well! That was an adventure,' muttered Carthinal as he strode across the market square.

People drew away from him and held their noses, but could not make out why he smelled so bad. Some of the rich folk held pomanders to their noses as he passed. His robe had kept out of the noisome water, and now covered his legs and feet, so the filth of the sewers could not be seen, only the smell became noticeable as people passed. They wrinkled their noses or pressed pomanders to them, giving Carthinal strange looks.

On entering their room, Fero and Basalt stepped away from him as though he had the plague. 'Where have you been?' Fero asked. 'You smell like a sewer rat.'

'Rather a polite way to put it, Fero. Carthinal, you smell like shit. Quite literally. Get a bath before you come anywhere near either of us. Or give us any explanations.'

Carthinal, with a grin at his friends, moved off in the direction of the bath house to get clean, after which he returned to their room ready to give the story of his trip with Thad and its results. At the end of the story, Fero expressed his surprise that Thad had been so cooperative.

'I had certain advantages that I used,' Carthinal told him, but did not go into any further details.

'Now, I think I'd better do some studying. The first test is History of Magic—not my best or favourite subject. I always thought history was a bit of a waste of time.'

It became obvious from his attitude that he did not want to make his remarks about his advantages any clearer so the other two left him to his studies and went to the bar for a drink.

Chapter 3
Asphodel

Asphodel reached the temple of Sylissa in a very, few minutes after leaving the others, though with some trepidation. What would happen to her? She knew she had been sent here in disgrace and that Mother Caldo could not do anymore with her, but what was the Great Father like here in Hambara? She rather felt he would be stricter than Mother Caldo would or she would not have sent her here.

She entered the temple through the great double-doors. Inside, she found a large, circular area. Seats surrounded a central altar and windows pierced the walls and the dome high above. These windows concentrated the light so that it fell on the altar and on the alcove opposite the doors where there stood a life-sized statue of Sylissa. All the walls of the temple shone with white marble and a beautiful mosaic, showing Sylissa giving the gift of healing to her first priestess, paved the floor. Asphodel stopped to admire the beauty.

'Yes, it makes everyone stop the first time they see it, sister.' The voice came from by her elbow.

Asphodel jumped. 'Oh! I didn't hear you coming,' she said, adding "Minister" and bowing her head as she saw his orange sash, indicating his rank.

'Sorry, sister,' replied the minister. 'I'm Minister Micory, and I'm on duty here today. Is there anything I can help you with?'

'I have a letter for the Great Father, Minister Micory,' replied Asphodel, bowing her head to a superior. 'Could you tell me how to get it to him, please?'

'If you give it to me, I'll get a novice to take it to him. Do you need a reply?'

'Yes. I will need some response from the Great Father.'

'If you wait here,' Minister Micory continued, 'The Great Father will send a reply to you as soon as he is able. I'll let him know where you are. You could use the time in meditation and prayer, sister.'

The time passed. Asphodel found herself thinking of the others. Where were they? What were they doing? Where had Carthinal decided to stay? In the Mage Tower or in the Golden Dragon Inn with the others?

Then, the service for the end of the day began and she had still not been seen. Afterwards, another minister came over to speak with her.

'It's obvious the Great Father won't be seeing you today,' she told Asphodel. 'You'd better stay in the guestrooms tonight. If your letter needs a reply, I expect the Great Father will send a message tomorrow. Follow me, please.'

She began to walk away to a door to the right of the altar. She walked along the corridor to the second door on the right.

'You can rest here tonight,' she told the young novice. 'You'll find an evening meal will be served in the refectory in about an hour, and breakfast at the second hour in the morning after the dawn service. I expect you'll want to attend that. It commences at the twenty-fourth hour of the day.'

The hours of the day were counted from the time of dawn on the equinoxes and there were twenty-four in each day.

The minister stood back to allow Asphodel to enter, and then closed the door behind her.

Well, that sounded more like a command. I'll get a wash and then go and eat. If I am to be up before dawn, I'd better get an early night.

It seemed that in the temple of Hambara the clerics washed in cold water and slept on beds harder than the ground she had been sleeping on recently. She sighed, put on a clean robe, and went out for some food that just about satisfied her hunger, if not her palate, as it seemed very basic. Asphodel went to bed feeling unsatisfied at her first experience of the Temple of Sylissa in Hambara.

The next morning, Asphodel awoke feeling stiff. She heard a bell somewhere nearby. This signalled the dawn prayers. She washed in cold water again and then dressed before making her way to the temple.

The service began with a choir singing a hymn to the dawn. Then, the rest of the service commenced. It continued with praises and thanks to Sylissa, and the officiating cleric, a deacon this morning, spoke at length about how all should be striving to eliminate evil in both themselves and the world.

He spoke of injury and disease as evils that had been brought upon the races of the world by their evil ways and how they were the punishment of the gods. He explained how the Most High, the leader of the Church of Sylissa, wanted to eradicate all evil beings in order for the gods to lift their punishments from the peoples of the world.

He gave a long talk; Asphodel estimated an hour at least. She wondered how anyone could manage to talk for so long about the need for the elimination of evil, and her mind wandered. She began to wonder where the others were and what they were doing. Was Carthinal getting ready to take his tests? She realised that she had no idea when the tests were to begin. Would he have to wait in Hambara for a while or would they begin straight away today? She thought that Basalt and Fero would be seeking work, and sent up a little prayer that they were both successful.

By the time the service ended, Asphodel's stomach embarrassed her by beginning to rumble. The service had taken well over two hours. She left for the refectory where she found bowls of porridge and glasses of water. She sighed as she took her portion to a table and began to eat. Did Sylissa want her servants to live like this? Surely not! All these rules and abstinence, even having to eat poor, quality food. It had not been like this at the temple in Bluehaven when she left, and she found herself wondering if this were the only temple where they practised such abstemiousness.

After her breakfast, such as it was, she returned to the temple to wait, again admiring its beauty. Just before the sixth hour, a novice approached her with a message to follow him. He led her along a corridor off the first one she had gone down with the refectory at the end and the guestrooms. They came to a door on the left. A Temple guard dressed in white, the colour of Sylissa, guarded it.

The novice knocked and a harsh male voice called, 'Come in.'

Asphodel opened the door and at once saw a large man in front of her with gold-edged, white robes. The Great Father. She immediately fell down onto her knees, as she had been taught, and kept her eyes on the floor. She could see nothing but the carpet beneath her feet, a very rich one, in deep blue and gold. The voice spoke from somewhere above her head.

'I have read Mother Caldo's letter, child, and I find it most disquieting. She thinks that you would be better here and that I can do more with you than she can. I think that perhaps she is right.' Feet paced the floor towards the window to her left.

'Firstly, I think that we should effect a means of teaching you discipline—a virtue that you seem to be sadly lacking if Mother Caldo's letter is anything to go by. I have therefore decided that you will join with the Daughters of Sylissa.'

Asphodel stifled a cry at this. She had never even contemplated a life with the Daughters, knowing instinctively that she did not have the right personality for such a life.

The voice went on, 'I do not think we will expect you to take the vows and become a full Daughter, unless, that is, you decide that you are called to them, but as long as you remain with them, you will abide by their rules.'

Here, the Great Father paused and his feet resumed their pacing.

'You will have no contact with anyone other than your fellow sisters, except when you are healing. Of course, as far as the other Daughters are concerned, you will become a full member in due course. Only the Mother will know that it may only be temporary. Do you have anything to say, daughter?'

'H-how long will I be with the Daughters, Great Father?' Asphodel stuttered, appalled at the idea.

'That depends on you, child,' came the reply. The feet turned towards her. 'You must show that you have learned the discipline required of a true cleric, which includes obedience to your superiors. Now, I will call for a novice to take you to the House of the Daughters.'

Asphodel felt faint. She could hardly believe what the Great Father had said. Not to have any contact with anyone except the Daughters for an unspecified length of time. She felt as though she had just been sent to jail.

When she arrived at the House of the Daughters, which a windowless corridor connected to the Temple, the Mother took her to a room, told her to sit down, and then cut off all her long, black hair. Her protests that she was not actually joining the Daughters permanently fell on deaf ears.

'As long as you are within our walls, you are a Daughter. The Daughters all have their hair cut off. It's a temptation sent by Allandrina, that evil goddess of deceit, to tempt men into lustful thoughts and deeds and young women into the sin of pride and vanity. No, it's better that the hair is removed. It's obvious that you've already fallen into the sin of vanity by your objection to having your hair cut.'

Asphodel watched as her hair fell to the ground. Afterwards, she put her hand up to her head to feel what had been done. It now just reached her ears. She almost asked for a mirror, but two things stopped her. Firstly, she thought that she did not really want to know what she looked like, and secondly, she thought that Mother would accuse her of the "sin of vanity" once more.

After that, a novice showed her to a cell in another part of the building. If she thought the guestrooms were primitive, it seemed luxury compared with what she now had. There was a narrow bed with a blanket over it, but no pillow and only a very thin mattress that would do nothing to soften the hardness of the bed. A small shrine to Sylissa stood in the corner of the room, with a statue and a triskel, and a tallow candle in a candlestick. Nothing for any personal items either or even any chair or chest. Just a bed and the shrine.

'Mother has given me permission to speak to you,' murmured the novice who showed her to the cell, 'so that you'll know exactly what to do. The washing place is at the end of the corridor. You'll wash at night before retiring and in the morning on rising. No other time is permitted.'

'Is there no bath house?' asked Asphodel. 'I do like to bathe sometime to get properly clean.'

The girl looked shocked. 'No! Bathing is strictly forbidden. It's a luxury, and we eschew all luxuries as they can lead to the sin of avarice. We always wash in cold water too for the same reasons.'

She looked closely at Asphodel as if she could not understand her wish. 'We're not allowed to converse with one another except for one hour after the evening meal. We attend all services in the temple. We work in the infirmary and any days we're not there, we spend in meditation and prayer. We've been instructed by the Most High to pray for the eradication of evil from the world, and for the help of Sylissa in doing so. I think that's all that you need to know. If you want to ask anything else, you can ask me now, or after the evening meal.'

She paused and then remembered something else. 'Oh, yes. We are allowed no personal property except our robes and triskel, and a cloak for if we have to go out to attend a sick person outside the temple. Any other property you have you must hand over to Mother.'

Asphodel told the girl she thought she had explained well, and that if there were nothing else she would now like to go into her cell and meditate. The novice then smiled and left.

Asphodel entered the room and sat down on the hard bed. Tears pricked at her eyes. Her head felt wrong without the weight of her hair, and she felt ugly. She rose and closed the door. She would not let them know how she felt. She felt violated. Her hair had been taken away without her volition. She had had all contact with the outside world removed from her, and her few meagre possessions were forfeit.

How would she find out about her friends? They would think that she did not care about them. She wanted to know if Carthinal had passed his tests. What about the others? Bas and Fero? If they got jobs that took them out of the city, she would not know, and may never see them again. The tears began to flow. She turned onto her stomach and allowed them to continue. She cried until she felt wrung out, then, still sobbing, she turned to the shrine and the statue of Sylissa. She spread her hands and prayed.

'Why are you letting them do this to me? Deep down inside me, I know this is not right. Most of what is happening here don't feel right. Even praying for the eradication of evil doesn't feel right.' She sighed. 'Surely, you and the other gods put evil here as well as good for a purpose? We don't know why you did so, but I feel inside that it's necessary. I know the Most High is the leader of your clergy, but could he not be wrong in this? Or is it blasphemy to think that he could be fallible? Give me the strength to get through this ordeal. I'll do my best to do as they wish so that I can once again go out into the world and heal as I wish to do.'

She spent the rest of the day attending services, and meditation and prayer. The Daughters were allowed to do their meditation in their cells, or in the gardens in the centre of the House.

Asphodel decided to go into the gardens, as she thought she could feel a bit of freedom in the open air. Elves loved the natural world and felt stifled if they could not get outside into the woods and open country. The gardens looked beautiful even this early in the season, with some early spring flowers already beginning to bloom in the shelter of the high walls and covered walkways. Flowering trees put out their blossoms and the scent of spring perfumed the air, but even so, Asphodel found the atmosphere oppressing, so after a while, she went back to her little cell.

The next morning, after another long, dawn service in the temple, Archdeacon Jenoria, the Mother of the Daughters of Sylissa, told her to report to the infirmary for duty. Several other Daughters of different ranks accompanied her, all going on duty, with bent heads in a gesture of humility and submission. Asphodel did so as well but found that she kept glancing around her. She found it almost impossible to keep her head in the bowed position.

They eventually reached the infirmary. It was a light and airy place with a white, marble floor and white-painted walls. The whole room had a feeling of cleanliness and efficiency. A senior cleric gave the Daughters a number of tasks or simple healing to do. He told Asphodel to clean a nasty cut on a child's knee and to bind it up to keep it clean.

During the course of the morning, Asphodel had to do some binding of wounds, but little actual healing. She did do a simple healing on one small boy with a head wound, got from falling out of a tree he was trying to climb, as he was obviously in pain, but there were no serious injuries to deal with.

In the afternoon, however, all seemed to change.

A woman came in with a bad knife cut on her hand where a knife had slipped while she was gutting fish. A vicar asked Asphodel to see what she could do to save the use of the woman's fingers. Firstly, she gently removed the pad that someone had placed on the injury, and wiped away all the excess blood. She cleaned the wound as best she could, and prayed to Sylissa for healing. She felt the strength of the goddess entering her and then passing to the woman until the bleeding stopped, but the ligaments concerned were still in danger of not knitting properly, so she prayed once more to Sylissa for her strength. This seemed to be sufficient to ensure that with further, natural healing the woman would keep the use of her fingers.

Shortly after this, a man came rushing in carrying a boy. He seemed to be panicking. A poisonous snake had bitten the boy in the grass outside the city. The man, the boy's father, had carried him to the temple as quickly as possible. The vicar told Asphodel to try to help him.

She prayed to Sylissa again. She knew that she would only be able to carry sufficient power from the goddess to slow the passage of the poison, that she was nowhere near strong enough to break it down and render it harmless. The goddess granted her power through Asphodel, and she felt the strength going out of her once more. After that, a more experienced healer would take over, but the immediate panic was ended.

She felt as though she could do more healing, for although she felt tired, she did not feel as drained as she did when she had used up all her strength. This pleased her because it meant she was getting stronger and could perhaps end her noviciate.

The next hour was quite simple, prescribing herbs for a cough, cleaning grazes on children's knees and the like, but nothing requiring any serious healing work. Then, a young girl came limping in on the arm of a young man. The girl's ankle was swelling very badly and she could hardly bear to put it down.

'She slipped down the stairs coming out of the temple of Parador.' explained the young man as Asphodel gently felt her ankle.

'Can you move your toes?' she asked the girl.

'Yes, I think so,' she replied, trying.

'I don't think it is broken, just a bad sprain. I'll do a simple healing on it that will help with the pain and then give you a poultice. You must rest it after that until the swelling goes down. I'll give you some more of the herbs so you can make another poultice.'

This she did and felt the strength go out of her as the healing took effect. She felt some elation as it meant that she had now performed more healing than she would previously have been able to do. Vicar Helzel, who was passing, also noted this and wrote it down in her little book.

Finally, Asphodel performed a final, simple healing on a man with a bruised head, and at last was feeling exhausted.

'Well done, Sister,' Vicar Helzel said. 'I will inform the Great Father that in my opinion, you are ready for promotion.'

She smiled at the young elf and said, 'Go back to the House of the Daughters and get some food and rest.'

Asphodel bowed her head and replied, 'Thank you, Vicar Helzel,' and gratefully left.

The second day of her time with the Daughters of Sylissa was again spent in prayer and meditation except for the time in praise of Sylissa in the temple. The services were beautiful if indeed the preaching was a little over-long.

That morning, a novice brought her the lilac sash and lilac-edged white robes of a curate, and she felt proud to be wearing it. She now addressed the novices as Sister, and they had to call her Curate Asphodel.

Asphodel's second day of healing dawned after the day of rest, and she made her way through the corridors to the infirmary once more. As a curate, she could now use the novices and give them simple tasks to do as other, higher-ranking clerics had done with her previously.

The day was passing quickly with a busy morning when a young man came in. He looked around somewhat furtively and then took a seat at the end of the queue to wait. He was obviously in some considerable pain and Asphodel noticed that he was bleeding from a nasty wound in his shoulder, although he was trying to keep it from being noticed. In her opinion, the wound should be attended to quickly due to the loss of blood and the dangers of infection if it were not cleaned, not to mention the shock that must accompany such a wound.

Strangely, though, the clerics all seemed to be ignoring, or even actively avoiding the man. This puzzled Asphodel and she went over to him. As she approached him, the day's duty vicar called to her. It was Vicar Weslon. He was a severe man. Not quite what Asphodel thought of as a caring healer. Still, he was good at his job and she respected that.

'Curate Asphodel,' he said as she approached. 'We must not see that man until we have attended to everyone here and then only if there is time, perhaps. Is that clear?'

Asphodel could not believe her ears. Was she being asked—no, told—not to heal someone who desperately needed it, and quickly at that? This was against what she understood to be her vows. She dared not argue with the Vicar if she wanted to be released from the Daughters, but it worried her. She could not help but ask the reasons.

'That man is evil,' Vicar Weslon answered. 'He is an assassin and has killed many people in his life. We cannot condone such, especially since the Most High wishes the elimination of all evil. By withholding treatment, he is likely not to live, and so another of the evil gods' minions will have been eliminated.'

With that, Vicar Weslon walked away to attend to a seriously ill woman.

Asphodel continued with her work until she heard a sudden cry from the direction of the assassin. She looked over in his direction. He seemed to be about to lose consciousness, and his wound was bleeding again rather more profusely. He was shivering violently although it was warm in the infirmary thanks to the hypocaust under the floor.

I cannot ignore a sick man, even if he is an assassin, It is for the gods to judge us, not other people, Most High or not.

She made her way over to him, in spite of her earlier instructions, and did what she could. A couple of simple healings soon stopped the bleeding and then she carefully washed and dressed the wound with healing herbs. She had just finished, and the man was thanking her profusely when she heard Vicar Weslon call her. He wore an angry look on his face.

'Disobedience,' he spluttered. 'Rank disobedience of an order by a superior. Go back to the House of Daughters immediately. The Great Father will hear of this. You are not to return to the Infirmary, but to remain in your cell. I will speak to the Great Father personally about this. It may take a few days for him to see me and you will remain in the House of the Daughters until he sends for you. Pray, girl, for the humility to be obedient.'

He watched as she left the room and walked the corridors back to her cell. What was Sylissa doing allowing such disobedient girls into the ranks of the priesthood? How come she had not been weeded out before this, and why was she on *his* duty roster? Admittedly, she was a good healer for a newly promoted curate, but still, disobedience was disobedience, and he dismissed Asphodel from his mind until the end of his duty.

The next morning, Asphodel received a summons to the office of the Great Father soon after breakfast as she was praying in her cell. Maybe it was not about the incident the previous day? It was a bit quick for Vicar Weslon to have seen the Great Father. The Great Father did not see lesser ranks very quickly as evinced by her own wait in the temple when she first arrived, and she thought that would have been longer if Mother Caldo were not known to the Great Father. Still, she would have to go to find out.

She walked down the corridor approaching the office with some trepidation and as she reached the door, the guard outside said, 'You are Asphodel?'

She replied in the affirmative.

'You are to go straight in.' Then, he smiled and said, 'Good luck. He seems to be rather angry this morning. I hope it's not you that he's angry with!'

'I rather think it may be,' Asphodel replied, opening the door and crossing the threshold.

As soon as she saw that the Great Father was present, seated behind his desk, she fell to her knees.

'Words fail me.' The voice of the Great Father came to her from over her head. 'Mother Caldo said you were defiant, but I did not fully realise how defiant. You disobeyed a direct order yesterday I understand, and you have only just come to us, too!'

Asphodel said nothing. It was not permitted to speak to the Great Father unless given specific permission to do so.

'You were told not to heal an evil man, yet you went ahead and did so anyway. This in spite of the commands of the Most High, that we work to rid the world of evil in all its guises. That man would not have survived if you had not interfered, and another evil soul would be gone from this world to be judged and punished by the gods.'

He paused. 'I do not know what to do with you at the moment,' he went on, 'Do you have anything to say for yourself? What is your excuse for your disobedience?'

Asphodel took that as an invitation to speak and answered quietly, 'Your Holiness, when I took my vows I swore to help the sick and injured wherever I may find them. I did not promise anything about selective healing or only healing good people. The man was in need and I fulfilled my vows. That's all.'

This seemed to infuriate the Great Father still further. Asphodel heard a chair scrape back as he got to his feet, and then she heard him walk around the desk. She saw feet and a white robe edged in gold.

'YOU—DISOBEYED—A—DIRECT—ORDER!' The words were almost shouted at her. 'YOU, A NEWLY PROMOTED CURATE, DISOBEYED A VICAR'S ORDERS!'

'I obeyed my conscience and my vows,' replied Asphodel, still in a quiet voice.

'Now, you speak before being given permission! Is there no end to your defiance?'

Asphodel looked up. It was forbidden, but she was beginning to become angry herself. Who was this pompous man in charge of the Church of Sylissa in Hambara? She saw in front of her a rather, tall man with grey hair, thinning on the top. He was overweight, indicating overindulgence, and his round face was red with anger. Fortunately for her, he was not looking in her direction, and so did not see her looking at him.

'Girl, I have decided.' He turned towards the window. 'You will join the Daughters on a permanent basis. You will take the vows of the order. You will learn discipline. You will be confined to your cell until I decide that you can once more take up the duties of a Daughter of Sylissa, and then you will take your vows. You will, until that time, be fed only on bread and water.'

Asphodel forgot all protocol and surged to her feet, her grey eyes, almost black with anger. She could no longer contain herself.

'You cannot force a free person to take vows they are unwilling to take. If you do so, those vows are null and void, and you know it. I will *not* become a Daughter of Sylissa.'

Asphodel's hands clenched and unclenched at her side as she looked the Great Father in the eye.

'I've every respect for those who wish to take up that life, but it's not for me. I cannot live like that, and I will not. I'm going to leave this temple now, and you will not stop me. I'll become a travelling cleric and heal where it's needed according to my conscience.

'It's not our place to decide who will live and who will die, to put ourselves in the place of the gods. Surely, if there is evil in the world, the gods put it here? If we are evil, then the gods gave us that capacity. We cannot understand the gods and the way they work, only do what we can.

'If this means that I do not progress any further in the ranks of the Church, then so be it. I'll remain a humble curate for the rest of my days, but I—will—help—people. Whoever they are, or whatever they have done, as long as they have a need. Maybe seeing what good is, some bad folk may reform. That is surely better than condemning them to death, and surely much more pleasing to the gods. As to my advancement, Sylissa will give me strength to increase my healing capacity. Only she can do that. It matters not what I am called—novice, curate, archdeacon or bishop.'

With that, she turned and headed for the door.

As she hurried down the corridor and into the temple, she did not pause to look at its magnificence but swept through the main doors and down the steps into the late winter sunshine.

Chapter 4
Job-Hunting

When they re-entered the city, Fero was immediately struck by the smells. They had seemed considerably less in the parkland of the Duke, and he could almost imagine he was back in the countryside. However, when they left the gardens and park, the stink of the city hit him again.

How can people live like this?

When Carthinal and Asphodel left for their respective destinations, he and Basalt wandered around the city getting to know it a little better. It did not improve with the knowledge in his opinion.

'The sooner I can get a job that takes me out of here, the better,' he grumbled to Basalt. 'I really don't like cities. They are crowded and they smell.'

After a morning of wandering round, they found themselves once more outside the walls of the Ducal Palace in the centre of the city. The square outside the palace divided the city into four areas, and Basalt and Fero had just come from the area known as the Warren.

This was the poor quarter of the city and the place where the thieves, assassins, common whores, beggars and honest poor lived out their lives. It was also the reason for Fero's complaints about the smells. Although the city boasted a sewer system, the homes in the Warren were not connected, as the inhabitants could not afford it. That, and the close proximity of the dwellings, and the unwashed bodies, not to mention the piles of horse dung, all added to the noisome atmosphere.

The road cleaners did not clean up these streets, as they did not go into this area, it being deemed not important enough. All these things went to make the Warren a stinking place. The two of them, therefore, decided to return to the Golden Dragon to get cleaned up and eat a meal.

The next morning, Fero and Basalt left the Inn to go in search of work. Fero decided to first go to the hiring hall where people looking for work could meet with potential employers.

There were quite a lot of people putting themselves up for hire in various capacities, the largest being agricultural workers, as it would soon be time for the spring planting.

Fero stood in the area where the scouts and guides stood. Caravan leaders approached him several times, but each time they went away without finalising an agreement. Sometimes Fero saw someone speak to them before they went away.

'It almost seems as though someone doesn't want me to get work,' he mused.

He had not found employment by the eleventh hour, so he returned to the inn where he found Basalt just coming in. Bas, it appeared, had done no better than himself in the job-hunting. He told Fero what had happened.

After leaving Fero at the door of the inn, he decided to go straight to the barracks to try to get a job with the city guard.

He approached the gates and pulled on the bell that hung there.

Shortly, a man approached the gates saying, 'Yes! What do you want?'

'I am looking for work as a guard,' Basalt explained.

'Oh! Come on through then,' the man replied, opening the gate. 'The captain'll see you in a few minutes. He's busy at the moment. You can wait in the common room.'

The guard showed Basalt into the common room where there were a number of off-duty guards sitting around. Basalt went to sit near a bar in the corner. The barman struck up a conversation with him.

'New recruit?' he asked.

'Hope so,' Basalt replied. 'I'm waiting to see the captain now. I believe he's busy.'

The other snorted. 'I doubt it, but he'll pretend to be to make it seem he's important. He'll keep you waiting for a bit, then call you in as though doing you a favour.'

Just then, a young sergeant came into the room from a flight of stairs opposite the bar. He approached Basalt and told him to follow him up the stairs to see the captain. The stairs led to a small landing and the sergeant knocked on a door at the top.

'Recruit to see you, sir,' he said.

A voice said, 'Come in then,' and the sergeant opened the door to admit Basalt.

The room was very organised with a large desk in the centre behind which sat a large man with greying hair, and one of the largest moustaches Basalt had ever seen.

'Want to be in the Hambara guard, do you?' the captain asked. 'Why?'

The question took Basalt by surprise. 'I've got experience as a fighter, and I need the money,' he told the other man. 'As there aren't any wars at the moment; there are no army jobs going, so I thought of the town guard and here I am.'

'I'd like to give you a job. You look a strong and determined man, but I'm afraid my hands are tied,' the captain told him. 'Duke Rollo sent a message out yesterday that we are not to employ anyone not born in Hambara or lived here for at least five years. Left to me I'd give you a job right away. If you come back in five years, having lived here all that time, I'll be delighted to employ you.'

He stood up and offered Basalt his hand to shake, which the dwarf did, saying, 'I doubt I'll be here or anywhere else in five years unless I can find a job soon.'

The afternoon he spent going round the blacksmiths' forges in the industrial area. He had no more luck here than he had with the guards. Since he was getting hungry, he made his way back to the inn where he found an equally disappointed Fero waiting for him.

The two of them sat down to eat a meal and were sitting drinking when Carthinal came back. They asked him how he felt his tests had gone, but he was rather brief in his answers. He said he felt the need to go and do some work in preparation for the next day, and so Fero and Basalt decided to sample the taverns around the town

Basalt had a similarly disappointing time the next day while enquiring amongst the metalworkers as he had with the Guard and the smiths. As with the blacksmiths, they all seemed to want someone with less experience than the dwarf or did not want to employ anyone at all. In a large town such as Hambara, Basalt found this state of affairs strange in the least. He wandered back to the inn, musing to himself.

When he arrived, Keloriff approached him with a note from Fero. He thanked the man but did not open it, as it would have been a waste of time since he had never learned to read. He had not needed to read, working in the mines as a youngster, and he had not bothered to learn since. He would wait until Carthinal returned and ask him to read it.

He did not have to wait too long before Carthinal came through the door. He was in a buoyant mood, as he had now received the results of three tests and had passed all of them, the second with distinction, and the third with a merit. Basalt was pleased for him and after congratulating the mage, he handed him the note.

'It's from Fero,' Basalt told him. 'I think it's telling us he's gone out of town. He was rather restless and feeling the need for some fresh air, I think. Can't blame the lad. I feel a bit like that myself.'

Carthinal opened the note and read,

Carthinal and Bas,

I have been unable to find work in the city and I am becoming suffocated here. I cannot breathe this air or stand the press of so many people any longer. I am going out of the city and into the woods for tonight. I will return tomorrow to try my luck again in the Hiring Hall. I will come to the inn after that and eat with you, at least.

Fero.

Carthinal and Basalt ate their meal, fish from the lake, baked with a kind of sweet potato and tomatoes and onions. They finished the meal with goat's cheese and bread and washed it down with ale.

'I'm afraid I won't be able to keep you company this evening, Bas,' apologised Carthinal to the dwarf. Tomorrow's test is to be the most important, the practical, and I must ensure that I have enough rest. I hope you don't mind if I go to our room now.'

'Of course not, lad,' replied the dwarf. 'Your test is important. I'll find someone to while away the time with.

Basalt found a group of men who were playing Rond, a popular card game, and asked if he could join them. They readily agreed. By the end of the evening, he had a nice pile of crown pieces stacked up by his side.

These he placed in his pouch and said, 'Thank you, gentlemen. Anytime you'd like to play again, I'll be pleased to join you.'

One of the three, other card players grunted that he was too good for them, and maybe they should try a different game next time. They bid him goodnight and Basalt climbed the stairs, feeling a little more pleased, as he now had some money. Not being able to find a job still concerned him, though.

The next morning, when Basalt woke, he was not looking forward to the day searching for a job. There were still a lot of options open. There were other metal workers he had not yet approached, and he could also carve wood quite passably, so failing metalwork, he would try his hand at woodwork.

The morning passed in a similar vein to the previous days, but in the late afternoon, in a narrow back street, he came across a small, metalworker's shop. The goods in the window were of a high quality and so he entered. A young man was there, working on an intricate piece.

'I'll be with you in a moment, sir,' the young man said. 'Just at a tricky bit. Look around while you wait.'

Basalt took the young man at his word and looked. The goods were of a very well made. Not quite as high as he himself could make, but if the young man was responsible, he was not very experienced yet and eventually, Basalt thought, he would make a top craftsman.

'There! That's done,' said the young man with feeling. 'Now, what can I do for you? Sorry to have kept you waiting. Is it a commission, or do you want to buy something from stock?'

'Neither,' Bas replied. 'I'm looking for work.'

'Really?' The young man looked surprised. 'Are you any good? Do you have any examples of your work? Sorry to have to ask, but I'm new here in Hambara, and have yet to make my reputation. If I take on a substandard worker, my reputation will suffer.'

'Yes, I understand. Don't fret yourself, my lad,' replied the dwarf, fumbling in his backpack. 'Now, where is it? Ah! Here you are.' He handed a piece of jewellery to the young man who took it to the window to inspect. 'I don't have any larger pieces on me, but I can do wrought iron work for whatever function you require,' Basalt told him.

'This is superb work,' said a rather, breathless, young man. 'Why has a craftsman like you come to me for work? Surely, you could get a job with one of the more, established shops in the town?'

'No. It seems no one is looking for a master craftsman at the moment, surprising as it may seem,' replied the dwarf.

'Well, I am,' said the young man, surprising Basalt, as he was expecting the usual reply. 'We'll need to negotiate your pay, of course. I can't afford the wages that are paid by most of the others in town, but I would really like to have you work for me. This work is the best I've seen. You'll make my shop famous if your larger work is as good. Maybe we can become partners, in time.' The young man's enthusiasm threatened to overwhelm him, then he said, 'Are you sure you want to work here?'

Basalt replied in the affirmative, and the two of them negotiated the rate of pay. It was considerably less than he was hoping for, but he knew the young man, (whose name turned out to be Nitormon), was in no position to pay more, and so he made a token show of bargaining so as not to embarrass Nitormon. He also knew that in the future, Nitormon was going to make his name such was the quality of his work. They agreed for Basalt to begin work the following morning at the second hour.

That evening, Basalt returned to the inn in a much more cheerful frame of mind. He had a job, and he was looking forward to seeing Fero again, hoping he had also been successful, and Carthinal too, as he was sure that he also would have something to celebrate.

He ate alone. Neither of his friends had come in. The evening was spoiled for him. He was worried. Fero said he would return to at least dine with them, and Carthinal should have been back from his practical test by now. Basalt hoped the worst had not happened to Carthinal. He heard sometimes mages died during the practical tests. Probably, he had gone out to celebrate the end of the tests with the other candidates and would be back late, but his worry did not go away, and he fell into an uneasy sleep.

The next morning, when he woke and saw that Carthinal's bed had not been slept in, he was even more anxious. Perhaps, he should go to the Tower and find out what had happened? Then, he thought he would look foolish, like an anxious mother if Carthinal was fine, and had slept off his celebrations at the Tower.

He could do nothing about Fero, but he imagined all sorts of things happening out in the wilds. Therefore, he set off for Nitormon's shop. He entered, was greeted warmly by Nitormon, and set to work on a complex piece of wrought ironware. It was to be a serving table for a rich house, one of those on the outskirts of the city. Nitormon worked alongside him, and chatted about himself and asked few questions of Basalt, for which the dwarf felt grateful. He did not feel in the mood for talking very much.

Lunchtime came and he determined to go out of the shop. He walked as far as the nearest tavern. At one point, his footsteps began to stray towards the Tower, but he made himself return. After lunch, he returned to the shop to find it closed. The door was locked and there was no sign of Nitormon.

He stood there puzzling out what had happened, when a passing woman said, 'He's gone. Don't know where or why. I saw two men go in, and a few minutes later Nitormon came out with them, locked the shop, and they all went off down the street. Nitormon looked uneasy, as though he didn't want to go with them, but the men were big fellows, so he probably had no choice. Hope he's all right, though. Nice chap, Nitormon. If you want to buy something, try Tendex in the main street. He's almost as good. Goodbye.'

With that, she walked off leaving a puzzled Basalt standing looking at the shop. Bas could not think what Nitormon had done to be carted off like that. He could do nothing standing there, though, so he spent the rest of the afternoon worrying about his friends and his job and wandering the streets of Hambara until he decided to return to the Golden Dragon.

Chapter 5
Yssalithissandra

Carthinal left the tower to wander around the gardens. He managed to get through the practical test, for which he was grateful. In fact, he was the first one to complete it. Hammevaro only just managed it, much to his dismay, and Ebressaria failed to complete at all. Unfortunately, one of their number, Laurre, had died in the test and all the apprentices, no, now new mages, were very upset by this.

Each apprentice had been watched magically by an archmage, and it so happened that Yssa had watched Carthinal's progress. When the test was ended, she had invited him to come to her rooms to talk some more about the finding of the ancient book.

Carthinal left the Tower to walk in the gardens. He sat down on a seat near a stream and leaned back to enjoy the late afternoon sunshine. The winter was almost at an end, and there was beginning to be a little strength in the sun at last.

He heard footsteps behind him and opened his eyes to see the archmage who had briefed the apprentices. 'I hope you don't mind me joining you, Carthinal,' he said as he sat down on the bench next to the younger man. 'I wanted to congratulate you on passing your tests. I believe you passed very well. I cannot tell you more than that at this juncture, though, but Mabryl would have been proud of you.'

'Thank you,' replied Carthinal with a smile. 'I hope that Mabryl would have been pleased. You don't know how sorry I am that he couldn't be here. I sometimes feel there must have been more I could have done so he could be with us now.'

The young half-elf's face filled with sorrow as he spoke.

'I am certain there's nothing at all you can blame yourself for, Carthinal.' Tharron placed a reassuring hand on Carthinal's arm. 'Just be glad for his life and remember him as he would have wanted you to remember him. And,' he added, 'If he can see you from where he's gone, I know he will look on you with pride.'

'You're right of course,' replied Carthinal. 'I'll never forget his kindness to me. I owe him more than I could ever repay. I'll try to live as he taught me and maybe that'll be some repayment of my debt.'

'Well said,' smiled Tharron, 'but this is a time for celebration, not sadness. You've made it into the ranks of the mages, and there's nothing to stop you from going further. There are no more tests like the ones you have just taken, only your own growing powers and experience will take you through to the ranks to the arch-mages and maybe even magister some day in the future.' He shivered suddenly. 'It's beginning to get a little cooler out here. It must be nearing half after the eleventh hour. I usually eat something at around the twelfth hour. Would you care to join me? The dining room will be opening fairly soon, or we could go to an inn. There's quite a good one not far away. I knew Mabryl very well when he was in the Tower and would like to talk about him with you.'

Carthinal suddenly realised he had not eaten for a long time. He accepted Tharron's invitation and the two of them decided to go to the inn, away from the confines of the Tower so they could have some privacy and for Carthinal to escape the reminders of the tests just undertaken.

The meal was excellent, and Tharron insisted Carthinal drink some of the extremely good wine he ordered as a celebration of his success.

'You'll get your results officially tomorrow when you'll find out how well you've done overall,' Tharron told him. 'The practical is weighted in the results and carries twice the marks of the others, but you'll get your final results tomorrow at the Ceremony of the Presentation of the Robes.

After a very good meal, for which Tharron insisted on paying, Carthinal excused himself and left to make his way to see Yssalithissandra. It was about an hour after sunset by the time he knocked on her door.

'Come in, Carthinal,' called a warm, feminine voice from inside the rooms.

He opened the door, entered, and found himself in a cosy room. There was a fire burning in the grate on the wall to the right as he entered, with a pile of logs ready to replenish it as it burned down. In front of the fire were two settees set facing each other. They were upholstered in red velvet with gold covered cushions scattered over them. On the floor was a rug of red and gold and gold brocade curtains hung at the window on the opposite side of the room from the fire. A window seat filled the window alcove and the curtains were closed against the chill of the night air.

The room was lit by candles in holders rather than by torches, and between the two settees was a low table supporting two wineglasses and a bottle of wine. Sitting on one of the settees was Yssalithissandra. She was wearing white robes, and her hair was unbound. It seemed to be made of spun gold in the flickering light of the candles and fell down past her shoulders, reaching almost to her waist. Carthinal stopped in the doorway. He knew he was staring, but could not help himself. She was beautiful.

'Come and sit down, Carthinal,' she said, 'and have a drink. I've opened a bottle of Perimo in honour of your success.'

Carthinal was not sure he should have any more to drink as he had wine with his dinner, but Yssalithissandra was already pouring a glass of the sparkling pink wine for him. He thanked her and sat on the opposite settee.

'Now, I want to know about Mabryl. Tell me all about your life with him. We knew each other well when he was at the Tower. Then, he decided he didn't want the academic life anymore, went adventuring, and we lost touch after a while.'

'He told me after he left the Tower, he had gone adventuring for a number of years until he felt he was too old. Then, he settled in Bluehaven, working for the Duke and other nobility. I believe he occasionally had the odd job from King Gerim, too,' Carthinal replied.

'Did he now?' Yssalithissandra sounded impressed. 'I always knew he had it in him to go far. If he had been so minded, I believe he could have been Chief Magister of the Tower, but he preferred to live more freely than that job would have allowed.'

They talked about Mabryl for quite some time, each remembering tales of him, and laughing over some of the exploits he had got up to as a student, as well as Carthinal relating some of the antics of himself and the other apprentices, which annoyed Mabryl. Carthinal felt much better as the evening wore on. He felt that talking of Mabryl to someone who had known him well and had been a valued friend was, at last, helping him to come to terms with the death of his foster father.

'I'd almost forgotten the other apprentices,' said Carthinal suddenly. 'They'll have to find another mentor now. They also don't know of Mabryl's death. I'm ashamed to say I'd completely forgotten about them until just now.'

'I'll send word to them, and tell them they can come and join me here at the Tower. I'll take them on as my apprentices. I don't have any at the moment.'

'Thank you Yssalithissandra. That will be a great help,' replied Carthinal.

'Please, Carthinal—Yssa. I hope we'll be friends after this evening,' protested the elf, pouring out another glass of wine.

Carthinal laughed. 'Of course, we will be, Yssa,' he replied, 'but I really shouldn't have any more wine. I'm feeling a little light-headed as it is. I had some with Tharron over dinner, too.'

Yssa looked up from pouring the wine. Her eyes were unreadable. She set down the bottle and moved over to sit down by Carthinal.

She stroked his hair, saying, 'It is the most beautiful colour. Those reddish glints! How I envy you.'

'But your own hair is so beautiful, Yssa,' replied the bemused half-elf. 'How can you envy someone who has red hair? I was always teased about it when I was younger. It came from my mother, you know. Now your hair is like spun gold—a precious metal, while mine is mere copper.' He took a strand in his fingers as he spoke. 'And it feels like silk,' he continued.

Yssa blushed as he spoke. She was feeling a little light-headed from the wine, as indeed was Carthinal. A log in the fire popped, but neither of them seemed to notice it. They continued to talk to each other of inconsequential things and became acutely aware of the proximity of the other and seemingly unaware of their surroundings. The world had contracted to just the two of them and the settee on which they were sitting.

Before he knew that he was going to do it, Carthinal took her hand and kissed her palm. She looked into his eyes, which seemed a darker blue than ever. Her hand came up to caress his cheek and as she did so, he leaned forward and kissed her lightly on the lips. It seemed to whet his appetite for her because he then pulled her towards him and kissed her again, this time, more passionately. Yssa responded to his ardour and her lips parted as she accepted his kiss.

After a few minutes, she stood, took his hand and said, huskily, 'Come into the bedroom. It'll be more comfortable,' and she pulled him towards a door in the back wall of the room.

Carthinal followed her and once in the room, they made love on her large and comfortable bed.

The daylight streaming in through the window woke Carthinal. He could not place where he was for several minutes and then he realised as the memory flooded back. What had he done? He was in the bed of a respected arch-mage, and he merely newly promoted. She would be so angry at allowing this to happen he was sure. They had both been a little tipsy from the wine, but he should have been more responsible. After telling Tharron that he wanted to live as Mabryl had taught him, he immediately went and took advantage of a woman under the influence of alcohol.

At that moment the door opened and Yssa entered with coffee.

'Yssa! I'm so sorry. Last night should not have happened.'

She laughed. 'Why ever not? Didn't you enjoy yourself? I know I did. You are a good-looking, young man and an excellent lover. Didn't I please you? Don't you find me attractive?'

On receiving replies of a positive nature, she continued, 'Then, what's to regret?'

'But you are an eminent arch-mage and I'm just newly promoted!' Carthinal also felt some guilt about Asphodel, although he told himself that he would probably never see her again.

'Rot!' replied Yssa. 'Since when does that matter? What is rank anyway? Simply something saying that I have more experience than you do. And I'm willing to bet that at some time in the future you'll be a better mage than ever I am. Now, drink your coffee and get dressed or you'll be late for the ceremony. There're soap and things on the washstand in the corner. I've heated up some water for you.'

With that, Yssa left the room. Carthinal sipped his coffee and then got out of bed. True to her word, Yssa brought water, and when he was washed and dressed, with his beard trimmed to the short stubble he preferred, he strode out of the room.

Yssa looked him over. 'That's better. Now, you look fit for a presentation. You'd better go on down. Please don't be concerned over last night. It was something that happened that neither of us planned. There are no strings, Carthinal, remember that.'

Carthinal left the room and descended the stairs feeling relief at Yssa's words. They could still be friends without last night getting in the way. The young half-elf was pleased to think that, as he truly liked Yssa and enjoyed her company and wanted to think that she also liked him and equally enjoyed his company, which, it seemed, she did. Yes, they could be friends.

He came to the Great Hall, which seemed even larger than before. It was filled with chairs, and a platform was erected on one side. The other four, newly qualified mages were already there, and they called him over. Hammevaro did not seem very pleased to see him, but the other three were very welcoming.

'Now, we'll see how well we really did,' remarked Grimmaldo. 'They'll give us our overall results at the ceremony.'

Shortly afterwards, they were told to take their seats at the front of the room, and the other chairs quickly filled up. Soon the magisters - the highest-ranking mages, entered in the golden robes that were reserved for these high-ranking men and women and took their place on the platform.

They went up one by one and collected their robes. At the same time, their final grades were given. Grimmaldo had achieved a good pass, as had Hammevaro. Olipeca obtained a merit, but Carthinal had achieved a distinction. All except Hammevaro were pleased with their results, but even he managed to relax a little during the celebratory meal after the ceremony.

Eventually, everything drew to a close, and the group was free to don their new robes, which they did with alacrity, and to go out to celebrate in their own way.

Chapter 6
Quest

Carthinal had been celebrating with the other newly-appointed mages after the presentations and the celebratory feast, and drinking a farewell to Laurre. They found they missed the lanky apprentice, although they had only known him for a few days.

'He would want us to have a drink for him, I'm sure,' commented Grimmaldo. 'To you, Laurre, wherever you are now.' He raised his glass. The others did the same.

They were all still feeling rather tired after the practical tests, and so they bid one another farewell by mid-afternoon and Carthinal returned to the Inn.

As he began to climb the steps of the inn, a figure detached itself from the crowds and grabbed his arm. 'Carthinal! At last! Where've you been? It were a woman, weren't it? I hope she were worth it, 'cos I've been waitin' 'ere all bleedin' night and all day for you.'

'Yes, she...' Carthinal began, then checked himself, annoyed at being caught off guard. He looked down at the figure holding the sleeve of his robe.

It was Thad, grinning all over his face. 'I knew it! Don't worry, I'll not tell anyone, especially that elf cleric you had with you when I robbed you,' he said with a knowing look at Carthinal. 'But, hey, it's best you've forgotten her as she's now out of bounds.'

'What do you mean?' asked the mage.

'She's gone an' joined the bloody Daughters of Sylissa, ain't she? They're an enclosed order and only meet the public in the infirmary,'Thad responded. 'They're not allowed to even speak to each other except during those times they're healing. Didn't you know?'

Carthinal thought for a moment. This did not seem like Asphodel. He could not imagine her in such an order.

'How can you possibly know that?' he retorted.

'There's this man, an assassin, see. (I can't tell you his name for professional reasons. Right?) Anyway, he was bleedin' stupid enough to get injured rather badly, a botched job I think, and 'e went to th' infirmary for some 'ealin' yesterday. Well, it seems that a young curate called Asphodel 'ealed him partially, but against orders. Br... th' assassin I mean, thinks she may be in trouble over it.'

'I hope not,' worried Carthinal. 'Anyway, I'm sure you didn't just come here to gossip.'

'No. Got your damn horse statue thingy, ain't I,' replied Thad, handing it over. 'Told you I'd get it back.'

'I hope you didn't have to do anything drastic to get it,' said Carthinal.

'No. Just more promises to my fence, that's all.'

Carthinal sighed. He was sure Thad could manage the man who "liked boys", streetwise as he was. He had, after all, been brought up in the Warren and survived to reach his mid-teens, but he could not help being a little anxious for him all the same. He thanked the young thief and turned to go into the inn.

Carthinal hefted the figurine in his hand as he continued into the inn. He examined it and there was no doubt in his mind that this was indeed the one Danu gave to Mabryl as surety of his validity. It seemed like months since that happened. So much had passed in a few, short weeks. He sighed, opened the door, and entered. He was immediately rushed by a delighted dwarf, and nearly knocked off his feet.

'Whoa there, Basalt,' he exclaimed, 'Don't kill me, please.'

Basalt then launched into a tirade of abuse at Carthinal for staying out without telling him.

'Hang on, Bas,' Carthinal said when the dwarf paused for a breath. 'It was something that came up on the spur of the moment. I'm sorry if you were anxious, but you and Fero seem to be able to have a good time on your own. Where is he anyway? I thought he'd still be here.' Carthinal looked round the room.

'That's just it. He never came again, although he said he would,' Basalt replied, sinking into his seat again. 'Carthinal, I'm worried. I know we've not known Fero long, but I didn't have him down as someone who would break a promise.'

'No, nor did I,' frowned Carthinal, sitting down by the flustered dwarf. 'In that case, I'm sorry that you had to worry about me as well.'

'Well, you know the rumours about those practical tests—that they can sometimes injure or kill. I was thinking the worst about both of you,' grumbled Basalt.

Carthinal remembered Laurre again. 'Yes. The rumours are true. One of our number never made it.' He rubbed his hand over his face. 'He was a good man, too.'

'Well, you did,' responded the dwarf, brightening somewhat.

Carthinal told Basalt about his test (but not about his night) and showed him the figurine. The other took it and looked at it carefully with the practised eye of one who knows jewellery.

'Yes, I'd say it's the genuine thing. A bit late now to take it to the Duke, but I suggest we go first thing tomorrow and then begin asking around about Fero.'

Carthinal agreed and Basalt then told him about his doings and the mysterious way that his new employer, Nitormon, had been removed without any explanation. He was in the middle of this tale when the door opened and a figure in a white cloak with the hood over its head, appeared in the doorway.

Carthinal recognised the figure immediately.

'Asphodel!' he exclaimed, moving a chair to their table so she could sit down with them.

She came into the room, but made no move to remove her cloak, keeping the hood firmly in place.

Sitting down in the chair Carthinal had drawn up, she said, 'I've come to tell you that I'm leaving Hambara tomorrow morning. I'm going on the road as a wandering cleric.'

'Then you didn't join the Daughters of Sylissa!' exclaimed Carthinal surprising himself at the relief he felt at that. 'Someone told me this morning that you had joined their ranks.'

'No. They tried to make me, so I decided to leave instead. I told them what they could do with their "Daughters".' That was all Asphodel told them of her ordeal at the temple. 'I thought I owed it to you to tell you what I was doing.'

'As it happens, I'm at a loose end myself,' continued Carthinal. 'With Mabryl dead and his other apprentices coming to the Tower to be apprenticed with a new master there, I have little to keep me here, or anywhere come to that. I may leave and come with you. If you have no objections that is.'

Asphodel looked relieved at this, and said that she would be pleased for his company. Bas also said he would like to leave the town; since there seemed to be no work for him there since his employer had disappeared, and so the three of them decided to leave after seeing the Duke the following morning.

They all hoped to find Fero on their travels. Basalt and Carthinal told of what had happened to them in the few days that had passed since Asphodel left them, and then Asphodel called to Keloriff to see if there was any chance her room was still available.

'I'm sorry, Sister, but we let it to a young couple just this morning. Horselords if I am not mistaken, from beyond the

Western Mountains,' replied the innkeeper. 'However, we have a single room up in the attic. It's not usually let out to guests, as it is not quite up to the standards that we have set ourselves, but you're welcome to have it if you wish. There would be a considerable reduction in our usual prices, of course,' he added. 'If you don't wish to take up the offer, however, I can recommend you try at the Jolly Gnome on Bull Street. Their accommodation is not as good as ours is, but it's clean and friendly. Alternatively, there's the Blue Boar, a high-class place near the Palace, but with prices to match. I wouldn't recommend many of the other inns in the town to a member of the clergy, though.'

'No, the attic will be fine for tonight. We're planning to leave tomorrow,' replied Asphodel.

'Are you not going to stay for the Equinox celebrations then?' queried Keloriff. 'They're really something here in Hambara. This square is quite spectacular, and I hear there's a specialist coming to show us some new thing he calls "fireworks". They are lights and fire in the sky, so I believe. It sounds like magic to me, but I'm assured it's not.'

On being told that it was unlikely they would be there for that spectacular event, Keloriff went away to get his wife to prepare the attic room.

Asphodel was still wearing her cloak and hood, and Basalt asked her why she had not removed it in the warmth of the inn. She told the pair of the cutting of her long, black hair, and that she did not want anyone to see her as she felt she looked ugly.

'Come on now, lass,' soothed Bas. 'We're your friends. We would never think you looked ugly. In fact, I don't think there is a mortal alive on Vimar who could find it in themselves to proclaim you ugly, even if you were bald.'

With much more coaxing, Asphodel finally removed her cloak. She certainly looked different. Carthinal privately mourned the loss of her beautiful hair, but to his eyes, she was still a beautiful and delicate elf, and he told her as much.

'Thank you for saying that, Carthinal,' replied the elf. 'It's kind of you, but I don't feel beautiful, and probably won't until my hair grows again.'

She then looked at him with a half-smile on her face. 'By the way, I never congratulated you on your success in your tests.'

Soon after, the three decided to go to bed, Asphodel after a nice, long soak in the bath.

'*To the Ninth Hell with eschewing luxury,*' thought Asphodel as she soaked in the warm water. '*If this is a sin, then I am guilty as charged.*'

The next morning, just as the trio finished their breakfast in preparation to visiting the Duke, a boy came rushing into the Inn. He looked round until he saw them and then, slowing his pace, walked around the tables to the group. The boy stopped and looked at Carthinal, breathing deeply as though he had been running. (Which indeed he had).

'Ye be the mage, Carthinal?' he panted.

When Carthinal replied in the affirmative, he handed him a letter, sealed with the Duke's seal. He then walked out of the inn and they could see him running through the crowd after he left, jinking this way and that to avoid collisions.

Carthinal opened the letter, and read the neat handwriting within.

'*To Carthinal and Company*

Please come to the Palace as soon as possible this morning. I have something to discuss with you. It relates to the letter you brought to me the other day. I have now come to a decision and want to put a proposition to you.

Rollo. Duke of Hambara'

'Well, what do you think of that!' exclaimed Basalt. 'Just a little longer and we'd be there anyway. Wonder what it's all about?'

'Well, we won't find out by lingering here over our breakfast, Bas,' replied Carthinal, drinking the last of his coffee and standing up.

Since the three had finished eating, they decided to go immediately to see the Duke. As they left the inn, Asphodel once more donned her cloak. It happened to have started to rain and so it did not seem at all unusual for her to have her hood up. The other two also donned cloaks and they walked through the town, heads down against the rain, trying to avoid the inevitable muddy puddles, and saying very little.

The walk through the Palace grounds was not as pleasant this time, owing both to the rain and their continuing anxiety about Fero's whereabouts. When they got to the inner gates, they were open as well, and the three were waved through. They hurried through the formal gardens and past the fountain with its wonderful, golden fish with barely a glance, and through the door that was being held open for them by the elf, Daramissillo.

Daramissillo took their cloaks, and if he noticed Asphodel's hair, he was too, well bred for it to show on his face. He took them to the study and showed them in, saying that they were to make themselves comfortable until the Duke could be with them. He would only be a few minutes.

The three sat down by the fire and got warm and dry. They waited for about fifteen minutes before the Duke finally arrived, apologising for keeping them waiting. After shaking the hands of each of them in turn, he sat down beside them.

'Firstly, may I apologise for bringing you out in this weather and also, to you, Basalt, for hindering your job-hunting. However, I wanted to ensure that you were free of any commitments if I needed you.'

'You were behind all that difficulty?' Basalt was amazed.

The Duke smiled ruefully at the dwarf and said, 'Yes, I'm afraid so. I think, also that you, Asphodel, were subject to some—how shall I put it—inconvenience? I hope to explain myself shortly.'

He then stood and went to the door of the study. He opened it, and beckoned. Through the door came a tall man in black, dirty and unkempt, with his hair hanging down in untidy locks. A guard gave him a push into the room, at which action, Duke Rollo reprimanded him. The man had his head bowed so his hair was obscuring his face, but even so, the three companions recognised Fero.

'You may go,' the Duke commanded to the guard.

'But, Your Grace, suppose the prisoner decides to attack you?' The guard was reluctant to leave.

The Duke spoke in a voice, which although quiet, brooked no argument. 'I told you to leave. Do not cause me to have you disciplined.'

The man left and the Duke led Fero to the remaining chair. 'I must also offer my most sincere and humble apologies to you, Fero. You have been most badly treated.'

Fero looked up at this, but his black eyes seemed dull and lifeless.

'It is true that I gave orders that you, none of you, were to leave the city as I thought I may need you,' went on Duke Rollo, 'But someone went too far here. It was never my intention you be treated so badly. The lieutenant concerned has been punished. Demoted to the ranks. I was always a little concerned about him anyway. A bit too enthusiastic in his duties, if you know what I mean, and to frame you for theft and throw you in jail was going too far.'

Asphodel went over to Fero during this speech. She laid a gentle hand on his arm tentatively as though expecting a rebuff.

Fero, however smiled slightly at her through his hair and said in a quiet voice, 'I'll be all right now, Asphodel. Now that I'm out of that place.'

Asphodel looked up from Fero as the Duke began speaking again.

'I want you all to listen carefully to what I have to say. Firstly, I've concluded that you are what you told me, just a group of people travelling to Hambara who met on the road. Quite why I believe that I don't know. There seem to be blanks around you all and I've been unable to find out much about any of you.'

'The figurine!' Carthinal had forgotten all about it. 'You said you wanted the figurine. I've managed to get it back.' He fumbled in his pockets. 'Here it is,' and he passed it to the Duke who went over to the window and examined it carefully.

'Yes. This is my old friend Danu's horse figurine all right. I have its twin right here on my desk. How did you manage to get it back? No matter, there's business to discuss.'

The Duke came back to his seat and sat down. 'Danu's letter held some disquieting information. At the moment, I don't want to disclose everything that it said. It's not certain yet, but if Danu's suspicions are correct, we are all in grave danger. His words were, "Danger lurks on all sides if my suspicions are true." I believe his suspicions are true. This is where you come in. If, and as I said, I believe him, if Danu is correct, I want you to take on a quest for me. I want you to find Sauvern's Sword.'

With those words, the Duke sat back in his chair and, steepling his fingers, looked from face to face of those before him to gauge their reactions.

Carthinal sat in stunned silence, staring at the Duke as if he had just asked them to fly up to Heaven and speak with the gods themselves. Then Basalt broke the silence.

'Begging your pardon, Your Grace, but what is this Sword, and who is Sauvern?'

'Of course, you are not from Grosmer, and neither are Asphodel and Fero, so I'd better explain. Please bear with me, Carthinal.'

Carthinal nodded.

'Once, Grosmer did not exist. There were six separate kingdoms, roughly corresponding to the six dukedoms of the present day. These kingdoms were constantly warring with each other, so when the raiders came from across the ocean and sailed up the Three Seas to get slaves and plunder, the kingdoms were easy pickings for them.

'This happened numerous times over the centuries until Sauvern came along. Sauvern was the king of what eventually became Hambara, my own dukedom. His origins are somewhat mysterious. Some said he was the trueborn son of the king, hidden to prevent some mysterious prophecy from coming true. Others said that he was a bastard son of the king, raised by a peasant woman, and yet others claim he was a bastard of the queen. Whatever the truth, he eventually came to the throne and it is said, ruled wisely and well.

'One day an old woman came to the palace begging. Sauvern called her in and feasted with her at his own table. After the meal, she threw off her cloak and revealed an elven priestess. She took a magnificent sword from her side and presented it to Sauvern.

"'This Sword is called Equilibrium," she said. "And it will protect the Balance in the lands and help you against the evils that come from over the sea."

'With that, she withdrew leaving all gasping at the beauty of the Sword.

'Then the raiders came again. Sauvern saw them decimate Bluehaven and Sendolina and begin their march up towards Hambara. He realised that Hambara could not stand alone, so he made alliances with all the other kings and together they drove the raiders back to their lands over the sea.

'Then the kings realised that it was much more sensible to cooperate than to fight and they elected Sauvern as High King. He built Asperilla as his capital rather than rule from one of the kingdoms. Of course, as you realise by now, this eventually led to the old kings becoming dukes, and Grosmer becoming one kingdom.

'As to the Sword—well, it is said that it was buried with Sauvern, but the whereabouts of his tomb is lost, if it were ever known, but legends say that it will be found again when the land of Grosmer is in dire need. The letter you brought from my old friend Danu of Bluehaven suggests that time is now.'

Fero spoke up. 'So, you expect us to search for a sword that may or may not exist?'

'Yes,' replied the other. 'As to its existence, that much is true. The Sword existed all right. Danu agrees with me on this. I have no real proof, but just call it intuition if you wish. Don't make a decision right away. You must have the chance to discuss it.

'If you agree to go on this quest, I suggest you begin by doing some research in Hambara. You have, between you, access to a number of sources that any one individual can't see. Even the Duke! You, Carthinal, can look in the libraries of the Mage Tower. You, Asphodel, have access to the libraries of the temples, and I give you the run of my library here in the Palace. It's quite extensive, you know. Some of my ancestors were avid readers it seems, and no one here has ever catalogued all the books and scrolls, so we don't know exactly what we have, though my daughter likes spending time in the library.'

He smiled. 'It's nearing lunchtime, so I'll allow you to discuss the matter in private. Through the door there,' he indicated a door next to the fireplace, 'you'll find a small room. I use it to sleep in sometimes when I'm busy late into the night.

'Daramissillo will bring you some food. Please, don't hurry with your decision. This evening will do. I'll be in here when you want to speak to me and you can go out through the doors onto the terrace and walk around the grounds if you wish, although in this weather I prefer to remain indoors.

'By the way, if you agree to go on the quest, I will pay all your expenses here in Hambara, and any treasure you may find, except the Sword, that is, you may keep.'

He opened a door at the far side of the fireplace and the four of them entered the room.

Asphodel sat down in a chair next to a fire that had been lit in the room's fireplace. She reached over and put another log on the blaze. The rain had made the day feel cooler than many they had recently and the warmth of the fire was welcome. Carthinal perched on the narrow bed, which was along one wall, while Basalt sat down in another chair. Fero strode over to the fireplace and leaned on the mantelpiece.

'Is this some elaborate, practical joke?' he growled. 'First, I'm put in prison for something I didn't do, then I'm asked to go on some, what do you call it in Grosmerian? Wild, wyvern chase? Is that right?'

'I think that Duke Rollo is serious about this,' replied Asphodel. 'Very serious. So serious that he decided to prevent you from getting work and leaving the city. That has to be a massive job to tell everyone not to employ us.'

'He didn't! He missed Nitormon,' grinned Basalt, pleased that the Duke's men failed in something. 'I hope he's all right now. I must ask the Duke later.'

'I agree that he's serious about it,' responded Carthinal, 'but he told us to decide if we are to join in with him and his impossible ideas.'

The discussion continued until the door opened and, true to his word, the Duke had sent Daramissillo with lunch. The elf brought a steaming tureen of soup and fresh rolls, with pastries and fruit to complete the meal. He also included a pot of tea, which they welcomed for its warmth. The companions stopped discussing their options while partaking of this meal.

After they had eaten, a little mousy girl, who looked frightened to death of the strangers, cleared the meal away. Fero then stood up and told them he could no longer remain cooped up and decided to take the duke at his word and go for a walk in the grounds, rain or no rain. He crossed the room to the doors onto the terrace, and as he opened them, the rain seemed to cease. The smell of freshly washed vegetation drifted through the window and they could all hear the drip,drip, drip of water as it dropped from the eaves of the Palace and branches of trees. Suddenly, they all felt a desire to walk in the gardens and feel some grass beneath their feet. Picking up their cloaks, they all, with one accord, passed through the doors onto the terrace just as the sun's rays found a way through the banks of cloud overhead.

Later that day, after much further discussion, they had formulated a plan to lay before the Duke, and so they re-entered his office.

'You have decided then?' the Duke asked them, getting up from his desk and indicating they once more take seats near the fire. 'I hope you decided in my favour.'

'Not exactly,' replied Carthinal. 'But we haven't rejected your offer, though. In fact, we have a proposition to make to you,'

The Duke raised his eyebrows questioningly.

Carthinal resumed speaking. 'We suggest that we postpone agreeing to this quest immediately.' He raised his hand, as the Duke started to protest the urgency of the pursuit, and continued, 'What we suggest is that we spend time in research, trying to find something out about this mythical Sword. If we find the whereabouts, or sufficient clues as to where the thing is, we will reconsider going on this quest of yours. We will, however, gratefully accept your offer to pay our expenses while we are searching as we are running short of cash.'

The Duke thought deeply for a few minutes and then said, 'I suppose that's fair. I shouldn't have expected you to commit yourselves to such an open-ended task. However, I'll give you a note to show at your inn and any shops that you use to further your research. Oh, and Basalt,' he went on. 'Your former, brief employer has been recompensed for his inconvenience. I have given him new premises in a much more accessible area, and he has my permission to use my personal recommendation. He has my arms to hang above his shop. He is a remarkable craftsman. Should go far.'

'Thank you, sir,' replied the dwarf, relieved. 'I was worried about him.'

Having given the quartet the promissory note, the Duke bid them farewell, after assuring them that the library at the Palace would be available to them at any time. Daramissillo led them to the door, and bowed his own farewell and they walked slowly back to the Golden Dragon, wondering how they had managed to get themselves into such an impossible seeming task.

Chapter 7
Research

The four of them had returned to the inn the previous evening and gone to the room which Carthinal, Basalt and Fero were sharing. Asphodel sat down on Fero's bed, which stood nearest to the door and sighed. She had been wondering all the way back from the Palace why they had agreed to this and she had said as much. Fero said moodily that as he could not read, he would be of little help in the research so did not deserve the payment of his expenses. It had been up to Carthinal to reassure him that both he and Basalt would be helpful in interpreting anything they found. Their brains were of use he had told them, even if they had to have things read to them.

The next morning found them approaching the gates of the Palace once more. They had agreed that Asphodel would go to the temple of Zol with Fero to help her since she did not want to approach Sylissa's temple after her precipitous exit only a few days before. Anyway, Zol was the god of learning and knowledge, so it seemed reasonable to go to his temple first. Bas and Carthinal would begin their search in the library at the Palace. Their ways parted at the gates of the Duke's residence, and Carthinal and Bas, after leaving their weapons at the gatehouse as usual, and with Bas's usual grumbling about it, walked through the park and gardens to the house.

Here, they were let in and Daramissillo, after bowing to them, led them to a door on the opposite side of the hall from the Duke's study.

'The Library, sir,' he said, bowing as he opened the door.

They entered a large room, which seemed to run the length of the eastern side of the Palace. Dark oak panelling covered the walls on one side, but to keep it from appearing too dark, glazed windows filled the other. Carthinal could not even begin to think how much the glass would have cost. The Duke of Hambara was obviously a very, rich man, or rather his ancestors, who had the library glazed, must have been. The room stretched away to their left, and from the ceiling depended crystal chandeliers. They had candles in them ready to be lit if needed, but as the morning light streamed through the windows, there was no necessity. However, this was not what caught Carthinal's attention, marvellous as it seemed. Bookshelves, all full of books and scrolls, filled the room. He had never in his life seen so many books and all in one place. The shelves ran down the long side of the room opposite the windows and were from floor to ceiling, broken only by the two doors that led to the great hall of the palace, and one which led to the central quadrangle and its garden. Occasionally, there were other freestanding bookshelves arranged at right angles to the wall and windows. Now their task seemed even more daunting than ever.

'Look at those chandeliers,' whispered Basalt. 'They must be a magnificent sight when the candles are lit, with the glass refracting the light.'

Just at that moment, two figures appeared through the door nearer the far end of the library. One of them they recognised as Duke Rollo. By his side walked the most beautiful girl either of them had ever seen. She was tall and slender with silvery-blonde hair and Carthinal estimated she was about eighteen-years-old.

The Duke approached them and said, 'This is my daughter, Randa. I've told her to help you to find what you require or you'll be here forever, and we haven't got forever, I'm afraid. Randa has spent a lot of time in the library and is the most likely person to be able to find anything you need. Randa, this is Carthinal and Basalt.'

Carthinal bowed slightly to the young woman, and nudged Basalt hard to remind him to do the same.

'Pleased to meet you, my Lady,' he said.

Lady Randa sniffed. 'At least you have some manners, for a half-elf,' she replied rather imperiously.

'Father, do I really have to work with common riffraff, and a dwarf and half-elf at that? Not even human!'

'Now, Randa,' replied the Duke. 'You know how important this is. Carthinal and Basalt will not be able to find what they are looking for until the next time both moons are dark without some help from someone who knows the way things work in this library. Please, do this one small thing to help. For me?'

Obviously, the Duke did not often impose his will on her, and she sniffed again, but, turning to Carthinal, she said, 'Well, half-elf, if I must do this unpleasant task and work alongside you and the dwarf, we'd better get started. I have fencing practice just after the seventh hour of the day, so we'd better begin immediately as it is already…' here, she glanced at an hourglass on one of the tables. 'Half an hour past the third hour. I will leave you so I can eat with my father at half an hour after the sixth hour, so that leaves us with only three hours. I cannot be with you after the noon meal as I have fencing practice.'

'Randa, can't you miss your fencing for a couple of days?' pleaded the Duke.

'Father! I will get rusty if I don't practice. I must also exercise Storm. You know how he gets if he doesn't get a gallop each day, and no one else seems to be able to control him.'

With that, Lady Randa walked away from the Duke, beckoning Carthinal and Basalt to follow. The Duke held his hands out as though to say 'What can I do with her?' Then he turned and left the library.

'Are you coming, half-elf?' called the girl from half way down the library. Her movements were beautiful and graceful. Carthinal remembered the portrait in the Duke's study. She looked so much like the woman in that portrait. Of course, that was her mother who, according to the guard at the gate, died in childbirth. Her mother's hair in the portrait had been black, so Carthinal presumed she inherited her blonde hair from her father.

'*A pity she's not inherited his character as well,*' he thought.

'She's going to help us?' queried Bas in a whisper. 'She looks as though she'd rather run us through with her fencing sword.'

'She does seem to be rather a spoiled brat doesn't she?' whispered Carthinal back. 'Still, we've only got to put up with her for a short while. As soon as this research is over, we can leave her to her father. And good luck to him. Come on. We'd better follow her.'

The three hours in the library with Lady Randa were not quite as bad as Carthinal and Basalt thought they would be. True, Lady Randa insisted on calling them "half-elf" and "dwarf", and not by their names, until Carthinal decided he had enough and said,

'We have names, my Lady, and we would both prefer you use them. I am Carthinal and my friend is called, Basalt. Please, remember that.'

Lady Randa looked at him askance at being spoken to in what she thought as far from respectful but she said nothing and afterwards called them by their names as requested. She made some scathing comments about the fact that Bas did not read, though, but none the less they found her a great help. She located the scrolls and books on Sauvern and helped to read them and to make notes in her beautiful and elegant handwriting.

During that day, they found little certainty about the life and death of Sauvern, except that he had somehow united the warring cities under his rule, and the united provinces had then gone on to repulse invaders from across the sea. Most of these tales had the invaders coming from the east. They also discovered that his body disappeared just after his death. All the tales were clear on that. There were various tales of the enchanted Sword but nothing seemed clear as to its ultimate fate. Several accounts, however, hinted that there were clues to be found as to its whereabouts. All this they gleaned by much cross-referencing and deduction. True to her word, Lady Randa left the pair in time for lunch and did not return. Daramissillo brought a tray of lunch for the pair in the library, and after that, they worked alone. Carthinal managed to teach Basalt the letters that made up the name of "Sauvern", and "Sword", which meant he could help a little with the search. By the end of the day, they were both feeling tired and left to return to the inn.

The other two were already there when Basalt and Carthinal entered the inn's common room. They greeted the newcomers and told them they ordered dinner for them all. Fero seemed to be coming out of his depression now that he had his freedom once more, but Asphodel thought privately that he would not be himself until they were out of the city completely.

They exchanged the information they had found. There were again conflicting stories about Sauvern and the Sword. However, tales said had been named "Equilibrium" in all the tales that Fero and Asphodel had found, and to have powerful magic.

Asphodel and Fero had found a poem, seeming to refer to Sauvern's tomb and the Sword. They showed the copy they had made to Carthinal who read it aloud.

"'Deep in the forest lies the tomb
Protected from all evil.
Sauvern lies as in the womb,
Safe from man or devil.

"His Sword is resting by his side
Awaiting call to action.
When danger lurks on every side
You need the Sword's reaction.

"But first, 6? 8? Questers bold must go
To Sauvern's tomb, surrounded
By Guardians strong, no fear must show
Or from there they will be hounded."

'Asphodel, you have two numbers with question marks in the last verse. Why?'

Asphodel replied that the ancient scroll was unclear in places. They managed to piece together the rest, but could not distinguish the numbers very well. Context did not help here. They felt they had made some progress with the discovery of the poem, though. Maybe, this was the time for the Sword to be rediscovered and the clues were beginning to come to light. After all, was it just coincidence that the words used by Duke Danu of Bluehaven were almost exactly the same as a line in the poem? Duke Danu told Rollo that 'Danger lurks all around'. Nevertheless, whatever the truth, they were still a long way from finding the tomb. In a forest somewhere in the world, although most probably on the continent of Khalram, the continent on which Grosmer resided. They still had much to be done, so they retired to bed to continue the following day.

The next day, Carthinal and Basalt returned to the Palace to try to find anything about the whereabouts of the tomb. Lady Randa arrived again, saying she had risen early in order to exercise her stallion, Storm, and she did not have any weapons practice that day. She should have gone to practice her music, but her music master reported that he felt ill, so they had all day. Her expression said she was glad of this excuse to get away from her music, even if it meant spending the day with "riffraff." Truth to tell, she found the work interesting. She never took much interest in history before, and it surprised her how fascinating she found it.

Carthinal and Bas exchanged a glance at this dire prospect, but both wisely refrained from making a comment.

Lady Randa did not make it any easier, however. She did, most of the time, remember to call them by their names, but made it abundantly clear that she considered herself above them in all ways, and that only her father's request made her come to work with them.

Shortly after lunch, just after Lady Randa returned from lunching with her father as usual, and as Carthinal searched for a specific scroll, he noticed an unusual crack around a particular bookshelf. He called Lady Randa over and asked her if she knew of any secret passages in the house.

'There are tales and rumours of course,' she replied, 'as there always are in old houses, and this house is very old. It has been rebuilt, modernised, and extended many times over the years. Why do you ask?'

'Because,' responded Carthinal, 'unless I am very much mistaken, there is a hidden door here which may lead to a secret room.'

'This is part of the old house,' Lady Randa told him, 'but I hardly think that a secret passage would have gone unnoticed by my father, or me—or my grandfather come to think of it. Why would a half-elf find something in a few minutes that the family hasn't found in generations?'

'Elvenkind have very good eyes and we are good at spotting such things,' retorted Carthinal, keeping his temper with difficulty.

Basalt spotted the warning tone in Carthinal's voice and glared at him. It would not do for him to lose his temper and anger the daughter of the second most powerful man in all of Grosmer. However, Carthinal managed to hold onto his temper and suggested that he try to open the disputed door.

'If it will satisfy you,' replied Lady Randa imperiously and turned away.

A few moments later, a grinding and rumbling came from behind. She turned and her eyes popped. Where there had been a bookcase hole had appeared with steps leading downwards.

The three stood looking at each other in amazement. Carthinal was sure the bookcase concealed a hidden door, but not that it would open so easily, nor that it would reveal a secret passage. He thought at the most it would reveal a hidden room.

The stairs looked dark and cobwebby. Carthinal shuddered to think of the spiders running around. They had generations to breed down there. However, he would not reveal his feelings of revulsion to Lady Randa.

Instead, he said, 'Lady Randa, do you think it pertinent to explore this passage at this point? We are not sure it will aid us in our quest.'

He secretly hoped not to have to go down the stairs with their cobwebs and spiders, and that she would say others could explore. However, Lady Randa decided that since they had found the passage, they should be the ones to explore it.

'Why give the pleasure of discovering something new to people who did not find the passage?' she said.

Carthinal had to admire her guts. She reached for a torch on one of the walls and lit it, then made her way to the entrance.

'My Lady,' murmured Bas, 'we don't know what's down there. Maybe, we shouldn't go down without some weapons.'

'Are you afraid, Dwarf?' retorted her ladyship. 'If you are, then stay here. I'm going down.' She started to move towards the open door.

'Basalt is right, Your Ladyship,' Carthinal backed up his friend. 'At least get a sword or a dagger.'

'Hmm... I suppose that makes some sense,' Lady Randa eventually agreed. 'You two stay there and I'll get some weapons. What's your preferred weapon, Dwa...er... Basalt?'

'A battle axe, if you have one, your ladyship,' replied the dwarf.

'Typical. A messy weapon, but I understand the dwarves prefer it to a sword. A sword takes so much more skill to use.'

With that, she disappeared through one of the library doors to go in search of weapons. It was just as well she did, for she would have had Basalt taken to the nearest prison and the key thrown away if she could have heard him cursing at her condescension.

'A battle-axe takes as much bloody skill in wielding as a bleeding sword,' he spluttered. 'Dwarves begin to learn at a young age to become proficient. To become a master of the weapon takes years. That little minx knows nothing. How old is she? Seventeen? Eighteen?'

Fortunately, Carthinal had managed to calm him down by the time Lady Randa reappeared with the weapons. She had a fine long sword, which she claimed as her own, and a rather less than fine battle axe which she gave to Basalt, for once having the grace to apologise for it.

'It's the only one I could find,' she explained. 'My father captured it in some war or other, I believe. We don't have anyone here that uses a battle-axe now. Carthinal, just in case, I've brought a dagger. I understand that mages often use one, as they do not have the time to learn more subtle weapons.'

This she handed to the mage, hilt first as was polite. It appeared she did know some of the niceties of life.

'Diplomacy is not her second name, is it?' hissed Basalt to Carthinal.

The mage grinned at his friend in reply.

After they were armed, and Bas had hefted his battle axe a few times and proclaimed it 'Not too bad, considering', they made their way to the hidden entrance to the staircase. Basalt insisted on going first, much to Lady Randa's annoyance. She told him that she had trained in weapons with her father's master at arms and could use the sword, and since it was her father's own house, and she outranked the others in the group, she should lead the way.

Basalt pointed out be that as it may, but her father would have their heads if anything happened to her, and he was not going to allow her to go first.

Carthinal held his breath, waiting for the explosion from Lady Randa. She did not disappoint him.

She rounded on Bas like a whirlwind. 'You…you…Dwarf!' She said the word as though it were the worst insult in the world (which to her it may have been). 'You DARE to speak to me like that! Me! The Honourable Lady Randa! I am my father's only heir and will inherit this Dukedom. Yet you tell me *you* will not allow *me*! How dare you?'

However, she had not met with the stubbornness of the mountain dwarves. Carthinal thought they would remain there for the rest of their lives with the two arguing, and finally with Basalt standing, arms folded in front of the doorway so no one could pass. Lady Randa tried to push him out of the way at first, but Bas stood his ground. A dwarf standing his ground is very hard to move, even for a grown man, and Lady Randa was no grown man.

Eventually, her curiosity over the passageway overcame her anger and she said, rather reluctantly, 'Go in front if you wish then—and hope that whatever's down there kills you before I do.'

So, the three crept stealthily down the stairs, Basalt in the lead, Lady Randa next, and Carthinal in the rear. Carthinal was grateful for that as most of the cobwebs were swept away by the others, but he still had to steel himself not to cry out as a stray one swept his face. It would not do for them to think him such a coward as to be afraid of spiders, even if it were the truth. He kept a look out both to the side and behind, trusting to Bas to watch for anything in front, but they had an uneventful descent of the stairs, although the stairs were old. No one had passed that way in many, many years and their feet sent up clouds of dust, which made them sneeze. The stairs were not worn away either, in spite of their age. Another indication that they had not been much used.

To his consternation, Carthinal saw many, small, glowing creatures with his infra-vision. Spiders he assumed, that had lived and bred there for aeons. He shuddered, then suddenly, after what seemed like a long descent, they found themselves in a passage leading straight ahead.

He called to Basalt and the dwarf looked round. 'We seem to have come down a long way. You dwarves are used to being underground. How far down do you think we've come?'

Basalt frowned, did some calculations in his head and replied, 'We're very deep, Carthinal. Well below the foundations of the present Palace. If you ask me, we are at least 200 feet down. This looks like old stone. About 1,000 years, maybe a bit more, maybe a bit less.'

The three looked around in awe. The dry air in the room preserved the stonework well. The fact that no more cobwebs hung from this ceiling pleased Carthinal, too. The walls were well built and strong. They walked slowly and quietly down the corridor. They passed doors on either side, but none of them could manage to open them, no matter how hard they tried. They walked until they came to the end of the corridor, where another door stood in the end wall.

'Should I try?' whispered Basalt. (It did not seem right to speak normally in this ancient place).

'Go on then.' said Lady Randa and Carthinal together, and Carthinal added, 'Although, why this one should be any different Majora alone knows.'

He hardly got the words out of his mouth when he saw the door swinging open with a loud creak. Bas hardly had to try. It had not been either locked or stuck. As they entered the chamber in front of them, each drew a breath of amazement.

Fabulous carvings decorated the room. Unicorns and satyrs played in woods where dryads peeped shyly from behind their trees. A Centaur appeared to be discussing something with a nymph, half in and half out of her pool. Dragons basked in the sunlight and elves and humans were gathering flowers and making garlands to adorn each other. Here a group of dwarves, hard at work, dug minerals from their mines; there some merfolk sat on rocks in a cove while the waves broke around them. The surf looked so realistic they almost thought they could actually hear its booming as the waves crashed against the shore.

The room was circular in shape and in the centre stood a large, round table. On the table lay a number of books, a quill pen in its stand, rather tattered after all the years that had passed, a knife for sharpening the quill and an ink well, which had dried up. The books were stacked neatly, all except for one, which lay in front of a chair drawn up to the table, as though the room's occupant had been working there and just slipped out for a moment. A piece of paper in the book seemed to mark a place.

The three walked slowly around the room, gazing at the superb workmanship of the carvings. Basalt declared that it must have been dwarves who carved the stone, and no one, not even Lady Randa, disputed this statement. Eventually, Carthinal left Lady Randa and Basalt admiring the room, as he felt drawn to the books. He picked up one at random. It was a spell book. He carefully opened it, and it crackled with age. It seemed to be the spell book of a powerful mage. There were many complex spells in it, which Carthinal could not begin to comprehend. He put it down in its place and picked up another. This one he recognised. These were the simpler spells that he himself had in his own spell book, but it was written in an archaic style and he had some difficulty recognising some of the words. Then he noticed that Bas had gone to the desk and picked up the book with the "bookmark" in it.

Basalt thought he would look at the book, although he could not read. Maybe, he would be able to recognise the word shape Carthinal taught him stood for 'Sauvern'. To his surprise, part way through the text, he thought he recognised the word. He was not certain. These letters were formed in a slightly different way from the way Carthinal taught him, but it was enough for him to call Carthinal over.

Carthinal looked over Bas's shoulder, and Lady Randa came to see what Bas had found.

'It certainly seems to say "Sauvern",' Carthinal confirmed.

'But the rest?' queried Lady Randa. 'What about the rest? It looks like no language I've ever seen.'

'No. You won't have, and probably won't again,' Carthinal told her. 'If I am not much mistaken, this is an archaic form of Elvish.'

'Can you read it?' asked Randa.

'Unfortunately, no,' Carthinal replied, 'but I know someone in the Mage Tower who may, or at least, she may know someone who can translate it for us.'

'There's some writing on the paper that kept the place too,' observed Bas. 'It looks different.'

True enough, the writing was in Grosmerian. Again, it was an old form of Grosmerian, but Lady Randa had learned something of this during her extensive education as the heir to a Dukedom.

'It's a poem,' she said. 'Should I read it?'

'We'd better not ignore anything. Especially in view of the fact that the book seems to mention Sauvern,' Carthinal said. 'Go ahead.'

'It's called "The Wolf Pack."', she went on.

> *"The wolves will fight 'gainst every foe*
> *The balance to maintain.*
> *Though far and wide the pack must go*
> *All borders they disdain.*
>
> *"The pack contains the strangest group*
> *One whose pride comes with her,*
> *And one who slips through every loop,*
> *The wilful one, the tracker.*
>
> *"The leader with his anger held,*
> *The ones who hunt the horse.*
> *The rock that's strong completes the meld*
> *And makes the pack a force.*
>
> *"The wolf pack's members are filled with zest*
> *And all do have their place.*
> *They hunt their foes with ruthlessness*
> *Then vanish without trace.*
>
> *"In times of danger, all must know*
> *The wolf pack will be there.*
> *They work as one; they keep their vow.*
> *For each other, they will care."*

'Doesn't seem to make a lot of sense. I think it's just something the writer of this book used as a bookmark.'

'I think you're right there, Your Ladyship.' Basalt always seemed to make his use of the honorific sound like an insult, and Lady Randa bristled. 'No reference to Sauvern or his Sword.'

Carthinal replaced the "bookmark" in the place in the book where it came from, remarking that they may as well use it for the job the original writer did.

He went on to remark that the books were extremely old, and moving them may damage them, so, with the Lady's permission, he would bring his friend to the Palace so she could translate it in situ as it were. Randa agreed, and with that, they left the hidden room, almost having to drag Bas out from his examination of the carvings.

When they came up the stairs to the library, they found that darkness had fallen. The candles had been lit in the chandeliers and the light bounced around the room, split into colours by the glass, and making rainbows everywhere. The slight draughts moving around the room caused the candles to flicker and the light looked like thousands of fireflies dancing around.

'This never fails to impress me,' said Lady Randa, momentarily forgetting to be the Duke's Daughter. 'My grandfather had it done. Look at the way the windows reflect the light back into the room. Isn't it beautiful?'

The others agreed and reluctantly tore themselves away from the beautiful library to make their way back to the inn and dinner.

They found that Asphodel and Fero had their own successes. It seemed that in Sauvern's time, the humans and elves were living all through the lands that are now human, alongside each other. Although in times past, the land was shared amicably by both groups, by the time of Sauvern, many humans considered the elves to be inferior beings and were persecuting them. Some even blamed the elves for the ills that had fallen on the land, including the Raiders. The elves in their turn thought that humans were inferior, having such short lives and being a later creation of the gods.

Sauvern had, so the account went, set up the elven homelands on the far side of the Mountains of Doom. It appeared his friend and counsellor was an elf or half-elf and he wanted to end the conflicts between the races. Quite how all this would help them in their search for his burial place, they did not know, but, as

Fero pointed out, every piece of information helps to build up a picture of the man and his time, which may be important. With that, they agreed on a plan for the next day. Carthinal should seek the help of Yssa in the Tower and see if he could find any further information there and Bas would go with Fero and Asphodel. He would not be allowed into the library in the Tower as a non-mage, and Carthinal did not want him to go to the Palace to work with Lady Randa without him being there, knowing the way they rubbed each other the wrong way. Basalt readily agreed, not wanting to be left to work alone with the haughty, Lady Randa.

They all set off together the next morning for their respective destinations as they were in the same direction. When they reached the road to the Tower, Fero suggested meeting for lunch at a nearby tavern. Carthinal pointed out that he did not know how long the translation would take, or whether Yssa could even do it. He may have to wait until later in the day until someone became available. They all agreed to meet back at the inn that evening.

Chapter 8
Translation

Yssa lay back in the bath in the Tower bathhouse and sighed. She was very tired. She had been up all night again trying to perfect the spell she was working on, but something was not quite right. She needed a good night's sleep. The spell was one that was reputed to have been known in the distant past, but which had been lost during the time known as "The Forbidding." Her speciality was researching these lost spells.

Once there had been a dreadful war between two groups of mages for power. Many innocent people had died as well as many mages. The king at the time vowed it would never happen again and banned the practice of magic. The Forbidding lasted 500 years and had only been lifted 150 years previously The mages were still trying to find or re-create the spells of the past.

Many people still mistrusted magic and mages, although things were getting a little better she mused. Mages were no longer burned, thank goodness, but in the past, this had happened to both mages and their spell books, hence many spells, were lost. It was part of Yssa's job to recreate some of these spells, but with only rumours passed down, and probably changed by word of mouth, she did not find it an easy task. However, she enjoyed the work, so it did not worry her to sometimes get little sleep.

Just then, a knock came on the door of the bathhouse and a voice called, 'Are you there, Yssa? There is someone asking for you in the Great Hall.'

Yssa recognised the voice as one of Tharron's apprentices, a girl by the name of Soocardith.

She sighed and answered the girl, 'Did this person give a name or say what they want?'

'No. I-I'm sorry. Should I have asked? He's a half-elf probationer. Tall, good looking, with auburn hair.'

Yssa needed no more information. '*Carthinal! I wonder what he wants?*' she whispered to herself, then called out to the girl. 'I know who it is, Soo. Tell him I was up all night working and must have some sleep. I'll meet him in the dining hall in four hours time. Oh, and if Tharron doesn't want you, you may entertain him for that time, please.'

With that, Yssa reluctantly rose from her bath, squeezed the water out of her long, golden hair, and after drying herself, dressed, and returned to her rooms to fall into her bed.

Just before she fell asleep, she thought, '*It will do him no harm at all to have to wait. I don't suppose he often has to wait for females to come to him,*' and she smiled.

Carthinal waited rather impatiently and scowled when Soocardith returned with her message from Yssa. He knew she could tell he was not too pleased with having to wait but he did not care.

She said, rather shyly, 'Yssa asked me to look after you until she came to meet you.' She looked up at the half-elf. 'My name is Soocardith. My friends call me Soo. What's your name?' She looked at Carthinal through her lashes, which were incredibly long.

He secretly appraised the girl. She was small and slim with big, brown eyes fringed with incredible lashes. She wore her dark, brown hair shorter than many women, it not being much longer than Carthinal's own, but he liked the cut and it suited her. Her mouth asked for kisses and she had a cute little nose with a sprinkling of freckles. It would be pleasant to spend time in her company, and maybe kiss that lovely mouth, too. Then, Carthinal heard in his mind the voice of Mabryl:

'*Never toy with the affections of a young girl, Carthinal.*'

He replied to her question, 'I'm called Carthinal. Thank you for the offer of your company, but I'm actually here to work, believe it or not. While I'm waiting for Yssa, I'd like to go to the library and do some research.' He saw disappointment cross her face, and continued, 'I'm very new to the Tower, having only come here to do my tests in the last group. I'm afraid I don't know where the library is. I'd be grateful if you'd show me.'

Soo's face brightened at this and she took Carthinal up the winding stairs, chattering all the way. She expressed fear at the practical test and asked Carthinal about it. Rumours said someone had died in his group. Carthinal told her, yes, indeed someone died, but if a mage were up to it, he or she had no real need to fear. Just keep your head. Anyway, the real blame lay with the master of that apprentice. Obviously, he was not quite ready.

'I'm sure Tharron would never allow an apprentice to take the test without being absolutely certain they were capable of passing, so I don't think you have any need to worry.'

He smiled at the girl. She was quite pretty, and he would have liked to spend some time in her company, but he told the truth when he said he came to the Tower to work. He could not return to the Golden Dragon and say that, apart from seeing Yssa, he had wasted his time with a young, pretty apprentice.

They went up nearly to the top of the Tower, and eventually entered a long and curving corridor with a high, vaulted ceiling. There were a number of bookcases in this corridor, and between these were doors. Soo explained that these all led to the same, large room in which both students and their masters worked.

They entered through one of the doors and found themselves in a very high and impossibly, large room. It must have been 150 feet across, and Carthinal, again, felt it was larger than it should have been. There were, he saw, a great many desks, and these were separated into groups by tall bookcases crammed with books and scrolls. There were a large number of people in the room, of all levels of mage, from apprentices to even the odd magister. Only the occasional rustle of a page turning, or a chair scraping, disturbed the silence.

To his surprise, a few gnomes scuttled around, removing books from unoccupied desks where the occupant had left them before leaving, and replacing them on the correct shelves. He looked at Soo and raised an eyebrow. She quickly interpreted his meaning.

'Librarians,' she whispered.

Carthinal nodded. Yes, it made sense to have these people. They were industrious and learned, even if not magical. They were clever inventors and scientists but did not look down on magic or claim, as did some, that science was the new magic, and that magic would eventually die.

Soo continued in a whisper and got a severe look from a passing gnome. 'They work here in return for being allowed the use of the books for their own research. I believe they are working on some mathematical model of the flight of an arrow. Don't know why. If an arrow flies, it does, and if it doesn't, well, keep practising or get new arrows.' She shrugged, dismissing the problem. 'What section did you want?'

'Ancient History,' replied Carthinal.

'Over there, on the third shelf to the left,' the girl whispered back. 'I see now why you want to see Yssa. That's her speciality.'

Soocardith smiled to herself. She wondered if Carthinal wanted to see Yssa to make some romantic assignation. Yssa was certainly beautiful with her delicate elven looks and long, golden hair, but it seemed he only wanted her for work. Maybe she, Soo, stood some chance with him, then. Provided she played her cards right.

Carthinal resisted the temptation to express surprise at the revelation of Yssa's speciality and nodded instead. After all, he should know about such things if he came asking to see her. He then made his way over to the shelves and began to examine the books there. Out of the corner of his eye, he saw Soo sitting down in a seat where she could easily see him. He sat down in a vacant chair, picked up the quill pen that lay on the desk, examined the point, found it sharp enough, then dipped it into the ink and began to make notes from the book he took from the shelf.

After he estimated four hours had passed, Carthinal took his notes and rose. As he walked towards the door, he saw Soo casually rise, stretch and wander towards the same door, carefully not looking at him.

As they neared the door, she feigned surprise and said, 'Oh, Carthinal! Are you going down to the dining hall? So am I. I just realised how hungry I am. "*It must be lunchtime,*" I said to myself. Do you mind if we walk down together?'

Carthinal entered the dining hall with Soo. He looked round for Yssa, but could not see her, so he and Soo went and got something to eat and sat down. While they were eating, Yssa entered and waved across to them, went and got something to eat for herself and then came over to them. Carthinal stood and kissed Yssa on both cheeks twice in the elven style, drew out a chair for her to sit on and then sat down himself.

'I'm sorry to make you wait,' smiled Yssa, sitting down, 'but I was dog-tired. I stayed up all night researching a lost spell. I hope Soo has been good company.'

'I'm sure she would have been excellent company, Yssa, but the truth is that I deserted her for the library, I'm afraid,' replied Carthinal, smiling at Soo.

'Not very gallant of you,' Yssa smiled back. 'Let me finish my meal and then you can tell me what you wanted to see me about.'

The three of them ate and talked until Yssa said, 'Let's go outside, Carthinal, and you can tell me what you want while we walk in the grounds. It's such a nice day and I'm fed up with being shut inside. Thank you for your help and company, Soo.'

'Sorry to desert you again, Soo,' Carthinal apologised, picking up his cloak from the back of the chair, 'but I must discuss my business with Yssa now. Thanks for being such help. I hope we'll meet again, sometime.'

He shook her hand, and Soo walked away to where some other girl apprentices were waiting all excited to find out whom the handsome stranger was that she had spent so much of the morning with.

Yssa and Carthinal left the tower and wandered through the grounds. The earliest, spring flowers were beginning to come out in the mild weather. Some of the trees had a hint of blossom, and the sun seemed at last to have a little strength. They could feel its warmth on their faces.

'I have been given a job,' Carthinal began to explain. He went on to tell Yssa about the quest that he and his friends were offered and how they had agreed for the moment to do research, but not to undertake the quest. He went on to tell her about the finding of the secret room, and the book with the archaic writing in it. Yssa listened in silence, her eyes bright with interest.

'So, I'm looking for someone to translate the writing,' concluded the young man.

'You've found her then,' replied Yssa.

'Are you sure? I know you're very busy with your own work at the moment,' Carthinal found it hard to keep a smile off his face knowing that Yssa seemed to want to do this but did not want to tear her away from her own work.

'Try to stop me! Anyway, although I say it myself, I'm the best here for knowledge of archaic Elvish. Yes, I'll come with you immediately. Are you ready?' and with that, she started for the gate.

'Yssa,' called Carthinal after her retreating back.

She stopped and turned to him.

'Aren't you going to get a cloak? It gets cool in the early evening at this time of the year,' he reminded her.

'Oh! Of course. In my excitement, I forgot.'

She hurried to the Tower, and within a short while she returned. Then, the two of them made their way to the Palace and the secret room.

Lady Randa waited in the library, reading a scroll. She looked up as they came in. Carthinal introduced Yssa to her. The Duke's daughter gave her a brief glance, and turned back to her scroll.

'Did you find anything further, your Ladyship?' asked Carthinal.

'No. Nothing,' came the brief rejoinder.

'Then I'll go and show Yssa the book we found. With your permission, that is. She thinks she may be able to translate it.'

'How in the name of the gods does she know that? She's not even seen the book. It may be beyond her,' said Lady Randa imperiously.

Yssa felt rather annoyed by this young woman who spoke as though she were not present, but masked her feelings.

Instead, she told Lady Randa, 'I'm an expert in archaic Elvish. In fact, I'd go so far as to say I'm the best, and that's no boast. If I can't translate it, no one here in Hambara can. Maybe, not anyone in the known world, either.'

A rude reply sprang to Lady Randa's lips when a voice sounded from the doorway.

'She's right, Randa. Yssa, my dear. Welcome to the Palace.' The Duke walked quickly to Yssa and kissed her on both cheeks twice. 'Yssa, it has been far, too long since you came to visit me, but I suppose you've been busy. However, fifteen years is a long time.'

'Not for elves, Rollo,' replied Yssa, smiling.

The other two could not help noticing that she called him by his given name, and did not use the usual courtesies given to a duke.

'However, I apologise for my remiss. I'll try to visit more often in future,' she continued.

'Please, do. You may not change, but I'm not getting any younger. One day I'll be dead and gone but you'll still be as young and beautiful as ever,' the Duke told her. 'But I think you'll be visiting me more often in future when you see in that room.'

The beautiful carvings on the walls amazed Yssa when she entered the rooms deep beneath the ducal palace, just as they had amazed everyone else who had seen them. They allowed her to examine them thoroughly, as they knew exactly what she felt seeing them for the first time. Eventually, though, she approached the table and saw the books. Carthinal and Lady Randa stood back to allow her to examine them in her own time. She picked up one at random, much as Carthinal had done. She opened it with great care as it was obviously very old, and once she began to read it, she gasped, looked up at the others and then back down at the book in amazement.

'Carthinal, pinch me, please,' she requested.

'What?' replied the half-elf. 'Pinch you did you say? Why?'

'Because I think I must be dreaming and if you pinch me I'll wake up.'

'What is it, Yssa?' Lady Randa, after realising the elf was a friend of her father's, became rather more respectful than usual.

'These books are priceless. They are the spell books of a mage from ancient days. Many of the spells in here have been lost and we are trying to re-create them. With great difficulty and an enormous expenditure of time and money, I may add. When translated, these books will save us years of work, centuries maybe. So, that's what your father meant when he said I would be visiting more often!'

Carthinal interrupted her.

'I can understand your excitement, Yssa, but these were not what I wanted you to translate. The problem lies in this smaller book here.' He indicated the book where they thought they had found the name of Sauvern.

She picked it up and looked at it. 'The first part seems to be full of all sorts of notes. They don't make much sense at the moment. Random jottings of experiments, etc. What exactly did you want me to translate?'

Carthinal pointed out the part marked with the paper. Yssa glanced at the poem, and then put it down on the table, sat down on the chair, and picked up a pen and paper. She then began to read. After a few minutes, she looked up at the other two.

'Do you know who wrote this?' she asked, her eyes lit up with wonder. 'No, I don't suppose you do. It seems to have been written by none other than Sillaranoshedes.'

'Who?' exclaimed the other two in unison.

'Sillaranoshedes. Otherwise known as Sillaran, the elf who was Sauvern's counsellor.'

If she had said Kassilla wrote it herself, they could not have been more astounded.

They both looked at her in silence, until she laughed and said, 'Close your mouth Carthinal. You look like an imbecile.' Then, she became serious again and went on, 'Yes, I am sure, before you ask. Please, would you not speak to me now, as some of the words are not very easy to translate. I'll read the whole text to you when I've finished.'

Randa suggested they leave her to get on with the work while they go and continue in the library. Carthinal, however, could not seem to settle. His mind kept wandering to the room below where Yssa worked away at her translation, wondering how long it would take her. It seemed Lady Randa's mind ran along similar lines as she, too, kept glancing at the door to the stairs. Eventually, after what seemed like an eternity, but probably only about three hours passed, Yssa emerged from the door. She looked tired, but elated. Before leaving the Tower, she had bound her hair, but it came loose from its bindings and tendrils hung around her face. She pushed them back, irritated.

'Are you ready to hear this now, or do you want to wait until later?' she asked them.

On hearing her footsteps on the stairs, the two sprang to their feet. Carthinal strode over to her and solicitously lead her to a comfortable chair.

As he did this, he said, 'Yssa, don't tease. You know we're anxious to hear it as soon as you're able.'

'Well, stop treating me as though I'd just crossed the Mountains of Doom on foot,' she smiled. 'I've been sitting down all the time I was working down there. Although, I must admit to feeling rather tired now, and this comfortable chair is rather more conducive to sleep than Sillaran's. I could easily sleep here, you know.'

She leaned back and closed her eyes.

'Yssa! Stop it!' Carthinal scolded.

Yssa opened one eye. 'Still here? Well then, I suppose I'd better read it to you or I'll never get any sleep will I?' She opened the paper she had in her hand and began to read.

"'*Diary Entry of Sillaranoshedes.*

"*This day, the fourth day of the third week in the month of Candar, in the 2,268 year since humans began to measure time, is the worst of my long life. Today, my king, my friend has lost his life.*

"*I am distraught. It should not have ended so. Not yet 50-years-old! True it is that humans have brief lives, but Sauvern should have reigned for another twenty or thirty years, long enough for the boy to grow to manhood. A child as king!*

"Already, the accusations begin from those seeking power. Witchcraft, poison, and fingers will be pointed. I do not need magic or omens to foretell that war once more will visit this land, yet omens tell me that your enemies will revile your memory and your body, my king.

"But, my lord, my friend, you must be treated with all honour in death as in life. I will take your body and your Sword, and together with some true knights, we will take you to where you wished to rest for all eternity. We will travel to..."

Yssa paused and looked at Randa and Carthinal. 'The page had crumbled away here,' she said. 'I'm sorry.'

Carthinal swore a blasphemous oath, and then, remembering himself, looked at Lady Randa and apologised. She looked at him with steel in her blue eyes.

Yssa went on, 'There is some more. Should I go on?'

The others agreed and she continued reading.

"'Over the mountains we will go to the forest that you declared must be enchanted, so beautiful did you find it, with its mysterious mists and sudden sunbeams. By the lake where you loved the nymph, I will lay you to rest.

May the gods look on you with favour, my king, until such time as your Sword is needed once more. I will now seal this room with magic so that it can only be opened by..."

'The page has again crumbled here,' Yssa told them, but it finishes...

"...clues I have left which will only be found when the world is again in grave danger. Guardians I will put to watch over you. Your Sword is safe by your side and you may rest in peace until that time when the wolves roam free."

'And there the entry, and in fact the whole book, ends,' concluded Yssa.

After a few moments of silence when they stood looking at Yssa, Carthinal spoke:

'This is incredible. A diary of the elf, Sillaran! We must re-read it so we can fully digest what it says. What about the rest of the books, Yssa?'

'I think the books should not be moved. The atmosphere down there seems to be just right for them to have been preserved in near perfect condition,' she replied. 'Moving them may do irreparable damage. I will ask your father, Randa, if I may come here to translate and study them.'

Randa looked none too pleased that Yssa should call her by her given name, as though she were just any young lady and not the heir to a dukedom. Then, she remembered her father, the Duke himself, had not turned a hair when the elf addressed him thus, so she supposed she should forbear from making the sharp retort which sprung to her lips. Instead she replied, if a little coldly,

'I'm sure he will be pleased for you to come and work down here, Yssa, isn't it?'

Lady Randa went off to look for her father to tell him what they had found.

After re-reading the translation, Carthinal turned to Yssa and asked her to have dinner with him that evening as a thank you for her work. She had just graciously accepted, when the Duke and his daughter returned. Yssa read the paper again, this time to a visibly, excited Duke Rollo.

'How I wish I were younger, and didn't have all these responsibilities. I would love to go on the quest to find this place where they buried Sauvern. I had a number of adventures in my youth, you know; before I married and had Randa, and before my father died and I inherited the title. I sometimes wish my brother had been the elder and that I could have gone on adventuring for longer. What a life that was. Excitement and danger. And fun. Yes, lots of fun—and companionship, too. Also, sadness at the death of friends. But in spite of death being an ever-present companion, and the danger, or maybe because of it, those were the times I felt most alive.'

Here the Duke's eyes took on a faraway look as he remembered past times and companions. He suddenly seemed to come back to the present and asked to read the translation that Yssa had in her hand. She also brought up the poem in case the Duke thought it was of any importance. He firstly read the poem, and after a comment about bad poetry, he put it down on the table.

He read the diary entry and became excited again, 'We need a map to see if we can work out where this may possibly be, but not tonight. It's getting near dinnertime, I think. Yssa, would you do me the honour of dining with me this evening? We can reminisce about the days when you were a regular visitor to the Palace.'

Yssa smiled. 'I'm sorry, Rollo,' she replied, 'But I've just agreed to have dinner with Carthinal.'

'Not to worry,' replied Rollo, nevertheless looking rather disappointed, 'There will be other times, I'm sure.'

'Most certainly, Rollo,' replied Yssa. 'I'll be working here for some time to come, I think.'

The Duke visibly brightened at that prospect.

Carthinal picked up the translation and with it the poem and put them in the pocket of his robe.

As he and Yssa walked away towards the library door, Rollo called after them, 'Carthinal!'

The half-elf stopped and looked round at the Duke, who said, 'Use that letter I gave you to pay for dinner.'

Carthinal grinned at him. 'I intend to, sir,' he replied.

An hour later found Yssa and Carthinal in a secluded corner of the dining rooms in the best tavern in Hambara. At first, Yssa objected, saying Carthinal could not afford those prices, but Carthinal replied maybe he could not run to it, but the Duke certainly could, and the Duke was paying. Yssa laughed at that, and then made no further protests. So, here they were in the most, expensive eating place in the city, enjoying a meal, and each other's company.

After the meal, Carthinal told Yssa that he would walk her back to the Tower. It was a pleasant night, and both moons were in the sky. Lyndor was waning, shining gibbous in the sky, and Ullin was just past full. As they passed through the gates, Yssa asked Carthinal if he would like to go to her rooms for a last drink. Carthinal declined, saying he must get back before it was too late, and suggested a walk in the grounds instead, as the night was so beautiful. They strolled through the trees, and talked of this and that, each acutely aware of the other, until they came suddenly on a small summerhouse set on a slight mound in the middle of a clump of trees. The moons shone down through the trees and the moonbeams played over the little building.

Yssa shivered. 'It may be nearly spring,' she said, 'but it's still a little chilly. Let's go in and sit for a while.'

Carthinal thought about going back to the inn. He had not heard the striking of the hour bell and had no idea of the time. However, he enjoyed Yssa's company, and it seemed a pity to waste such a beautiful night, so the two went into the summerhouse. There were large windows on one side, which just happened to be the side where the moons were shining. They cast a silvery light inside the room. Yssa sat down on a wicker sofa next to a fireplace. A pile of wood stood ready at the side of the fireplace and a fire set in the grate. Yssa explained that some of the mages used this hut to get some quiet, and they used it summer and winter. There was always wood and a fire set ready for lighting. Carthinal knelt down and lit the fire. A cheery glow soon permeated the small room, and a feeling of cosiness and contentment filled the pair. Carthinal knelt back on the rug and looked at Yssa. She had removed her cloak, and her hair tumbled down her back having been freed from the restraints of the hood and the braiding she had put in before going to the Palace. Carthinal thought how beautiful she looked with the combination of firelight and moonlight on her golden hair. He stood up and went over to where she sat and bent down to kiss her. She responded to his advances and they made love on the floor of the summerhouse.

Afterwards, Carthinal apologised, but said he must leave. They walked hand in hand to the door of the Tower. Once there, Carthinal bent to kiss Yssa once on each cheek, and then once on the lips for good measure. He then turned to walk away towards the gates.

'Carthinal… You remember what I said last time…?' Yssa began as he left.

'Yes. I know. No strings,' he replied as he disappeared into the shadows of the trees.

'Yes. No strings. I said that, didn't I?' sighed Yssa to herself, looking with infra-vision at the reddish shape that Carthinal made until it disappeared. Only then did she seem to come to herself and with a shake of her head she entered the Tower and closed the door behind her.

Chapter 9
Decisions

'You were late in last night!' said Basalt, looking hard at Carthinal. 'We thought you'd forgotten where the inn is. Asphodel wanted to send out a search party, but we convinced her that you'd probably got involved in the translation and forgotten the time.'

Carthinal yawned. He hated people who woke up bright and cheerful.

'Yes, we finished a bit late, and then I took Yssa to dinner—as a thanks for her help, you know.'

'Hmm!' the dwarf said.

'What's that supposed to mean?' demanded Carthinal, looking at Basalt rather sharply.

'Nothing at all,' replied the dwarf.

Carthinal continued to get dressed and then told Basalt and Fero he would read the translation to them at breakfast when Asphodel could hear it, too.

When they got down to the common room, Asphodel smiled to see Carthinal. He explained that he had taken Yssa out to dinner as a thank you, and that he did not eat with them the previous evening because of that. Asphodel remained silent as she received the information, but he thought he saw a strange expression, pass fleetingly over her face. It went so quickly that he thought he must have imagined it. He went on to tell of the events of the previous day in the Palace and took the paper out of his pocket. As he did so, the paper with the poem on it fell to the floor.

Fero picked it up. 'Is this important, Carthinal?' he asked, passing the paper to the mage.

Carthinal looked puzzled for a moment, then he said, 'Oh! I didn't realise I'd picked that up. It's only a poem that someone used as a bookmark. I must have put it in my pocket without realising it.'

Asphodel took it off Fero and read it. 'It's not even good poetry,' she observed, handing it back to Carthinal, who decided he had better read it out so that the other two would know what they were talking about, even if it were not relevant.

All agreed it was probably not important, as they could not see what wolves had to do with it. However, Basalt counselled against throwing it away. 'Just in case,' he said, but did not explain "just in case" what.

They all became excited when Carthinal revealed just who had written the words in the hidden room, and Asphodel called Mabrella over to ask if she had any paper, a pen and some ink. She explained to the others that she thought they should write down all they had discovered so far.

When the pen and paper arrived, she began by writing, "Sword in tomb. Evidence: poem and diary."

Eventually, they ascertained the tomb, and hence the Sword, must lie over some mountains and by a lake in a forest in which lives or lived a nymph. Something guarded the tomb but they could not determine what. They agreed that the prophesied time for finding the Sword had arrived. Sillaran had stated the room would remain sealed and hidden until danger again threatened the world and the powers of the Sword required once more.

Which mountains, though? They discussed this at length, coming to no conclusions. None of them had any knowledge of the lands over either of the mountain ranges. Only Asphodel had been east of the Mountains of Doom, since she had been born there, in the elven capital city of Quantissarillishon. She told them that she had hardly been out of the city and knew little of the surrounding country beyond the immediate area around the city, and could not in all honesty say whether a valley such as Sillaran described existed or not.

Carthinal turned to the others and said, 'I'm sure we can find the answer to this last question. If this is truly the prophesied time, then the answer will be there if we can only find it. I'm inclined to tell the Duke that I'm willing to go on this quest for him. I've become fascinated by this while we've been doing the research. Much more that I thought I would. I don't want to think that we've done it all for someone else to go and find this fabled Sword. If you're with me on this, I will be delighted, but if you don't want to agree, then I don't blame you, either.'

'I have to go on the road anyway, Carthinal,' Asphodel replied. 'I'll go with you.'

'Me too,' said Basalt. 'You need someone with a bit of common sense to see you don't do anything foolish, also, you need someone who can use a decent weapon. What about you Fero?'

'Try to stop me, dwarf,' Fero replied. 'You're not going off to have fun without me. Anyway, you need a drinking companion, don't you?'

'So, all we need to do is to find out whether to go east or west,' said Carthinal. 'I think we can dismiss the Roof of the World. No one has crossed that range ever, or so I've been told. I'll go to the Duke and tell him we'll take his job and I'll look at some of the maps he has there. Maybe, that will help. See if I can see a lake in a forest over either range.'

He paused for a moment, then continued, 'If we're going on the road, we'll need some supplies, so you and Fero could take care of that, Bas. Asphodel, much as I respect your clerical dress, does your Church permit the wearing of armour? If it does, then I suggest you get some, and you need to get a weapon, too.'

'The Church allows armour, but not edged weapons, as Sylissa is the goddess of Life and Healing. It's too easy to extinguish life with a sword. Blunt weapons can stop and not kill,' she replied. 'I'll see to it. If we're going to go on a long journey, as I suspect this will be, may I suggest we buy a horse to carry our things? It'll save our energy and mean we can make quicker progress.'

'Good idea,' replied Fero. 'Bas and I will see to it.'

They all went their separate ways to complete their allotted tasks. Firstly, Carthinal went to tell the Duke they would go and try to find the Sword for him, and then he looked at the maps the Duke provided. There were no lakes marked over the Mountains of Doom, and the only ones marked over the Western Mountains were not in woodland, so he approached the Mage Tower little wiser. He took Mabryl's staff to the Tower to see if he could have some light thrown on its possible magical effects. He had forgotten all about it in the past few days of tests and research. As he entered the tower, he saw Yssa crossing the Great Hall and called to her. She came over. He told her about the staff and how he would like to know more about it and its powers.

'You say it Mabryl left the staff to you?'

Carthinal nodded.

'Well, I already know it's magic,' she continued, 'so I don't need to check that. I daren't touch it, as many magic staves will react badly if anyone but their rightful owner tries to touch them—a wise precaution. However, Mabryl gave this to you on his deathbed, so you are obviously all right at least to pick it up.'

She paused for a moment to think. 'Hmm!' she went on. 'Have you felt anything when you pick it up?'

Carthinal remembered the slight tingling he felt as he carried the staff after Mabryl told him he must have it, and the warm feeling that came after it. He told her of these sensations.

'Fine, you should be able to use it then. It seems to have accepted the change of ownership,' Yssa replied.

'You speak as though it is alive!' Carthinal raised his eyebrows.

'Well, it is and it isn't. It can detect who should and who should not be using it and it will only obey the commands of that one person. Beyond that, it is just a bit of wood,' she explained.

'I see,' said Carthinal, who did not really, 'but how do I know what it can do?'

'Look carefully at the carvings on the side,' she told him.

Suddenly, he thought that he could see letters and then words in intricate carving among the other decoration. They were so ornate that it was no wonder he had overlooked them before. Yssa, however, explained. The words would not be able to be read by anyone with no right to do so. That is anyone who did not own the staff. Secondly, she explained that he had been unable to read them before, as he had not yet passed his tests and become a full mage, although Mabryl had bequeathed the staff to him.

'I expect that Mabryl had the staff in his hand when he told you that you were to have it,' she said. 'He must have managed to touch you with it, too, so that it would know you.'

Carthinal thought back to the moments when Mabryl told him to leave him as he lay dying. The memory still hurt. After all, it was only a very short while ago. Yes, he remembered that Mabryl had his hand on the staff, but that had not struck him as unusual, as it had rarely been far from the man's side. He also thought he remembered a very, light brush by the staff that he had put down as an accident. It seems now that Mabryl had probably deliberately touched him with the staff. He pushed the pain away. Now was not the time to indulge in mourning.

They went on to discuss what the words that Carthinal could see meant. Yssa told him they would most probably be the command words for the various powers of the staff. She thought the first one Carthinal could read would give him magical protection against weapons. Yssa explained that it made a thickened layer of air around the mage making penetration by anything extremely difficult. It was a spell in the domain of Matter, she said, which affected physical things around. The second one would release some magical bolts of energy. (From the domain of Energy). All magic affected a variety of aspects of the world. As well as the physical world and energy, there were spells that affected the Mind of living creatures, spells affecting Time, and spells of the Spirit.

Yssa went on to explain that the staff was very old, having been passed down from master to apprentice over many generations. Therefore, it must be a rechargeable staff or it would have long since lost its powers. It had a large, quartz crystal on the top. Carthinal knew little of crystals, it not being a part of the initial training of mages, so Yssa explained the power of quartz and how it recharged the staff by drawing in the mana from all around the world. (Mages could study Crystallography if they desired to take up magical research after they had passed their tests).

After Yssa explained about the staff to him, he turned to her and said, 'We've decided to take up Duke Rollo's quest and go in search of the Sword. There are only four of us, and the poem that Asphodel found seems to indicate six or eight people should go. I'd be pleased if you'd accompany us. We plan to leave as soon as possible. Tomorrow, if we can manage to be ready.'

The idea tempted Yssa. To go adventuring. To go with Carthinal. To find a long-lost, legendary sword. Despite herself, Yssa began to have feelings about this handsome and charismatic half-elf, and she would love to spend more time in his company.

However, she replied, 'Much as I'm tempted, I have my work here. There are all those books in the Palace that have to be translated and Mabryl's book to study. I couldn't bear someone else to get their grubby paws on them and find out their secrets first. Thank you for asking me, Carthinal, but I must say no.'

When Carthinal got back to the inn, he found the others already there. Asphodel looked businesslike, dressed in studded leather armour and she had a tabard in white with a scarlet triskel worked into the cloth covering it. Leather trousers protected her legs. She looked very different now that she was no longer wearing her clerical robes. She produced a sling saying the weapons master she consulted suggested this weapon for her to learn on, since she could not get the practice on another in time to be sufficiently proficient by the time they set off. She could practice using the sling while travelling. He had also made his views known about temples that allowed their curates to go on the road without sufficient weapons training.

Basalt and Fero had a successful morning, too. They purchased dried food and more water skins. Basalt replenished his dwindling supply of dwarf spirits and they acquired a couple of skins of good wine, as well as several skins of ale and cider. Basalt pointed out that they had to ensure they would be able to drink, even if they could not find water. The alcohol would help to purify the water, too, if they could not boil it for any reason. It also made a good basis to cook in. He had eaten dried, rabbit meat cooked in cider with mushrooms and herbs and thought it delicious, he told them.

'All right, you don't have to make excuses for your purchases of alcohol to me,' laughed Carthinal. 'I expect I'll drink my fair share. What about a horse to carry all these supplies? Did you have success there?'

'We were certainly lucky, Carthinal,' Fero told him. 'We went to a livery to try to buy a horse. As we were looking them over, rather inexpertly I hasten to add, a young couple came in. They were Horselords from over the Western Mountains. The ones who are staying here as it happens. The stableman gave us a price for the animal, and they overheard. They came over and told us that although the animal was a good one, we should not pay as much as he asked. They talked to us, or rather the girl did (the man seemed not to speak Grosmerian so well) and persuaded us not to buy that mare, but to look over theirs. They were reluctantly having to sell her in order to feed themselves.'

'Where is the horse, now?' asked Carthinal.

'We've brought her to the stables, here,' Bas replied. 'But, Carthinal, I'm rather concerned about this horse business. I had no experience of dealing with the mine ponies when I was mining, and Fero tells me that he knows nothing about them. This is a beautiful horse of the Horselords. I'm worried we won't be able to take care of her as she should be.'

'The elves don't use horses, either,' said Asphodel. 'I know nothing about your background, Carthinal, but I would be very surprised if it included horses.'

Carthinal shrugged and shook his head.

'We'll have to learn quickly, then.'

'Carthinal, I have had an idea,' Basalt said suddenly. 'Those two Horselords have little or no money left, so they want to find some kind of employment. I don't suppose they would really enjoy working at anything they would be likely to get in Hambara, so why don't we ask them if they'd like to join us in the capacity of grooms?'

'Do you think they would?' asked Asphodel. 'They are known for being very proud. The man also looks very fierce. I saw him yesterday. He frightened me a bit, to be honest.'

The discussion proceeded for a few minutes until the entire group agreed the suggestion had sense.

'Anyway,' Carthinal pointed out, 'The poem Asphodel found suggested six, or maybe eight, should go on this quest, and we are only four. If they come, that will make six. Besides, as we all know, six is a sacred number, and so that would perhaps give us some luck.'

The planet of Vimar took 360 days to travel around the sun, and the people had divided the year into twelve months of thirty days, which were in turn divided into five "weeks" of six days. This led to the idea of six being an important number, and it also included all multiples of six, especially thirty-six, (six squared), and numbers with all sixes, such as sixty-six, six hundred and sixty-six, and so on.

They agreed to ask the couple when they returned, having ascertained from Keloriff that they were not in yet. While they were waiting, they ordered some food as the usual time for the mid-day meal had passed.

While they were eating, the door opened and the Horselords came in, hand in hand. The man was not exceptionally tall, about five-feet-ten and the girl was tiny, barely five-feet-tall. They both wore leather, there being little difference between the dress of either of them. Both wore brown, leather trousers tucked into brown, leather boots. They had leather tunics over coarsely, woven shirts. The girl had long, brown hair tied in two plaits and clear, hazel eyes, fringed with long lashes. Her eyes were her best feature, and beyond that she was not particularly pretty, with a small, upturned nose and a wide mouth. Necklaces of beads and feathers hung around her neck and she had feathers hanging from the rings in her ears. The man, however, was extremely imposing. He had a proud bearing, and a good-looking face that looked fearsome due to a tattoo going up his straight nose and over his brows and was in the shape of a bird with outstretched wings. He had very, dark hair, done in the fashion of the tribes, long and braided with beads and feathers, and he had light, brown eyes. Intricate designs covered his leather clothing.

The girl caught Basalt's eye and she smiled in recognition. Her smile transformed her face, and Bas thought that here was the face of someone who had a happy and cheerful nature. Carthinal looked over to them, and stood, beckoning them over. Fero reached out and pulled two more chairs to their table so the pair could sit down.

Once they had sat, Carthinal made the suggestion to them. 'We are none of us experienced in the tending of horses, and yet we feel the need to have one on our journey. We are going on a quest for Duke Rollo, and may be gone for some time. Basalt here suggested that we asked if you two would accompany us to tend the horse. We cannot pay much, but would be willing to share in any treasure we may find. The Duke will pay our expenses here in Hambara, so your bill at the inn will be taken care of if you join us. I'll need an answer fairly soon as we wish to leave first thing tomorrow morning if possible.'

The man replied in halting Grosmerian, 'First we talk. Private. We go to room. Return half-hour.'

With that, the pair rose and went up the stairs to their room leaving the other four looking after them.

Just over half an hour later, true to their word, the Horselords reappeared in the common room.

The girl turned to Carthinal and said, in much better Grosmerian than her husband, 'We have thought about your offer. We would know the nature of this quest before we can agree.'

'That's fair enough, Carthinal,' said Basalt. 'Would you go somewhere without knowing some details?'

Carthinal replied to the couple. 'I can tell you that we go east to try to find a long, lost artefact. The details I cannot reveal unless I know you are with us. It will probably be dangerous though, that I can tell you.'

'Danger never disturb Horselords,' the man replied, drawing himself up. 'We accept offer and come on journey.'

He stood, and, crossing his hands on his breast, bowed to each of them in turn.

'I, Davrael,' he said, 'This, my wife, Kimi.'

Kimi then also rose and bowed to them in turn as Davrael had done. The others rose and bowed to the two Horselords, introducing themselves. Once the introductions were over, Carthinal gave Davrael and Kimi a brief run-down on the quest and read them the poems and diary extract they had found. Davrael said he thought they were right in deciding to go over the Mountains of Doom, since he had no knowledge of lakes in woodland on the plains of his homeland. Indeed, although there were lakes aplenty on the plains, the woods were small and far apart. Being plains, there was little that could be reliably termed a valley anywhere that he knew about.

They spent the rest of the afternoon talking and getting to know one another a little. Davrael and Kimi seemed reluctant to open up about their homes, but the Horselords were noted for their reticence, so the others ignored this. However, they felt the pair would fit in and were happy with the decision to ask them to join.

The last afternoon in Hambara ended. A few, short, six days ago, none of the group knew of each other's existence, and now, here they were planning an expedition where they might have to entrust their very lives to each other.

'*Life is very strange,*' thought Asphodel. '*I came here to the temple to become a healer, and now I'm going chasing after a magical sword in the company of a half-elf, a dwarf, a foreigner from beyond the Great Desert and two barbarian Horselords. Who would have thought it?*'

The afternoon darkened and evening approached. The group decided to rise early and leave at the first hour. They all retired to their rooms to make whatever preparations they needed.

Interlude

He set the bowl of black ink before him and began to chant. The ink began to lighten and then showed him a clear picture. He saw a group of six people passing through the gates of a city. He did not recognise the city. It had changed much since he had last seen it, but he knew it to be Hambara, in the centre of the land of Grosmer, for there he had directed his search.

'So, they are coming from there. I'm glad I was right. A pity I can't scry them out personally, but I've never met any of them; I just happen to know Hambara. At least, I did!' he muttered to himself, looking at the new buildings outside the gates of the said city.

Then, he laughed. 'They'll never find the Sword. They don't fulfil the prophecy.'

He chuckled to himself. 'However, I'll send them something to think about, anyway. It's always possible they could pick up two more.'

He had read every prophecy he could lay his hand on about the Sword and had deduced that the seekers would come from Hambara at around this time. Therefore, he had carefully scried the gates leading in all directions for likely folk, and this motley band seemed to be the most likely to be those searchers. Of course, he could be wrong, but he doubted it. He felt in the marrow of his bones that this group was the one destined to search for the Sword of Sauvern, and he had learned over his many years to trust those feelings.

He carefully poured the scrying ink back into its bottle and wiped out the bowl. These he carefully placed in a cupboard, locked it and went to the door. He called down the stairs for his assistant who came running with alacrity. It did not do to displease the Master.

'What is it you want, magister?' the young mage asked entering the room somewhat breathlessly from running up the stairs.

'There is a group of people that I want to see the end of,' the magister told the other. 'One of them is your erstwhile fellow companion in your Tests, Carthinal Mabrylson. He has just left Hambara in the company of five others. They are a conspicuous group composed of the half-elf, a female elven cleric of Sylissa, a dwarf, a man from the southern lands and a Horselord couple. I think we should send my new pets out to see what they can do about them. Release a couple and tell them to get there quickly. I suggest they hide themselves with the more normal of their kind. Release a few of those, too. They'll follow the others with no problem. Oh, and speed them on their way by using a Gate. You can do that now, can't you?'

On receiving a reply in the affirmative, he gave a key to his assistant who nodded and went back down the stairs.

The magister, for he was indeed one of the highest-ranking mages on Vimar, then smiled to himself. 'We'll see how they cope with my little pets then,' he chortled. 'I hope that youngster gets out of their way quickly enough. I've still got things planned for someone like that one.'

With that, the magister sat down to wait.

Part 2
The Journey

Chapter 10
Followed

They all met the next morning and after eating a substantial breakfast, gathered up their things and went to the stables. Here, Davrael and Kimi loaded the things onto the mare and led her out of the inn yard. She was a pretty dapple-grey with the elegant bearing of the animals reared by the Horselords. Kimi said she named her Moonbeam. Moonbeam seemed reluctant to leave the warm stable for the cold of the early morning air, and she whickered to the other horses still there. There was a snort or two and some stamping of feet from the other animals, but then they passed through the stable yard gates and the horse sounds were left behind, to be replaced by the sounds of the city.

The little group made its way along Doom Road towards the West Gate with the slums of the Warren on their left and the Merchant area where their inn was situated on their right. Kimi wrinkled her nose at the smells issuing from the Warren.

'How can people live in places like that?' she wanted to know.

Carthinal looked at her and replied quietly, 'Most of them have no choice, Kimi. It's live there or die.'

They were quiet then until they passed through the arch of the gates as they thought on Carthinal's words. The guards saluted them as they passed, except for one, a surly-looking fellow who gave them a black look and then spat on the ground.

'He's the one who "found" the stolen necklace in my pack,' whispered Fero. 'It seems the Duke has done as he said and demoted him. He's just an ordinary guardsman now I see.'

'And, with a great deal of resentment it seems,' responded Basalt. 'Most of it turned towards us if his look is anything to go by.'

They walked through the outlying districts of the town, which were very similar to the areas they came through when they entered, until at last they left the last building behind.

Fero took a deep breath. 'At last I can breathe,' he said. 'I felt suffocated in that town.'

To a greater or lesser extent, they all felt that way. The atmosphere of Hambara troubled Carthinal the least, although it was a much bigger town than Bluehaven. Davrael seemed as pleased as Fero to be out in the countryside again, although he had not been in the town for as long. They were passing through farmland, and every so often there a little well-fortified farmstead appeared.

The countryside was undulating outside Hambara. Low, green hills rose on either side. It was a gentle land with many, small woodlands and streams. A few fields with crops and some cattle lay on either side of the road.

Then, when they rounded a bend, they saw a farm at the side of the road. Dogs ran out barking as they approached. Moonbeam shied and Kimi, who had control of her at that time, had trouble calming her down.

One rather angry looking black and tan beast ran up to Carthinal snarling and showing his teeth. Carthinal prepared a spell to send the animal to sleep when the farmer appeared with a crossbow ready loaded and pointing at them. He looked as though he knew how to use it and was not reluctant to do so if necessary. The farmer was tall and muscular with dark hair and eyes. He was deeply tanned from working outdoors, and wore a boiled, leather jerkin and trousers with a thick, woollen cloak, dyed green fastened around his shoulders against the chill of the day.

'Down, Bramble,' he called to the dog.

The animal cowered down, still growling and looking at Carthinal in a menacing way, teeth bared in a grim smile. The other three dogs were slinking around obviously ready to attack if the one called Bramble did so. He was the obvious leader of these dogs. The others were smaller. One black and white animal had a rather piratical look as it had a black patch over one eye, and one ear cocked and the other down. The other two were both all black, but one was almost as large as Bramble, and had a ragged ear as though it had been chewed in a fight. No doubt a challenge for supremacy amongst the animals had occurred, but whether Bramble had been the original leader and had beaten down the challenge, or whether he had won the leadership off the chewed ear dog, none of them could say. Although if asked, Carthinal would have plumped for Bramble having been the challenger as he looked the younger dog.

'If ye be friends, then ye need have no fear,' said the farmer, still pointing his crossbow, 'But these be dangerous times and we've a need to be careful. No sudden moves now or Bramble there'll attack. Not to mention how me finger might slip on this here trigger. State yer names and business.'

With a nervous look at the dogs, especially Bramble, Asphodel replied for the group.

She gave their names but did not tell why they were travelling. She told him that they were a group of friends on a journey to Roffley, naming a town to the east.

'Guard, Bramble.' The farmer addressed the dog, and he lowered his crossbow.

Bramble looked ready and anxious to have a piece of Carthinal for lunch, with Bas for afters. He showed his teeth again.

Carthinal ignored him, although it took all his willpower to do so. He knew the dog was only being controlled by the slenderest of threads and the farmer could lose control at any moment if he did anything to upset the animal.

'*The others dogs will follow the lead of Bramble,*' he thought, '*as he is the pack leader, here.*'

'Don't ye move,' said the farmer, 'and ye'll be fine. A man can't be too careful. There're bandits around these days and they have all kinds of wiles t'get into th' house.'

He walked round the group, went up to Moonbeam, and patted her.

'This be a grand mare,' he said. 'Horselord stock if I'm not mistaken, and you two are Horselords too. What brings Horselords over the Mountains?'

Kimi decided, to tell the truth.

'We ran away,' she said. 'Our parents didn't want us to get married so we left and came to Hambara where we met these others.'

'Mmm. That explains why ye're going further east. Why are the rest of ye travelling?'

Asphodel told him the truth of her exile from the temple and he muttered in sympathy. Carthinal, Fero and Basalt said they decided to accompany her for the adventure.

The stories seemed to satisfy the farmer and he turned to the dogs. 'Come. These be friends. Bramble! Friends!' With that, he went and patted each of the companions on the back. 'Ye'll be fine now. Bramble and his pack'll do ye no harm.'

The four dogs came and sniffed each of the companions one by one. Bramble even licked Asphodel's hand, much to the surprise of the farmer.

'Well, I never!' he exclaimed. 'Ye be greatly honoured, Sister. He's never done that to nobody save in the family. Well, I be Borolis and this here be my farm. It were me father's afore me and his father's afore him. I hopes it will be me sons' and their sons' too, the gods willing. It's hard farming here. The land is good, but it be dangerous times, and lonely hereabouts, hence the dogs. Come on in and have a bite and meet the missus and kids.'

'I don't know about us having a bite, I thought we were going to be the bite,' whispered Carthinal to Asphodel.

They followed Borolis into the farmhouse where the warmth made them feel most welcome. There was a delicious smell of cooking, obviously, the midday meal being prepared. A pretty, blonde woman came up to them wiping her hands on her apron.

Borolis addressed her. 'These here be travellers heading for Roffley. Do we have enough food for us all?'

'Well, Borolis, you know how as I always cook too much food. You're forever telling me about it. We can find plenty for yon strangers. Are ye going to tell me who they are?' scolded his wife playfully.

'Oh! Sorry. Forgot me manners,' and he introduced them.

At the sound of his voice, two young boys about ten-years-old, obviously twins, and a girl of about five came running into the room. The boys were dark of hair, like their father, and like him had dark brown eyes, full of mischief. Their sister was blonde but had also inherited their father's brown eyes. All the children were dressed simply in brown trousers and jackets, but all had immaculately clean shirts underneath. The girl had a shirt of primrose yellow which seemed to match the colour of her hair, while one boy had a green shirt and the other an orange one.

'Did you say there was an elf here, Papa?' cried the girl.

'Now, now, calm down, Amerilla,' said their mother fielding the twins, but missing her daughter, 'Yes, The young lady there is an elf, and her name is Asphodel.'

'Ooh! I've always wanted to meet a real live elf,' exclaimed Amerilla

Borolis laughed. 'That be my daughter, Amerilla, in case you haven't guessed. The boys be my twin sons. Voldon be wearing the orange shirt, and Kram, he be in the green. Unless they've changed over shirts again!'

'No, Papa,' replied the boys, looking innocent, as though such a thing would never enter their heads.

'My wife be called Elpin, and she be the best wife a man could have.'

This with a loving glance at the said lady, who blushed and said, 'Go on with you! Now, I'll just set some more places at the table. Would ye like to put your cloaks over by the door on the stand, and sit ye down by the fire to get warm? It's mighty cold outside.'

With that, she bustled off to get some more plates and cutlery out of the kitchen. The boys were questioning Basalt about his weapons and Amerilla was gazing in awe at Asphodel, who in her turn was trying to put the young girl at ease so Carthinal had time to look around and take in his surroundings.

The room was large, taking up most of the ground floor of the house. The fire was in a large fireplace built on the left-hand wall as they came in through the door, and next to it stairs went up to an upper story. There was a door in the wall opposite the fire, where Elpin had disappeared, and Carthinal surmised that it was the kitchen. Next to the entrance door was a window with pretty curtains and there was another window on the back wall. The door through which the children came was obviously a door into the farmyard and was next to the back window. There were five, wooden chairs around the fire, made comfortable by having plenty of cushions and a large table in the centre of the room, which Elpin was now setting with six, extra places. Altogether, it was a clean and happy place, although obviously not very rich. Carthinal thought the love and care he felt in that house was worth all the riches on Vimar.

'Come and eat,' called Borolis, disturbing Carthinal's musings. They all sat around the table while Elpin spooned large helpings of stew and bread onto each plate.

The stew was delicious and the bread still warm from the oven. To the hungry travellers, the meal seemed like the nectar of the gods. Borolis insisted on them having second helpings, and plied them with ale. They were feeling full when Elpin left to go into the kitchen. When she returned, she was carrying a bowl of late autumn's fruit she had dried for use in the winter. This had been soaked in a syrup of honey and water and then cooked. It was still slightly warm, and the sweet, warm syrup perfectly complemented the slight tartness of the mixed fruit. All told, it was a delicious meal, and the companions sighed, replete with good food. They thanked their hosts gratefully.

'We did not expect so gracious a welcome or such wonderful food,' said Carthinal to Elpin, who beamed at his compliments.

'Not after the welcome ye received from me and me dogs, eh?' responded Borolis with a twinkle in his dark eyes. 'But ye can't be too careful round here these days,' he went on more soberly. 'There be all sorts on the road now. Thieves and brigands, aye, and worse.'

'Shh! Don't frighten the little ones,' Elpin quickly hushed him, but Voldon replied, drawing himself up as tall as a ten-year-old could.

'We be not frightened, Mama. We be men now. We be nearly eleven, and Papa has told us we can have short bows for our birthday so we can learn to fight to help to protect the farm. With Papa's crossbow, us with our short bows, and the dogs, nothing can harm us.'

'I want a bow, too. Papa, can I have a bow? I want to fight for the farm as well,' cried Amerilla, who was bouncing up and down in her seat. 'I want to be a fighter when I grow up. Or perhaps I'll be a healer like you Asphodel,' she said, turning to the elf.

'She wanted to be a travelling entertainer last sixday and the sixday before it was a druid. We never know what she's going to come up with next. Thank the gods the boys are not like her. Farming is all they ever wanted to do,' smiled Elpin.

'Parador has smiled on us with those two,' went on Borolis picking up his wife's thoughts quite naturally, and referring to the goddess of agriculture. 'Not that I'd change Amerilla in any way, shape or form,' he went on to say fondly. 'I expect she'll get married and settle down with some farmer, eventually.'

This was a truly happy and devoted family. All the travellers hoped that everything would turn out well for them for their kindness.

Carthinal then spoke, 'We thank you kindly for sharing your food and shelter this cold day, but we really can't impose on you any longer.

'Ye be welcome to stay longer. We seldom see visitors. We can find beds for you for the night if ye don't mind straw mattresses on the floor. It be getting dark out yonder and it's not safe to be wandering after dark.

'Elpin'll pack some food for ye tomorrow and ye must fill all yer water skins from the well. The water is good, and does not need boiling,' replied Borolis.

The first night out from Hambara, the six travellers had a restful night in the farm of Borollis and Elpin.

The next morning, farewells having been said, the little party continued on their journey. The dogs, led by Bramble, accompanied them for a little way along the road, but then turned back, Bramble having given Asphodel's hand another lick. Their journey was once more under way.

'We must visit them again,' said Asphodel, 'and bring them something for their kindness.'

The others all agreed.

As they walked, Fero began to hum. It was a tune in a minor key, but it had a rhythm that seemed to encourage them to walk.

Even Moonbeam seemed to prick up her ears and walk with more vigour.

'Does that song have words, or is it just a tune?' Asphodel asked him.

'It has words. It's a work song of my people,' Fero said.

'Could you sing the words for us?' Kimi enquired, coming alongside the other two.

Fero began to sing. He had a deep, bass voice, and the others felt a tingle run through them as he sang. They could imagine the dark, sweating bodies toiling under a hot sun.

'What do the words mean?' Basalt asked the tall ranger.

Fero translated it into Grosmerian for them.

> *"'I rise before the sun each morn*
> *And sometimes wish I'd ne'er been born.*
> *For life is hard here in the heat*
> *But I must toil or I won't eat.*
> *And soon I will be dead and gone*
> *But still, the work goes on and on.*
>
> *"I plant the grain and sow the seeds.*
> *The sun looks down on all our deeds.*
> *His sister rain falls from above*
> *And nourishes the seeds with love.*
> *The sun himself gives warmth to all*
> *And makes the plants and grain grow tall.*
>
> *"Now I am glad to have been born*
> *The land is kind, it gave us corn*
> *And grass for all our cows and sheep*
> *And you and I can soundly sleep.*
> *For once again through winter's chill*
> *We'll once more live. It will not kill.'"*

'Rather sad, but it does end on a hopeful note,' Asphodel observed.

'It's a very old song,' Fero explained. 'It dates back to the time when my people scratched a living from the land. It's hard to farm on the edge of the Great Desert. Sometimes, the rains failed and then people starved. Now, it's better. We've learned how to cope and what to grow, and about water conservation and irrigation. Many people live in the cities and towns, which are usually near some kind of water, either a river or an underground reservoir. We are, however, very careful. A rich man is one who has his own water supply. We recycle as much water as we can.'

After this speech, the longest that Basalt, Carthinal, and Asphodel had heard from the ranger, Fero began to sing again, this time quietly.

Then, Carthinal had an idea. 'Teach us your song, Fero,' he said. 'It'll help to pass the time while we're walking and it's a good tune to walk to. It has a good rhythm to it.'

So, for the rest of the morning, they sang each line after Fero, and when they stopped for lunch as the sun reached its zenith, they all knew the first two verses in Fero's language.

Davrael tethered Moonbeam to a tree, loosely so she could graze, then removed her pack. The mare shook herself, and would obviously have liked to roll, but Davrael spoke softly to her in his own language and she seemed to content herself with a shake. He patted her and then came to sit with the others.

'How long it take get Roffley, Carthinal?' he asked, taking a piece of bread and dried meat, biting it, and then looking at it questioningly. He casually draped an arm over Kimi's shoulder.

'Over a sixday,' came the reply. 'Probably about eight days, assuming we continue to make good progress. We should be there by the Equinox with any luck. Asphodel wants, if possible, to be able to honour Grillon at this time of year.'

'I thought you were a cleric of Sylissa?' Kimi asked the elf.

'Yes, I am, but we are not forbidden from celebrating the festivals of other gods. In fact, we are encouraged to do so. Grillon is the preferred god of the elves and so I like to celebrate the New Year.'

'Grillon is also my god, as a ranger,' Fero told them, 'So I would like to be able to celebrate him, too. I also would like to get to Roffley by the Equinox.'

They rested for about an hour after eating, and then Kimi and Davrael re-loaded Moonbeam and they set off again along the road. Again, they sang as they walked along, continuing to learn Fero's song, and they hardly realised how the time had passed until they noticed the sun beginning to set, and the evening had come suddenly upon them.

They walked on until they found a place by the road where they could set up camp. They were just beginning to leave the farms behind and enter wilder lands. Soon, they would be in the forest. A small stream ran alongside the road here, and they used it to firstly replenish their water supplies, and then to wash. Asphodel found some soapwort growing near to the stream, and they gathered some both to use then and to take with them in case they could not find any later. The herb, when squeezed in water, gave out a soapy substance that was useful for washing. Peasant women had known of the herb for centuries.

Fero went on his usual hunt, but this time, he took Asphodel with him so she could practice with her sling. Whilst they were away, the other four set up camp, Kimi grooming the horse with some dry grass she pulled up while Basalt, Carthinal and Davrael collected wood to build a fire, and dug out the turf, setting it round with stones to form a primitive hearth. By the time Fero and Asphodel returned with some rabbits and a partridge, the fire burned brightly and the blankets had been set out around it.

Just as they finished their meal and were deciding on the order of watches, Fero stood and said, 'Excuse me a moment. I think I heard something.'

'Yes,' replied Asphodel. 'So did I. I thought it was probably a squirrel. It seemed to be in that tree.'

Fero walked towards the tree in question and peered up into its branches. He could not see anything although the leaves had barely begun to sprout. He walked back to the others, signing them to say nothing. They continued with their discussions, and Fero walked away from the group, but not in the direction of the tree. He made as though to go amongst the sparse woodland to relieve himself, then doubled back, keeping to the darker shadows and moving slowly and quietly towards the tree where he thought he heard the noise. He stood in the shadow of a large, oak tree, remaining motionless and waited. After a few minutes, the sight of a slight movement in the tree, and the sound of a sigh rewarded him. He continued to wait, and eventually his patience was rewarded. The smell of the cooking partridge and rabbit wafted his way. Then, there came the sound of a stomach rumbling. It came from up the tree, followed by further scrabbling as someone descended. That someone got lower in the tree as Fero made out a definite, human shape. Just as they were about to jump from the lowest branches, Fero moved quickly and grabbed a leg. Someone squeaked.

'All right. Get down, but don't try to run. I'm a good shot with my bow.'

The figure jumped down and said, 'I'll come quietly.'

Holding onto the arm of a slight figure, encased in a cloak with the hood pulled up, Fero re-entered the camp. The others stood up as he approached, except for Basalt who was, at that moment, turning the spit on which the two rabbits and the partridge roasted.

He walked into the light of the fire and yanked the hood off saying, 'Let's see what we've caught, shall we?'

'Thad!' exclaimed Carthinal when the hood revealed a crop of curly, red hair. It was indeed the young thief from the Warren in Hambara. 'What are you doing out here?'

'I followed you,' replied the boy. 'Things was gettin' too bloody 'ot for me in town, like. I thought you wouldn't take me if I asked, so's I followed, like. I were goin' t' come out tomorrer, see, but I were so 'ungry smellin' yer food. I thought I might be able to "acquire" some if I waited, but Fero bloody well caught me.'

Carthinal then asked the boy why he felt he had to leave his home, so Thad explained that his fence found out he had stolen the figurine back and was out to get him, so he had to get away.

'What about your family?' asked Asphodel. 'Won't they be worried?'

'Got no family.'

'Have you ever been out of Hambara before?' asked Basalt.

'No! Don't send me back! Please, don't!' The anxiety in the boy's voice and eyes was real enough. 'I'll do anything. Anything at all.'

'Thad,' said Carthinal gently. 'We are on a dangerous mission. We are not sure where we are going except over the mountains. Lives will be in danger, of that I am sure. You are only a boy—and one with no experience of living in the wilderness at that. We may have to send you back with a caravan in Roffley.'

The boy dropped to his knees and grabbed Carthinal's robes. 'No! No! It can't be more bloody dangerous 'ere than there! Please, Carthinal.' Then, regaining his composure, he got to his feet. 'I'm a damn good thief. You said so yourself, Carthinal, right?'

'What would we want with a thief?' asked Kimi. 'We're not planning on robbing anyone. Surely a lawbreaker will be more trouble than he is worth.'

'I c'n 'ide in th' shadows and scout wi' Fero,' he replied. 'I'm real good aren't I, Fero?'

He noted the ranger's nod with satisfaction.

'I c'n use this short sword and a dagger as well if there's any fightin'. I'm real good with throwing daggers, too. I c'n also find any 'idden traps so's to keep you safe from that danger, right? I promise not to use me skills against any o' you. There! Now, what d'you say?'

'That you not use skills to take from folk we meet. We get needs honestly.' Davrael spoke for the first time.

Thad looked over at the Horselord and seemed to shrink back a little.

'I…I promise,' he said in a small voice.

Carthinal sighed. 'You can accompany us at least to Roffley. Once there, we will reconsider sending you back, but you must behave yourself and prove yourself until then.'

'Yeah, Carthinal,' he replied, trying to appear meek, but rather spoiled it by a cheeky look from the corner of his eye.

So, they sat down to eat their meal and then, with Davrael and Basalt taking the first watch, they rolled themselves in their blankets and slept.

The next morning dawned rather misty. They tidied up the campsite, put out the fire and replaced the turf. When they had loaded all their gear onto Moonbeam, they began their journey once more.

Basalt suggested that today he teach them a song of the mountain dwarves to help to pass the journey, and by lunchtime, when the sun had burned off the mist, they were halfway through learning it. They were also entering thicker woodland, leaving the farms behind. Here were more signs of spring. Catkins grew on some of the trees and bushes, and there were occasional clumps of early spring flowers like snowdrops and celandines. There were even a few of the small, wild daffodils coming out. Birds were marking out their territories in song in preparation for finding a mate and rearing young. A smell of growth and renewal hung in the air. They all felt an elation that had been missing in Hambara, even Thad, who found all this new and exciting. He kept exclaiming at all kind of things, from a shy squirrel they disturbed to the newly-growing flowers. The others were forced to see the wildwood with new eyes. At their mid-morning half-hour rest, he barely sat down but spent the time looking and exclaiming at everything there.

They stopped for lunch as the sun reached its zenith, and rested again for an hour. Just as they were getting up and clearing all their waste away, they heard galloping hooves coming up the road. A rider on a black horse came galloping down the road. The horse was being ridden fast, but just as it drew alongside, the rider caught sight of them and quickly reined in. The horse reared up and slid to a halt. The rider jumped from the saddle almost before the animal had stopped and ran over to them.

'Carthinal. You've got farther than I thought.'

'Lady Randa!' Carthinal's eyebrows rose. 'What are you doing here? Is there a message from your father? He is all right, isn't he?'

He wondered at Lady Randa coming herself with a message. Surely, her father would have sent a messenger and not his only, precious daughter.

'I've come to join you. No, there is no message and yes, he's all right,' she replied.

Lady Randa was dressed in chain mail armour. She had a helmet on her head with her long, ash-blonde hair tucked into it, and she carried a longbow slung over her shoulder and a quiver of arrows on her back. She had a rather fine longsword in a tooled scabbard at her hip, and she was drawing off a pair of leather gauntlets.

'I've ridden hard to catch you up and my horse needs a rest. We'll wait here for another half an hour before moving on,' she ordered turning to Davrael. 'You! Horseman! See to my animal, but be careful, he can be vicious to people he doesn't know.'

Carthinal saw Davrael bristle and quickly gave him a warning look. Davrael was an intelligent man and saw what Carthinal was trying to tell him with that look.

'*Don't say anything, just do as she asks, and I'll get rid of her as soon as I can,*' he read in Carthinal's eyes.

He walked over to the blowing stallion. Talking all the time in gentle tones, he slowly approached the horse and managed to pick up the trailing reins. The animal put back his ears and pulled back, showing the whites of his eyes, then made as if to bite the man who had so unceremoniously taken the reins that the stallion considered to be the property of his mistress. Davrael, continuing to talk all the time, gradually coming nearer to the animal until he could put up his hand and stroke his nose. The horse made no objection and so Davrael began to walk him in circles to cool off.

Carthinal spoke to Lady Randa. 'This is no place for you, my Lady. We're on a mission, as you know, that may be dangerous. As soon as your horse is rested, you're to go back to your father.'

'You cannot make me. This is a free highway unless I am much mistaken. I can travel it if I wish. If I happen to be going in the same direction as you, then that's just too bad.'

Carthinal sighed and looked at Basalt who shrugged but looked dismayed at the thought of having the Lady Randa in their company.

'All right. I can't make you go back now,' Carthinal conceded. 'However, once we are in Roffley, you may change your mind. There's probably a caravan going back to Hambara from there and you can travel with that.'

'Carthinal, I am not useless. Nor am I unintelligent. I'm aware of the dangers. I've travelled the roads before, albeit, with my father's guards, I admit. I can use these weapons I carry with competence. I've trained with some of the best. You will not find me a shrinking violet when it comes to a fight.'

'All right. Carthinal says you can stay until Roffley, but if that's the case, we are not going to mess around with "My Lady" this and "My Lady" that,' Basalt retorted. 'You will be called Randa. You'll address us by name as well. In case you've forgotten, my name is Basalt, not Dwarf. The elf is Asphodel. She's a curate of Sylissa…'

'I can see that. I said I was not stupid, Dw…Basalt.'

'The ranger is Fero and the two Horselords…' he emphasised the "lords" part of the word, 'Are Davrael and Kimi and they are not grooms to be ordered around. We are all equal here.'

The arrival of Randa seemed to put a blanket over the good humour of the morning. They continued towards Roffley, Randa riding her magnificent, black stallion she said was named, Storm. He was pure black except for a star of white hair on his forehead and one white hind foot. He was also very temperamental and highly-strung. It said much for Randa's riding skills that she could control such an animal.

The others walked, Kimi leading Moonbeam with Davrael at her side. He held her free hand, the one not holding the reins, and they talked quietly together in their own language.

The day progressed in this manner. Fero left them once or twice to scout ahead or behind, and once returned with a hare he managed to shoot. Asphodel found some mushrooms and other edible herbs and vegetables, so they progressed towards their destination.

About half an hour before sunset, Carthinal called a halt. They found a small clearing in the forest and decided to make camp there. As they all busied themselves making camp, Randa sat on a log and waited.

'Randa,' called Asphodel. 'Will you put some of these herbs into the pot and then put the pot over the fire?'

'Why can't you do it?' came the petulant reply.

'Well, I would, only I'm skinning the hare. Kimi and Davrael are seeing to the horses, Bas and Carthinal are collecting wood and making the fire pit and Fero has gone hunting with Thad. There's no one else.'

Randa reluctantly went to help Asphodel. She had obviously never cooked before, and Asphodel had to tell her, step by step, what to do. It would have been easier for Asphodel if she had just done it all herself, but she was determined to not let this spoiled and arrogant girl just sit there while everyone else worked, so she persevered. She sighed and ran a hand through her hair. Carthinal, just finishing the job of building the fire pit looked over. He smiled and rolled his eyes to the heavens as he saw her frustration with Randa. She smiled back and shrugged.

They ate well again that evening. Carthinal insisted Randa take a watch, and for a moment, it seemed she would refuse. Asphodel thought she could foresee a struggle for power between these two. Randa obviously thought she should be in charge by right as the Duke's daughter, and did not realise that one earned true leadership and did not merely consist of giving orders. Eventually, she agreed to stand the first watch with Carthinal and the others lay down in their blankets to sleep.

Chapter 11
Attack

The attack came just before dawn. Fero and Thad were on watch. Carthinal suggested the watch be arranged as far as possible with one person with infravision and one without. Fero, he decided with his ranger training, was almost as good as an elf or dwarf. Carthinal watched with Randa, Basalt with Kimi, and Davrael with Asphodel, leaving Fero to watch with Thad.

Dawn had just begun to light the eastern sky when Fero thought he heard a sound in the bushes to his right. He stood, drew his sword, and looked over towards them, signalling to Thad to be prepared. Then, before he had time to take a step, the bushes parted and a wolf rushed him. He shouted to wake the others, and at the same time, swung his sword to injure the animal. He only managed to catch a glancing blow, and then his sword slid off, but he managed to slow the wolf down.

He heard, rather than saw, the others coming to their feet. The wolf, far from being afraid, as Fero had expected, came again. He slashed once more and again made contact. This time, the animal fell at his feet, its lifeblood seeping into the ground from the severed jugular. Fero heard the sound of Carthinal chanting and knew there were other wolves. Over the sounds of fighting, Basalt's battle cry resounded. Then, he heard a sound from in front of him. Another wolf appeared. This was an enormous animal. Much bigger than a normal wolf. This was going to take some killing. The huge animal looked at Fero with an evil intelligence in its yellow eyes. Sounds of the battle were raging around him, but he scarcely heard them anymore, giving himself over to his own task. He swung his sword again, but the wolf seemed to anticipate him and moved off to the side. They circled each other like two fencers. Fero feinted to his left and the wolf moved away. Fero then changed his thrust to the right and caught the wolf, cutting it on the side of its head. The animal backed away, but it suddenly changed tactics and sprung for Fero's throat. He put up his sword to protect himself, but the huge beast dropped, a bolt sticking out from its ribs and a throwing dagger from its eye. Fero turned, sword still raised until he saw there were no more of the beasts alive. The others were all standing, panting, and leaning on weapons. Asphodel tended a bite on Davrael's arm, while Kimi tried to calm the terrified horses.

'There was eight of the bleeders,' Thad told him. The young thief shook visibly now that the action was over. 'There were another like that bloody, gynormous one you was fightin'. What remains of it's over there. Carthinal killed it with 'is magic. Two silvery bolts of energy from 'is fingers, like. It were real cool.' He looked at Carthinal with admiration.

'Those big ones were dire wolves,' Fero told them later when they had cleaned the blood from themselves as best they could, while Asphodel tended the wounds of those who were injured. 'They don't often come this far south, especially at this time of the year. There was something else, too. Dire wolves are more intelligent than normal wolves, but these seemed even more intelligent than the average dire wolf. The one I fought seemed to have more knowledge of sword fighting than it should, and the fire didn't seem to put them off, either. There's something strange going on here.'

'Let's move on before breakfast. I don't think I could eat with these bodies around,' shuddered Asphodel, and the others agreed.

They broke camp. The horses calmed down once away from the smell of the wolves and blood, and the little band trudged on down the road.

'You fought well,' Carthinal said, coming up beside Randa where she rode a little distance from the others.

'I told you I could use my weapons, half-elf,' came the reply.

Carthinal turned to Thad. 'You too, lad,' he said.

The boy seemed pleased with the praise. 'I did good with th' throwin' dagger didn't I¿he replied. 'I got him right in th' bleedin' eye. 'Ave I earned me place in your company, Carthinal?

'Yes, you did well with the dagger, and with your sword before that,' Carthinal told him. 'It took some courage to get up close enough to those wolves so you could use it. As to earning your place, I will think about it and discuss it with the others.'

Thad smiled and then looked away, almost shyly.

Eventually, they found a clearing where there was a small pool of water surrounded by bushes. A stream fed it from the north and left from the western end of the pool. They decided not only to break their fast here but also to bathe and rest for the remainder of the day after their ordeal.

'I suspect it's not our last fight, though,' Carthinal warned them.

Davrael took the horses to the pool first to allow them to drink, and Asphodel filled the water bottles that were empty. They decided the girls should bathe first, and the men would prepare a fire. It would be cold in the water, and they would need a fire to get warm since the sun had little warmth yet. Asphodel, Kimi and Randa set off and soon sounds of splashing and squeals could be heard from behind the bushes.

Soon the three reappeared, dressed in their armour, but with hair dripping wet and hanging loose. Fero stared at Randa with an open mouth. She had not had her hair down since she arrived, it having been in her helmet, or bound around her head. Basalt heard a slight intake of breath. He looked at Fero and noticed the expression on the tall man's face. Fero saw the dwarf looking at him.

'Such hair!' he breathed. 'It's like moonlight rippling over the sea. Never have I seen such beautiful hair.'

'Yeah!' replied the dwarf. 'A pity she's not as beautiful in character as her hair.'

Fero sighed and drew his eyes away from the girl. 'Yes. A beautiful exterior, but inside she is ugly. Maybe an adventure such as this would change her. However, Carthinal seems determined to send her home.'

'I wouldn't bet on her going, my friend. That young lady is used to getting her own way and can be as stubborn as we mountain dwarfs,' Basalt replied, remembering their tussle of wills in the library over who should go down to the secret room first.

Carthinal, Fero, Basalt and Davrael then moved to the pool. Davrael noticed Thad was sitting by the fire and making no move to go with them.

'Come on then,' he called to the boy.

'I don't need a damn bath. I've got the flippin' blood off,' the boy replied in a rather surly manner.

'Oh, yes you do. You owe it to us. We don't want to be smelling you for the rest of the journey,' Basalt told him.

'Nor tempting any more wild animals. They will be able to smell you for ten leagues at least,' Fero told him, smiling.

'No!' The boy shrunk back.

'We'll have to strip him and throw him in then,' Fero and Bas advanced menacingly towards the thief.

'Stop! I can't bathe with you.'

Tears stood in Thad's eyes as he spoke.

'What's the problem, Thad?' asked Asphodel gently, signalling to the others to stop teasing.

'Promise you won't tell anyone?' he looked at them all. 'All of you! Promise! Swear by Kassilla?'

They all looked puzzled, but then, one by one they all agreed not to tell whatever Thad was about to reveal.

'I can't bathe with you guys because I'm not a boy, I'm a girl!'

A thunderous silence met this revelation.

Then, Asphodel said, 'All right. You men go off and bathe and Thad can come after on his, er… her own. Go on then.' This last as no one had moved.

After they had all bathed, they sat around the fire to get warm and Thad said, 'I think I'd better tell you the truth. I didn't leave 'Ambara because o' my bleedin' fence. 'E still, like, don't know as I stole the damn horse thingy back. I'd better begin at the beginning.'

'A good place to begin,' remarked Basalt, gaining himself a glare from Carthinal.

'Me mother's a whore,' the girl began. 'She used to be one of Madame Dopari's girls, right? From what she told me, she was bloody good at 'er job. She 'ad a number of regular clients, right, and made damn good money. Mother got large tips from some bloody rich clients, see? Then she made a mistake. She forgot to, like, take the 'erbs to prevent a soddin' pregnancy. If the girls become pregnant, they either have to, like, get rid of the baby or leave, right? Mother decided to leave and 'ave me. OK? She 'ad money, and could live well. So she thought. The money didn't last long, o' course, and so we 'ad to go to live in the bleedin' Warren. Mother 'ad to return to whorin' to keep us alive. She don't know no other way to make money, see. But the whores in th' Warren don't earn much of a livin', no matter 'ow good they are. Rich clients go to places like Madame Soddin' Dopari's, and th' poor can't pay much. Some clients was a bit rough too.

'One day, when I were about nine or ten, I over'eard a conversation in which Mother's like: "When Thadda's a woman, I'll take 'er ter Madame Dopari. She c'n then earn enough money fer us t' live better and' I c'n stop being a 'ore."

'I knew what me mother did for a livin'. There were only a thin wall between 'er room 'n' mine, right? I c'd 'ear everythin', like. I couldn't bear ter think o' that 'appenin' ter me. Not for soddin' money, like. Takin' any man who bleedin' well comes? No! That's so not cool.

'Then one day, just after me twelfth birthday it 'appened. I had me first bleedin', an' so I packed up a few things an' left, right? I called meself Thad, cut me 'air to look more like a damn boy, wore boy's clothes, an' disappeared into th' Warren. OK? (That's quite easy y' know). For a while, I begged. There're good pickings near th' temples for beggars. People feel so guilty and all that. Want ter salve their consciences or summat. Then, I were found by a man, whose name don't matter, an' 'e taught me ter be a thief, see?

'Just afore you left 'Ambara, I learnt that Mother 'ad found out that I were posin' as a boy, like, an' that I were now a bleedin' good thief, right? It wouldn't be long afore she found me, see, an' so I went to th' inn ter look for you, but you'd already left. I followed and 'ere I am.'

'Carthinal,' said Asphodel, turning to the half-elf, 'You can't send her back! Not if her mother is going to find her and send her to that…that place!'

'No. No, I can't, you're right, Asphodel.' He turned to the frightened, young girl. 'Thad, I will not be responsible for you being forced into prostitution. I'm not happy about the dangers you'll face with us, but I will not send you back against your will.'

'Also,' said the girl shyly, 'Me name's Thadora. Me mother called me Thadda sometimes when I were little. You c'n call me either, but I would like to leave Thad be'ind now. He don't exist no more.'

Chapter 12
Roffley

About four days later, at around noon, the little band reached the small town of Roffley. It was situated on the banks of the Brundella near to where it made a southward turn, heading for the Inner Sea. There were signs of the flood that had so tragically taken the lives of Carthinal and Asphodel's travelling companions, but it had now retreated leaving the ground at the side of the road soggy and wet. The party had stayed at an inn they came across about half-way between Roffley and Hambara. They were grateful for the comforts it offered after sleeping rough for some days. Now, as they entered Roffley, they were again looking forward to sleeping in proper beds and eating food that was not either rabbit or dried rations.

The town was very small. It boasted of little more than a main street and a market square. They entered the town from the West through a gate in the surrounding walls. The walls did not look very strong, and in fact were in poor repair in places. Basalt commented that with a few dwarves, he could make the town a fortress in a week, but he could not understand how the townsfolk had neglected their defences.

'I suppose it isn't necessary in times of peace,' pointed out Randa, 'and it's only a small town. Not one of great strategic importance for it to warrant much input from elsewhere. I expect the townsfolk are too poor to pay for the upkeep of the walls.'

The seeming callousness of the remark appalled Asphodel, intimating as it did that the people of Roffley were of no importance, but she bit her tongue and refrained from making the comment that sprung to her lips. After all, Carthinal intended Randa to return to Hambara from here, so they would no longer have to put up with her arrogance.

They walked along the main street, a cobbled road between close buildings on either side. They were looking for an inn so they could have somewhere to stay. The people on the road made it difficult for them, to pass, especially as they all seemed to stop to stare at the group. After all, a half-elf mage, an elven curate of Sylissa, a dwarf bristling with weapons, an exceptionally tall, dark-skinned stranger, a young, red-headed girl, two Horselords, and a tall, aristocratic, young lady made strange travelling companions.

Eventually, they arrived in the market square, and all stopped to admire the market hall. It dominated the square to the extent of almost completely filling it. It comprised of a low wall, about three-feet-high, interspersed with occasional gaps for entry, down the two, long sides, which were about fifty-yards-long. The two, short sides were open, with steps leading up to a raised floor. At intervals all around the building were pillars of oak supporting a roof. On the two open sides, they were mounted on stone pillars, and on the longer sides were on the low wall. These columns were also inside the building in two rows, holding up the roof. When they looked up, they saw the structure of beams supporting the roof, a strangely beautiful pattern, but very strong.

'This hall will be here for centuries to come,' commented Basalt, his dwarven admiration for construction coming to the fore.

'P'raps so, but we so don't want ter wait ter see if you're right,' Thadora said. 'Look, isn't that a damn inn over there?' and she pointed towards the far end of the square to a building which seemed larger than the shops on either side of the market hall.

They made their way towards the building, which proved indeed to be an inn, called the Black Cat. They entered and were greeted by the proprietor.

'Ah! Strangers, I see. And what can I be getting for you? Ale, wine, spirits, rooms, maybe?'

'Yes, we would like rooms, first,' Randa stepped forward and took over just as Carthinal was about to speak. 'I need a room to myself, of course, and I suppose the Horselords would like one for themselves as well. Two others will suffice for the rest.'

While the others stood open-mouthed at her presumption to decide sleeping arrangements for them all, the innkeeper replied, 'I'm sorry, but I can't accommodate your demands. We're rather full with the Festival coming up. I could manage to squeeze you into two rooms, but four is out of the question.'

Randa was about to remonstrate with the innkeeper, but Carthinal quickly interrupted her.

'We'll take the two rooms, please,' he said, throwing Randa a glare that made her physically recoil, 'and I'll have some ale. What about the rest of you?'

When they ordered, Carthinal once more reminded Randa that she was not travelling with her father, or even as herself. She was, he reminded her, incognito. She would not get, nor even ask for any preferential treatment. The alternative to staying in the inn, crowded as it may be, was sleeping out in the woods again.

To her credit, Randa appeared sorry and said as much to Carthinal.

'I am so used to having everyone run around and do whatever I wish that it'ss very difficult to remember I'm not Lady Randa, here,' she replied somewhat uncharacteristically.

The landlady, a plump, good-natured woman in her middle years, seemed eager to talk to them about the town's celebrations whilst there was a lull in the business of the inn.

'We have to work so hard here in Roffley and the surroundings,' she told them, 'That we really look forward to the festivals. We always dress in our best for the gods.'

She looked pointedly at the group of adventurers in their armour and dusty travelling clothes.

'We don't have much in the way of decent clothing with us, I'm afraid,' apologised Asphodel. 'We have had to travel light, but we would very much like to celebrate the New Year here. Several of us worship Grillon in particular, and the rest of us revere him. Will it be particularly bad if we are not dressed in our best?'

'Oh, don't you worry too much about that,' smiled the landlady. 'I have seven daughters, ranging in age from fifteen to thirty. I'm sure we can find you something that fits. If you would be willing to borrow clothes, that is,' she added, looking at Randa.

Randa seemed to visibly swallow her pride, and she replied, to the surprise of the others, 'That's very kind of you. I think we would be very grateful to take up your offer,' but she looked as though she had eaten something nasty as she said it.

'I'll send Mandreena, my youngest, to you. She'll help you to choose, and maybe do any alterations that are needed, but we'll need to see about it quickly. And you young men', she went on, 'can look through the shirts and trousers belonging to my sons if you have none of your own.'

'I have a change of clothing in my pack,' replied Fero, 'but thanks for your kind offer.'

The other men also thanked Tramora. She told them that was her name, but Basalt noted that she was unlikely to have anything to fit a dwarf. Davrael said he had a clean shirt, but Carthinal accepted the offer as his change was a clean scarlet robe, and he wished not to wear his robes at an occasion such as this.

The girls spent the rest of the afternoon trying on dresses in the company of Mandreena. She was a lively, talkative girl, and made friends easily. She especially took to Thadora, being almost the same age. Randa made a special effort not to order anyone around or be too snooty about the dresses, although they were much inferior to even her oldest clothes. They chose dresses and Mandreena took them away for the small alterations that were needed, saying she could soon have them ready. The others bathed and got themselves clean, then felt much better.

That evening, the little band of questers decided to have a meal and to go to bed early since the next day promised to be long. They all wished to rise at dawn to worship at the stone circle as well as to take a part in the celebrations later.

The next morning, they all rose before sunrise. They wore their travelling clothes as no one had to dress up until later for the feast, but Carthinal decided to wear his clean robes as they were going to worship the god. So, leaving their weapons and armour behind in the inn, they walked the short distance to the circle just outside of the town, along with most of the rest of the village and surrounding farms. Many farmers were carrying lambs or kids, or leading calves, the first born of the new season, to be sacrificed to Grillon.

When they reached the circle, they were surprised to be ushered into the centre. It seemed that because of Asphodel's status as a cleric, the villagers gave her a place of honour, and her companions were included. They found themselves sitting next to the Baron of Roffley and his family, although they said they would be happy with the rest of the crowd, the priestess in charge insisted, so they were accommodated inside the circle.

Farmers then began to progress towards the altar in the centre of the circle, which had been decked in a green cloth and green branches. Then, the farmers brought their young animals forward in a procession towards the altar. Huntsmen with a live catch followed them. To their surprise, Fero stood and joined the huntsmen, pulling a small, wriggling rabbit out of his pocket.

'It's not much, but some sacrifice from us may persuade the gods to help us in our quest,' he whispered to the others, who looked amazed, wondering where he had got the animal. Fero said nothing but just grinned at their expressions.

The priestess spoke words of blessing over the animals and then selected one lamb for immediate sacrifice. (The rest would be sacrificed later in the morning). She placed the hapless creature down onto the altar and, with a sharp knife, quickly killed it by slitting its jugular vein and then allowed the blood to run into a bowl.

When the blood filled the bowl, she held it aloft saying, 'Lord Grillon, accept the offer of the blood of this lamb, and give fertility to all our beasts so that we may prosper in the coming year.'

She then drank some of the blood and placed the bowl back on the altar with the lamb's carcass.

Then, she raised her hands in the air, saying, 'All praise to the Lord Grillon.'

The congregation replied, 'All glory to the Lord Grillon.'

Finally, she said, 'All honour to the Lord Grillon.'

Then, she blessed the farmers and huntsmen who came with animals and called down Grillon's blessing on all the people of Roffley and its neighbouring farmsteads.

After this, she spoke to the assembled people. She had, she told them, studied the moons and the almanacs for this day, and the portends were not good. Tonight, the first of the New Year, it was the dark of the moon, Lyndor, but Ullin would just be seen as a sliver of light as it was waning. This indicated a time of evil and despair to come in the year just dawning. They must trust in the gods of good to help all mortals through this time that was coming.

After some more praise and prayers, the congregation left the circle. It was still only one and a half-hours after the dawning of this first day of Grildar, and so people had time to kill before the feast. Since there would be merrymaking throughout the night, the adventurers decided to go back to the Black Cat to rest until it was time to change for the rest of the day's festivities. Once there, Mandreena accosted them. She insisted that Thadora go with her to see the Wanderers. These people were travellers who rarely stayed in one spot for long. They were reputed to have the second sight, and able to predict the future as well as being excellent entertainers. They would be giving the entertainment during the feast, Mandreena told them, but maybe they would be willing to tell the girls something of their futures. Glancing at Carthinal as though for permission, Thadora left for the excitement of the Wanderer camp. Asphodel reminded her of her promise not to steal from anyone, and to return in time to get ready for the feast.

The girls exited the inn in great excitement. They passed through the Market Hall, which was being decorated in greenery for the coming feast, and went on through the village. A delicious smell of baking bread rose from the baker's shop, but all the doors were closed.

'That's for the feast,' Mandreena told her. 'Everyone gives something today. The Baron lends us his cooks, farmers give meat, and we at the inn give the wine and ale. The fish is from the river, courtesy of the fishermen, and there is always game from the huntsmen. I defy you to eat some of everything!'

Eventually, they came to the Wanderers' camp on the north side of the town. There were brightly coloured wagons everywhere in a seemingly haphazard pattern. Children and dogs were underfoot on every side. There were adults cooking, changing, washing clothes and themselves, and practising the various skills they were going to show at the feast. It was a noisy, lively place, the like of which Thadora had never seen before. She considered herself worldly wise, coming as she did from the Warren in Hambara and surviving on the streets there, but so far on this journey, she was finding out that there were many things she did not know. Far more than she did know in fact, and she was a little nonplussed to find there was so much new in the world. It also surprised her to realise she would have difficulty surviving in the countryside, just as those from here would have problems where she came from.

Soon, they found what Mandreena was looking for. A wagon with an eye painted on the side stood near the northern edge of the camp. It had a variety of other signs and symbols painted on it, none of which Thadora recognised. Mandreena approached the wagon and ascended the steps leading up to the door. She knocked loudly, and a voice called out.

'Who seeks knowledge of the future?'

'It is Mandreena of the Black Cat and Thadora of Hambara,' Mandreena replied.

'Enter, then, Mandreena of the Black Cat and Thadora of Hambara. You may come in either singly or together, as you wish. Have you the customary payment?'

'Yes,' both girls replied, as they opened the door.

The interior of the wagon was dim, to say the least. There was a smell of oil lamps, but only a single, red candle burned on a table. The girls could make out a thick, red cloth covering the table, and plenty cushions scattered about. These were large and comfortable looking, and were largely in red, deep greens, blues, and gold. Seated on the only visible chair behind the table, they could make out the figure of an old woman dressed in the colourful dress of the Wanderers. She beckoned to the girls.

'Come in, come in. It's not warm enough for these old bones to be in the draught from the door, although I doubt I'll be willing enough for it to be open come summer. What have we here, then? A girl and her sweetheart, maybe? I thought you gave two girl's names! But wait. Now I see. You are indeed two girls, although one of you is dressed in boy's clothing. No doubt it will all be clear after your readings. Well, who wants to be first?'

'You go first, Thadora,' whispered Mandreena, seeming to lose her courage a little in the oppressive atmosphere of the wagon.

Thadora stepped forward, offered the customary silver piece to the old fortune-teller, who waved her to a seat.

'You sit down over there,' the old woman told Mandreena, then proceeded to hand a small, crystal ball to Thadora. 'I want you to hold this in one hand while I look at your other palm, so it can absorb some of your aura. Let me see your left hand first please.'

Thadora did as the old woman bade her and the old woman took her hand and pondered it deeply.

'I see you have had a happy childhood, in spite of great deprivation,' she whispered. 'Then something happened, and after that, life became very tough. You are a strong girl, and you overcame this. I think this was why you dress as a boy. You have had little in the way of the love of a man, yet. There is also something missing in your past. Maybe, you never knew your father? Yet, you have a sister, I see.'

Thadora looked sharply at the old woman.

'No. No sister. Nor brother either. There were just Mother and me.'

The old woman continued as though Thadora had not spoken.

'You seem to have been seeking something or someone.'

Thadora opened her mouth to deny this, but the old woman continued.

'Let me see your other hand.'

Thadora changed the crystal ball to her left hand and gave her right hand to the clairvoyant.

'Whatever or whoever you sought, you seem to have given up, but you will find it fairly soon. A change is about to come about in your life. It may have just happened, or it is just about to happen. You have a great destiny, child,' She looked up into

Thadora's eyes. 'If you accept this destiny, life will be difficult and dangerous. If you refuse it, life will be easier for you, but the consequences for the world will be dire.'

She reached out and took the ball, at the same time extinguishing the candle. They were plunged into complete darkness. Mandreena gave muffled scream, and then was silent.

The old woman's voice came from the blackness, 'You have the health and strength of mind for the task ahead of you. That much I can see from your aura, which is very strong in this darkness. There are Guardians watching over you, to protect you, though you are not aware of them.' She then looked in the crystal. 'There are images here also of seven companions. Eight are needed for the task ahead, which is but a beginning and all may not see its end. I can see mountains, snow, and death very near. Help from unexpected sources. Now a valley, beautiful it is with a lake set in a beautiful, magical forest. Yet, there is dark magic here. You must beware. I can see no more. The rest is hidden in swirling mists. Choose your path well, young Thadora. The right path is not always the easy one. May the gods go with you.'

There came the sound of flint on steel and the candle once more fluttered to life. The old woman peered at Thadora through the dimness, but said nothing more. She then turned to Mandreena for her turn.

Mandreena's fortune seemed much more mundane, but she seemed happy with the usual predictions of a happy and fulfilled life as the wife of a handsome farmer with lots of children to come.

As the girls left the wagon of the fortune-teller, Mandreena could not help but ask Thadora a little about what the fortune-teller told her. Thadora told the other girl that although she had no sister she knew about, she did not know her father, and he could have another daughter somewhere. She did not say anything of her mother's profession, however. Mandreena then asked about the quest they were on.

'I can't say nothin 'bout that,' replied the young thief, importantly. 'I'm sorry, Mandreena.'

'What about your friends?' went on the other girl. 'That Carthinal is very fit. I bet you fancy him, don't you? I know I do. Are you going to try to get him to go to the woods with you tonight?'

Thadora blushed. 'No. O' course not,' she replied.

'Why not? If you don't, someone else will. Trust me. A man that good looking will not pass this night alone.'

'He's got a girlfriend already, like,' Thadora retorted.

'One of your group? That tall, beautiful girl or the pretty elf? I must say, I don't like the blond much. She's a bit too fond of herself if you ask me.'

'No. Some elf back in 'Ambara, I think, but I've never met 'er. She's a mage, too.'

'Well, tell me about him, anyway. Where's he from?'

'He comes from Blue'aven, right, and came to 'Ambara to take his apprenticeship exams. 'E passed very well, I think. With distinction, me sources tell me. But, 'e, like, scares me a bit. 'e has a fierce temper, yer know.'

'It's the red hair,' said Mandreena, knowingly, glancing at Thadora's unruly, red curls. 'To tell the truth, that other one, the Horselord scares me more, but go on.'

Thadora suddenly realised she knew nothing more of Carthinal, and when she considered more deeply, she realised she knew no more about the others, except for Randa. The conversation began to get too personal, and she wanted to think about what the clairvoyant told her, so she told Mandreena that she wanted to go back to the inn to rest in preparation for the celebrations later.

As she walked, she wondered. Here she was with seven people she knew nothing at all about. She was about to go off into the wilds with them. Her mother would have a fit if she knew. She smiled at that thought, then began to wonder if she was wise to trust these strangers. Yet, trust them she did. She entered the inn, still deep in thought, and ascended the stairs to the room she shared with the other girls. They were all three there, asleep, or resting, and she threw herself on her bed and fell asleep herself.

Kimi aroused her a little later telling her it was time to begin getting ready. Already, the others had bathed, so she went down to the bathhouse and had a bath. On her return to the room, the others were getting into their dresses and doing their hair. Kimi had tidied Asphodel's roughly cut hair with a pair of scissors borrowed from Tramora, and it looked much better. She offered to do the same for Thadora. Afterwards, Thadora had to agree that it was a great improvement. Her red curls seemed to fall around her face in a way that flattered her features and she smiled at the result as she looked into the small, silver mirror that Randa produced.

'You look more like a girl, now,' said Mandreena, entering the room to help them to dress, 'although you'll look much better when your hair's grown. You'll be really pretty with long hair and wearing a dress.'

Thadora grimaced at the thought of wearing dresses and privately vowed that even if she got back to Hambara she would revert to her previous persona if it were the only way to avoid it.

Mandreena brought with her some jewellery for them to wear. It was only cheap, imitation jewellery, but they thanked her for her kindness, and although Randa had to bite back some remarks about it, she accepted it gratefully.

Eventually, after much laughter and discussion about how to do Randa's hair, the girls were ready. It was fifteen minutes before the sixth hour, but Randa suggested they keep the men waiting.

'It doesn't do to seem too eager,' she told them. 'We'll make an entrance. We'll wait until we hear them go down, then wait another five minutes or so before going down ourselves.'

This they agreed to as Randa knew more about this sort of thing than any of the rest of them, but they waited impatiently as they were all eager to get to the festivities. Eventually, Randa told them the men had waited long enough.

The four girls came to the top of the stairs and decided to go down one at a time for maximum effect. Each of them paused briefly at the top of the stairs and then slowly descended.

Thadora was wearing a green dress almost the exact colour of her eyes, which sparkled with excitement. The imitation emeralds at her throat and ears gave off green fire in the light, and her red curls set off the image to perfection.

'Thadora,' smiled Carthinal, 'You look lovely. I hadn't realised how pretty you were under all that dirt.'

Thadora then spoiled the image by sticking out her tongue at him and coming out with a few, choice swear words, and they all laughed.

Kimi wore a lemon dress, with a skirt that trailed slightly at the back. She had "diamonds" at her ears and throat, and had a "gold" bracelet on her wrist. Her hair was done in its usual braids, but they had been pulled up onto the top of her head, revealing her lovely neck. Davrael was entranced at how lovely she looked and hugged her hard, earning a reprimand for disturbing her clothes.

Randa looked very dignified, having done this sort of thing many times before, although never in an inn. She chose to wear a dress of her favourite sky blue. It had a very, low neckline revealing her exquisite breasts and it clung to her as she moved, revealing her almost, perfect figure. Round her neck, she wore a necklace of imitation aquamarines the exact colour of her eyes. The girls eventually decided her hair was her best feature, (although Mandreena remarked that all her features were her best feature), so they left it loose, falling in a silvery-gold rain down her back.

'Close your mouth, ranger,' Basalt whispered to Fero as the tall man gazed at her in awe.

Finally, Asphodel came down. She paused and looked down at the men. Fero in his usual black hair tied back with a black leather thong and a silver earring in one ear and. Basalt, in a brown shirt also wore black breeches. She looked at Davrael. He wore what was obviously the dress of his tribe. Dark brown, leather breeches with a green shirt, covered by a tunic of brown leather, tooled with many symbols. On his head he wore a multicoloured headband to keep his long hair out of his eyes.

Finally, she regarded Carthinal. He had put on an indigo, silk shirt. His breeches were a pale, fawn colour and he brushed his auburn hair until it gleamed and hung loose around his head. She smiled at him, as she came down the stairs. Her red dress made a dramatic statement against her black hair. She had a shawl of black wool draped over her shoulders, adding to the drama of the dress. The dress itself fitted to her figure and both revealed and concealed. Around her neck, she wore a necklace of a single piece of jet set in a gold surround, and she had similar, jet earrings in her ears. She slowly descended the stairs, noticing she was making quite an impression, not only on her own party but also on others in the common room, too. Once all the girls were down the stairs, the eight of them moved out of the inn to the market square where the town held the feast.

It was a merry occasion, held in the market hall. Everyone in the town came. The four girls were glad they took the opportunity of borrowing dresses, as everyone else looked their best. They had set a table at the near end of the Hall across the others and there the Baron and his family sat. The other tables were set down the long sides of the hall, one on each side to allow space in the centre for both the entertainment and the ease of serving.

Carthinal found eight seats, four on each side of the table, and they sat down. After a brief benediction from the cleric, they found themselves plied with drinks. Then those designated as waitresses served the first course, a spicy, mutton soup. The serving girls served each course and then went to sit down to eat their own food. Entertainers did their acts between each course. First came jugglers who came in juggling balls, but eventually were juggling anything that came to hand; knives and forks, drinking goblets, fruit of various kinds or anything else left loose on the tables. When the jugglers left, the serving girls came round with plates of steaming fish, caught in the river, and eaten with a fine, white wine from the cellars of the Baron. After the fish, the acrobats entertained them and who amazed the feasters with their agility. Then, came the main course. Platters of meat were carried out and set on the table. Much of the meat came from the sacrificed animals, and so there was a great variety. Bowls of fresh vegetables and bread warm from the oven were also served with the meat, along with a choice of red wine or ale. Basalt chose to drink the ale of course, but the others drank the wine, which flowed freely. As soon as someone emptied their goblet, a server or a neighbour re-filled it. It seemed everyone intended to get everyone else inebriated.

The next entertainment was a "mage" whom Carthinal said was nothing more than a man clever at sleight of hand, and not true magic. His 'magic' did not disturb the mana at all, as true magic would do. However, this did not detract from the enjoyment of the spectacle as he drew doves from a hat, and coins from behind people's ears.

After this, there were chunks of local cheeses with butter and more fresh bread, and of course, wine or ale, and finally the meal concluded with a dessert made with apples and sweet pastry, and a variety of other sweetmeats.

During this course, a bard came into the centre of the Hall and began to pluck his instrument. Silence fell as he began to sing. He sang the song of the legend of Grillon and Parador.

'One day, the Lord of Nature was walking all alone
When beside a hidden pool a lovely sight was shown.
For bathing in the moonlight, where no-one should have been
Was a beauteous maiden, the loveliest he'd e'er seen.

'Lord Grillon lost his heart to her
This maiden oh so fair.
He vowed that she would be his own
His life with her would share.

'He showed himself at once to her
As forward he did tread.
She said "And who are you, good sir?
Should you not be abed?"

"'Oh lovely maid, my love, my life,
I ne'er will rest again.
Unless you come to be my wife
My heart will feel such pain."

'And so fair Parador was wed
To Grillon. She agreed
To always sleep within his bed
And others ne'er to heed.

'But evil now will turn to dust
That love and bliss
For Barnat after her did lust
And swore she'd be his.

'He poisoned Grillon's mind and said
She was untrue
That she had been into his bed
And others too.

*'Lord Grillon he was truly sad
That she should treat him so.
He thought that he'd go truly mad
So far from her, he'd go.*

*'Now Parador had done no wrong
To deserve this fate.
She could not anymore be strong
Beneath Lord Grillon's hate.*

*'So mourn she did and all the world
Did join with her in sorrow.
All green things died and creatures curled
All safely in their burrow.*

*'But in good time, Lord Grillon found
How false the god of war.
He came to her and he reclaimed
The love of his wife once more.*

*'So once again the land grew green
And springtime came again.
And summer's warmth and life serene
While she forgot her pain.*

*'And so each year the land remembers
The love of Parador
And autumn comes and winter's embers
Till Spring returns once more.'*

The story of Parador and Grillon having been told once more, the tables were cleared and moved out of the way. There was to be dancing until sunset when the priests would light the bonfires. Small tables were set around the outside of the hall, and the taverns set out tables as well. It seemed that people still expected drinking to be done, here. A small group of musicians set themselves up at one end of the building and began to play. Soon, dancing people filled the space. Fero and Basalt were not too sure of the dances as they were Grosmerian dances, but the others joined in with gusto. Soon, with a little more ale, and not a small swig or two from Basalt's flask of dwarven spirits, the dwarf and ranger were persuaded to have a go at a dance that was danced in a circle and performed quite competently.

Just as the sun set, someone rang a bell to indicate that the bonfires were being lit. There were fires at all the cardinal points of the town, and so the throng of people went in four different directions. The friends were in the middle of the hall and found themselves separated by the milling people. Carthinal saw Fero's dark head above the crowd, being swept away towards the south. He could see no one else except Asphodel, and he quickly grabbed hold of her hand.

'We'll go with the flow, Asphodel,' he told her. 'The others can take care of themselves. We'll see them at the inn later, or tomorrow morning.'

'But what about Thadora?' Asphodel looked a little concerned. 'She's hardly more than a child. Not yet sixteen.'

'Two points, Asphodel. One, Thadora is only a few days away from sixteen, if she is to be believed, and two, she's looked after herself in the Warren at Hambara for about four years, so I don't expect harm to come to her here. Anyway, you're not her mother.'

'Well, yes. You're right of course. Let's go and enjoy the fires.'

The two went towards the eastern fire. By the time they reached it, it was burning brightly. A circle had formed, and the people were dancing round and round the flames. The pair managed to insert themselves into the ring, joining hands with the others, and were soon being pulled madly round in a circle. This dance dated back to the earliest times and represented the turning of the seasons, the fire being the sun around which the planet of Vimar moved. Some folk said it represented the wheel of life, with souls being constantly reborn. Whatever the meaning or origins, it was a tradition, and great fun. Soon, people became hot and thirsty and they moved to the tables where they found more drink at a table near the fire. The tables by the fires were run by the taverns and inns in Roffley, and were run as a business, so now the drinks were paid for. Water was free, however, so Carthinal and Asphodel had a goblet of water each, then they followed it with a goblet of wine. They sat down on a log placed there for that purpose.

'I'm feeling a little giddy,' Asphodel confessed. 'How much have we had to drink this afternoon?'

'I washn't counting,' replied Carthinal, 'but I exshpect it was rather more than we think. My wine goblet sheemed to be alwaysh full. Maybe it wash one of those fabled magic onesh that never runsh dry!' He laughed at the idea.

'You're slurring your words, Carthinal,' said Asphodel. 'I think you're drunk!'

'And you're not, I suppose?'

'A little merry, maybe. Look, the fire's burning down. People are disappearing, too.' She shivered.

'You're cold. Do you want to go back to the inn?'

'No. Not tonight. Not on Grillon's Night. Let's walk for a little. I've got my shawl, and walking will keep us warm.'

They set off walking around the outskirts of the village. After they had walked for a while, talking of this and that inconsequential thing and laughing a lot, a light shower surprised them. Ahead of them, they could see a dark shape suggesting a farmer's barn.

'Let's shelter there,' said Carthinal, pulling Asphodel after him in the direction of the barn.

'As long as there are no dogs like Bramble,' she replied, running hard to keep up.

They reached the barn, pushed open the door, and nearly fell in. They were both wet. A surprised cow turned her head to look at them. Her expression of surprise made them both begin to laugh again. Never had a cow seemed so funny. They clung together, laughing until their stomachs ached. Then, an impulse took Carthinal. He bent his head and kissed Asphodel. She stopped laughing immediately, put her arms round his neck, and kissed him back.

'Let's go up into the loft. There will be some hay there,' Carthinal whispered in her ear, tracing its pointed shape with his finger. In reply, Asphodel led the way towards the ladder, climbing it rather unsteadily.

Carthinal heard a cock crowing, then a slight tickling on his cheek. He opened his eyes slowly and saw light beginning to creep through a high window to his right. He felt something thump lightly onto his chest, and then small, sharp needles began to prick his skin. He opened his eyes wide and looked down. On his chest, he saw a small black and white kitten. As it settled down, purring, it began kneading his chest with its tiny claws.

'Hey! No, you don't! That hurts!' Carthinal protested as he gently removed the small creature, setting it down into the hay. 'Although maybe not as much as my head!'

Then, last night came back to him. He looked over to his left and saw Asphodel asleep in the hay, her nakedness covered by the black shawl she had been wearing. He groaned. He had not intended this to happen, although it had been Grillon's night when such things were allowed, and even expected. He admitted to himself that he felt a strong attraction to the young elf, though. He did not remember the walk from the village much, but recalled a sudden shower, and running into the barn for shelter.

He remembered kissing Asphodel and, all too clearly, the rest of it. He knew he should not have allowed it to happen. He was not worthy of her, and he respected her too much. He remembered his past life and buried his head in his hands. Asphodel would not understand the things he had done when he was an orphan boy living with the gangs in the poor quarters of Bluehaven. How he had fought and thieved to stay alive. He could not hurt her by admitting his past life. She would not accept that at all. No, he decided. She deserved more than the man he was. He would let her believe that it was just a Grillon's night celebration. Yes, that was the best thing. That way she would be hurt the least. He leaned over to her and gently shook her awake.

'It's dawn, Asphodel,' he murmured. 'We should get back to the inn. We walked farther than I thought last night.'

The young elf stirred in her sleep and then opened her clear, grey eyes.

'Oh, yes,' she said, and smiled at him.

He thought her smile would break his heart. He hardened it to her and said, 'Last night. I'm sorry. It should never have happened,' he told her. '*I seem to be apologising for this sort of thing a lot these days,*' he thought.

The girl's smile faded. 'I suppose it's because of your girlfriend in Hambara,' she replied.

Carthinal frowned as he framed the words, 'What girlfriend?' when she continued. 'What is her name? Yssa, isn't it?'

Carthinal decided to let her think that Yssa was the reason for his reluctance, but could not bring himself to say so in so many words. He looked away.

Asphodel took that as an affirmation of her assumption, 'Don't worry. I'm no threat to her. Last night was Grillon's night after all and these things are expected to happen. I expect she celebrated in a similar way.'

During this speech, Asphodel dressed and had her back turned to Carthinal so did not see the look of pain that her words brought to his face. He found himself surprised at how he felt hurt at her seeming indifference to the previous night's activities. So, it was nothing more than a Grillon's Night assignation to her, was it? Well, it was best that way, he thought. She wouldn't be hurt if that were how she felt, but he felt sad nevertheless that she should look on it as just that, in spite of the fact he was also relieved she would not be hurt by his reaction to the event.

'Come on, then, get dressed, and we'll go back. I expect we both need some more sleep. It wasn't incredibly comfortable up here.'

They finished dressing and then climbed down the ladder. The cow looked at them again, this time pleadingly. She evidently thought they would milk her.

'Never mind, old girl,' Carthinal said as they passed her. 'I expect they'll be late this morning, but it's only once a year,' and he patted the animal as they passed.

So, they returned to the inn.

Chapter 13
Wolf

They remained for two more days in Roffley in order to gather provisions and to rest, for they knew they had an arduous journey in front of them. They had to cross the formidable Mountains of Doom. Thadora asked Davrael to teach her to use a short bow. She spent some time practising under his eye, and Asphodel practised her skills with the sling, too. Kimi continued her knife practice she had started on their way from their own lands, and now used two knives that Davrael bought for her in Hambara.

Randa and Carthinal argued after discovering that a caravan would be departing for Hambara in the next sixdays. Thadora, rather surprisingly, settled it by telling the group that the old clairvoyant mentioned eight companions to her, and as she pointed out, the number in the original poem had been unclear. It could well have been eight. So, Carthinal agreed, if reluctantly, to Randa's demand that she accompany them. Basalt was less than convinced and told Carthinal so. He disliked the heiress to Hambara's dukedom intensely, and she reciprocated. However, he accepted Carthinal's decision on the matter but did not have to like it, as he pointed out.

They decided to leave the horses behind at the inn to be cared for by Fat Ander, as the innkeeper was known. The animals would doubtless find the journey over the mountains difficult, as neither of them were bred for mountain work. The horses that did travel the passes over the Mountains of Doom to Erian were a sturdy, mountain breed, sure-footed, and with thick coats. Fat Ander told them he would allow their animals to run in his fields with his own horses. Payment for any feed or other expenses could be made on the traveller's return. If they did not return, they agreed Fat Ander could have the horses. He grinned at this, as the value of Storm alone would be worth more than his inn could earn in a year, not to mention the value of a horse like Moonbeam, from Horselord stock.

Randa smiled, 'I hope he knows what he's letting himself in for with Storm. He can be very difficult. I wouldn't put it past him to jump out of the field and go home!'

She was obviously very fond of her wilful stallion.

During the night, Asphodel had a vivid dream, but in the morning, she found it very difficult to recall.

'I know it had something to do with the way we have to go,' she told them. 'I can remember thinking in the dream that this was a true dream, and not one brought about by our discussions earlier. Oh, why can't I remember it now?' she exclaimed in frustration. 'There was a man sitting on a stone. He looked like a scribe, I think. I think he had ink stains on his fingers and carried quills in his pocket. I can't remember anything else.'

The description seemed familiar to Davrael and Kimi.

'It sounds very much like the man whom we saw in the clearing when we were coming to Hambara,' Kimi told them. 'The man who married us. We suspected he was Zol. It was so very mysterious.'

'Try to think as we walk,' Carthinal told Asphodel. 'Maybe more of your dream will come to you.'

Relations were a little strained between them since Grillon's night, each trying to distance themselves from the other. The rest of them, if they noticed, did not show they did, and they set off on their travels once more.

Mandreena walked to the edge of the town with them and waved goodbye.

'I hope you stop again on your way back,' she told Thadora. 'We had a good time together, didn't we?'

'Yeah, we did. I'm sure we'll stop. After all, your dad's got our 'orses!'

With that, they left the town of Roffley behind them.

They stopped for the night by the side of the road. The Mountains were coming nearer, and the land began to rise in low hills as they left the small town. They had seen some farms as they walked, but now they were few and far between, and the forest began to encroach on the road once more. The river still ran alongside them, and they made use of it for water and washing.

They found a small dell in the forest, near the river, and they lit a fire, both for cooking and warmth, for the temperature dropped suddenly at night. They were more tired than they were before coming to Roffley because they now had to carry whatever they needed, and consequently they travelled slower. They were going to have to rely on catching some game to supplement their rations, too. Fero had insisted they buy a rope just in case they had to climb up something in the mountains, and now they had little money left.

They took watch, as they had become accustomed to. Fero was watching with Kimi, and they had the last watch before dawn. As they were sitting there, they heard a howl. It did not seem too near, but Kimi looked across at Fero for confirmation of her assessment that there was no danger. Seeing Fero's relaxed attitude, she allowed herself to relax, too. Then, they heard a sound from near the fire. Fero looked round, and saw that Thadora had woken at the sound of the howl, and sat bolt upright clutching her sword in her hand. Fero went over to her.

'It's all right, Thadda,' he said, using her pet name to reassure her, 'That is the cry of a normal wolf. They don't attack people, especially a well-armed group like we are. Nor do they come near fire.'

'Those others damn well did,' she replied. Thadora looked wild-eyed and Fero tried to reassure her.

'That group seemed very strange. I told you at the time. A pair of unnaturally, intelligent dire wolves led them. These others near here are just a normal pack.'

''Ow d' yer know?' Thadora demanded.

'I saw them yesterday when I went out to scout,' he told her. 'When the others wake up, we'll go and look at them. If you watch them for a while, you will see what they are truly like. They are not the fearsome beasts people tell about in children's stories and tales related by travellers in the taverns. Those tales are all made up or greatly embroidered to frighten people or make the tellers seem brave and bold.'

The early morning saw Fero and Thadora moving through the forest towards where he had seen and heard the wolves. 'Do you know how to walk quietly, Thadora?' asked Fero as they neared the place for which he was heading.

'You know it!' came the reply. 'Hey! It's a requirement o' th' job o' a bloody thief. It'd be so no use if yer wake folk by bangin' about.'

So silently, they slipped through the rapidly lightning forest until they came out on an escarpment overlooking some flatter land. The trees disappeared here, and they could see the Grosmerian plain spread before them. To the east, the hills continued to rise to meet the mountains, but to the north and west, the plains began.

Tracts of forest and open countryside separated small farmsteads They could just make out the lights coming on in Roffley, a day's journey away, as people rose to their morning tasks. Then Fero held out his hand to warn Thadora to be silent. They wormed their way forward on their stomachs and looked down from the cliff top to the plain below. They found themselves about twenty feet above the plain here and below them they saw a pack of wolves.

Thadora watched the animals in fascination. They were obviously a closely-knit group, with the exception of one animal, much paler than the rest, who seemed to hold itself aloof, or the others were ostracising it. Fero whispered that she (for it was a she-wolf, he told her) was a stranger, and probably trying to join the pack. She had not been there when he caught sight of them yesterday. Maybe she had lost her own pack. He told Thadora that pack sizes were usually between six and ten, but ten was rare. 'More than about eight, and one kill would not suffice, and less than six and the pack would find it difficult to hunt down larger animals like deer,' he whispered.

He pointed out the alpha male and female to her. The alpha male was a reddish-brown animal, quite large, and the alpha female was a smaller, black creature. Fero told Thadora that as a rule, only these two would mate, and the others would help in the rearing of the cubs. Another large, black male began to sniff at the pale she-wolf. She was cautious and bared her teeth at him, at the same time, crouching down, ears flattened to her head. Of the others, one, obviously much younger, had a reddish coat again. She was obviously one of the cubs of the alpha male. There was another black wolf, slightly smaller than the large one, and two greyish ones, one of which was a small female and the other was a very small, adult male. Fero thought the smaller, dark wolf and the greyish female were probably littermates, the way they seemed to stick to each other's company.

They watched for some time, and Thadora became fascinated. Then the large, black wolf sniffed the air as the wind gusted and seemed to change direction and he swung his head in their direction. He gave a sharp bark, and the leader turned and led his pack at a loping trot away from the cliff.

'Damn!' swore Fero, 'Wind changed direction and he smelled us. We'd better get back to the others. They should be ready to leave and we've still got our things to pack up.'

'Thanks, Fero,' said Thadora on their way back, 'But, hey, those wolves didn't seem scary. I don't think I'll be such a bloody wuss as far as wolves are concerned in future.'

Fero smiled.

When they got back to the camp, they found the others had indeed packed up, including Fero and Thadora's things, and that Basalt had made oatmeal porridge that he said would sustain them well for their trek. Fero and Thadora sat down and took the wooden bowls of porridge they were handed. The group sat around eating, then when they were finished, they wiped out the bowls, tied them to their packs, and were ready to leave. Fero saw to it that they had put the fire out completely before they left and returned to the road.

Thadora was very quiet as they walked along. She had a frown on her face. Fero hoped what she had seen of the wolves would help her with her fear.

She came up to Fero and asked, ''Ow common are th' colourings o' that pack, like?'

'Well now—wolves come in a range of colours ranging from very pale to black. However, the very pale coat of the she-wolf we saw trying to join the pack is not common this far south, although they are more so in the snowy north. Maybe that was why she didn't have a pack. Sometimes, albinos are turned out. However, she wasn't a true albino. Her eyes were brown and she had some colour to her coat.'

'Hmm!'

When they stopped for a midday break, Thadora suddenly said, 'Carthinal, that poem about soddin' wolves that you 'ad, right? D'you still 'ave it?'

'Somewhere in one of my pockets, I expect. Did you want me to read it?'

'No, Mother taught me ter read, so I c'n read it by meself. She learned at Madame soddin' Dopari's, right? It were somethin' th' damn Madame insisted all th' girls learn. Would yer lend it t' me for a while?'

'Of course. You can keep it. I don't know why I've still got it since it seems to have no relevance to us or our quest.'

So Carthinal gave the poem to Thadora; she took it and began to read it.

All the afternoon, Thadora kept perusing the poem as they walked. No one seemed to be able to get anything out of her, and they all thought her behaviour a little odd and out of character, but she had obviously been working something out. Fero thought she was trying to work through her fear of wolves, but Kimi had the feeling it was something more. She expressed her thoughts to Davrael.

'I expect she'll tell us when she's good and ready, and not before,' her husband replied. Davrael was a man of few words.

'Yes, you're right of course,' Kimi replied, linking her arm through his. He placed his other hand over hers and smiled down at the small, young woman with love. They continued in this way in silence.

Thadora did not reveal her thoughts until after they stopped for the night. After they had eaten, she opened the paper with the poem on and began to read it aloud.

> *"The wolves will fight 'gainst every foe*
> *The balance to maintain*
> *But far and wide the pack must go*
> *All borders they disdain.*

"The pack contains the strangest group,
The one whose pride comes with her
And one who slips through every loop
The wilful one, the tracker.

"The leader with his anger held,
The ones who hunt the horse
The rock that's strong completes the meld
And makes the pack a force.

"The wolf pack's members are filled with zest
And all do have their place
They hunt their foes with ruthlessness
Then vanish without trace.

"In times of danger, all must know
The wolf pack will be there.
They work as one. They keep their vow.
For each other, they will care."

'I think this bleedin' poem refers to us.'

The others looked at her in surprise.

'What makes you think that?' queried Basalt

'It was, like, when I were watchin' th' wolves wi' Fero. They seemed in lots o' ways ter be like us, see. Th' leader was a big, soddin', reddish-brown animal that made me kinda think o' you, Carthinal, right? There were somethin' about 'im that seemed so kinda dangerous, but hey, 'e didn't show any behaviour to th' others that made my feelin' logical, see? I think it were just that 'e seemed ter be holdin' somethin' inside o' 'imself, right? You give me that feelin', too, Carthinal. An' that, wi' 'is colouring an' all were what made me, like, think o' you.

'Then I looked at th' others. We was all bleedin' well there. A small, black wolf, the alpha female Fero called 'er, was you, Asphodel. Small and pretty, but wi' plenty o' spirit you know. Then, there were a damn big, black wolf that were obviously Fero. A little distant, yer know. I noticed that 'e sometimes wandered off, sniffin' around—fer game I suppose, or danger.

'A small, reddish one, much younger than the rest were me, see, while th' two 'oo was littermates and was always together was Davrael and Kimi. Th' male o' these was black, too. Th' other two were obviously Basalt, a small adult wolf, and a light-coloured female for Randa. The pale wolf were findin' it hard ter get accepted inter th' pack, a bit like Randa is wi' us, like. (Sorry Randa, but it's true, ain't it)? Then th' large black, Fero, showed interest in th' pale wolf. Don't look away, Fero. I've seen yer eyes on Randa when you think no one's lookin'.'

At this comment, Fero looked embarrassed and Randa looked annoyed, but Thadora continued, 'So I wanted ter look at th' damn poem again, right? Here is 'ow I sees it. Th' wolf pack in th' poem is us. OK? I'll ignore th' first verse as I don't know what that means. Th' second starts to describe th' wolves. "The one whose pride comes with her" is Randa. Hey, you are rather proud an' 'aughty yer know, Randa, and th' "one who slips through every loop" puzzled me at first, but I think it's me. I seem to allus manage ter get away when some bleedin' person is on me track for some damn scrape or other.

'Now the "wilful one" I think is Asphodel, right? You told us you 'ad to leave 'Ambara because you 'ad annoyed the bleedin' Great Father o' th' temple by disobeyin' orders because yer didn't agree wi' them. That's wilful! And "tracker" is obviously Fero, OK?' She paused for breath and looked round at them. They were all looking at her with interest.

'"The leader" is Carthinal, right?' she continued. 'You seem to 'ave a 'idden anger, too, Sometimes not so idden, either, Carthinal, so that fits in wi' "with his anger held." "The ones who hunt the horse" are Davrael and Kimi, though strictly speaking you don't 'unt 'orses, but 'erd 'em; and finally, Basalt is "the rock that's strong." Basalt is, I think, a rock. Is it strong?

'I've not got no further wi' th' meanin' o' th' first verse, but th' last obviously means that we must stick t'gether and be as a wolf pack.'

'Maybe,' said Basalt sceptically, 'but it could just be coincidence, couldn't it?'

'I think Thadora is right,' Randa disagreed, surprisingly agreeing with Thadora and earning a sharp look from Basalt, and a murmur of 'Of course. Never do to agree with a dwarf!'

'Basalt, don't be like that,' whispered Kimi. 'She's a right to voice her own opinion.'

The dwarf stopped grumbling and sat scowling to himself instead.

Randa continued, 'Look at it this way then. We were unsure as to how many of us there should be. This poem makes that quite clear. There should be eight of us. It makes it clear who should be here.' Here she threw a glance at Carthinal and Basalt who were reluctant to have her in the group at first. 'Those wolves Thadora and Fero were watching served to jog Thadora's mind about the poem and to set her thinking. Yes, I agree that it refers to us, and someone has put those wolves where we would see them. Everything seems to be happening rather too conveniently for it all to be accidental.'

Asphodel had been thinking as well. 'The first verse,' she said slowly, frowning as she spoke, 'refers to the Balance. Some clerics believe that in order for the world to work, there must be a balance between good and evil. Just as there are night and day, so we can sleep at night and wake in the daytime refreshed for our daily tasks. We, it seems, must maintain the Balance and to do so, we must cross borders and travel far.'

'And the last verse say we must "Work as one and keep our vow," and look out for each other. Much like wolf pack. But we have make no vows, do we?' This came from Davrael. 'Well, not all to whole group.' He looked at Kimi as he spoke of vows, and smiled.

'Well, that can be remedied,' Carthinal spoke for the first time in the discussion. 'We have a representative of the gods here.' He gestured towards Asphodel. 'I'm willing to swear to protect you and treat you as the brothers and sisters I never had.'

The others agreed, and they all stood in front of Asphodel.

Carthinal thought for a few seconds and then said, 'I think I have the words. I will let you decide if they are appropriate before we swear.'

When they had heard his thoughts, the others concurred and he said, 'I will be as the wolves, and learn from them how to live for the pack. I will put the good of the pack before my own good, and protect the other members to the best of my ability. I will follow my destiny wherever it may lead, and through whatever dangers may befall, serving the pack and the land in all things. This I swear and may the gods hear my vow.'

They all agreed the words were good, and then they all joined hands and repeated them.

Then Thadora said, impulsively, 'We are Wolf.' and the others repeated her words.

So was born Wolf, from a group of unlikely companions, sworn to each other and to the world.

Chapter 14
Mountains

They walked on for the next couple of days, a growing companionship gradually forming between the disparate members of the group. They knew little of each other, but none of them felt it mattered. What lay in the past of each individual had gone, and what they were now was what was important.

Some uneasiness still existed between Asphodel and Carthinal. Carthinal decided he would not allow any deepening of the feelings he had towards the elf since he convinced himself that he would bring her nothing but grief. She was a cleric, after all. How could she possibly care for such as he? So he treated her with some coolness determining not to show her that he cared for her Anyway, he reasoned, she had given him little reason to be encouraged. She implied that what happened on Grillon's night was just that—something that happened to celebrate the Equinox and Parador's return to Grillon.

Asphodel in her turn, believing that Grillon's night meant nothing in particular to Carthinal, treated him with the same coolness, equally determined not to show him her hurt.

Then at about noon, they reached a place where the road split. One road, a narrower path, continued on the right bank of the Brundella, in a northeasterly direction, while the other road, obviously the main road, crossed the river by a bridge and continued eastwards. A stone had been fixed at the junction, and it had an arrow pointing to the north, with the legend: High Pass to Pelimor. The other arrow pointed south and read: Berandore, Erian and Rindissillaran

They had not banked on this split in the road, so they stopped to decide the way to go. Several of the group thought they should continue southwards across the bridge since the main road went that way, but Asphodel did not join in with their assertions. In fact, her face suggested that she did not wish to travel that way. Basalt ventured to ask her what worried her, but she did not reply.

Then she said, realisation dawning on her face, 'I recognise this place. It's the place from my dream. The man, the scribe, was sitting on that stone.' She pointed to a large boulder at the base of the signpost. 'He said...' here she paused, frowning as she tried to remember... 'He said: "Here lies a choice. You can take the easy road and go to Berandore and the lands to the east, or you can take the difficult path through the high mountains towards the land of Pelimor. Much rides on your decision. You must choose correctly or you may be too late."'

Basalt sat down heavily on the stone that Asphodel indicated the stranger was seated on in her dream. 'How are we supposed to make a decision then,' he asked. 'We may just as well toss a coin.'

They all seemed to slump.

'"If we make the wrong decision, it may be too late." What does that mean? That the Sword will be gone? That we may never find the valley? Or that something else will happen?' asked Randa.

Then Thadora's eyes lit up. She pointed to the left, up the road to the High Pass. 'That's the way,' she exclaimed.

'How you know?' queried Davrael. 'How you so sure?'

'You remember th' fortune-teller in Roffley? Yeah? Well, I didn't tell you what she said, did I? She said some damn weird things I didn't really understand, but she told me th' easy path were not always th' correct one. If I chose that, I would live a comfortable life, but that it would, like, be so bad for the world, or somethin' like that. So we take the difficult path—the High Pass, right?'

'Hmmph!' grunted Basalt. 'Those fortune-tellers are usually charlatans if you ask me. They seem to say what you want to hear. Wouldn't base my life on what one told me.'

'He's right there, Thadora,' responded Fero 'but there are some genuine ones,' he told the dwarf. 'Maybe yours was one of them,' he said, turning back to Thadora.

'I think she were. Genuine, I mean,' replied the girl. 'She told me things she shouldn't have been able to. It so spooked me.'

'Even if she were genuine, I think she was probably referring to life choices, not an actual physical path,' Randa said.

'There's another thing,' Thadora spoke quietly. 'I went back to 'er wagon th' next day. I wanted ter know 'ow she bloody well knew so much about me. Not to consult 'er again, but ter snoop around an' see 'ow she operates, like. It had bleedin' gone. 'Er wagon, that is. Maybe there's nothin' real strange about that, but when I asked th' other Wanderers, they seemed ter know nothin 'bout 'er. She'd arrived just afore we went ter see 'er, an' 'ad gone th' next mornin'. Almost as if she came specially ter see me. That's so creepy!'

Then Carthinal spoke. He had been listening to the arguments carefully and came to a decision. 'We'll take the High Pass,' he said. 'We have to go one way or the other, and as we have no other clues, we must decide based on what we know. The only help we have is Thadora's clairvoyant, genuine or false. I think we should eat something before we continue, too. It's nearly the sixth hour and I, for one, am getting hungry.'

After they had eaten, Asphodel suddenly said, 'I remember now. The man in my dream also said something along the lines of not taking the easy path. I think he pointed towards the High Pass, and told me of unexpected help along the way, too.'

'Hey, that's what she said an' all,'exclaimed Thadora. 'Th' bloody fortune-teller, I mean. She said I'd find unexpected help or summat, too.'

They decided to take the northerly path. Not all of them were entirely in agreement, but since they had to go one way or another, and they had all come to look on Carthinal as their leader with perhaps the exception of Randa, they reluctantly went along the road leading to the High Pass. The road, if it could be called such, continued to wind its way through the foothills of the Mountains of Doom. The mountains towered above them and it began to seem they would never reach them. They finally crossed the river, which continued in a more northerly direction, whilst the road carried on towards the northeast.

It took them several days walking over these wooded hills before the track began to ascend the mountains proper. They all carried wood they had collected in the forest since in the high mountains no trees would grow and they knew they would need to light fires at night. Although the lowlands could feel the coming of spring, it would still be very cold in the high pass. Each carried as much wood as they could manage, but Carthinal still worried that it would be insufficient to get them over the pass, not knowing how long it would take, nor how high it went.

Soon after leaving the woods, winter seemed to descend on them once more. Pockets of snow lay in shady patches where the sun had not warmed the ground, and it became noticeably colder. They all donned warm cloaks and pulled them tightly around their bodies to protect themselves from the teeth of the icy wind. They found less and less game the higher they climbed and eventually Carthinal called for rationing of their supplies of dried food. They ate only in the evening, and, having walked all day with gnawing hunger, slept at night to the sound of rumbling stomachs.

'In 'Ambara, it seemed so cool to run away and join this adventure. Now it just seems cold,' Thadora remarked to no one in particular. 'Even sleepin' in th' soddin' sewers sounds good. At least it'd be out of this blasted wind.'

'Down there in the valley, I felt I never wanted to eat rabbit ever again,' observed Randa pensively, 'Now a nice rabbit stew would seem like a king's banquet.'

'Sleep,' put in Asphodel. 'A nice, warm hayloft. Even prickly hay would seem a comfort.'

Carthinal looked at her sharply, but she showed no emotion on her face and she did not look in his direction. He shrugged.

'The desert,' Fero recollected, 'is hot and dry, but it would be preferable to this cold, wet snow,' as he shook some of the offending stuff from off his boots.

They trudged onward and upward, through the mountains, making only slow progress. Maybe they would end their lives in these mountains. One day seemed to flow into the next until it seemed they had never done anything but climb and shiver. Their fires at night did little to warm them. The air seemed so cold that it sucked all the heat from the fire. Basalt even considered if it were possible for a fire to burn with cold flames instead of hot, but he felt so cold and exhausted that his mind refused to co-operate with his musings.

They climbed for several days. Carthinal had strapped his staff onto his back, as it had now become a hindrance since he required both handsfree to climb. Each evening he studied Mabryl's spell book to see if he could find anything to help them. He couldn't. The path became narrower and narrower until they thought they would be unable to pass. In places, it seemed to cling to the side of the mountain. They had to travel in single file and shuffle along close to the mountainside. Clouds descended from time to time and they became wet with the condensation in it as the path climbed relentlessly, ever upwards.

'I can't go on. Leave me 'ere,' cried Thadora one morning.

'Get up and stop whining, girl,' snapped Carthinal.

Tears welled in her eyes and she turned away but made no move to rise.

'Do you make a habit of upsetting women, half-elf?'

Basalt came up and gave Carthinal a push. The mage's face took on a feral and dangerous look. He looked like the wolf from which the group had taken its name.

'Don't push me like that, dwarf,' he snarled. 'Don't ever push me like that again.'

'You deserve pushing,' growled the dwarf, not at all deterred by Carthinal's look. 'First Asphodel, now Thadora. Now you've no consideration for a young girl not yet sixteen! Look at them, Carthinal. They're spent. We'll not make it over the mountains like this.'

Carthinal looked round. Thadora still sat wrapped in her blankets, sobbing. Asphodel slowly and reluctantly folded her blankets, looking pale and drawn. Kimi and Davrael sat, arms around each other, all but propping each other up. Randa listlessly pulled a comb through her silvery hair, and even Fero stood slumped against a rock, not even watching Randa comb the hair that so fascinated him.

Carthinal's anger evaporated as quickly as it had come when he saw his little band.

'Accept my apologies, Bas,' he said. 'You're right. We can't keep pushing ourselves. I'm anxious to get over the highest part of these mountains before we run out of fuel and food, but I don't suppose it'll help if we die of exhaustion in the process.'

Therefore, he called for a day of rest. Thadora curled back gratefully into her blankets and quickly fell asleep again. Carthinal spoke to Asphodel about the food situation and they agreed to have an extra ration that day, even if it meant going hungry later. So they rested and slept for the rest of that day.

During the following night, two things happened. Firstly, the wood ran out, and then it began to snow. Carthinal and Randa were on watch when the first few flakes fell, an hour before dawn. By the time the sun rose behind the clouds, the snow had begun to fall heavily.

'We should find some shelter if possible,' said Randa.

'We're out of wood, too,' remarked Fero.

They shook the snow off their bedding and rolled it up into their packs; then, with cloaks pulled firmly around them and hoods over their heads, they trudged on.

Davrael first saw the footprint (to Fero's chagrin, as he felt he had let them down by not noticing it). It was huge. Much larger than the largest human footprint could possibly have been. It was also the print of a bare foot.

'What is it? What could possibly have made such a footprint?' asked Kimi, drawing closer to Davrael. He absently put an arm around her.

'Yeti,' responded Fero, hunkering down to look at the print more closely.

'What's a Yeti?' asked Thadora.

'A large beast of the mountains.' Fero looked up at her. 'Few people have seen them, but then few people come so high. They are said to look vaguely human but are much bigger. Some say nine or ten feet, but that may be an exaggeration.'

'That print's big enough for that,' pointed out Randa.

'They're supposed to be covered in long, white or grey hair,' continued Fero as though no one had spoken, 'and are said to be very savage. It has been said they'll eat human, dwarf or elf flesh if they can get it. That may well be true as there's little enough to eat up here, and the only reports brought back have been distant sightings. No one seems to have seen them close—or at least to have returned with the tale.' He stood once more, then continued, 'That print must be quite fresh. It would have been covered in snow else.'

'Even a blind gnome would be able to tell that,' mumbled Basalt. The others ignored him.

'We look out then,' said Davrael. 'Maybe we take turns for scout ahead.'

'No!' Carthinal was adamant. 'We stick together. In this weather, it would be too easy for someone to get lost. In fact, Fero, where's your rope?'

The snow continued to fall, perhaps even harder, and the path became hard to see.

'Good idea, Carthinal. Everyone slip the rope through your belt so no one can get lost.'

This they did, and then continued on their way. None of them were happy at the prospect of running into the large, fierce Yeti, and everyone listened and strained their eyes to see any shadows looming through the snowstorm. Eventually, Randa realised they seemed to have lost the path. At least to her feet it did not seem to be a path they were on. She called to Carthinal to tell him.

Dusk had arrived, although the day had been so dark it was difficult to tell, so Carthinal called a halt, hoping to retrace their steps if the snow stopped the following day, if indeed they had lost the path.

They lit no fire that night but huddled together to try to get some warmth from each other. They had set a watch, but it seemed useless in the blizzard as nothing could be seen. Soon, they did fall asleep one by one, even the watch. They all drifted into that pleasant, dreamy sleep said to overcome people lost in the snow. They did not hear the soft footsteps approach, nor see the gigantic shadows fall over them.

Chapter 15
Yeti

She awoke with the feeling that something was not quite as it should be. Slowly, as she came awake, she realised she was warm. Not only that, but she felt dry. Blankets and furs were heaped over her, and when she opened her eyes, she saw a flickering orange light. Someone had lit a fire. She remembered drifting off to sleep in the snow. She remembered someone in a distant life telling her that you could easily drift off to sleep in the snow and die of exposure. She felt it was the easiest thing to do, out in the cold and wet. It had been pleasant, drifting into sleep and death. Maybe she had in fact died and was in the afterlife? Then Thadora saw rock around her. Ahh! She was in a cave.

'I 'spect th' others found th' cave an' carried me 'ere,' she thought, 'Though, where they found th' wood ter light a flippin' fire I can't imagine. Anyway, thanks, dudes.'

She turned to look to her left. She saw the fire and what looked like several other mounds of fur. Sounds of breathing and occasional snores came from them. The others, she surmised. One of the mounds stirred slightly. She saw a pair of light blue eyes and a wisp of silvery- blonde hair. Randa. Randa made a shushing shape with her mouth. Thadora frowned. Why must she remain quiet? She could smell cooking now as her senses returned. Who was cooking if the others still slept?

She heard the sound of footsteps approaching the fire. Then an arm reached over her and added some logs to the blaze. Her heart began to beat rapidly. The hand seemed far too large for human, elf or dwarf; then she noticed the arm attached to the hand. Long, snow-white hair covered it. At first, she thought it a garment, but soon realised it was part of the creature.

Thadora tried her best not to scream, but a small squeak escaped her. She shut her eyes tightly. The little girl in her told her to do this. If she could not see these creatures, they could not see her. It was not rational, but she was too frightened to be rational. She heard Fero's voice in her head. "Savage beasts. Eat human, elf and dwarf flesh..." They had been caught by Yeti.

The snow-white yeti made a harsh, grunting noise of several sounds. It moved away and another one took its place. This time, Thadora saw when she ventured a peek through tightly squeezed eyelids, a more greyish colour. The creature seemed about nine-feet-tall and covered head to foot in grey hair. Hair almost obscured its face, but a pair of black eyes in which no whites could be seen gleamed from above a small, black nose and a lipless mouth. Then she squeaked again, this time in surprise for the yeti spoke. It spoke Grosmerian, very badly and very slowly and obviously found it difficult to form the words, but the creature could just be understood.

'You wake,' it said. 'You slep' long. Much days. Eat food. You be better.'

With that, it put some meat down in front of Thadora. Her mouth watered, and her stomach growled, but she did not take the food.

'Oh no,' she said. 'No way. I got no idea what this is, man.'

'You eat. You need strong. This, bird from mountains. Good eat. Good for cold and warm folk.'

Thadora puzzled over the speech. 'You mean I should eat this—bird from th' mountains. That it's good ter eat fer both cold and warm folk? I don't get "cold and warm" folk!'

'You from warm. Die in cold. We from cold. Die in warm.'

She could not resist the meat put in front of her any longer. She picked it up and took a large bite. It burned her mouth and she almost spat it out. She breathed cool air in through her mouth over the meat to cool it. The yeti made a grunting noise, almost like a laugh. The meat was delicious. Like a cross between chicken and pork.

The yeti wandered away saying, 'I go. Too hot here. Br'ng food for rest warm folk.'

When it had disappeared, Randa rose onto one elbow. 'Thadora,' she hissed, 'The food may be poisoned or drugged. You shouldn't eat it.'

'Randa, I don't give a toss. I'm bleedin' starvin'. If I'm gonna be killed by these bastards, then I'll die wi' a full belly.'

The greyish yeti returned with more food, which it put on the ground.

'Not poison or drug. You must strong. Not kill. Why you think kill?' This last it said to Randa.

There were movements from several of the other mounds of furs as the others came awake. The yeti turned its head and looked at the emerging people.

'Who you chief?' it said.

Carthinal started to stand and then quickly lay down again as he realised he was naked under the furs, as indeed were all the others. The yeti curled back its lips in what Thadora supposed was a smile, but it was rather fearsome since it showed its long, canine teeth.

'You warm more quick with no close,' it said. 'Have close when leave.'

Carthinal looked embarrassed but spoke to the creature. 'I am the leader of the group. My name is Carthinal.' He spoke slowly and clearly to the yeti. 'What do you want with us?'

'I Grnff.' The yeti pointed to itself. Grnff was obviously its name. 'Mate she called Zplon. She beautiful, no?'

He was proud of his mate, who lurked in the cave entrance. His black eyes gleamed in the firelight as he looked lovingly towards her. She lowered her gaze and then looked at Grnff through her lashes in a very human and coquettish way, giving him a savage "smile".

Grnff had trouble with Carthinal's name. 'Crthnal,' he repeated, slowly. 'Crthnal.'

Carthinal looked at the yeti. Fero called these creatures "beasts," but they were obviously more than beasts. Beasts did not light fires and talk. They would have to move with care.

'We would feel better with our clothes. We can then get up and move around.'

'Why not up with no close?' asked Grnff, frowning. 'Warm here. No need close.'

Carthinal sighed. He could not begin to try to explain the customs and taboos of the "warm folk" to a yeti. Asphodel helped him out. She had woken during this exchange.

'In the culture of the warm folk,' she said, 'it is taboo for members of the opposite sex to see each other unclothed unless they are mated.'

'Strange custom,' said Grnff, musingly, then added, 'Grnff giv close.'

He went to the side of the cave and rummaged among some furs. Then he brought their clothes, armour and weapons, and also some furs. 'Fur better than cold le'ther and m'tal. Why you wear cold le'ther and m'tal?'

'It helps to protect us from attack.'

'Hmmm. But not good in cold. You eat. Talk after when you str'ng.'

Basalt whispered something to Carthinal.

'I think it's all right, Basalt. We'll have to eat something anyway. I don't see we have a choice. Anyway, if they wanted us dead, we wouldn't be discussing whether to eat or not to eat. We've been at their mercy for quite a while, I think, and they've not harmed us at all. Quite the contrary, in fact. I rather think we'd have died out there in the blizzard if not for these…' he hesitated, trying to find the right word, 'These people.' He had decided the Yeti were, in fact, people rather than beasts.

The members of Wolf ate their meal in silence. They were all now awake. The cave smelt slightly of yeti, but it did not seem too unpleasant, and not enough to put them off the delicious food. While they were eating, they speculated on their position.

'It seems reports of these creatures were inaccurate,' observed Fero. 'The little I've heard, they were said to be animals, but these obviously have speech and fire, so they cannot count as beasts. I'd say they need to be re-classified as being amongst the sentient races of Vimar.'

'They don't seem hostile either,' put in Kimi. 'Grnff seems friendly, and I think his mate is just rather wary of us.'

'Now we've got our clothes back, I suggest we dress,' Carthinal said. 'As long as we're here in the cave with the fire I think we can dispense with armour and wear these furs. Grnff was right about armour not being good to keep out the cold.'

'Why's he doing this? What's in it for him?' asked Thadora.

'Let's ask him when we're dressed,' replied Carthinal.

They agreed the four men would dress first, then go outside to see Grnff while the girls dressed. They soon accomplished this, and the eight travellers sat just inside the cave mouth with Grnff and his mate, Zplon.

'Now, Grnff. Tell us why you rescued us and fed us. Never has it been known before for yeti, that is cold folk, to help warm folk as far as we know,' Carthinal began the conversation.

'Man come. Man speak Grnff language. Strange. Never warm folk speak Grnff language. Man magic. Cold folk no magic. Man say you come. Man say you need help. Man say Grnff and Zplon help. Man say you called Wolf. Man say you eight warm folk. Man say chief is magic man, too. Magic man have red hair. Man say four female, four male, one male small with hair on the face like cold folk. Man say one female have hair colour of cold folk. One female have red hair, one black hair. Man say one male very dark and big for warm folk. We look. We find near dead. You cold. Make fire. Wrap in fur. You thaw like icicle.'

They all felt as though someone had dropped cold water down their backs as shivers ran up and down their spines at this. Who was this strange man who knew all about them, and how did he know they were going to need help in the snow? Carthinal asked a question that made it even stranger.

'When did this man come?'

'Many darknesses ago. We not count time. Man here in cold time. Man here just before light is shortest.'

'He came before the winter solstice? But that's impossible! We hadn't even met then. In fact, that was even before the flood on the Brundella!' exclaimed Randa. 'You and Carthinal had not even left Bluehaven, Asphodel!'

'How you learn speak Grosmerian?' Davrael asked.

'Man teach. Man say Grnff need to speak with you or you 'fraid.'

'That's the best crash course in a language I've ever seen,' commented Basalt. 'It took me months to get to the stage that Grnff is at. How did he do it?'

'Grnff say. Man magic. Man teach by magic. And Grnff very clever. Quick to learn, man say.' He puffed himself up with pleasure at relating the man's words.

Asphodel touched Carthinal's arm. He turned, heart beating wildly at her soft touch.

'There is more here than meets the eye, Carthinal,' she said. 'No one could possibly have known we were coming here as far away as the winter solstice. For Sylissa's sake, we didn't even know ourselves. Someone described us to Grnff before we'd even met!'

'The description could be after the event. After all, Grnff here has seen us and could have put in our descriptions himself to make a mystery and win our confidence,' pointed out Basalt, 'and as to speaking Grosmerian, he could have learned it at any time in the past from any passing traveller.'

'True enough, all you said, Basalt, my friend. Just one thing I'd like to see you explain,' Fero said. 'How did he know we've called ourselves "Wolf?"'

'We-el,' Basalt considered, 'That is a bit of a problem.'

'One o' us could 'ave talked in our sleep,' suggested Thadora.

'Yes, I suppose we could have, but I prefer to think that we are being watched and guided by the gods,' Asphodel said. 'What did the man look like, Grnff?' she asked, turning to the yeti.

'He look like other warm folk. He not tall, not small. Him close have many p'kets and ink m'rks on. Him h've long feather in p'ket. He use to m'ke marks on white stuff him c'll paper.'

'Sounds a bit like the man in my dream.'

Kimi then butted in, 'AAnd the man who married us in the glade on our way to Hambara.'

They left the problem unsolved, as the group continued to talk to Grnff. The fact of the matter remained that, for whatever his reasons, man or not, Grnff saved their lives, and for that, they were in his debt. They were not all completely without suspicions. They could, as Fero pointed out later, be getting fattened up for later killing and eating, a thought that Thadora did not want to think about at all. On the other hand, they were given their weapons and armour back. Not something anyone would do if they wanted to kill you. They decided to play the whole thing by ear.

Grnff told them he would show them the way to their destination. "The man" told him where to take them, apparently. He insisted they were not yet ready for the journey and the dangers they would encounter once there. They must continue to rest and eat. He and Zplon found food and cooked it for them. How they managed to find it in the wintry conditions existing outside the cave, the others could not guess. Certainly, it seemed bleak up in the mountains, but they managed to find meat and enough fresh, edible, vegetation to make the travellers begin to feel strong and healthy.

During this time, Thadora seemed to strike up a strange rapport with Grnff. He showed her how his long hair covered an undercoat of soft fur. He also confided in her that Zplon was pregnant.

'She have cubs in warm time. Soon go to birthing place. Cold folk have two cubs one time,' he told her. 'Many cubs not live. Life hard in mountains. Cold folk have hunger. Cold folk have enemies who eat them. Animals. Some warm folk kill cold folk. Call us beasts. Say we savage and a danger. We stay away from warm folk. But Grnff like you, Red Cub. You friends not bad, too.'

'You're a real cool dude, too, Grnff,' Thadora told him.

The yeti frowned, not understanding. Basalt translated for him.

'She means you're a good man,' he said.

During the next sixday, they stayed in the cave with Grnff and Zplon. Then one day, Grnff stated they were ready to move.

'You now strong. We go,' he said. 'Must leave or too late for Zplon to get to birthing place. Then cubs die. We very sad. First cubs.'

'Oh, Grnff, we can't risk your cubs dyin'' said Thadora, appalled at the idea. 'Tell us th' way an' take Zplon to th' birthing place. We'll be OK. We're strong now, right?'

'You not find way. We go through mountain. We take path of fire god. You good, Red Cub, but fire god angry if warm folk go alone on paths.'

'What happens if the fire god's angry?' asked Basalt looking anxious.

'He wake. He shake with anger and ground shake. He breathe fire from mountain.'

'A volcano!' exclaimed Bas. 'By Kassilla's tits, I think we're going to go through a volcano!'

'They must worship the volcano as a god,' Asphodel said.

Grnff overheard this exchange and obviously understood most of what was said. He replied, 'We have two gods. Fire and Ice. God of fire destroys if angry. Must keep him happy. He sleeps now. He sleeps for hundreds of seasons. He not like to be wak'nd. God of ice good. Makes water hard so it not run away. Makes snow to keep cold folk cool, but not too cold. Must give gift to fire god to keep him happy.'

'What must we give?' asked Carthinal.

'Something you hold dear.' Grnff replied. 'Must be sacrifice or not good enough for god.'

They all thought hard about this, and then Kimi stepped forward. The thing I hold most dear is this ring, given to me by Davrael. It symbolises our love. No beginning and no end.'She looked sadly at Davrael. 'I'm sorry, my love,' she said, 'but if it is required for our safe passage through these mountains, I must give it up. It will not change the way I feel.'

They all then searched for something they held dear. Thadora handed over a locket that had belonged to her mother; Davrael gave an eagle's feather, symbol, he told them, of his standing in his tribe; Asphodel reluctantly gave a ring that was given to her by her sister. Then Fero added a stone carved in the shape of a lion's head, which was carved by his mentor, a ranger in his homeland, and Randa, a silver pin that was her mother's. Basalt gave a black opal, one of the first to be found in his parents' mine, and Carthinal pulled out of his pocket an exquisitely painted miniature of a handsome couple, he an elf and she a human.

'My parents,' he said as he laid it on the little pile.

The Wolves looked at the pile of belongings sadly, each remembering other times, people and places.

Grnff swept them up in his huge hand. 'Give to god in deep place,' he said.

He then went to the back of the cave, accompanied by Zplon. The pair took a bundle of torches from a natural shelf there and lit one each. Grnff then beckoned the others and they followed him into the deeper part of the cave.

After travelling for a while, the Wolves realised Grnff was right. They would have soon been hopelessly lost in this maze of tunnels. However, Grnff and Zplon seemed to know exactly where they were heading and took turn after turn. They seemed to be continually going down. Basalt grumbled at first about having given their most treasured possessions to a volcano. He would not have minded; he told them if it had been a genuine god, but a mountain was ridiculous. Asphodel reminded him that they had to get Grnff to lead them, and he would not have done so without the sacrifice. Basalt said no more but continued to stomp along, making his displeasure clear in his body language.

'You friend not happy, Red Cub,' Grnff said to Thadora.

'No! He don't believe th' mountain's for real. Least not godwise.'

'He gave. He safe. It not matter if he believe in god of mountain, god of mountain believe in him,' came the reply.

They continued deeper into the caves. Basalt felt the most at home here, since he was a mountain dwarf, but even he jumped when they heard a rumbling deep in the bowels of the mountain.

'Must go quick,' said Grnff. 'Giv' sacrifice. God wake. Angry with strangers in him.' And with that, Grnff began to move more quickly. Basalt, with his short legs, had to almost run to keep up with the long stride of the two yeti. Even Thadora and Kimi found they had to break into a trot every now and then to prevent themselves from being left behind.

Shortly the tunnel opened out into a large cave. A deep crack ran across the cave and from this crack came the rumbling sounds. Grnff and Zplon went to the edge of the crack and fell to their knees. Bowing deeply, they began to chant in their strange, guttural language. It sounded more like the growling of angry beasts that a known language and they understood how people had thought of it as such. However, they came to recognise several distinct sounds and phrases in the growling, and Thadora even learned some words, although Grnff and Zplon laughed their feral laughs at her attempted pronunciation. After a few minutes of this chanting, Grnff prostrated himself, then drew out their treasures and dropped them one by one into the fissure, saying the name of the owner, even though his pronunciation sounded rather strange.

'Tadra, the Red Cub. Dvrel, the Savage One. Littl Kimi. Black Fero. Strong, hairy Bslt, Pale Rnda. Priest of strange god, Asdel. Chief and Magic man, Crthnal.'

Then they stood, turned round three times and backed away from the fissure. Immediately after this little ceremony, there came a much louder rumble that made them move instinctively closer together and farther from the fissure. Davrael and Kimi clung together, and Carthinal suddenly found himself holding Asphodel in an instinctive desire to protect her. He quickly dropped his arms and took a step back. Then just as quickly, the rumbling stopped, and there were no more sounds.

'You gifts accepted,' said Grnff. 'God say gifts good. We pass now.'

Then they saw, for the first time, the bridge that spanned the fissure. It was a natural, stone bridge, but they would only be able to cross in single file and there was no parapet. Davrael visibly paled on seeing the narrow path they would have to walk. He was a man of the plains, and while a fierce warrior, who knew no terror in battle, he had no experience of crossing such a path. He swallowed, and glanced to the fissure. Then Zplon murmured something to Grnff.

'You give rope,' he said to Fero. 'Zplon take. Cross bridge. Grnff hold end here. You cross holding rope.'

Zplon duly crossed the narrow span and between them the two yeti held the rope taught.

Thadora quickly skipped across the bridge without using the rope. She stopped once in the middle to look down, calling cheerfully back, 'I can't see th' bottom. 'S real deep!'

'Shut up, Thadora. You're not helping,' growled Carthinal to her.

She grinned and ran nimbly across to the other side. After all, in her career as a thief she had run across rooftops and climbed walls.Heights did not frighten her.

'Of course, you'd expect a thief to be able to cross high stretches. I expect it's in the job description,' mumbled Randa disapprovingly, as much to herself as to anyone else, which was as well as no one else seemed to be listening.

The only other person who had no qualms was Basalt. Being a dwarf and used to wandering about in mountain tunnels, the bridge held no fears for him so he crossed next.

Carthinal insisted that Davrael go next. He noticed the paling of Davrael's face when he realised they needed to cross the bridge. If he left the young warrior with too much time to think, they may never get him over.

'Go on, Davrael,' he urged. 'You've seen Thadora and Basalt go. It's not too bad.'

'I not afraid,' said the plainsman, but his face belied his words.

However, he stepped forward slowly and carefully placed his foot on the stone. He gripped the rope so tightly that even in the dim light of the cavern, they could see the whiteness of his knuckles. He inched his way across, slowly.

'Don't look down,' called Basalt, which was the wrong thing to say as Davrael's eyes were immediately drawn downward.

Then he froze. He saw a deep, dark drop beneath him. His fear was almost palpable. Almost half way across, his feet refused to move. His heart began to beat frantically. He thought he was going to have a heart attack it beat so fiercely. He had fought enemies and been in danger of his life. He had tamed the wildest of horses. He could ride better than anyone in his tribe, and perform death-defying feats on horseback. He had even come face to face with a mountain lion that wanted him to feed to her cubs, and lived to tell the tale, which was more than the mountain lion did. He had never known fear like this, though. Never again would he call anyone a coward for being afraid. All he could see was the dark beneath him. Then he heard a voice at his elbow, urging him on. Thadora had run onto the bridge and talked him across. Slowly, inch by inch, she got him to move. The span seemed to go on forever until at last the black abyss had disappeared from beneath his feet. His legs gave way under him and as he sank to the ground, Zplon pulled him away from the edge.

When the others were all across, they found Davrael still slumped on the ground shaking.

'I coward. I not think me coward, but I be.' He seemed unable to say nothing else.

'No,' said Asphodel, kneeling beside him, 'That was one of the bravest things I've ever seen.'

Davrael looked up at her sharply to see if she were mocking him. 'I afraid. I not able to move. You should send away in disgrace. I be outcast to show such cowardice in my tribe.'

Kimi held him but carefully did not say anything. She knew whatever she said to reassure him he would take as an expression of her love, and not take any notice. She let the others do the talking.

'Have you ever been afraid before, Davrael?' asked Fero.

'No. I thought to be bravest in tribe. I not fear anything.' The warrior drew himself up a little in pride but quickly slumped again. 'Until now,' he finished.

'That's not bravery,' continued the ranger. 'Anyone can seem to be brave if they don't feel fear. True bravery is to feel fear, face it and overcome it. That is what you did.'

They continued to talk to him in this manner until they had convinced him he was not a coward and bolstered him enough to be able to continue. He suggested several times they should leave him in the mountain for his perceived cowardice. Grnff and Zplon waited patiently while this was going on, and when Davrael at last rose to his feet, they continued to lead the way through the mountain.

They continued walking until Grnff decided they must rest.

'It night,' he said suddenly, and lay down, put out the torches, curled up into a ball with Zplon and promptly fell asleep.

The Wolves unpacked their bedrolls and spread them onto the rocky ground. They lay in the pitch-blackness hearing the soft breathing of the yeti pair as they slept. The darkness was complete. Only the dwarf and those with elf blood could make out anything at all. With their infravision, they saw warm reddish mounds. Kimi and Davrael snuggled together under the furs and blankets to conserve warmth. As he looked around, Carthinal wished he could snuggle with someone, too. Although not cold in the mountain, it did feel cool. He pulled the furs closer round him and turned over.

Sleep was a long time in coming even so, and it seemed that he had no longer dropped off than felt Grnff shaking him and saying, 'Eat. We go.'

He ate the piece of meat thrust at him and saw the others being woken with a meagre breakfast thrust at them. He wondered how long this passage through the volcano would take and ventured to ask Grnff.

'We out wen sun highest,' Grnff replied. 'Now sun get up.'

True to his word, about six hours later they emerged from a cave to see a beautiful, wooded valley spread out before them.

'We leave you now,' said Grnff. 'We go birthing place. Just time before cubs come.'

Carthinal turned. 'We can't thank you enough, Grnff,' he said. 'You saved our lives and guided us through the mountains. If there's anything we can ever do for you, we will.'

'Finish task is what you can do,' he replied. 'Make world safe for cubs to grow up.'

The others said their goodbyes and began to descend the slope, but Carthinal and Thadora remained where they were. Thadora flung her arms round first Zplon and then Grnff, giving them a hug. She came only about up to their waists. They hugged her back, gently. Zplon said something to Grnff and he translated.

'We talked. We decide on naming cubs. Cold folk have two cubs, always. One male and one female. We call male Crthnal for you, red magic man and chief, and female we call Tadra, for you, Red Cub. Go. You friends wait.'

With that, the two yeti re-entered the cave and were gone.

'Cool,' said Thadora. 'I never thought I'd 'ave a yeti cub called Thadora after me, an' there's to be one called Carthinal too, after you.'

'At least Crthnal and Tadra, anyway. Come on, Red Cub,' he replied, grinning at her. 'We'd better join the others.'

Chapter 16
Valley

It was a truly, beautiful valley. It opened towards the east and the sunrise. Dense woods covered the ground but with open glades between mature oak trees. The snow-capped mountains towered high above them to the north, west, and south, but gradually fell away towards the east. Below them, spring had begun to burst out. Trees were showing the first pale blush of green and there were spring flowers blooming. They wondered how long they had spent with the yeti. They worked it out by the height of the sun that it must be the middle of Grildar at least.

'Then I'm not a child anymore,' stated Thadora. 'If it is the middle of Grildar, my birthday has gone. It was on Grildar 8. I'm sixteen!'

'That should have been cause for a celebration, then,' responded Basalt. 'We must have a birthday party when we finish this quest.'

They slowly walked down the slope towards the woods, listening to the birds singing their songs in the trees and bushes until they entered the woodland. It seemed an almost magical place. The large oak trees spread their branches high towards the sun as though in welcome and all with the hint of new greenery. Beneath their feet, last autumn's leaves crunched. The huge trees every now and then gave way to open glades where the sun's rays filtered down making the place look almost magical. Then they stepped out of the forest to see a lake spread before them. It steamed in the sunshine. Kimi wondered why that should be so.

Basalt explained to her. 'This is volcanic country, Kimi. There is heat below the ground, which feeds the volcanoes. There are often hot springs nearby. I suspect this lake is one such, fed by a hot spring from below the volcano.'

They decided that they all needed to eat and bathe, as they had left Roffley, and their last bath, a long time ago. Settling down by the lake, they ate the cold food Grnff gave them before they parted. As they looked towards the lake, they saw strange birds flying in the sky.

'What are they?' Thadora asked the words that had been on everyone's lips.

No one seemed to be able to say. Then one of the birds, followed by two or three of the others, dived into the lake. They expected to see them rise into the air shortly, probably grasping a fish or something, but to their surprise, they remained swimming in the water. Then Asphodel noticed something with her superior, elven sight.

'Strange birds, with four legs as well as wings,' she said.

The others looked closer.

'The wings look rather leathery, not like birds' wings at all. They look like pictures I've seen of dragons in my father's library. I used to like to look at his books on the animals and plants of Vimar when I was a child,' said Randa.

'You know, I think she's right. They do look like dragons,' responded Basalt. 'Just our luck. I suppose we couldn't have hoped for our good luck to continue,' he grumbled.

'Well, they're a long way away. Maybe we'll be able to avoid drawing their attention,' said Asphodel. 'We'll have to be very wary. Anyway, they looked rather small. Mayb they're just babies.'

'Or maybe they only looked small through distance. Or maybe they're babies, but if so, their mother won't be far away,' groaned Basalt. 'Well, at least I'll end my days in pleasant surroundings in the company of friends.'

'Don't be so pessimistic, Bas,' Kimi scolded him. 'We may not see any more of them, and even if we do, if we're careful, we may not alert their parents.

'Always expect the worst, Kimi, lass,' Basalt retorted. 'Then, when it doesn't come to pass, it's a pleasant surprise.'

'You don't always go by that philosophy, though, do you Basalt?' Fero put in. 'I've known you to be a happy sort of fellow at times.'

Basalt grunted in reply.

After they had eaten, the dragons seemed to have disappeared, so they walked slowly and quietly down towards the water. They were looking for places where they could bathe in privacy, the men apart from the women.

A small beach appeared in front of them, and as they approached it, Fero, who went ahead as usual, held up his hand and stopped. They drew along side of him and saw, sprawled on the beach and basking in the warm spring sunshine, a small, iridescent shape. It was one of the baby dragons they had seen flying over the lake. It was about three-feet-long from the tip of its snout to the tip of its tail. It had spread its wings out to catch the maximum warmth as it snored gently. It had the horns of an adult dragon on its head, but they were rather small in comparison to its size. It did not seem to be a definite colour, but its scales shone with many colours in the sunlight. There it looked red, here blue, and then again green. Sometimes, it seemed to be black. It was a beautiful creature.

'The pictures of dragons in my father's books were definite colours,' puzzled Randa. 'Not this iridescent mix. I think the books said there were blue dragons in the mountains.'

'Yes, but p'rhaps th' young're different. P'rhaps th' colours come later on, but dragon or not, it's so-o beautiful,' put in Thadora.

'True enough. Many youngsters look different from their parents,' responded Fero. 'Think of frogs and toads to name but two. Dragons may be like that. Anyway, it seems there are dragons around here after all.'

Asphodel then murmured in Elvish. 'Dragons! Typical! How are we to fight dragons?'

Thenshe turned to the others. 'That poem said there were guardians near the tomb, but didn't specify what. Maybe the guardians are dragons.'

The sleeping creature suddenly leaped up. It looked around itself, saw the friends and made some sounds.

Asphodel looked surprised. 'That sounds like a form of elvish!' she said. It sounded as though it said, "Dragons? Where? I'll sort them out for you."

The Wolves looked at one another.

Asphodel replied, in elvish, 'You're the dragon, even if only a baby.'

The creature looked incensed. 'Baby?' it said. 'Baby? Who are you calling a baby?'

'But aren't you a baby dragon then?' asked Asphodel.

'Indeed I am not! I am a fully-grown dragonet,' it responded.

Asphodel translated the conversation to them.

'I've heard of dragonets,' Randa said, 'but they are considered to be myths by most people nowadays.'

Asphodel translated when the little creature asked what Randa had said.

'Do I look like a myth to you? My name is Muldee, by the way. If you'd been properly brought up, you'd have introduced yourselves to me first, since this is my home.'

Asphodel again translated for the others and Randa then looked towards the creature and said, 'I, at least, have been properly brought up. I am Randa. My companions are,' and she indicated each one in turn, 'Carthinal, a mage, Asphodel, a curate of Sylissa, Fero, Thadora, Basalt, Kimi and Davrael. May I apologise for our poor manners.' After more translation, the dragonet replied, 'That's better. Now we know each other I must ask you what brings you to our valley?'

The companions looked at each other and then at Carthinal. The young half-elf spoke for the first time.

'Asphodel, tell Muldee that we are passing through. We became lost in the mountains, and a pair of yeti showed us the way through the volcano.'

The dragonet put his head on one side and looked at Carthinal. 'Most unusual. In fact, unheard of. Yeti helping people?'

Suddenly, a flurry of wings sounded over Muldee's head. Another dragonet appeared, this one paler in colour, but still with the iridescence of Muldee. It made a series of whistles and clicks. Muldee responded with his own series of whistles.

'My clutch mate, Amonine,' he told the Asphodel. 'She hatched after me, and so is more of a baby.'

'Huh! Baby, indeed. I only hatched seven hours after you! Come on, Deedee. We're waiting for you.' (She spoke in the form of elvish Muldee used so Asphodel could understand her). With that, she dived into the water and swam away.

Muldee's concentration seemed to evaporate as he saw his siblings swimming and diving, and he turned to the travellers saying, 'I don't suppose "they" will let you do any harm, anyway, so I may as well go and play.'

With that, he ran to the water's edge and swam out to join the rest of the dragonets out in the lake.

Once he had gone, the others looked at each other.

'Not only do they damn well exist, they talk, too. That's real cool,' said Thadora in delight at the little creatures.

'At least, they're not dragons. They seem harmless enough,' Kimi replied.

They decided to continue their search for bathing places. The men quickly found another beach about 100 meters away, and so the party split. The girls quickly undressed and ran to the warm water. Randa had some soap in her pack, and she soaped herself, and then her hair. She threw the soap to Asphodel who did the same, and then the other two had the soap. They swam in the water and splashed each other. It felt good to be clean again.

The men had also stripped off. Basalt seemed quite happy to wade into the water as far as his waist but pointedly refused to go any deeper. 'If dwarves were meant to swim, we'd have been given webbed feet,' he replied to the urgings of the others.

As Davrael stood in the shallower water trying to persuade Basalt to come in deeper, all of a sudden, he found himself swept from his feet and took a severe dunking in the water. The normally proud and dignified Horselord looked far from proud or dignified as he thrashed around to regain his feet, and came up spluttering. He automatically felt for his knives, but of course, they were not there as he was naked. He looked at the others. They were all laughing. How could they laugh when something nearly drowned him? Then he saw a flurry of water in Basalt's direction. Something was beating the water and covering the dwarf in a fountain.

Basalt spluttered in anger and he, too, reached for his non-existent axe. Then a shape burst from the water beside him and he realised what had happened. Muldee decided to join them in their swim. The loss of his dignity still smarted but he had to smile when the playful dragonet dragged Carthinal down, and he came up spluttering and angry. Muldee then flew high in the sky and dived into the water. Soon, they were all, except for

Basalt, swimming and diving with the little creature and enjoying themselves immensely.

When the men saw the four young women had left the water, they too climbed out onto the sand and sat there drying off before putting on their clothes, also to give the girls time to dry off and get dressed. They saw ripples in the water and thought one of the dragonets was approaching, but nothing emerged. Davrael thought he saw a figure that looked vaguely human beneath the water, but could not be sure. They watched but saw nothing. Eventually, they decided it must have been a large fish of some kind. Then, just as they were dressing to go back to the others, Fero dashed into the water and managed to catch the shape. He drew out a beautiful woman, who spat and scratched at him. She had blue hair and a faintly greenish tinge to her skin. Her ears were pointed like an elf's, and she had elf-like slanted eyes of a deep blue colour, but her pupils were elongated like those of a cat.

Fero held her gently, but firmly whilst the others looked in astonishment.

'It's a nymph!' exclaimed Carthinal. 'This must be her lake.'

'Yes, half-elf,' she spat, 'This is my lake. You did not ask my permission to swim.'

'I apologise,' he replied, bowing slightly to her. 'We didn't realise a nymph lives here. We'd have been more respectful if we did.'

'So I would hope,' she said. 'Now let me go!' she said to Fero. 'No one has visited this valley for hundreds of years, and I have been left in peace,' she said. 'Now you come. Why are you here?'

'We are on a quest,' Carthinal told her. 'We are searching for a magical item.'

'Oh-oh,' the nymph said. 'Well, I don't expect you'll get far. The Guardians will soon see you off. No one comes here now. The stories of the Guardians are enough to frighten would-be treasure seekers. It suits me. Although sometimes it does become lonely with only the dragonets for company. They are amusing, but at times can be rather irritating.' She cast a sidelong glance at Fero. 'I occasionally feel the need for company of a more, shall we say, grown-up kind. The dragonets get a bit tiresome at times.'

'Don't look into her eyes, Fero,' Basalt whispered out of the side of his mouth, 'Nymphs can spell humans into thinking they are in love with them.'

'Don't worry, Dwarf,' she said, 'I had a human lover once. He loved me of his own free will and I him. That is better than a sorcerous love. I have never wanted anyone under magical coercion since.'

'That not usual?' asked Davrael. 'Nymphs not usually love humans, I think.'

'That's true. He found his way into the valley when he and his army got lost in the mountains. He wandered away from them to be alone. He had just lost a battle and was feeling despair. I saw him and loved him immediately.

'He was proud and dignified. A bit like you, warrior,' she looked at Davrael. 'I was going to cast a spell on him, but he saw me and I then realised I didn't want him to love me through magic but for my own self. I showed myself to him and comforted him. He truly loved me. He could not stay with me forever though as he had a wife, and had his duty to his country; so, he left.'

The nymph sighed.

'He returned many times, though. His adviser, an elf, cast a spell on his men so they would forget where the valley is. Only my lover and his adviser could find it again. But hundreds of years have passed since then. I've been alone ever since, except when the advisor came with others and created the Abominations.'

She shook her head as if to remove an unpleasant thought.

'My lover came back to me, you see. To stay forever near me—not her, his wife. He was dead, of course. I've mourned his passing ever since. Don't worry, handsome, dark stranger,' she said to Fero. 'I would never want to have love through magic again when I've had the free love of a man.'

They were silent for a while. Then, Carthinal asked, 'Why are you telling us this? Nymphs are usually shy and don't talk readily to mortals such as we.'

'I don't know,' she replied looking puzzled. 'I felt that it was important you know. Whether to you or to me, I don't know.'

With that, she turned and slipped back into the water and was gone.

The men looked at each other. 'I think we've found our valley, guys,' said Carthinal. 'Let's go and tell the girls!'

They all sat around the fire they had built from dead branches gathered from the woods around. Carthinal repeated what the nymph had said.

'It was most odd,' he told them when he had finished. 'Nymphs are the shyest of creatures, and don't usually succumb to loneliness, yet this one was quite voluble, telling us things I would not have expected.'

He left them to draw their own conclusions about the valley, which they quickly did.

'There are tales of Sauvern falling in love with a nymph, aren't there?' asked Asphodel

'Yes, indeed there are,' replied Carthinal, 'and if you take into account we've been warned about "them" and also told of the "Guardians" it seems to add up. As I said to the others, we seem to have found our valley.'

'Or rather, had it found for us,' said Basalt. 'We would have been hopelessly lost, if not dead if Grnff and Zplon hadn't saved us and brought us here.'

Asphodel frowned in thought. 'And what about the mysterious man who told Grnff about us—before we even knew each other existed. We've definitely been directed here. I think this is the valley, too.'

Just at that moment, there a flurry of wings sounded overhead and then, in a spray of sand, Muldee arrived. He landed on his hind feet, and sat, to all intents and purposes like a dog begging for food, his strong tail balancing him behind. In his front talons he carried a large fish.

Asphodel translated his words.

'I thought you may like this,' he told them, dropping it straight into Randa's lap. 'I'm sure you would like a change from those birds the yeti seem to enjoy so much.'

Randa grabbed the wet and fishy creature when it landed on her and she dropped it quickly. The lively fish flopped about, wetting Randa further.

The others smothered laughs as she picked it up gingerly and said, 'Thank you, Muldee. We'll enjoy this immensely. Will one of you kill it please?'

'Why can't you?' said Asphodel.

'I've never killed anything before. I'm not sure I can.'

'That's not true, Randa,' Fero told her, 'you managed to kill those wolves that attacked us, and very efficiently too, I might add.'

'That was different. They were attacking us. It was our lives that were at stake.'

Fero looked at her, and pointed out, 'It could be our lives at stake here, too. People die without food as well as by being killed by wild animals. It's necessary to kill in order to survive. Sometimes killing is to stop something from killing you, but more often it's in order for you to eat.'

'Yes, but someone else has always done it for me,' she whined 'and it's arrived on my plate looking nothing like an animal that gave up its life for me to eat.'

Asphodel responded to this by telling her that she should learn to face life's unpleasantness as well as the good things.

Carthinal glanced at her. She had learned a bit about life and death herself since her kidnapping by the orcs and having to live off the land.

'Killing a living being is never pleasant,' she went on, 'but sometimes it's necessary as Fero said. Before the flood, I'd never killed anything either, but I had to learn or starve. You kill the fish!' Muldee was listening to the exchange with a perplexed look on his face.

Randa, supervised by Fero, found a large stone, hit the fish sharply on its head and began the process of cleaning it. She screwed up her face as she used her dagger to split the fish and remove its insides. When she finished, Asphodel gave her a handful of herbs, which she spread inside the fish along with some wild garlic they found near the trees. Then she wrapped it, supervised by Asphodel, in leaves and placed it by the side of the fire, almost, but not quite in the flames.

'Now you burn it!' Muldee exclaimed. Asphodel laughed at the little creature's expression and translated again. 'Why do you ruin a good fish? I had a lot of trouble catching that. It's a big one. Enough to feed you all.'

Asphodel had to explain again to the dragonet. He sighed and replied to her explanation.

'It seems I know little of the world. We're very sheltered here in our valley.'

Then he seemed to be considering all he had learned.

They ate the fish and pronounced it good. They found they had some of the fish left over after they had all eaten their fill. They offered Muldee some, but he refused, saying he did not think he would like burned fish, even if they preferred it. Then he flew off, telling them it would soon be dark and he needed to go back to his clutch mates for safety.

They spent the night there on the beach. The nights were getting warmer, but not warm enough to want to be far from the fire, even if it were safe to do so, which they were unsure they were. After all, there were the mysterious Guardians to consider.

The following morning, they finished the remains of the fish, which tasted even better than it had the previous evening. Each of them expressed a feeling that eyes had been on them all the time they were on watch. It was an eerie feeling, as nothing could be seen or heard. Fero moved silently towards where he felt the eyes were but saw nothing. They quickly dismissed it as imagination. The warnings of Muldee and the nymph had been on their minds, they decided.

After breakfast, they set off in search of the tomb that they were now quite sure must be in this valley, somewhere. They walked towards the head of the valley, in a westerly direction, with the intention of circling the lake, and returning by the northern and eastern shores. The mountains towered over them, making them feel very small. There were small woods down here nearer the lake, interspersed with meadows, which now had flowers blooming. The day was warm, and the sky cloudless. In these less dense woodlands, bluebells were just beginning to form their blue carpet under the trees. Thadora was entranced. She had never seen a bluebell wood before and exclaimed continuously of its beauty.

'If I'd 'ave known 'ow lovely the damn countryside is, I'd 'ave never stayed in 'Ambara,' she exclaimed. 'I always thought as 'ow it'd be so not excitin' livin' outside o' th' town, y'know, nothin to do, nothin' 'appenin', like, but it's so bleedin' lovely, and I've not been bored one little bit.'

The others all laughed at her comments, and Fero pointed out that their journey so far had been an unusual one. People did not normally get attacked by wolves, traverse a difficult, almost impossible pass, nearly die from the cold in the snow, get rescued by yeti and walk through a volcano, not to mention meeting dragonets.

Yet, in spite of the idyllic surroundings, as they neared the western shore of the lake, they all began to have a sensation of being watched, much as they had during the night. The nearer they approached the western end of the valley, the more fearful they felt. They instinctively drew nearer to each other and walked with hands on weapons. Carthinal searched his mind for both offensive and defensive spells and used the staff to put protective armour of "hardened" air on himself.

As they emerged from one of the little woods, they saw spread out before them a meadow of wild flowers, much as others they had passed through. There was one difference, however. The feeling of menace here seemed stronger than ever, and standing before them amongst the flowers, looking somewhat out of place in the meadow, were twelve warriors with swords drawn ready to do battle.

Twelve, battle-hardened warriors against eight mismatched adventurers were not good odds, but that was not what brought them to a standstill. A feeling of utter terror emanated from the warriors. It washed over the Wolves. Wave upon wave of fear. They all struggled to stand their ground. In fact, Fero held out his hand to physically stop Carthinal from turning back there and then.

'We've not come this far to fail now,' he whispered to the half-elf. Carthinal looked at him.

'They are undead warriors,' he said. 'If there is one thing that I cannot face, it's undead. They frighten me more than anything else does on Vimar.'

Just then, one of the undead stepped forward. He wore a captain's insignia of an archaic design on equally ancient armour. He spoke, and it sounded as though the voice came from all around them, echoing from the mountains that surrounded the valley.

'Why do you come to the Valley?' he intoned. 'You must return and let the dead rest in peace.'

'We mean no harm,' Basalt said in a quavering voice.

'You are not the leader. We must speak with the leader,' went on the undead captain.

'Carthinal, speak to him,' prompted Asphodel as Carthinal made no move to step forward and respond to the creature.

All the blood seemed to have drained from Carthinal's face. He seemed as though he could not stand. Fero was all but holding him up.

'I-I can't,' he managed, 'I can't speak to those dreadful creatures.'

'You must or we can't get any further,' Asphodel scolded. 'Remember the rhyme. "No fear must show or from there you will be hounded." We now know what the Guardians are. You must control your fear and not let them see you're frightened.'

More protests formed in Carthinal's mouth when Davrael came to him.

'I understand, Carthinal,' he told him. 'I have fear such as you on bridge. You must face it. We here. We help you. I come stand by side. Face it and it seem less.'

With Davrael on one side and Fero on the other, Carthinal drew himself up to his full height. His legs felt weak, but he forced them to move and carry him forward.

The three approached the centre of the meadow, and the captain, with two of his men, did likewise.

'I am the leader of this group,' Carthinal ventured reticently.

'Then you must answer my question. Why are you here?'

Carthinal thought of a myriad replies then decided he must answer with the truth. These creatures would surely be able to tell if he lied.

'We are here to find Sauvern's Sword,' he told them. 'We have been sent by a man who believes the world is in grave peril.'

'What is this peril?' asked the undead captain.

'We don't know. We weren't told any details. We're only the employees doing our employer's bidding.'

The captain appeared to think about this reply. He turned to look at the other two with him. There were no words exchanged, but Carthinal had the distinct impression of a conversation passing between them.

Then the captain said, 'My youngest knight, Bry here,' he indicated the man on his right, 'wishes to ask you a question. It is unprecedented for the youngest to ask, but he has served bravely and well, so I grant him this boon.'

The young undead knight, who looked not much older than Thadora, said, 'Who are you?'

'I am Carthinal Mabrylson. My companions are...'

He got no farther before Bry interrupted him.

'No, Not your given names. That is meaningless. What do you call your group, if anything?'

Carthinal paused for a second, wondering if he should give the name as it suddenly seemed rather adolescent to call themselves a name, rather like the adolescent gangs in the cities he had once belonged.

Then Thadora suddenly ran forward. 'We call ourselves, "Wolf",' she cried.

The undead warriors looked at each other.

'They are the ones,' intoned the leader. 'Now, our vigil is at an end. We can at last go to our rest.'

With that, the twelve warriors seemed to slowly fade from view and the feeling of being watched vanished with it, along with the feeling of menace. All at once, the birds began to sing. They had not realised, due to their own fear that they had not been singing in this part of the valley until the song recommenced. A collective sigh came from the members of Wolf.

Chapter 17
Tomb

The Wolves continued their search after the disappearance of the Guardians. They were all subdued. They found it difficult to believe that Sillaran had created the undead warriors. The whole idea was anathema to them, as it would be to most people at that time.

'I can't believe Sillaran were evil,' Thadora mused. 'All th' stories 'bout 'im an' Sauvern said 'ow good they was.'

'Maybe they thought differently then,' Carthinal replied.

Asphodel then spoke in a quiet, thoughtful voice. 'Sometimes, good people do evil things, and sometimes evil people do good things. Equally, good can sometimes masquerade as evil just as evil often masquerades as good. I think this is what is happening here, evil being used to further the cause of good, just as at the temple in Hambara, good is being used for evil purposes.'

The others did not fully understand her thoughts, but all of them decided to keep it to think about later.

They soon came to a clearing in the wood. In the centre of the clearing were three grassy mounds. Two smaller ones stood on each side, with a larger one in the centre. Each of the smaller ones was about seven-feet-high in the centre and circular. They estimated they were about forty feet in diameter. The centre mound was much larger. It was twelve-feet-high and fifty feet in width, but instead of being round, it was about 100 feet long as far as they could estimate. They walked all round the three mounds to see if they could find an entrance to any of them, to no avail.

'Well, what now? We've not got the tools to dig our way in,' said Carthinal, sitting down on a fallen log and scratching his head.

'There must be a way in somewhere. According to the prophesies, the Sword would be needed again,' said Basalt. 'I can't believe that Sillaran would not put a door, or at least some easy way in, since he obviously knew of the prophecies.'

'That would make it too easy for tomb robbers, in spite of the Guardians,' put in Asphodel, sinking down beside Carthinal.

The half-elf jumped up, startling her. 'That's it!' he exclaimed. 'A door, but hidden or disguised.' He hit his head with the heel of his hand in exasperation. 'I should have thought of that straight away. Come on Asphodel,' He grabbed her hand and pulled her to her feet. 'We're going secret door hunting.'

The others looked at them.

'We c'n all 'elp, right?' said Thadora. 'I know elvenkind 'ave much better sight, an' an almost uncanny feelin' f'r these things, but even you c'n miss things sometimes. We might just find somethin' you didn't notice.'

Eventually, Wolf found three hidden doors. They were cleverly disguised with soil and vegetation, but they were there. They decided to search the largest tomb first, as it seemed the most obvious one to hold the body of a king. They scraped the soil away to reveal a wooden door.

'Don't open th' door yet, let me check ter make sure there's no soddin' traps on it,'said Thadora. 'It'd be a pity if we got bleedin' killed just opening th' door.'She examined the door and lock carefully and then declared it safe. 'But there're traps I've not seen before, an' this is very old so there's p'rhaps traps folk 'ave forgotten We should still be careful,' she added cautiously.

Fero volunteered to open the door. He approached it with caution, and standing to one side, he flipped the door open with his sword. The group stood for a few minutes, and then carefully entered the large tomb.

All drew weapons instinctively as they passed through the door. Once they were inside, they realised they needed some light. Thadora slipped out, gathered some dead branches from among the trees, and returned for Carthinal to light them with his useful little cantrip. It took a while for one of the branches to begin to burn, but eventually they had some light. A passage stretched out before them. On each side and at the end were doors. They opened the door on the left, first having Thadora check there were no traps. This she did and then Fero opened it in the same manner he opened the main door. When they peered in, they saw a coffin. In one corner, some weapons and armour lay piled up. There was a shield, chain mail and helmet, also a sword in its scabbard and a crossbow and bolts. They walked over to the coffin. On it, they saw the words:

"*Gallaron*
Faithful beyond death."

'One of the guardians, I suppose,' whispered Kimi. If she had been asked, she would not have been able to say why she whispered, but it seemed wrong to break the silence of this place.

They pressed on and entered the door on the right. There, they found similar weapons and armour, and a coffin bearing the same words, but the name of Lanroc. Another of the guardians it seemed.

Full of anticipation, they went to the final door. It opened readily, and there they found a third coffin, more armour and weapons, but instead of crossbow and bolts, they found a longbow and arrows. They cautiously and reverently approached the coffin, certain that Sauvern, the great King lay here. As they read the inscription their faces fell for it said:

> *"Craddok*
> *Captain and Friend*
> *He was loyal enough to guard his king*
> *even beyond the grave.*
> *He went to his fate willingly and with joy."*

'It look like only Guardians here,' said Davrael. 'Sillaran want hide body; he put in one of smaller tombs maybe?'

'Suppose 'e were so keen ter 'ide it 'e put a bloody false inscription on th' coffin?' Thadora responded.

'No,' replied Fero, 'I don't think he'd do that. Remember, there were prophecies about the Sword being needed again.'

'I think Fero's right,' Carthinal said decisively. 'Let's go search the other tombs.'

They went through the same procedure again. Again, they had the same results. One of the smaller tombs held five coffins and the other four. The only difference was a hand written, faded inscription on one saying:

> *"Stranger, if you have got this far, you are the prophesied ones and our task is finished.*
> *We no longer need our armour or weapons.*
> *Take whatever you need with our blessing*
> *Bry, the youngest guardian."*

There were a number of arrows they decided would be very useful; Fero and Randa examined some longbows, stating they were well made. These they appropriated in place of their own. It felt wrong doing so but in view of the inscription they felt they were permitted. The crossbow mechanisms were corroded and useless, so they only took bolts for Bas's crossbow. The rest of the weapons and armour were rusty and useless.

After Asphodel said a prayer over the remains of the guardians, as they all felt right and proper now they were truly at rest; they left the tombs.

Once outside, the little company sat down on the grass to discuss their next move.

'This just 'as ter be th' right place, right¿sighed Thadora. 'Lake, Guardians, tombs, even a nymph, but where's the main soddin' tomb? Sillaran 'as' idden it too well if yer ask me. I c'n see no sign of any other burial mounds.'

They sat for a time in silence, each trying to puzzle out the mystery. Then, Asphodel got to her feet. 'Secret doors and hidden passages again. Sillaran hid his journal in a secret room; the doors to the tombs were hidden; so he probably did the same here with Sauvern's body. Come on Carthinal, elf blood is the best for seeing secret doors. Let's go look,' and with that, he strode back towards the middle tomb.

'I'll come too,' called Thadora, 'It's an occupational requirement of thieves. Findin' 'idden things, that is'

'And me,' said Basalt. 'We dwarves know stones and can sometimes spot things, especially in stonework.'

Eventually, all eight went to look again, and Basalt suddenly noticed the slight gap in the slabs on the floor and the hollow sound his feet made as he walked over it. The gap was so small they could barely discern it. Even Carthinal and Asphodel, with their superior eyesight, had not noticed it. It was just in front of the coffin in the furthest room of the large barrow. Asphodel quickly found the lever that opened it and when she pressed it, a grinding noise sounded and the floor opened. One of the slabs tilted until it formed an angle and fitted into a slope leading downwards. Stale air wafted up from below.

'We'd better give it some minutes to clear that air and for it to be replaced by some fresh stuff or we could just about suffocate,' the dwarf advised.

'Then let's go eat while that's 'appenin',' Thadora suggested as her tummy rumbled. 'I'm so bloody well starvin', I don't know about the rest of you.'

Everyone thought this a good idea, so they exited the tomb once more.

A half-hour later they passed through the now familiar passage and stood at the top of the slope. Fero drew his sword. 'I'll go first,' he stated. 'I can be quiet and stealthy.'

'I'll come too,' said Thadora. 'I'll check there's no more traps, see. I c'n be quiet and stealthy, too, Fero,' she said to the ranger who looked as though he wanted to stop her.

'I know, Red Cub,' he replied, 'but it may be dangerous. We've no idea what's down there.'

'Poof! Th' 'ole mission's bleedin' dangerous, and what if you stumble across a trap unknowing and get bloody well frazzled?'

The two went quietly ahead. Halfway down they stopped and beckoned to the others that it was safe and they followed, weapons at the ready. They continued in this mode, Thadora and Fero went ahead and made sure no danger lurked there and the others followed until they reached the bottom. Here, the slope levelled out and they found themselves on the banks of an underground river. The surface steamed gently, like a pot on the coals, giving the air a misty and mysterious air.

'This must be the river that feeds the lake,' whispered Fero.

They continued along the banks of the river until they saw the wall ahead drop down to only a few inches above the water. The river rushed out from under the wall at such a rate as to make it impossible for anyone to attempt to go through to any caverns that may exist beyond. It seemed they had come to another full stop. They peered around them.

'Do you think the river has risen since the tombs were made?' asked Kimi. 'If so, it seems we are truly stuck, unless we swim through the water, on the off-chance that it comes out.'

'No way!' exclaimed Basalt, with feeling. 'I'll climb mountains and get nearly frozen to death in the snow, pass through lava tubes of a volcano, obviously only dormant, even face undead warriors, but never, never will I voluntarily attempt to drown myself in an underground river on the off-chance that I'll find air before I die.' He folded his arms over his chest and planted his feet firmly on the ground as though he expected them to drag him into the water at any minute.

Then Thadora called out, 'We may not 'ave to, silly bugger. I c'n see a dark patch up there, which is p'raps an entrance ter another passage.' She turned to Carthinal, ''Old up th' torch so I c'n see better.'

It was still inconclusive, so Thadora volunteered to climb up to see.

'Be careful, Red Cub. That wall looks difficult,' warned Carthinal.

'Oh, th' climb's easy enough,'she scoffed. 'Plenty o' 'andand foot 'olds. Much easier than scalin' th' wall of a bleedin' 'ouse.'

The others looked a little uneasy at the reminder of her profession, but Thadora did not notice as she had already climbed part way up the wall.

The climb was about fifteen feet. Once there, Thadora disappeared, and then her face reappeared and she waved and called down that she could see another passage, as she had thought, going off at an angle of about twenty degrees from the direction of the current passage. This made it just to the south of west, and probably into the hill behind the tombs.

The others were too busy watching Thadora to notice the river until it was nearly too late. A sudden sound made them turn as a large shape rose from the centre of the water. They saw a warty creature with large, bulbous eyes and a formidable mouth, which it opened and flashed out a long tongue like a frog or toad. Asphodel just noticed it in time to throw herself onto the ground and roll off to one side, or she would certainly have been caught. The creature withdrew its tongue and readied itself for another try.

Davrael and Kimi notched arrows to their short bows and let fly, but the arrows skidded off the thick skin of the creature. A bolt from Basalt's crossbow followed their arrows. To their surprise, Fero and Basalt's shots stuck.

'Well, I'll be a hobgoblin's breakfast!' exclaimed Bas. 'These arrows and bolts are truly good.'

Davrael and Kimi found their arrows were no use at all against the monster. Carthinal sent a couple of his small, energy bolts against it, and they managed to do some further damage. The creature roared in pain but readied itself for another attack. This time, it aimed for Fero, whom it obviously saw as one of its main tormentors. Fero had to take evasive action then and missed his shot, but the tongue also missed him by a hair's breadth. Carthinal used the staff to fire off the silvery bolts of energy, and to his surprise, it released six of them. Then, as the monster shot its tongue out again, this time at Carthinal, a knife came flying over their heads, turning in the air to embed itself firmly in the toad-like creature's eye. With another roar, it slipped beneath the surface of the water, which turned a pinkish colour.

From above, they heard an expletive. 'Shit! That were a good throwin' knife wasted,'Thadora called as she scrambled down the wall. 'I 'ope your ass is worth a good knife, mage.'

'What, in all seven hells was that thing?' said Davrael, leaning against the rough wall of the cavern and breathing hard, 'and what it do in here? If no us, what it eat?'

He looked surprised as the others laughed.

'Your Grosmerian is improving, Davrael,' pointed out Fero, 'If you are now beginning to swear in the language.'

'I learn from best,' he replied, smiling. 'I listen Red Cub there and learn. But I not like that thing in water.'

'"That Thing," Davrael, may have come in as a youngster. Maybe it has a tadpole stage, like true frogs and toads,' Randa said thoughtfully. 'As to what it eats, who knows? Fish can probably swim in here from outside, and maybe the occasional aquatic mammal. Perhaps there are fish living in these caves. I've heard of such things. They are white and have no eyes, as it's so dark that eyes would be useless. There may even be another exit from the tunnel Thadora's found and things come in and fall down here.'

'Have you seen that thing in your father's books, Randa?' Kimi enquired of the other girl.

'No, Kimi, never. I've no more idea than you as to what it was. I just hope it has no friends around.'

At that thought, they all turned once more to the river, but there were no further signs of life.

'Well, so much for the idea of going down the river then. Good job we didn't decide to do that. I'll go with Thadora's idea any day,' said Basalt.

They laughed.

'You wouldn't want to go up the river if there was nothing worse than a friendly otter,' teased Fero, his black eyes twinkling in the light from the torch he carried.

Bas replied with a 'Humph!'

Thadora had by now come down the wall. 'Well,' she exclaimed, 'I suppose th' wall an' that passage're th' only way forrad, so up we go.'

Davrael groaned. 'I'm not sure I can do it, Mouse,' he whispered to Kimi in their own language. 'I didn't know I had this height thing.'

'Are you a warrior and a Horselord, or just some kind of wimp,' she replied, also in the language of the Horselords. 'The only way to overcome your fear is to face it, as you said to Carthinal. So face it, warrior.'

Thadora took the rope from Fero and climbed nimbly up the wall again. She reached the top, tied the rope to a natural, rock pillar and let the end snake down over the lip of the opening. 'Use th' rope ter 'elp you climb,' she called down.

Fero went up first and he climbed well, scarcely using the rope to help him. After Fero came Randa and Asphodel, followed by Basalt.

Carthinal turned to Davrael. 'Warrior,' he said, using the formal form of address used in the Tribes, 'You helped me when I needed support. Now I will return your words to you. Face your fear. Decide why it frightens you. What is the worst thing that can happen?'

'I fear feeling I made to jump. I fear I give in to it. I fear I fall, or jump, I not die, but be maimed for all my life. Cripples in Tribes considered dead. They no use to our society,' then in almost a whisper he said, 'Women whose husbands crippled be free to remarry as they widows.' He looked at Kimi, pleading in his brown eyes.

She put her arms round him. 'We're not on the plains now, Davrael. Those rules don't apply here. Moreover, they'd never apply to us. I'll love you whatever you are, and wherever you are.'

'Come on, you three. We ve a Sword to find,' Thadora's voice came from above and a curly redhead poked out over the cliff face.

Davrael took a deep breath and stepped to the rope. He grasped the end and began to laboriously climb up, keeping his eyes always on the silhouetted figure of Thadora above him, who, realising that her face seemed to help, remained peering down at Davrael. He stopped once, half way up, and the others thought he was going to freeze as he had on the bridge, but then he continued to climb, and eventually made it to the lip of the opening and hauled himself over. He lay on the rocky edge for a few minutes, and then rolled away and sat up, breathing heavily with sweat beading his forehead. Thadora, in her demonstrative way, hugged him and praised his bravery. Then Kimi climbed up, followed by Carthinal and they were all in the upper passage.

Once they had all gathered their breath, and Davrael had once more regained his equilibrium, they set off along the tunnel that opened before them. The darkness spread around them but it was quite dry. Fero and Thadora walked in front, Thadora keeping an eye out for anything that might resemble a trap. Behind them came Basalt and Asphodel, followed by Randa and Carthinal. Davrael and Kimi brought up the rear, keeping a check behind in case they were followed by anything. They could not see very far ahead, even with the makeshift torches they carried with them, and so had no idea how far the tunnel went. Thus they nearly stumbled on the monster before they saw it. A large, caterpillar-like creature, white in colour, with many tentacles around its mouth, stood blocking their path. As soon as it saw them, it reared up on its hindmost legs, like some caterpillars do, in preparation for a strike. Fortunately, Fero and Thadora saw it and shouted for the Wolfpack to halt.

'Carrion Crawler,' Randa whispered to Carthinal. She called to those in front. 'Keep away from the tentacles. They have a poison that will paralyse.'

Carthinal seized the mana, and the familiar, silvery missiles shot from his fingers to hit the creature just beneath its raised head. At the same time, Davrael and Kimi released their arrows. Kimi's hit, but Davrael missed. Fero and Thadora scrambled backwards out of the way of the head, which now descended towards them. Basalt and Asphodel also moved backwards. Unfortunately, Thadora tripped on a slight hollow in the floor of the tunnel and fell directly under the creature's head. The tentacles struck. By this time, Fero had reached a safe distance and let off a shot, along with a bolt from Basalt's crossbow and a stone from Asphodel's sling. All three missiles hit. The final arrows from Davrael and Kimi, along with one from Randa dispatched the creature.

Fero rushed towards Thadora. 'Come on, Red Cub,' he said, 'You're all right. The thing's dead now.'

Thadora made no response, just lay motionless on the ground. Asphodel pushed Fero out of the way. She knelt down on the ground beside Thadora and gently felt her pulse and checked her breathing. That done, she felt all over her for wounds. 'Bring a light here, someone,' she commanded.

In the light of the lamp, she looked for any signs of wounds but found none except for a rash of reddish pinpricks on Thadora's neck where the tentacles had hit the young thief.

'She's alive, at any rate,' Asphodel told the others. 'Her breathing and pulse are steady, and I can see no wounds except for these marks where the tentacles hit her. The poison is fast-acting though. She went down immediately. Randa, do you know how venomous the poison is?'

'I'm sorry, Asphodel,' replied the girl, 'I can't remember what the book said. As I told you, I used to browse the books as a child. I wasn't looking for practical information, so I didn't take much notice of details.'

'I don't think it will be fatal to creatures the size of humans, elves and dwarves,' Asphodel went on. 'If it were, then I suspect Thadora's vital signs would be less strong, and showing signs of fading. I think she's just temporarily paralysed.' '*At least I hope so,*' she thought.

Just as Asphodel said, after five minutes or so, Thadora's eyes moved and looked around the Wolves, gathered around her, then slowly regained her movement.

When she could speak, she said, 'It's kinda cool you're all so worried 'bout me. Thanks. Nobody 'cept Mam ever seemed bothered afore.' Then, she sat up carefully. 'Me neck's bloody sore though,' she told them.

Asphodel tried a healing, praying to Sylissa for ease for Thadora's pain, and Thadora said that she felt a little better. Some of the stinging had passed away. She still wobbled a little as she tried to walk but expressed her view that she could carry on.

They continued down the tunnel, but at a slower rate and with frequent stops to look and listen but they met no further denizens of the underground. The tunnel then did a sharp left turn. They could see that a dozen or so feet ahead it ended, not in a stone wall, but with an iron-bound, wooden door. Thadora approached carefully, looking, and feeling for any traps. The others stood back as she instructed them.

'Take care, Red Cub,' called Bas. (The name given to her by the yeti seemed to have stuck).

In reply, she gave him a jaunty wave. She reached the door and inspected it on all sides before turning her attention to the lock. Careful examination in the light of the torch seemed to indicate that it had no traps on it, so she tried the door. It was locked. She searched the lock again and spotted a simple trap. If she had tried to pick the lock, a needle hidden in it would have struck her. She carefully removed the needle. There was probably poison on it, so she placed it in a leather wrapper in her pouch of thieves' tools so that she would not inadvertently prick herself with it later. After a final check, she inserted a lock pick and quickly had the door open. The others came forward. They looked into the cave beyond, and saw no dangers apparent. They cautiously entered.

Carthinal held his torch aloft and its flickering light illuminated the cave with leaping shadows. It was not a large cave, and it seemed to have been worked to make it larger. At least, that is what Basalt said when he examined some marks on the walls.

'Not very good work, though,' he opined. 'Done in a hurry, I'd say, and not by dwarfs either. Even in a hurry, dwarfs make better work than this.'

They walked around the cave, which was about fifteen feet across, and roughly circular in shape. In the centre of the cave stood a large, stone sarcophagus. They walked slowly towards it. They were not sure why, but hurrying did not seem appropriate here. Nor did the talking. They all had a feeling of righteousness and goodness about the place.

'A bit like a temple or other, holy place,' Thadora said later in describing their quest.

They spread themselves around the sarcophagus, each subconsciously standing at one of the cardinal points of the compass.

An engraved, brass plaque was fastened to the sarcophagus. It had some kind of writing engraved on it, but it had corroded somewhat with age. Carthinal leaned over and rubbed it with his sleeve. Some of the corrosion came off, and he read:

"'*Here Lie the Mortal Remains of*
The Greatest King Ever to Serve the Land
King Sauvern I
By his Side Lies His Famous Sword, Equilibrium,
Awaiting Its Call to Action Once More.'"

'Does that mean we have to remove the lid of the sarcophagus?' asked Kimi. 'That doesn't seem right. To disturb the last rest of a great King.'

'That's what is implied,' replied Carthinal.

We'd better get on with it then,' said Basalt, ever practical.

They pushed at the heavy, stone lid. It did not seem to want to move, but eventually, it shifted to the side. When they peered inside the coffin, they saw the bones of what had once been a tall man. The body had been dressed in chain mail armour, and had a beautifully worked helmet on his head, made to look like a winged hawk, with the head and beak forming the nose piece, and wings stretched backwards. A shield and a sword were grasped in his hands, bony fingers holding on tightly. It had a large sapphire in a setting at the top of the pommel of the longsword and the grip was ridged with what looked like gold. The quillons, or cross pieces, each had a smaller sapphire at the end and were decorated with gold, The blade had a blunt section, called a ricasso, at the top end just below the quillons. Here, another sapphire was set. The blade had a fuller running down the length.

'We can't disturb him,' Randa whispered, 'It would be sacrilege.'

'If anyone can, it must be us,' Carthinal replied, also in a whisper. 'We are the prophesied ones it seems, and now the Guardians have gone, anyone can get in here.'

'I suppose you're right, but it doesn't make me feel any better.'

Carthinal reached in carefully to grasp the Sword.

Suddenly, he withdrew his hand. 'It burned me,' he said, looking surprised and hurt. Thadora and Basalt suppressed chuckles.

'Let me try,' Basalt said, trying not to laugh at Carthinal's discomfort, but when he reached in, he could not lift the Sword at all. It seemed to him to be incredibly heavy.

He struggled and tried, all to no avail in spite of his strength. Eventually, he gave up, puffing and panting. By now, Thadora could not contain herself, and seemed to nearly explode with giggles. Kimi and Fero had also joined in with her amusement.

Fero decided he would try and received an electric shock for his pains. By now, they were beginning to feel they were not the right people. Randa decided to have a try, and then after her, Thadora said she would try, but that would be the last. No one else could use a sword since the Horselords used knives to fight, not swords.

Randa approached the last resting-place of Sauvern, the king who had united Grosmer and defeated the Raiders. To Randa's surprise, the Sword came out of the skeleton king's grasp easily, almost as though he had released it to her, and she lifted it up in salute to Sauvern. She swished it a few times, declared it to be perfectly balanced and the most incredible weapon she had ever held. Then she looked round at the others and it was her turn to laugh. The expressions on their faces were a sight to behold. There was a mixture of incredulity and amazement, mixed with not a little envy on the faces of a couple of the Wolves.

They were still looking surprised when they heard a sound. Those with their backs to the door, turned, and the others looked in that direction, all ready for action. They saw, silhouetted in the doorway, the figure of a tall man. He wore a robe that looked to be made of red silk, belted at the waist by a soft leather belt. Over his shoulders he wore a cloak of red velvet, and on his head was a circle of gold, with the symbols of all the gods surmounted at intervals. He held a sceptre, indicating rulership, in his left hand. It seemed a strange thing, Asphodel said later. He seemed to be here, and yet not here. They felt they could touch him if they reached out, yet he seemed distant. Not one of them felt afraid. They knew this was not an evil apparition. None of them could explain this afterwards, but they all agreed that this was what they felt.

Then the figure spoke. 'I am Sauvern. The gods have allowed me to wait for your coming before being born again on the Wheel of Life. I have returned to your plane briefly, although my time is short. You are those prophesied who are to come to claim the Sword.' He turned to Randa. 'The Sword has chosen, and will remain with you, my lady, until the day you die, unless you prove unworthy. No one else will it permit to touch it, as you have no doubt found. Use it well.'

He then turned to the others. 'Your task is not yet finished, your destiny not complete;, the gods tell me. They will not permit me to see what you must do, but the Sword and Swordbearer are needed at this time. Your paths will have many crossroads where you will need to make decisions that may impact on the future. Already, you have all made important decisions that have brought you together. Many of those decisions, I believe, were decisions involving some act of independence. This spirit of independence in each of you is what makes you who you are and ironically makes your companionship the stronger. The time ahead of you is uncertain indeed, and fraught with dangers. You will be tested in the future. You must all face dark times ahead, but you must be strong and overcome these trials. Remember your sworn oath. The gods heard you and accepted it. You must always remember you are the Wolves.'

With that, he slowly began to fade. As the apparition disappeared, they heard these last words. 'Take whatever you need from my tomb. All is yours. Swordbearer, I give you this.'

A tooled leather scabbard fell to the floor as the apparition finally disappeared.

After standing for a few minutes, Basalt recovered his senses. 'Well, you heard the man,' he said to Randa. 'Go get the scabbard, girl, and put the Sword away.'

Randa walked slowly towards the said piece of equipment as if she thought it might vanish any moment as its previous owner had. She slowly picked it up and examined it.

'It's a fine piece of workmanship,' she said, as she donned it and sheathed the sword.

'Of course it is,' Bas responded. 'It belonged to a king, didn't it? Can't expect him to have just any piece of old leather made into a scabbard.'

The others had recovered by now and again looked into the sarcophagus. They still did not want to take the armour, which amazingly still shone brightly, as did the helmet and gauntlets. Davrael reached in and lifted the helm off the head of the skeleton.

'A bird of prey,' he said. 'The totem of my tribe is hawk.'

'Put it on, Davrael,' Carthinal urged. 'Sauvern, or rather, his ghost, told us to take anything we needed.'

Davrael slowly lowered the helm over his head. The wings swept back over his head, and the head and beak of the bird came down to protect his nose. Its claws were made to cover the ears on each side. With this helmet and the tattoo on his face, Davrael looked truly fearsome.

'If I didn't know you, I think I'd be afraid,' Kimi said to him, smiling, 'but I know what a pussy cat you really are, even if you try to pretend otherwise.'

Davrael looked at her, put on a fierce expression and lunged towards her. 'You know what pussy cats do to little mouses,' he said as he lunged.

She jumped backwards, letting out a little squeal, then let him catch her up and swing her round. 'Ouch, Davrael. Those claws hurt,' she complained, as he hugged her to him, and he reluctantly let her go.

The others were looking at the mail and gauntlets still in the coffin.

'The chain mail may fit you, Fero,' said Basalt.

'No. Chain mail will make too much noise when I'm tracking and hunting. I prefer to stick to leather,' the ranger replied.

'Same fer me. It'd be no bleedin' use to a thief, even if it'd fit me,' said Thadora.

'It's too big for a dwarf,' said Carthinal' 'and no use to a mage either, as it would interfere with the magic.'

'That leaves Davrael, Randa and Asphodel as I'm sure it wouldn't fit Kimi; she's so tiny,' Thadora put in.

'I've already got chain mail,' Randa pointed out. 'I think the only one it will fit is Davrael.'

'Unless it's elven chain,' mused Asphodel. 'Sometimes, enchantments are put on by the elf mages to make it fit anyone.'

'Is that true, Asphodel?' asked Basalt. 'I've heard tales, but never quite believed them.'

'Only one way to find out!' said Carthinal. 'Someone must try it on whom it seems not to fit.'

After much discussion, they chose Asphodel. Kimi did not feel confident about using chain mail. She had never needed any armour at all until she had left her home, but Davrael insisted for her safety she should wear leather armour at least.

Asphodel removed the leather armour she wore and donned the chain mail. At first, it seemed to swamp her, but then a strange thing happened. The armour seemed to shiver, and then the rings seemed to slowly shrink, pulling it to a perfect fit. It was indeed elven chain mail with an enchantment on it to fit anyone. It felt so light that Asphodel felt as though she were not wearing armour at all. She pulled the tabard with the holy symbol of Sylissa over her head and was ready to continue. The question of the gauntlets now arose. Were they magical too? Randa had the Sword, Davrael the helm, Asphodel the chain mail. Carthinal could not use armour for fear of interfering with his magic, and Fero declined. The three remaining Wolves decided to try them on to see whom they would best fit. Thadora thus came by a pair of beautifully fitting leather gauntlets. She thought they might hinder her movements when drawing her bow she had been practising under the tutelage of both Fero and Davrael but she decided to give it a go since they would protect her hands in close fighting, minimising any damage that may affect her lock-picking skills. Finally, Basalt took the shield.

The Wolves left the tomb. They passed the body of the carrion crawler and climbed down the rope they had left back in the passage with the river. Thadora untied the rope and descended last, carrying it with her. The descent seemed very easy to her. Much easier than the ascent had been. When she reached the river bank, she once more protested the loss of her throwing knife but declined to follow Basalt's suggestion that she go into the water to reclaim it. They once more ascended the slope, closed the trapdoor, and exited the tomb.

When they got out, they were surprised to find it growing dark. They set up camp before the largest mound and prepared to eat some of their dried rations. They heard a rustle of wings over their heads, and Muldee descended before them.

He spoke to Asphodel in his version of elvish. 'They've gone! The Guardians. What did you do? How did you defeat them?'

She translated for the others, and replied, 'We came here for a purpose. It seems we were expected. The Guardians have finished their job and have gone to their rest.'

'About time,' Muldee replied. 'Their presence here spoiled the whole valley. Well, now you've finished, I expect you'll be leaving.'

Asphodel laughed. 'Are you so keen to be rid of us?' she asked him.

'No! Not at all,' replied the little creature. 'My brothers and sisters and I have been talking, and we've decided we should know more about the world, so they've elected me to be the explorer. I'm coming with you!'

The others looked at Asphodel's amazed face and immediately asked for a translation. When she had done so, she laughed at the faces of the others. They looked as amazed as she supposed she must have done.

'Is this a good idea?' queried Basalt, remembering the antics of the dragonet in the water, and how amused he had seemed to nearly drown them all.

'I don't see how we can stop him,' replied Fero. 'He'll follow us if we don't agree, and I for one would like to know exactly where he is.'

'My thinks too,' replied Davrael, remembering his own loss of dignity at the hands, or maybe one should say, claws, of the young creature.

They reluctantly agreed for Muldee to accompany them. The dragonet then went on to say they would not find their way out of the valley without him anyway, as it was not straightforward.

With that, the creature flew to the fire, curled up next to it and within moments fell fast asleep.

Interlude

Yssa woke still feeling tired. She must try to relax a bit more. She had been working too hard on those books Carthinal and Basalt had found. They were very interesting, though. She found it difficult to leave each evening. Yesterday, Rollo insisted she eat dinner with him. "For old time's sake," he said. She had agreed to do so. She and Rollo were lovers once. He was lonely after the death of his wife. She knew Randa did not remember her; the child was only three or four years old at the time she and Rollo were seeing each other, and she had not seen that much of her as the child spent a lot of the time in her nursery.

In the early days after his beloved wife's death, Rollo had not wanted to look at the child he blamed for this event. He had provided her with all the creature comforts she needed with the best nurses that money could buy, but he rarely went near the nursery to see his daughter. Yssa had once told him that a child needed love as well as food, shelter and warmth. She persuaded Rollo to visit his daughter more often. Fairly soon, Rollo discovered his love for the child, and, to assuage his guilt at neglecting her in her earliest years, he lavished her with not only love, but attention and showered her with gifts, giving in to her every whim. Randa had grown into a beautiful, but spoiled child who had become a beautiful, but wilful and snobbish young lady.

The door opened and admitted Emmienne. She and Tomac had arrived about three sixdays ago from Bluehaven. They were Mabryl's other apprentices that she had promised Carthinal she would take under her wing. They were proving to be very good. The girl, Emmienne, had taken to bringing her tea each morning along with hot water for her to wash, and Tomac was excellent at lighting fires. She could hear him busying himself doing that job at the moment. She smiled at Emmienne.

'Thank you,' she said. 'Put the tea there. I'll be up in a minute.'

The girl did as Yssa bade her and then left. She was a plain girl, Yssa thought—about seventeen, with a slender figure and chestnut hair. Tomac was younger. He was fourteen and had a shock of jet-black hair, which he found difficult to keep tidy. He tried to keep it tied back, but it kept escaping its confinement. She smiled. She liked her new apprentices very much, and if she were honest, she liked the attention they gave her, too.

After drinking her tea, Yssa rose. As she did so, a feeling of nausea and giddiness overtook her. It had happened once or twice recently. She hoped it was not some illness or other. She did not want to lose time on her translations of the books. She dressed and the moment passed.

Later in the day, she gave some instructions to her apprentices. She wanted them to try to learn a simple spell when Emmienne asked about Carthinal.

'When did he leave, Yssa?' she asked.

Yssa looked at her. She wondered if the girl had a crush on the half-elf. She would not blame her if she had. She herself had fallen under his spell and she was hardly an impressionable, young girl.

'He and his companions left on the twenty-second of Khaldar. That will be five and a half sixdays.'

Something began to dawn on her when she spoke of that time. She did some quick calculations and realised she had not had her monthly bleeding since before that date. She had been working so hard on the books that she had not realised. What with the translations and the new apprentices to settle in, she had been so busy. Now, she realised what her nausea and giddiness meant. She was pregnant. She had little doubt. She was always regular as clockwork, and now, she calculated she had missed two bleedings. She paled. What should she do?

Yssa finished her lesson with the two apprentices and then said, 'You two have worked hard since you came to me. You deserve a break. Take this and go and have a good time in Hambara.'

She threw a bag of coins towards them. Tomac caught it deftly, and thanking her profusely, the pair rushed from the room, as anxious to be gone as Yssa was for them to leave.

Once alone, she contemplated her position. She did not want a child. She had never felt maternal in any way, but having an abortion seemed quite out of the question. Elves have a reverence for all life, even that of the unborn, and Yssa was no exception in this respect. She was going to have a child, and she could not turn back. How had she been so careless? Her work, even before the finding of the hidden books had absorbed her so much that she had forgotten to take the herbs to prevent pregnancy.

As she thought about it, she thought she should go away, back to Quantissarillishon, the elven capital, and to find refuge with her parents. Her mother would be scandalised at first, of course, but she would soon come round when she thought of a grandchild. She could leave the child there, to be cared for by her parents, and Carthinal need never know. She did not want him to feel he had any obligation to her or the child. The mistake had been hers and hers alone. As the day wore on, she began to see that it was not that simple. She could not just go running off home like a little girl with a grazed knee. She had obligations here. She had taken on two apprentices, and she did not want to let them down after they had lost Mabryl in such tragic circumstances. She considered the translation. No one could do it like she could, and the importance to magic could not be exaggerated. No, she must stay here. She did not need to tell Carthinal though. He would probably be back before her pregnancy became obvious, and then he would go back to Bluehaven where he probably had family and friends. She suddenly realised how little she knew about this charismatic half-elf who had captured her heart in spite of herself; she, who thought herself so worldly-wise.

During the next few days, she seemed distracted. Rollo noticed and she confessed her pregnancy to him.

She asked him, 'Rollo, if someone were going to have your child and did not tell you, how would you feel if you later found out?'

'You are considering not telling the father, I take it?' the Duke replied.

Yssa nodded.

'I won't ask who it is,' he continued, 'but if it were me, and I found out later, I would be very hurt and maybe angry, too.'

'Yes, I thought you'd say that,' sighed Yssa. He had not solved her problem and she continued to think hard.

Part 3
Homeward

Chapter 18
Hobgoblins

The next morning, they left the vicinity of the tombs. Muldee told them they should follow the northern side of the lake as they wanted the exit on that side of the valley; so they duly followed him. He alternated between flying and walking, but he walked rather slowly, so he started riding on one or the other's shoulders. They put up with this as he not very heavy, and he did not stay long before taking off again. When he landed on Davrael's shoulders, he suddenly jumped making Davrael curse.

'Asphodel,' the dragonet called to the elf, 'This helm of Davrael's is magic. It startled me when I felt it. I didn't expect it.'

'How can you tell?' she asked him.

'Made me feel funny,' he said.

'Can you always tell if something is magical?' she continued.

The dragonet looked surprised. 'Of course,' he replied, 'Good magic or bad. Each feels different.'

'What about the other things we got from the tomb?'

He touched each item in turn and confirmed that they were all magical in some way and that it was not bad magic.

'All we need to know now is what kind of magic they have,' said Randa when Asphodel told them what Muldee was doing. 'We've no idea what they do.'

They followed Muldee's directions and found themselves heading much further north than they would have thought, but the little creature assured them that this was the only way out.

'All the branches towards the south are dead ends,' he told Asphodel when she asked about the direction. 'I told you that you needed me to find your way.'

The dragonet began to learn Grosmerian. He learned quickly. He experimented by trying to get into the minds of the companions. Unknown to the group, dragonets had a certain talent for telepathy. He discovered that Thadora and Asphodel were the easiest for him to read, but he found Basalt almost impossible. This talent made his learning of Grosmerian all the easier. One day, he surprised Thadora by managing to speak to her telepathically. It frightened the girl at first, but she became used to it, and even managed to respond. She did not seem very happy about the idea of the little creature "*rummaging around in me 'ead at me most private thoughts,*" as she put it, so Muldee said he would teach her how to shield her own thoughts, and also promised not to pry. This seemed to help Thadora come to terms with the idea of telepathic speech.

Two days after beginning their journey from the valley, they came to a place where it narrowed, passing between cliffs on either side. A stream flowed along the bottom, and a few trees managed to cling to the banks. By now, many of them were looking a pretty shade of pale green as they burst into leaf. Birds were well on the way with their nesting, and many animals were giving birth. They were all walking along and feeling very pleased with themselves when suddenly Randa felt a tingling from the Sword at her hip, and from the sides of the valley, where they were hidden from view by the rocks and bushes, sprang a couple of dozen hobgoblins.

Randa drew her Sword and began to fight, as did the others. Carthinal quickly gave the command to his staff to set armour on himself and then sent a ball of multicoloured light at one of the hobgoblins which blinded him as well as causing injury, followed by some missiles from his staff. The others were all fighting strongly, but in vain, as they were greatly outnumbered. Even Asphodel struck out with her mace, which she had hardly used since she had acquired it from the temple before leaving Hambara. She even managed to do some damage to the enemy while avoiding damaging her companions. When they were eventually all captured, they found there were only fourteen of the hobgoblins standing, and some of those were bleeding.

'We made them hurt, though!' whispered a voice in Carthinal's ear, sounding strangely satisfied. He turned his head and it surprised him to see Asphodel standing next to him, her arms tied behind her, and an uncharacteristically savage expression on her face.

A rough voice, obviously the leader of the ambush party, said something in a strange, guttural language, and they were searched and their weapons removed. They looked over to a large hobgoblin dressed in chain mail. He stood well over six feet, with a typically, animalistic hobgoblin face with tusks reaching up from his lower jaw. His eyes were brown, but had a hard, cruel look, and his mouth seemed to be in a permanent sneer. His men were obviously afraid of him and obeyed him with alacrity. The other hobgoblins were smaller and were wearing leather armour reinforced with metal studs. They all had crossbows and melee weapons, some with axes, some with war hammers, some even had short swords, and all looked as though he knew how to use his weapon of choice.

The hobgoblin who tried to remove the Sword from Randa, quickly dropped it, and ran around blowing on his hand. He had obviously been burned by the Sword's defence mechanism. The leader ordered another of the creatures to pick it up, but he failed. The Sword was just too heavy. He dragged it with the help of a second of the hobgoblins to the leader of the gang. The leader looked at the two, and then at Randa and said something scathing, judging by the looks of his two men.

Fero had managed to pick up a little hobgoblin on his travels, and he whispered to the others. 'He says they must be weaker than a mouse if they cannot lift a sword wielded so effortlessly by a mere woman.'

Randa looked incensed at being called a "mere woman," and almost responded when the leader came up to them. He kicked out at Randa and caught her on the ankle. She refrained from crying out, and just managed to stay on her feet.

'You not be hurt if you not fight,' he said in a harsh voice. 'Where your pet?'

Carthinal frowned, then realised he was talking about Muldee. Carthinal shrugged and the hobgoblin hit him across the mouth, for his insolence, so he said.

'No matter. It only small creature. It probably run away. Must be afraid of mighty hobgoblins. Would have made good sale, though. Bring lot of money for Khland. Khland take Sword for own. It do much damage to Khland's men. It good Sword.'

He walked over to the Sword and picked it up. It was no longer heavy, and Khland gave a disgusted look to the two who had dragged it to him. Randa did notice a wince, however, and after he had strapped on the sword round his waist, she caught him looking surreptitiously at his hand.

The hobgoblins marched the party along at a brisk pace, allowing no talk at all between them. Thadora wondered where Muldee had got to but then decided he probably thought it was too dangerous in the world and had flown back to his siblings. Suddenly, one of the hobgoblins at the rear of the line put his hand to his head and crumpled up in a heap, moaning about a loud noise in his brain. They stopped, and the leader, Khland, demanded to know why.

They held a hurried discussion in hobgoblin, which Fero tried to hear, but failed, and then one of them dispatched the injured creature an axe, stripped off his armour, weapons and money, and the column moved off again. This happened again during the day, and the hobgoblins repeated the same procedure.

That evening, they made camp in a barren place. They had been going steadily northwards since leaving the valley, and the mountains had given way to hills covered with heather. These moorland hills were bleak, and the east wind cut across them with an icy blast. There were little valleys with small streams in them, and every now and then, a rill joined a bigger stream, tumbling down through the heather in a series of little waterfalls. There were few trees here, and what few there were, were poor stunted things that leaned away from the prevailing wind, which usually blew from the west and gave no shelter from the icy blast.

The hobgoblins set up a large tent for their commander, and while this went on, he amused himself by taunting the captives.

'You be cold tonight,' he told them. 'Not possible to make fire. Heather burn easy. Too easy. You be hungry too. Have only small foods for you.'

'Why have you captured us? Where are you taking us?' demanded Randa imperiously.

'You not speak to Khland unless told,' and he kicked her in the stomach.

She doubled up in pain, tears springing unbidden to her eyes, but she was determined not to let them fall and give Khland the satisfaction that he had hurt her, so she straightened as best she could and, with her most proud look, gave him a disdainful glare. Khland raised his foot to kick her again when one of the hobgoblins came up and said something to him.

He said to Randa, 'Wait till later. Khland hurt you then. Not damage badly, though. Orders not to, but no orders not to hurt you.' With that, he strode off to where the others had erected his tent.

The Wolves stood and stared after Khland.

'If he touches you again,' said Fero, 'I swear I'll kill him myself. Somehow.'

''Ow, wi' yer 'ands bleedin'-well tied and no weapons?' asked Thadora, somewhat scornfully, Fero thought.

'I'll find a way,' snarled Fero, slumping to the ground. 'I'll not let him hurt any of you girls,' he went on.

The others also sat down and eventually one of the hobgoblins placed a bowl of thin stew before them, with eight spoons dipped into it. He brought no bread.

'How are we supposed to eat with our hand tied behind us?' Carthinal complained.

'I go ask,' replied the hobgoblin, and disappeared towards the tent of his commander.

It seemed that they could do nothing without the permission of Khland. They watched as he spoke to the guards, and then Khland came out, said something to him and cuffed him around the head. The chastised creature came back and untied their hands, but tied their feet together, one left foot to the next person's right. All except Carthinal. He had his feet tied as did the others, but his hands were not released.

'Hands of mage stay tied so he not do magic,' the hobgoblin soldier told them.

'I'll feed you some of this stuff if you want, Carthinal,' said Kimi. (She sat between him and Davrael).

'I'm tempted to say that I don't want any of it, but I suppose we should all eat something,' he replied, 'but goodness knows what it is. I'd rather not think about that.'

They ate, and afterwards, their hands were retied, but this time in front of them, except for Carthinal, whose hands remained as they were. An icy wind blew around the hills, getting up more strongly as darkness fell. They could see a brazier around which the hobgoblins were sitting or lying down sleeping, and a light flickered in Khland's tent showing that he, too, had some heating. They huddled together as best they could for warmth but passed a very uncomfortable, cold and sleepless night.

The next day, they were all very tired. They were dragged roughly to their feet and made to march again, still over the rough, moorland terrain. They were given nothing to eat this morning and only a minimal drink of water. They stumbled on, each wondering whether they were more miserable now than they were in the mountains. At least in the mountains, they had been free. They found it difficult to walk, as their feet were still tied, and they found they stumbled frequently, much to the amusement of the hobgoblins.

Just as they stopped for a brief respite for the hobgoblins (but not their captives) to have a brief bite and drink, one of their number suddenly clasped his head. He said something that Fero translated as "Blinding headache." Khland told him to get to his feet and to continue marching with the others. They almost felt sorry for him as he obviously felt very rough.

'You should not drink so much while on the march,' Khland told him. (Translated by Fero). In reply, the afflicted creature moaned that he hardly had any last night. The hobgoblin chief kicked him and told him to go ahead as a scout. Later in the day, they found his body lying in the heather, quite dead. As with the others, they stripped him and left him for the wild creatures.

'Do you think it's some disease that's killing them?' asked Kimi nervously.

'Possibly,' Asphodel speculated, 'but it seems very quick acting. I've not heard of anything like it.'

'Let's just hope it only affects hobgoblins, then,' said Carthinal.

Later in the day, it began to rain. A light drizzle only at first, but soon they were all wet through. The rain continued harder as the day progressed, and the captives were thoroughly miserable. The easterly wind continued and it seemed to go right through them, wet as they were. They could not talk any more as they were punched or kicked if they tried to communicate. They saw a creature flying high above them once or twice, but could not make it out clearly. Thadora hoped it was Muldee and that he could somehow get some help to them, but whenever it came lower, the hobgoblins fired bolts from their crossbows, and one came very close to hitting it, and it flew away again.

In this manner, the next day passed. That night, Fero began to shiver and sweat. He complained of aches and feeling unwell. Asphodel diagnosed "flu," but she hoped secretly it was nothing worse. She demanded to see Khland, and when he eventually came to them at dawn, she expressed her view that Fero could not travel; that he needed rest and warmth to recover. Khland growled that they had no time. Fero must continue with them or be left for the wild beasts.

'Have headache?' Khland asked Fero.

'I ache everywhere,' the ranger replied.

'You not got same illness as men?' he asked.

Asphodel replied for Fero.

'I'm sure it's not. Your men had a headache and then dropped. Fero has a fever and aches all over. I'm sure it's "flu" brought on by us being so cold and wet.'

'We be at hobgoblin camp less than two days. Only one more night on road.' With that, he hobbled back to his tent.

They all noticed he had started to limp rather badly, and that he still had Equilibrium strapped to his waist, and they each decided that caused him some pain. They found a grudging admiration for the hobgoblin captain to endure such pain as they knew the Sword could inflict. Then, the creature in the sky descended and drew their attention away from Khland. One of the hobgoblins raised his crossbow and took aim, but immediately he fell down clutching his head, unconscious. The other hobgoblins murmured among themselves, but one harsh look from Khland silenced them quickly.

'Kill him and we go on,' said Khland, and the others quickly complied.

They marched on for a while until Thadora felt what she later described as a "scratching in her brain." She tried to make it go away, and it did indeed fade a little, but then it began again more forcefully until she thought she could hear words in her head.

'Stop blocking, silly girl.'

She looked around but could see no one.

'It is me! Muldee!' she heard. 'I follow. I attack. I try chief next. He a big man. Hard to hurt. Others afraid. Think they have illness.'

She tried to think back to the little creature.

'I 'ear yer, Muldee. You're causing this "illness" in th' bleedin' 'obgoblins? 'Ow cool is that?'

'Yes. I make loud noise in heads. It kill little creatures. Many dragonets together can kill bigger creature. One dragonet only hurt hobgoblins. Maybe it enough. I go. Mindspeak make me tired. Need strength for hurting.'

Thadora passed on what she could to the others when no hobgoblins were looking so she would not get beaten. The news seemed to raise their hopes somewhat, even Fero, ill as he felt.

After about an hour, as they were marching along, Khland raised his hand to his head and stumbled, but he managed to regain his balance and limped on with a pained expression on his face. The rest of the party of hobgoblins looked at each other, then quickly away again. After a few more miles, Khland again stumbled, this time falling to his knees. He allowed a groan to escape his lips, but he struggled to his feet and staggered off down the road. Almost immediately, Muldee landed in the heather ahead of them. Carthinal hoped he had not landed too close to the hobgoblins, but they did not seem to notice as they were all looking anxiously at their leader, Carthinal thought, with hope in their eyes. The heather rustled as the dragonet tried to get nearer to the hobgoblin leader, and then he again fell down, this time, to lie face down on the track. He did not move. The other hobgoblins stood frozen for a few minutes and then one cautiously went forward and poked the immobile Khland. Still nothing. He came back to the others and said something in his own language. The hobgoblins held a brief discussion and then they came over to their captives and roughly searched them for any valuables, while two others went and systematically robbed Khland. The hobgoblins took all the gold the Wolves had on them but left them their armour. Carthinal supposed they did not consider it valuable enough to be worth carrying the extra weight. The Wolves' packs they were carrying, including the group's weapons, were dropped as they fled away from their captives and vicious leader.

After they were gone, Muldee appeared from the heather.

'Hurry. He not dead, just unconscious. Must leave quickly.'

'Thank you, but we can't move well tied up like this,' Carthinal told him. 'Can you do anything to help us escape?'

'I've spent time tryin' ter work meself loose,' Thadora responded, 'an' I think I've nearly succeeded in loosenin' th' rope enough ter slip me 'and out.'

'I bite through rope, too.'

Between them, they managed to get out of their bonds. They searched the hobgoblin leader and found no gold, but only the Sword. It seems the other hobgoblins had not dared to touch it. As Randa removed it from Khland, she noticed that his left leg looked as though it had frostbite and she felt a grudging admiration for the determination of the creature that he had continued to wear it, in spite of a great deal of pain.

'I think we should kill 'im,' said Thadora. 'After all, 'e bloody well 'urt us and wasted some of 'is own men when they was 'elpless. He's a soddin' brute.'

'And make us as bad as he is?' replied Asphodel. 'No, Thadora. I will not kill a helpless creature, nor be party to such an action, even if he is an evil brute.'

Picking up their dropped packs, they set off down the road, free once more.

Chapter 19
Shepherd

Fero could barely walk now, his fever getting worse; Davrael and Carthinal were half-carrying him. Asphodel declared they would have to find some shelter quickly, but this barren land had little in the way of buildings.

'There must be some people living around here,' exclaimed Basalt after they walked slowly on for around an hour, 'After all, there seem to be sheep on the hills. Someone must look after them.'

Then Carthinal spotted what he thought looked like a dwelling some distance ahead.

'Let's hope the occupants are friendly if the place is occupied at all,' he said. They all concurred with this hope.

When they eventually reached the hut, for it could be called little else, they noticed smoke coming from the chimney, indicating someone did live there. A pen stood at the side of the hut built with stone, like the hut itself, and the pen had a shelter, as well. A woodpile leaned at the other side of the hut, covered by a lean-to. Carthinal knocked on the door and called out.

'We are travellers who are in dire need of shelter. We will not harm you. Please, may we come in?'

A man's voice called out from inside, 'Few come this way. You are welcome. Enter.'

Carthinal suggested to Muldee that he remain outside at least for the moment, as they did not want to frighten whoever lived in the hut. They would call him if they felt the owner would welcome him. When the little creature agreed, they opened the door and found themselves in a small, one-roomed place. A fire burned in a hearth at one end of the room, in front of which were lying two, black and white sheepdogs. The room had little in the way of furnishings. A small bed stood against the opposite wall, a table in the centre with four chairs and two comfortable chairs by the fireside. The furniture was shabby and old, but serviceable, and fresh rushes lay on the floor. A delicious smell of stew came from a pot suspended over the fire. The companions' stomachs rumbled at the aroma.

'*Lamb and herbs, if I'm not much mistaken,*' thought Asphodel.

The sole occupant of the room sat in one of the chairs by the fire. It was an old man with grey hair and a gnarled face, but he had eyes of a bright and twinkling blue, indicating an intelligent and active mind.

'Pardon me if I don't get up to welcome you,' he said. 'My bones are not as young as they were. I keep saying I'll retire and go and live with my son and his wife down in the valley, but I know I'd miss these hills and the sheep. My son says I'm mad to not give up, but you know how it is. You are welcome to share my hut, such as it is. You are from Grosmer, I take it since you are speaking Grosmerian?'

'Yes, we are,' replied Carthinal. 'At least we came from there, and most of us call it home, even if we were not all born there. I take it that in our travels we've managed to cross the border. This is Pelimor, I assume?'

The man nodded.

'You crossed some way back, but on these moors, the border is not marked.'

'How is it that you speak Grosmerian so well?' queried Randa.

'I live near the border, so get the occasional traveller, and also, sometimes I used to take sheep over to the markets in Grosmer in my younger days, so I learned your language quite well.'

'Lucky for us, too,' replied Carthinal, 'None of us speak Pelimorese.'

'Please, may we get Fero somewhere to lie down?' Asphodel said rather sharply. 'He's nearly falling down as it is. We can do the introductions after he's settled.'

'Put your friend in the bed,' said the old shepherd. 'What's wrong with him? 'Flu is it? I ve a herbal preparation I take for that. It's very good, although the sickness has still to run its course, but it does help with the fever and seems to prevent the worsening of it.'

While Asphodel, with the help of Bas, got Fero out of his clothes and into the bed, the old man rummaged through a cupboard and found a bottle of some preparation. He and Asphodel went into a huddle to discuss the contents and dosage to give to the tall ranger. After a few minutes, he turned to them and told them to help themselves to the stew.

'You must be hungry. The stew is lamb. One of this winter's, only a few weeks old, but rejected by its mother. I failed to keep it thriving, so I killed it for the meat. It's good and tender.'

'I'm afraid we had all our gold stolen and so cannot pay you,' Carthinal told the old man, 'but we'll do whatever we can to help to recompense you for anything we eat or use. We are all fit and healthy, and can work for as long as we're here.'

'Don't worry about such things. You're my guests. Go ahead and eat.'

They did not need telling again, and quickly found bowls and spoons. They ate the lamb stew with gusto and after eating they all felt much better. Basalt got out his dwarven spirits that he had kept for "special occasions" and deemed this was one of them so they passed his flask round. The old man, who told them his name was Grandolin swallowed his share of the spirits and smiled. He spent the late winter and early spring in this hut as long as the sheep were lambing. He lived alone with his dogs, Fren and Crue, who helped him with the sheep.

'You are lucky to find me here. Lambing is almost over. A few ewes still to drop, then they will be turned out onto the moors. I'll visit from time to time to check on them, but this is the only time I spend any length of time here. Yon ranger looks in a bad way. You say you were robbed? By whom? There're few enough travellers hereby, and so no bandits and robbers.'

They told him about the capture by hobgoblins, leaving out the finding of the Sword, simply saying they were making their way to Pelimor in search of adventure. They also told him of the existence of Muldee and how the dragonet helped save them from the hobgoblins by using his mind skills.

'You young people!' he went on. 'Always so restless. You must go and find danger, although it seems to have no difficulty in finding a body even if you don't look,' Grandolin sighed. 'I suppose I was just the same at your age. You all look to be between sixteen and twenty-five. Am I right?'

'Actually, Asphodel, Basalt and I are above that in actual years, but in human terms, yes, I suppose you're right,' replied Carthinal.

Grandolin asked more about Muldee, and Carthinal fetched the dragonet indoors. The dragonet showed his pleasure to get out of the cold and he and Grandolin discussed the little creature's abilities.

'So what you do is not magic, then?'

'Carthinal say not. He cannot feel anything in what he calls "mana." I think what I do is something maybe anyone can do,' replied Muldee.

'Why do you think this?' asked the old man.

'I mind speak some of my friends. They hear me. I think they can block me, too, but they do not know what they do. Thadora can sometimes mind speak to me, too,' went on the dragonet.

Just then, Fero stirred and began to thrash about. Asphodel rushed over to him and listened to his breathing.

'Carthinal,' she called. The half-elf went over to her. 'I don't like this,' she told him. 'His breathing is bad. Listen to him. I fear he may have pneumonia. He can't be moved for some time.'

Grandolin came over.

'He's bad, isn't he?' he said. It was a statement, not a question. 'Poor young man. Pneumonia if I'm not mistaken. You must stay here until he's well, or…' His voice trailed away. 'My wife died of pneumonia,' he added softly. 'Twenty-five years ago tomorrow. And my first born… Still, this young man is exceptionally fit and strong. I expect he'll get over it. Many do, you know.'

That day, Asphodel remained by Fero's side, keeping him warm, and feeding him with a mixture the old man provided. Asphodel did not know this concoction, but reasoned it would do him no harm when she discussed its contents with Grandolin, and who knows, she reasoned, maybe this Peridorean old man knew something about healing, living as he did alone, and isolated for much of the year.

Halfway through the night, when the others were asleep on the floor of the hut, Randa came over to Asphodel where she still kept watch over Fero. Asphodel felt tired and had almost fallen asleep but would not leave her post. Randa approached and told her to get some sleep.

'I'll watch him and wake you if there's any change. You'll be no use to him or anyone else if you make yourself ill or too tired to function.'

The elf was only too grateful and impressed on Randa that she must wake her if there were any sign of change whatsoever. Randa took the cloth that Asphodel had been using to wipe Fero's head and sat down on the bed beside the tall man. Muldee sat at the head of the bed and crooned a little soothing tune to help Fero sleep more calmly.

In this manner, the night passed. The next morning, Asphodel once more took over and Randa got some sleep. The others all did some chores to help Grandolin. Basalt and Davrael chopped wood while Kimi and Thadora helped to birth a pair of twin lambs. This was much to the excitement of Thadora, who enjoyed yet another new experience, although Kimi had helped at the birth of foals. While they were doing this, Carthinal went with Grandolin and his two dogs to check on the other sheep on the moors.

Fero remained very sick and Asphodel began to despair, thinking they might lose him. He laboured in his breathing and he seemed barely conscious most of the time. Some of that time he was delirious, talking to people from his past.

'No. Papa, Please don't,' he cried one night and began to struggle to sit up and get out of bed. Randa sitting with him at the time, as she did most nights so that Asphodel could get some rest, and she soothed him with gentle words and stroked his hair. He settled again, saying, 'I'm all right, Mama. I'm not hurt. Are you hurt?'

'No, I'm not hurt, Fero. I'm all right,' Randa said to try to settle the ranger again, and at her words, he mumbled something she could not quite catch and drifted back to unconsciousness.

Another night, he began to cry.

'She's not dead. She can't be dead. I'll save her. Oh, my poor little Zepola. What will they do to you?'

This went on for five nights during which Randa soothed him, stroked his hair, and held him when he seemed in need of most comfort. In the quiet of the night, when all slept she wept. She realised how much the strength of this man had come to mean to her. She had been so dismissive of him, and the others, at the beginning of their quest, believing that all other classes and races were inferior, and put in the world to serve her and her class.

What a small-minded person she had been. How shallow her previous life seemed now. This band of adventurers, who would be treated as little more than thieves and beggars in some places, had taught her more of life and loyalty in a few weeks than she had learned in all her previous eighteen years. She wept at the thought of losing one of them. But it was more than that. Yes, she would weep at the loss of any one of them, but she felt deep within herself that this ranger from so far away had impacted her life in a much stronger way than any of the others. She felt drawn to him in a way she could not understand. His quiet voice, his steady presence, all filled her with a new sensation and when he looked at her as she combed her hair it felt as though his eyes were boring a hole in her head. She could scarcely prevent herself from looking around. She was always aware of his presence even when she could not see him. When he had touched her to help her over a difficult part of the mountain, she could feel his touch burning into her elbow for hours afterwards. And so she wept.

'Why are you crying, my Lady?' The voice sounded soft and a gentle hand brushed her long, silvery hair from her face. She raised her head and her tear-reddened, blue eyes met the almost-black ones of her charge.

'I thought you were going to die,' she replied, in a whisper, before she had time to think.

'And that gave you cause to cry? I'm honoured you thought me worth your tears.' His eyes held hers. She could not look away.

'I...I... Of course you're worth it. I...,' she paused, 'I promised to tell Asphodel if there was any change in your condition,' she said in a rush to cover her confusion, starting to get up. Fero reached out and held her arm.

'Sit with me for a few minutes longer. Please.' She obeyed his request and managed to look away from his gaze.

'How long was I sick?' he asked, 'And where are we? I remember being captured by hobgoblins, and being force-marched, and I remember some of them taking ill. Is that what I have had?'

'No. Asphodel said you had pneumonia from the exposure you had on the moors and the shepherd agreed. This is his hut. They've been dosing you with some medicine or other. We've been here five days now. The shepherd is very kind and is letting us stay in exchange for help with his chores. But I must tell Asphodel now or she will be very cross,' she gently removed his hand from where it still rested on her arm, 'and you must sleep. Proper sleep, not the restless kind you've had up to now.'

As she stood, he said, 'Wait, Randa. I've had such strange dreams. Of the past, and also I thought there was someone gently talking to me and holding me through the worst times.' His voice held a query.

Randa responded, 'I did what I could to help you, Fero.'

He looked up into her face and smiled.

'Go and get Asphodel now, my Lady,' and his eyes closed as he drifted into a normal and peaceful sleep.

Asphodel woke when Randa called softly to her and went to check on Fero. She declared that his sleep seemed more normal and that he seemed to have lost his feverishness.

'Randa, you go and get some sleep. I'll sit here now. It's nearly dawn anyway.'

Randa gratefully went and lay down in her blankets, spread on the rushes and soon fell fast asleep. She did not disturb until nearly noon, in spite of the others moving around her, and the two dogs coming over to sniff at her sleeping figure, wondering why she still slept in broad daylight.

Although Fero had mostly recovered from his illness, he still felt very weak. He remained in bed for two more days, then insisted on getting up. As soon as his feet touched the ground, he regretted his insistence as the room began to spin around him, but with typical determination, he struggled to one of the chairs by the fire. He felt as though he had walked ten miles. Asphodel watched him, though, and she settled him in, tucking a blanket round him. She and Randa took turns with caring for Fero, at Randa's insistence. The ranger seemed to take comfort from Randa's presence, a phenomenon that mystified the dwarf.

'He doesn't even like her,' he observed to Carthinal one day as the pair worked with the dogs rounding up the sheep.

'Doesn't he, my friend?' Carthinal smiled.

'He said to me once that she's beautiful on the outside and what a pity she's so ugly inside. That doesn't sound like someone who likes someone else.'

'Bas, Randa's changed,' Carthinal replied to his friend. 'She was a snob and, yes, something of a bigot as far as other races are concerned. Remember how she treated you and me in the library at the ducal palace in Hambara? We weren't humans, and therefore inferior. I think she used to think non-humans were not only inferior but also non-existent. She doesn't treat us like that anymore, does she?'

'Humph!' replied the dwarf. 'She's got used to us, but what about strangers? How will she feel about them? We'll have to go through S...Sill...the elven kingdom when we leave here.' Basalt struggled with the elven name for their land. 'That will be a true test of whether she's changed for real. She'll be surrounded by strange elves.'

One morning, Basalt came up to Thadora as she prepared some vegetables for the midday meal.

'I have something for you,' he said. 'Call it a belated birthday present if you wish.'

He held out his hand with a small wooden carving in it. Thadora took it and looked. She saw a young wolf, with its forelegs along the ground and its hindquarters raised. Its tail was obviously wagging. It was looking at a butterfly on a flower. A leather thong ran through a ring on the top of the carving.

'It's beautiful, Bas,' said the girl, passing the thong over her head. 'It's so, like, real. A young wolf cub playin' wi' a butterfly. What a cool idea. An' I've never had a real birthday present afore.'

Thadora showed it to the others and they all declared it a beautiful work of art.

'I suppose it supposed to be you, Red Cub,' said Davrael. His Grosmerian had improved with constant use and he made fewer mistakes now. He turned to the dwarf. 'It be nice for us all to have wolf symbol, you know, to show the world that we are one.'

Basalt decided to carve a wolf for each of them to wear. He tried to put some of each individual's character into their own particular pendant, and they all agreed he succeeded very well, and were pleased to wear their new symbols.

They remained there for two, more sixdays and then Fero declared he could travel. Asphodel and Randa would have liked to stay for a few more days to allow for a complete recovery, but they both thought they had put on Grandolin for long enough. The old shepherd insisted they took enough food with them to last for a sixday, as they had no gold to buy any more. They bade him farewell and he made them promise to call on him if ever they were in the area again. This they did, and they set off once more on their journey back to Hambara.

Chapter 20
Quantissarillishon

They travelled slowly, but soon left the high moorland and entered a country of rolling hills with little villages and farms studded between woods and fields. It was pleasant country, to the east of the Mountains of Doom, on a coastal strip between the mountains and the Bay of Pelimar. They walked steadily onwards, still pausing frequently until they came to a place where the mountains nearly met the sea itself. They strolled down onto the beach. It was a beautiful, sunny day and they felt very warm. The year rapidly progressed towards the summer solstice. The end of Kassidar approached, and the solstice would be in just over a month's time.

As they sat resting and watching the waves breaking over the rocks, Carthinal observed, 'The Duke will think we're dead we've been gone so long. We left Hambara on the nineteenth of Khaldar and still winter. Now here we are, nearing summer.'

'Over two months,' replied Randa. 'Poor father. Of course, he doesn't know I'm with you. He'll be worried about me by now. He'll have found out I'm not with my mother's people. I didn't expect it to take so long. I thought we'd be back within a month.'

'Most of us did, my Lady.' Fero had taken to calling her that since his illness, almost as a term of endearment. Randa smiled at him, and he smiled back, his eyes lighting up as he looked at her.

'There's something going on there,' whispered Basalt to Carthinal.

'You've noticed, too, then. I should have known you would,' replied the half-elf.

'A most unlikely pair, though. So different, and I'm not talking about appearance here. I don't know what's happened to him, but he certainly seems to have changed his view of her. I only hope she doesn't hurt him.'

'The attraction seems to be mutual, Basalt, my friend,' Carthinal reassured the dwarf, 'It's not unknown for a patient to fall for his healer you know.'

'Asphodel was his healer,' protested Basalt.

'Yes, but who sat with him, night after night, and held him when he was calling out and crying? They both think we were all asleep, but I saw how he cried, and I saw how Randa helped. I think she felt something for him before that, but his sickness eventually brought them together. Remember, you said something to me before?'

'Yeah!' Basalt remembered. 'I don't trust her, though. She's one of the upper classes. They don't marry the likes of us, Carthinal. He's bound to get hurt.'

Carthinal gazed out over the sea and thought maybe the dwarf was right. Nobility married other nobility, usually for some gain, either financial or political. They did not usually even mix with the common people. He hoped sincerely that Fero was not falling in love with Randa. He sighed. He could do nothing about it anyway. He had his own problems on that front. The more time he spent in Asphodel's company, the more he felt for her, but he could not allow his feelings to develop. He was not worthy of her.

Thadora interrupted his musings, 'Hey! Was that a dolphin out there? I thought I saw somethin'.'

They all looked to where Thadora pointed. Nothing could be seen, but suddenly, Asphodel cried out that she, too, had seen something. Soon, it became apparent that a pod of dolphins was driving fish into the bay. They watched the animals as they chased the fish, leaping out of the water as they did so. Then they disappeared as quickly as they had come.

'Wow!' exclaimed Thadora, 'I've never even seen th' sea before, an' now I've seen dolphins, too. Cool! What th' lads back in 'Ambara'd give ter see such things.' She grinned then. 'They'll never believe me when I tells 'em.'

The mention of "the lads" reminded them of Thadora's background and how she had been posing as a boy when they met her, a fact they had almost forgotten.

'You can't go back to your old life after this, Red Cub,' said Fero.

'What else am I to do then?' queried the young thief.

'You could come and train to be a ranger with me,' replied the other.

'That'd be real cool, Fero,' replied the girl. 'I'll think about it.'

It was such a beautiful day that they decided to spend the rest of it there on the beach. The mountains raised their heads behind them, looking slightly hazy in the blue sky, and no clouds drifted across the heavens. The beach was made of beautiful, golden sand and it reminded Carthinal of Yssa's hair. He felt a little guilty that he had not thought of her for weeks, but there were no strings attached to their relationship, so he put his guilt behind him in contemplation of the view. A slight breeze ruffled Asphodel's hair, which had now grown down to her shoulders. He thought how beautiful she looked, and then suppressed the thought ruthlessly. He must not think of her in that way. He lay back and felt the warmth of the sun on his face and drifted into a shallow sleep, listening to the murmur of his friends' voices and the cries of the seabirds overhead.

Within a day, they were at the border of Pelimor and Rindissillaran as the elves called their land. Asphodel stopped in surprise to see guards at the border.

The guards stopped them saying, 'Qua quioresti?'

'Llandorer quiero,' Asphodel replied. 'Sha broniler quieres?' then she turned to the others. 'He asks who we are. I told him we are travellers and then asked him why there is a guard here.'

'Shill llinoresti?'

'As Quantissarillishon llinero.'

Asphodel translated and told them the guard had asked where they were going, and she had told him Quantissarillishon, the elven capital.

'Are we going there?' queried Fero.

'Yes. We need to pass through it on our way back to Grosmer,' Asphodel replied. 'We'll also pass through Erian, too.'

The guard spoke again to Asphodel. Carthinal could make out a few words, but his elvish was none too good, and he could not get the proper sense of what they were saying. Asphodel told them the guard answered her previous question by saying there had been sightings of orcs and hobgoblins, and some said trolls, too, in the vicinity of the borders. They were concerned, so there were patrols all along the borders and guards at all the road crossings into the land. The guard went on to say that there was a strange creature, the like of which no one had ever seen before, around the border with Erian. He had not seen it himself, and descriptions were varied, so he could not tell them exactly what it looked like, but all agreed that it had a fearsome aspect, and was very large.

The captain came out of a small hut and spoke to the guard. Carthinal understood that he thought the guard should not talk so much to people who were foreigners and ordered him to get on with his job. The guard then spoke to Asphodel again.

'He wants us to show him what we have in our packs,' she told the others.

'Precious little,' pointed out Bas, opening his. The guard did a thorough inspection and then passed them.

'I held my breath a bit there; I have to admit,' Fero told them as they walked on down the road. 'I couldn't help but remember the last time someone searched me thoroughly.'

'We were safe there as long as we had nothing incriminating,' Asphodel told him. 'We elves may often be suspicious of others, but we don't frame people.'

Fero felt a bit ashamed of his reaction but smiled at her as she said, 'I understand your fears, though, Fero. It must have been most unpleasant being framed for something you didn't do.'

Randa looked uncomfortable, 'I apologise for that, Fero. My father was way out of order there.'

'Don't worry about it. It's over now. I'll forget it in time. I've forgiven your father anyway, if only because he has such a beautiful daughter.'

Randa blushed at these words and fell silent as they walked along the road leading to the Elven capital city.

The sun continued to shine all day and into the next. At first, they passed through lands with broom and gorse, all in flower, and the blue harebells were blooming at their feet. Then the vegetation began to change. There were hazels in their fresh, green leaves, elder with their creamy, white blossom, and bluebells carpeting the ground beneath the trees. Daisies dotted the grass along with red poppies in clearings, and there were foxgloves growing in every available space. Then they found themselves in taller woodland, mainly birch and alder, which gave way eventually to tall oaks and beech. The early summer flowers were in bloom and butterflies flitted between them. Bees buzzed, birds sang and so did the eight travellers as they walked, a habit they had got into at the beginning of their travels, but they had not felt much like it since being lost in the mountains. Suddenly,

Thadora stopped in her tracks, so suddenly that Kimi, who happened to be behind her, actually bumped into the young thief.

'Hey, Carthinal!' she called to the mage who was several yards ahead by now, having not been aware of the traffic jam behind him.

He stopped. 'What now, Red Cub?' he called back to her, 'Have you suddenly seen a butterfly or perhaps a squirrel searching for last winter's nuts?'

'No, don't be so silly. But, hey, yer know as 'ow we've, like, got no readies?' she called.

'It hadn't escaped my notice.'

'Well, we're goin' ter 'ave ter stay somewhere in Quanti… Quanti…whatsit, aren't we?'

'Quantissarillishon,' Carthinal corrected her.

'Yeah. Whatever. Well, we need, sort of, to 'ave some bleedin' gold for that, don't we?'

'Ye-es. What are you leading up to, Thadda?'

'Why don't we sing for our supper, then? We're not 'alf bad. In fact, I think our singing's wicked. I bet we c'd earn loads. It'd be real cool, Carthinal.'

'Hmm. Not a bad idea, Red Cub. Perhaps we should consider it.'

The idea of "singing for their supper" was thus put into their minds.

They passed a few, small hamlets and farms on their way towards the capital, but with no money, they decided to fend for themselves. It was different when they stayed with the old shepherd they argued. Then, they had a sick companion who needed a roof and proper food and care, and they could help him with some of his tasks. They were grateful for his kindness and vowed to return someday with gold to recompense him for what they had eaten.

Eventually, they approached Quantissarillishon, the capital of the Elven nation. At least, Asphodel said they were there, but the others could see little evidence of a city. The road continued to wind through the forest, but now there were a few sidetracks. They could be called little other than tracks, though, and no one could see any buildings. There were more people on the road than previously thought, indicating that there was a habitation nearby.

'Well, where is this fabled city of the elves, then?' demanded Basalt, looking round.

Asphodel laughed, 'All around you, if you look, dwarf.'

They looked and gradually became aware there were buildings, but all artfully constructed to look like trees. The walls were curved like trunks, and doors and windows looked like knots or holes in the wood. There were even dwellings built into the trees themselves, as well as some in the branches, high above the forest floor.

'It's marvellous,' said Fero. 'So artfully done, as to not impinge on the environment of the forest at all.'

'Yes,' replied Asphodel, 'the elves who designed the city didn't want to harm the wildlife or to destroy the beauty of the surroundings, so they came up with the idea of making it blend in.'

'We should find a place make our idea of entertaining people a reality,' said Davrael, practically. 'Are there inns near here, Asphodel?'

She took them down a side street until they came to a building that looked like an enormous redwood tree. She entered through a door cut in the huge trunk and the others followed to find themselves in the common room of an inn. A bar ran half way round the curved wall opposite the door and a minstrel's gallery to the left with steps going up to it on each side. Opposite the gallery stood a fireplace, which, since it was warm, had a large arrangement of flowers in lieu of a fire. A door opened off the room next to the fireplace.

Asphodel spoke to the bartender in elvish, told him they were wandering entertainers, and they would be willing to entertain his guests that evening for board and lodging.

After some negotiation, Asphodel turned to the others.

'He says we're welcome to entertain his guests but only one night is no use. He'd only have his usual clientele and would make no profit. In fact, giving us board and lodging would leave him out of pocket. He suggests we agree to stay for at least four days in order for the word to get around. If, after that time, he's not at least covered our expenses in profit, he'll charge us any excess. Anything we make over and above that is ours. (Subject to him making a profit, of course). I told him I'd put it to you and see what you think.'

'Sounds a good deal to me,' said Basalt.

'What if we don't make enough to cover our expenses, though?' said Kimi, practically.

'Let's consider that if and when we get to it,' said Randa. 'I'm sure we can make enough for a room and meals.'

'Four days,' Carthinal ruminated. 'We should really be getting on our way as quickly as possible. We've been delayed enough as it is.'

'An' 'ow 're we gonna pay ferr food an' stuff? Or are yer sayin' we starve? That's so not cool,' Thadora told him.

They eventually agreed to the terms and were shown to rooms upstairs behind the door by the fireplace. Shortly afterwards, a young elf maid appeared and shyly told them that a meal was ready in the common room if they would like to partake. They went down the stairs and entered the room where there was a small gathering of the landlord and bar staff, as well as several children who turned out to be the children of the landlord and his wife, who did the cooking and kept the books.

They ate a delicious meal, and when they had finished, Asphodel insisted they come with her "to hear something not to be missed," she said mysteriously.

It was getting towards dusk, and the Wolves followed Asphodel towards a grove of oaks in the centre of the city. Here, lamps were being lit, and many elves gathering. Then a beautiful sound filled the air. A choir of elves, all dressed in green, entered the grove from the West, singing.

> *'Ah equillin ssishinisi*
> *Qua vinillaquishio quibbrous*
> *Ahoni na shar handollesno*
> *As nas brollenores.*
>
> *Ah equilin bellamana*
> *Qua ssishinisi llanarones*
> *As wma ronalliores*
> *Shi nos Grillon prones.*
>
> *Ah equilin dama Grillon*
> *Pro llamella shilonores*
> *As nos rellemorres*
> *Drapo weyishores.*
>
> *Yam shi Grillon yssilores*
> *Grazlin everr nos pronores*
> *Wama vinsho prolle-emo*
> *Lli sha rallemorres.'*

'That is so beautiful,' whispered Thadora as the song ended and the choir made their way out of the grove. 'What's it mean?'

'It's the elves hymn to the evening star. Grillon's star, we call it. It is sung each evening in Quantissarillishon.It translates approximately as

*"Oh star of the evening
Shining brightly
You give us hope
In the deepening night.*

*'Oh beauteous star
Who heralds the evening
You tell us all
That Grillon guards us*

*'Oh Grillon's star
As you sink westwards
Return again
To guard the dawn.*

*'Ensure that Grillon
Through darkness keep us
Safe from all evil
Until the morn.'"*

So, each with the memory of the beautiful, elven song still ringing in their ears, the companions walked through the streets of Quantissarillishon, back to the inn where they were to perform for the first time that evening full of trepidation for what they had taken on.

Later, they stood in the room that Carthinal, Fero, and Basalt shared. They had changed out of armour and were ready to descend to the minstrel's gallery. They were surprised to see a hurriedly-written poster on the inn door proclaiming that during the evening there would be singing by, "Wolf."

"Come and hear the Wolves sing," it said.

'I feel sick,' said Thadora, suddenly, and rushed out of the room.

'Oh dear! I hope she'll be all right,' worried Asphodel.

'Just first night nerves, I expect,' Fero replied. 'She'll be fine once we get started.'

They had decided on a running order, and as soon as Thadora returned, they descended the stairs to the common room, crossed it and mounted to the minstrel's gallery. A ripple of applause ran round the crowd, but then people continued their conversations. Wolf stood on the gallery and looked down.

'Go on, Fero,' whispered Randa, digging the tall ranger in the back. Fero swallowed hard and stepped forward. Without a word, he launched himself into the work song he taught them on the way from Hambara. His deep, bass voice surprised the elves and the minor key of the song seemed to entrance them, too, because soon everyone stopped their conversations to listen. After the first couple of verses, the rest of Wolf joined in, harmonising as they had practised on the road so many times. Muldee, too, joined in, with his voice blending in a harmonious accompaniment with the others. At the end of the song, there was tumultuous applause. They went through their repertoire song by song, each individual beginning their own song with a solo, and the others joining in after a time.

Suddenly, between songs, Thadora, whom Carthinal had noticed fiddling with her boots, removed them and sprang up onto the rail that ran along the edge of the gallery. She ran along it from one end to the other and then walked to the middle. Here she stood on her hands, and slowly brought her feet over her head until she stood upright once more. She then flipped head over heels along the rail. Finally, she stood again on her hands, lowered herself to her head and rolled to a position straddling the bar. She again lifted herself to her hands, and with a back somersault, landed back on the gallery, facing the crowd. While the crowd applauded, Carthinal pulled her round to face him, rather roughly. He gave her a little shake. She could see by his eyes he was angry, but he smiled with his mouth. For the benefit of the crowd, she supposed.

'If you ever pull another stunt like that, Thadora, I'll personally leather your backside,' he said, through clenched teeth.

Thadora pulled free of his grip.

She grinned impudently. 'You'd 'ave to catch me first,' she laughed at him, 'But hey, the punters loved it.'

'I caught you once before, didn't I?' growled the mage.

'Yeah! But you, like, cheated. You used magic. That was so not fair,' grinned Thadora, unabashed by the half-elf's anger.

'You could have fallen and been injured doing all that acrobatic stuff on the rail.'

'Oh! That's why yer mad at me! I'm touched that you care,' the girl put her head on one side and looked up into Carthinal's blue eyes which at that moment looked like a stormy sea. 'You forget. I'm a thief. I c'n do all sorts o' cool things. Some acrobatics're sort o' useful when, like climbin' through winders or, runnin' across roofs to escape. I c'n even sometimes dodge arrows, and I once caught one out o' th' air.'

Carthinal's anger quickly evaporated. Everyone found it difficult to stay angry at Thadora's exuberance. 'All right then,' he replied, 'I'm sorry for shouting at you. I was afraid for you, that's all. I wasn't expecting it.'

'Can we keep it in, then?' Thadora asked.

Carthinal sighed. 'Maybe. We should talk about it. Just don't do it without prior notice, that's all.'

Wolf had been a great success. Randa and Asphodel went down to the common room to collect any money the customers wished to give, and they made enough to cover their costs if the innkeeper made no extra profit, and a little over. They were in high spirits, having enjoyed their foray into show business. They discussed having Thadora perform her acrobatics as a regular part of the act, as well as suggesting to Carthinal he add a little magic, too. He took some persuading, as he told them that magic was not an entertainment, but a serious business. Eventually, he agreed, though. At that moment, there a tap sounded at the door.

'Rill printheiron, Genori naravase,' the little elf maid said, timidly.

'Vandirrer dri ar yir llinisheress,' replied Asphodel, taking a tray from her.

The girl bobbed a curtsey, and left quickly, keeping her eyes down.

'The landlord thought we might like this, the girl said.' Asphodel told them. 'I thanked her very much.'

Basalt was investigating the tray. There were two bottles of wine, one white and one red, and a bottle of dwarf spirits. He studied the label.

'Ah! This is a really good one. You must try it, Fero. It's made near my home village, and, as we say in dwarvish "Thrin khlan grinnor rhikpe."'

'What's that mean in Grosmerian?' asked Thadora.

'You don't want to know,' Fero, who knew some dwarvish, hastily put in, and, raising a finger as the dwarf turned to him and said, 'Don't you dare translate that, Basalt Strongarm. There are ladies present.'

Basalt grinned and bowed to the ladies. 'I hear and obey. If you two gentlemen wish to know, I'm afraid it's too bad. My good friend here won't allow it.'

'I know some dwarvish, too,' pointed out Carthinal, 'and I concur with Fero. Ladies, it's a rather obscene dwarven expression used in the same context that we might say, "It will make a man of you."'

'Carthinal. I've 'eard every soddin' expression there is, an' know every bleedin' swear word in th' language, an' used most,'argued Thadora. 'By Zol's balls, I won't be shocked.'

'Too bad,' came the reply from Fero. 'You're not going to add dwarven obscenities to your repertoire.'

'No, Daddy. Sorry, Daddy,' This with an impudent grin. Fero made a half-hearted swipe at her, which she easily ducked.

Meanwhile, Basalt poured himself a generous measure of the spirits in a glass. He offered it round to all. Fero accepted, and so did Thadora, but the others refused.

'I'm not sure you should be drinking that stuff,' observed Randa. 'You're only a child.'

'I were sixteen in Grilldar,' pointed out Thadora. 'That makes me legally an adult. Anyways, you're only two years older. You're not even me big sister ter be concerned.'

'I'm not drinking dwarf spirits, in case you hadn't noticed, and big sister or not, I'm just showing some concern for your well-being.'

Thadora poked her tongue out and took a sip of her drink. She then nearly collapsed in a fit of coughing. 'Hey! That's strong!' she exclaimed. For her next mouthful, she took a much smaller sip and declared it good.

The next morning, seven of Wolf descended for breakfast.

'Where's Red Cub?' asked Basalt.

'Huh!' said Randa. 'She's a bit unwell. Thanks to you and your precious dwarf spirits. We left her moaning about wanting to die and throwing up.'

'She should get up and have a drink of water. Some fresh air would help, too.'

'Not allowing a young, inexperienced girl to drink strong drink would have helped even more,' Randa replied waspishly.

'Now, Randa, don't get mad at me,' Basalt pleaded. 'I'd like to see anyone stop her from doing what she wants. As to being inexperienced, no one from the Warren in Hambara can be described as such.'

Breakfast arrived in time to stop the argument. The dwarf and the Duke's daughter kept throwing unfriendly looks towards one another all through the meal. After breakfast, the seven companions who were fit set off to explore still further the wonders of this city. Asphodel wanted to show them the royal palace, supposedly one of the wonders of the world.

The seven travellers then spent the morning looking around the wonderful city of the elves. The elves lived as close to nature as could be possible and most of their dwellings were in the trees. Walkways hung from one tree to the next, all made to look like vines scrambling through the treetops.

Davrael was the least impressed of the Wolves, not having a head for heights, and he almost refused to go up at first, but Kimi teased him so much that eventually he reluctantly climbed up. Even he had to admit that the sight of the Royal Palace was worth it. It seemed to grow out of the trees and be a part of them too. It was not excessively large but the carvings were beautiful and elicited praise from Basalt.

All too soon, it was time to go back to the inn to see how Thadora was, and the party reluctantly climbed down from the trees.

Chapter 21
Bandits

The increase in his business due to the new entertainers pleased the innkeeper so much that he used his utmost charm to encourage them to stay for longer. In the event, Wolf agreed to stay for an extra two days over the agreed four. They hesitated to add even these two days, but they eventually agreed. The whole group decided they should not stay for more than two extra days for two reasons: Firstly they needed to return to Hambara as soon as possible, and secondly, the populace of the elven capital would eventually become tired of the "entertainers" and seek a new novelty. They gave this second reason to the innkeeper.

On Zoldar six, therefore, they once more took to the road, bound this time towards the land of Erian. With the gold that they made in their brief, but lucrative, career as entertainers, they booked their journey with a caravan heading to the town of Frelli, the capital of Erian. The journey took four days, but with wagons to sleep in, and a plentiful supply of food and drink, they found it much more comfortable than most of their journeying so far.

They found the capital city in a state of excitement. There were a lot of people on the streets, mostly heading towards one particular building, where they would enter, and a few minutes later come out again, with no apparent reason. Only Asphodel knew anything of the language, having lived there for a short time, and she asked the locals, what was going on, in rather halting Erian.

'It seems there is some sort of choosing of the government going on. They call it an "election",' she told them. 'Householders in each city, town and village go to a certain place where they choose whom they want to represent them on a council. The country is divided into a number of different areas. The councils from each area then choose someone to come to the capital city to form the government. The main person, who acts like a king, or the Elflord I suppose, is chosen from the people sent to the capital. He's called The Master. He chooses the people to do various jobs in the government, much as a king does. But'–and here she paused,– 'what is strange is that The Master only reigns for five years. He can be re-elected, but not more than twice. If he has children, they do not automatically go into the government or follow him into office. In fact, anyone in the country can become a councillor, member of the government or even Master. (If you're a householder that is).'

'It is indeed a strange system!' replied Basalt.

'I suppose it works for them,' replied Carthinal, 'or they would have scrapped the system.'

They discussed the merits of various systems of government until darkness fell and they retired to the rooms assigned to them in the inn where they had stopped. A king or similar ruler ruled most of the countries on the continent of Khalram. The Elflord, a hereditary role, traced through the female line, ruled the elves. The son (or daughter) of a ruler would not usually inherit, but the inheritance passed to the eldest child of his eldest sister, or nearest female relative if he had no sisters. Davrael then pointed out that in his country, there were many tribes, each with its own chief, and were constantly at war with one another. In some ways, it seemed a little like Pelimor that they had passed through. There, each city and town had its own government, forming a number of city-states. They were held together by little more than language and customs. They, too, warred with one another.

It took them a full sixday to reach the border. Here, Asphodel picked up that the elections were all completed and a new government had been sworn in. People were very surprised as a totally unknown man had emerged as the new Master. His name, they said, was Wolnarb, and he was a mage. In fact, he was a magister, the highest rank a mage could reach. A charismatic man, the people they asked told them, and the people had high hopes for the new regime. They could feel a sense of optimism in the air.

At last, they crossed the border into Grosmer and found themselves in the border town of Meridore. Asphodel knew the town, and found them an inn to stay in. They inquired about journeying towards Hambara, but they had just missed a caravan. The next one would not leave for another sixday the innkeeper told them, so they decided to make their way back under their own steam.

The Wolves only allowed themselves one night in Meridore, and then onward along the road towards the little town of Roffley. They left Meridore on a beautiful day with the sun shining in a cloudless sky. It had rained on the journey across Erian, and now the air seemed to have a sparkle. The Wolves were in high spirits, feeling they could see the end of their journey. Admittedly, they still had to cross half of Grosmer before they got back to Hambara, but at least they were in the right country, and the weather was sunny and warm.

'My father's going to be very angry,' Randa said one day. 'He'll have been worried about me. Well, there's nothing I can do about that now. I'll just face the music when I get home. He won't be angry for long. He never is.'

'What concerns me more is what he'll say and do to the rest of us,' Carthinal told her. 'He'll probably think we should have sent you home and not allowed you to come with us.'

'I'd like to have seen you try, Carthinal,' said Fero with a fond glance at Randa. He put his arm round her shoulders and hugged her to himself. 'This girl has a mind of her own.'

The romance between Fero and Randa continued to blossom as they travelled on their way westwards, and now they admitted to the others, as well as themselves, how they felt about each other. However, the group of friends had an unspoken agreement that they would say nothing about it to the Duke. It worried Randa as to what her father would think of her falling in love with a ranger—a man who could not settle in the city and help to rule it like the consort of a duchess should. The fact he came from a foreign country and was a commoner did not seem to be a problem she considered. That problem could easily be overcome, and her father never thought anyone was beneath him. (Unlike the Randa of a few months previously). He always said he had been given his position as one of service to the people, and not vice versa, trying to instil the idea into his snobbish daughter.

One day, as they were walking along a small ridge, with trees on either side, Randa became aware of the Sword vibrating and giving her a tingling feeling. She looked down and half drew it out of its scabbard.

'That's what it did just before the hobgoblin attack,' she whispered. 'Perhaps we should be on our guard.'

They had hardly begun to prepare themselves when a voice came from among the trees to their left. 'Halt and drop your weapons. Mage! Don't you make a move or a sound or you're dead. I've men all around with bows pointing at your hearts. A single move will be your death.'

The Wolves looked at each other.

'*Not again!*' thought Asphodel. She was beginning to get fed up with being captured. First, it had been hobgoblins and now bandits. A man stepped from beneath the trees to their left. They all reluctantly allowed their weapons to fall to their feet. Bows, slings, crossbow and swords all dropped to the ground.

'And your dagger, mage. But move slowly—very slowly.'

Carthinal drew his dagger from its sheath, which he kept fastened to his forearm. He did nothing to indicate he had another in his boot, and Thadora still had her throwing knives, he remembered. She retrieved them each time she used them, except for the one she used on the beast in the tomb.

Carthinal watched the man, carefully. He did not seem quite like the usual brigand. He was dressed in shabby clothes, but the cut and the cloth were good, and his speech indicated good education and breeding. His face was hidden both by the shadows of the trees, and the large-brimmed hat he wore. Carthinal suspected he may also have some kind of mask on, but could not be sure. The brigand called to his men in the trees and six approached, sheathing their weapons.

'Search them,' he ordered. Then, turning to the companions, he said, 'I've other men still in hiding, so don't think you can try anything.'

The men searched and found the hidden throwing daggers Thadora held back.

'Tut-tut!' the chief brigand tutted. 'What a naughty, little girl to try to hide her weapons when she's been told to drop them. Should we punish her, men?'

The men laughed. An ugly sound.

'What should we do with her, Boss?' one of them asked.

'I'll think about it and decide. I'll tell you later if you can have her,' replied his leader. 'Now, we can't let them go without armour, so we'll leave them that. And some weapons. There're bad people about on the road, you know. Bandits and the like!' He laughed. 'However, we'll have that pretty Sword there,' pointing to Equilibrium, 'and your helmet,' he said to Davrael. 'Of course, your gold and any jewellery or other trinkets you have, that goes without saying. Take those things, men. And that creature you have on your shoulder,' he told Thadora, pointing to Muldee, 'Should bring a small fortune. Dragonet, isn't it? Thought they were just a myth.'

The brigands pulled the helmets from their heads none too gently, and removed their other jewellery, then one of them went to pick up the Sword.

He quickly dropped it. 'It burned me,' he cried out, showing his blistering hand to his companion. The others drew back from the Sword, all reluctant to try to pick it up.

'I put a curse on it,' improvised Carthinal. 'No one can steal it.'

He did not want the bandits to suspect it was anything other than an ordinary sword, albeit an excellent one. He certainly did not want them to suspect its magical character, although they would have been unlikely to suspect its true nature.

The leader looked around the group, standing defiantly in the middle of the road. He looked at Randa twice. With the removal of her helmet, her hair and face could easily be recognised.

'Well! Well! Well!' he said, 'If it isn't the Lady Randa of Hambara. What are you doing with this riffraff, my Lady? A bit of a comedown, isn't it? And I always thought you despised the masses, especially other races, but here you are in company with a dwarf, elf and half-elf, not to mention three foreigners. What would your father think, my dear?' He stepped out into the road as he spoke.

Randa gasped in surprise. 'Sandron!' she exclaimed. 'What are you doing with a bunch of bandits?'

'I'm their leader, my dear,' replied Sandron, 'and now you are my captives. Tie them up and take them to the camp. At least one of them is worth a ransom. Make sure they don't see where we go.'

With that, the bandits bundled them up and tied their hands. The bandits blindfolded them and turned them around until none of them knew which direction they faced. They unceremoniously bundled Muldee into a sack that one of the bandits carried, before he had time to take off. Then, they were pushed forward, none too gently. They twisted and turned through the forest. Carthinal thought it was not so much because the way wound around, but to further disorientate them.

After walking for about half an hour, they eventually stopped, and their blindfolds were removed. It did not surprise Carthinal to see the man Randa referred to as Sandron standing in front of a tent, stripped of his leather armour, and drinking from a wine flask. He had obviously been there for some time, proving the bandits took a circuitous route to the camp. He looked round to get his bearings. The bandit camp was a conglomeration of tents set in a large clearing in the forest. Various sizes of tents clustered haphazardly around, with campfires burning in front of several of them. Carthinal estimated he could see about thirty men and twenty women, with a number of children scurrying about the place. This was obviously a well-established group of bandits who knew each other well. How Randa came to know the leader he could not begin to guess. Sandron addressing Randa interrupted his musings.

'Well, Randa. Now that I've captured you, I think I'll send word to your father. He'll pay a mighty ransom to get you back. Everyone in Grosmer knows how he dotes on you.'

Randa drew herself up, and once more became the imperious girl they had known only a few months before. She could still put on her haughty stare, it seemed. She used it now.

'And when he pays it, and I tell him just whom he has been dealing with, what then? How will your father react to his youngest son being a brigand?'

Carthinal saw this took the wind out of the young man's sails. He visibly deflated.

'You always could get the better of me, Randa,' he sighed. 'It would have been a good idea, but unfortunately you recognised me. With hindsight, I shouldn't have stepped forward as I did, but I was so surprised to see you there that I didn't think.'

'You never did, Sandron, at least not until later. Then, it was often too late. Are you going to leave us tied up? It is most uncomfortable, you know.'

'I'm sorry, my Lady,' replied Sandron, effecting a court bow. Then he turned to a man standing just behind and to his right. 'Undo their bonds and return their weapons. You!' he called to another man. 'Bring some decent food and wine to my tent. Enough for...' he paused to count, 'Nine. What about your dragonet? What does it eat?'

'I'll be fine with a little meat,' replied the said creature from his perch on Thadora's shoulder, which he had taken as soon as Sandron opened the sack to release him, 'although, I actually prefer fish. And for your information, I'm he not it.'

Sandron nearly fell down in surprise. 'I didn't know they could talk!' he exclaimed.

'Obviously,' replied Muldee, with a laugh. 'You should have seen your face just then. You nearly fell off your perch. (Metaphorically speaking that is).'

Muldee had perfected his Grosmerian, as he had picked it directly from the minds of his companions. Unknown to them, he was also nearly word perfect in Beridonese, Fero's language, as well as Dwarvish, and the language of the plains that Davrael and Kimi spoke. He had also picked up the thieves' cant spoken in the ghettos of the large towns from Thadora and Carthinal.

Sandron escorted the now, freed prisoners into his tent. It was lavishly furnished for a bandit leader's tent. It seemed Sandron did not wish to forgo too, many, creature comforts.

Two women hastily covered a table with a cloth. The tent only boasted two chairs. Sandron ordered more to be brought so they could all sit at the table. On the floor were rugs which, although they had seen better days, were of value. There were two comfortable chairs situated to one side of the tent on either side of a brazier which was unlit, it being a warm afternoon. A curtain hung across the back portion. Carthinal supposed that Sandron's sleeping quarters were there.

When the chairs were situated around the table, Sandron invited the friends to sit. This they did readily, except for Randa who remained standing, looking at her most haughty.

'I'm sorry, my Lady,' Sandron apologised. 'I forget my manners. I'm not used to grand ladies in my humble abode.' He went to draw out a chair at the head of the table for Randa to sit.

She was behaving just like a duchess, Carthinal thought, which was, of course, what she was going to be one day. He glanced at the others. Fero looked rather down, he thought. He had obviously just been reminded of how far apart their status was.

'*Poor Fero,*' thought Carthinal. '*I hope they can manage to sort it out.*'

'Now, Randa,' began Sandron, when the food arrived and was served, 'Tell me what you're doing with this group of adventurers, and does your father know?'

Randa looked towards Carthinal. Sandron followed her gaze with a look of surprise, realising she looked at Carthinal for permission to speak of their journey.

'We were on a journey for my father,' she told him, at a slight nod from Carthinal, being slightly economical with the truth of her part in the said journey. 'I am not at liberty to divulge the purpose of our quest, I'm sorry to say, but these, my companions, were chosen by my father for the task. Allow me to introduce them.'

She then went round the group telling Sandron their names and professions, introducing Carthinal as their leader. After she had finished the introductions, she gave a brief account of their journey, omitting any part of the finding of the Tomb. She did, however, explain how they found Muldee, and told of their rescue from death in the blizzard by the yeti pair. The fact that the yeti were not only intelligent creatures, but were not hostile either, surprised Sandron.

After telling their tale, she turned her blue eyes on him and asked, 'Now, you must tell us why you are here, leading a band of brigands, and not either in your father's castle or at court.'

'All right. That's only fair.' He turned to the others. 'Randa and I have known each other a long time. My father and hers are old friends, and we spent time together as children. In fact, we shared a tutor once. Do you remember old Snagtooth, Randa?'

Randa chuckled. 'Poor man. We did give him a hard time, didn't we?' She turned to the other Wolves. '"Snagtooth" wasn't his real name. That was "Professor Snaggletuf", but we called him "Snagtooth" because he had uneven teeth, and his name, unfortunately, adapted quite well.'

Sandron laughed aloud with pleasure at the memory. 'It was Brand who gave him the name if I remember correctly, but old, straight-laced Larrin told us we should have more respect for…' and here he put on a high-pitched voice with a nasal drawl, '"Our learned professor."' That was before you became "Her High and Mightiness the Duchess in Waiting, The Lady Randa." I'm glad to see you seem to have dropped that stand, at least with your friends.'

Randa ignored his comments and went on with her tale.

'Yes. Larrin was a pain, wasn't he? Always trying to stop us from getting into mischief. "For our own good," I think he said.' She turned to the others who were looking mystified. 'Brand and Larrin are Sandron's brothers. Larrin is the eldest, then Brand, and lastly comes Sandron. Larrin always thought of himself as an exemplary student. And a total pain. Brand was all right, though. How is he, Sandron?'

'Oh, he's fine. He's in the army now and a captain. Believe it or not, he's expected to go far. I think he's up for promotion again, soon. Anyway, that's part of the reason I'm here, which is what you asked, Randa, I think.'

'How can your brother be a reason for you to be outside the law?'

'Larrin has his career mapped out. He'll inherit both title and lands. My father is the Duke of Sendolina,' he added for the benefit of the others. 'My father arranged for Brand to go into the army. It's a good career, there are no wars or the probability of a war, and if there is one in the future, at least by then, Brand will have been able to get to a position where he needn't be involved in the fighting. I am a third son. There's little chance of me ever inheriting the title, and when father dies, there will be little left for me. I don't think I could take the discipline of the army. You know me, Randa. Always was a free spirit, as you liked to call it. (Father called it pig-headed disobedience as I recall). Now, I like my creature comforts. Many third and subsequent sons have ended up with little and died in poverty. Others have taken a career—merchant or something and made money like that. Me, I'm a gambler. I like danger and excitement. A staid job as a clerk or even a merchant would never satisfy me, and I most certainly could never go into the church.' He looked at Asphodel. 'I'm sorry if I offend you, Sister Asphodel, but I'm just not the religious type. So, I occasionally take myself to the woods and become a Robber Baron.'

Thadora had been thinking, and her thoughts, unknown to her, had run on the same lines as Carthinal's.

Carthinal now voiced a question she was wondering about, 'How old are you, Sandron, if you don't mind me asking?'

'Twenty,' he replied. 'Why do you ask?'

'It just seems very young to be the leader of such a group, especially since you're not born to the life. They must have been very suspicious at first. From what I know of robber gangs,' Carthinal thought carefully about what he said, 'There usually has to be some kind of contest, usually to the death, to become leader.'

'Ah! I see what you're getting at. Have I become a killer? No. I was just very, very lucky. I joined the gang as an ordinary member, just for fun. They had and still have, by the way, no idea as to my real identity. They knew, of course, that I hadn't come from their world, but I soon became accepted as I did everything they did and didn't stand on ceremony. Then the current leader was killed in a failed robbery attempt, and in the confusion, the rest of them were in a panic. I managed to calm them down and even get something from the robbery as I prevented them from running away empty-handed. They looked to me to make decisions automatically after that, and so I became their leader without bloodshed, or without really trying. That wasn't my aim, though. However, I can't say I dislike leadership. It gives my life some challenge as well as excitement.'

'What does your father think you're doing?' Randa queried.

Sandron smiled, 'In Asperilla, wasting my time in wenching, drinking, and gambling with my brother.'

'And what about Brand? Does he know where you are?'

'No! He thinks I went home to Sendolina to see my beloved parents,' Sandron grinned. 'No one in the world knows that Sandron, the bandit leader is one and the same as Sandron, third and youngest son of Duke Thoric of Sendolina. Except now you and your companions, Randa.' He grew serious all of a sudden and looked round the group. 'Are you going to grass me up?'

They looked at each other questioningly.

'Hey, I won't. I were, or rather am still, I suppose, a thief meself,' spoke up Thadora. 'I couldn't in all fairness squeal against another thief. Anyway, I think it's so real cool of you to be doin' this.'

'I, too, won't speak of this,' put in Carthinal. 'I've known times in similar circumstances myself.'

The others looked at him in some surprise. He had never said anything about his past life, or indicated he had some, hard times. Only Thadora did not look surprised. She deduced he must have spent time with the underworld somewhere, as only those people with close dealings with thieves and the thieves themselves, could speak the cant, the language of the underworld, and Carthinal could speak it well, indicating an intimate knowledge of such a life.

Randa assured Sandron that she also would not betray him.

'But only because of the harm it would do to the rest of your family,' she told him severely. 'I don't approve of this way of getting your kicks.'

The conversation then moved onto other matters, and Sandron seemed relieved by their assurances that they would not inform anyone of his activities. The rest of the day passed quickly, and dusk started to fall.

'Randa, you must sleep in my tent tonight,' offered Sandron, as he saw her stifle a yawn. 'I'll get some people to prepare somewhere for your friends and me to sleep. We'll use some of the other tents. It won't do my men any harm to sleep outside tonight. It's very warm.'

'No,' Randa replied, 'I won't take advantage of my position just because you know who I am. I'll sleep with the rest of Wolf. I've been roughing it since the end of last year, nearly three months now. Sleeping in a tent will seem like luxury.'

Sandron raised his eyebrows a little but acquiesced readily enough. He only made his offer out of politeness and breathed a sigh of relief that he did not have to give up his luxurious tent. He went to the door of his tent and called to someone outside to prepare tents for his guests.

A voice said, 'Do you want me to organise a guard for them as well?'

'No! Didn't you hear me? They are my guests, not my prisoners. One of them is an old friend.'

The voice muttered something else, and Sandron replied, 'No, I trust them. They won't betray us. They have their reasons beyond friendship.'

When the Wolves retired for the night, Randa found it difficult to sleep. She tossed and turned for a while, but then had an idea. She resolved to put it to Sandron the following morning. Once she had decided that sleep came quickly.

When the Wolves rose the next morning, having rested well in the tents, they found the camp already in full swing, with breakfast being prepared by some of the women who were obviously the wives and mistresses of the bandits. Some of the other women were with the men, sharpening and cleaning weapons and armour. These were mainly the younger women. The Wolves deduced that the women probably led the same life as the men until they were either pregnant or too old, then they prepared meals, looked after the children, and generally kept the camp life going. There were a few old men around, too, helping. These men were fulfilling various purposes from looking after children to tending the various animals that belonged to the bandit "city"—dogs, horses, chickens, a few goats, sundry cats, etc.

A large, muscular man stoked up a fire surrounded by ironware, an anvil, and hammers. The camp, it seemed, had its own smith. In fact, looking around, it seemed more like a mobile village rather than a camp. Davrael remarked that he felt at home as his life had been in a mobile camp. Some of the dogs came to sniff and bark at the strangers. One particularly large, skinny, brown beast growled menacingly when it saw Muldee. The little creature quickly flew up the nearest tall tree, where he sat looking down, eyes blinking fearfully.

Fero called up, 'Don't worry about him, Muldee.' He whistled to the dog, holding out his hand and talking quietly to it. The animal came and sniffed him, and even wagged his tail. After that, they had no more trouble from either that dog or any of the others.

'How'd yer do that?' asked Thadora in amazement.

'Just a ranger trick, my dear,' replied Fero with a smile, but it had impressed the girl. She was close to hero-worshipping the dark ranger as it was, and this increased her admiration still further.

Just then, they were interrupted by the approach of one of the men they recognised as one of their captors from the previous day.

'Boss says yer're t' come t' 'is tent t' break your fast,' he growled.

They made their way across the camp, trailed by the brown dog, to the large tent Sandron used.

'Come in and eat with me,' he smiled at them. 'I'm due for a return to Sendolina, I think. I've just realised how I'm missing some educated company. These people are good for many things, but not for intelligent conversation. Don't get me wrong. I like them all well enough, and they are excellent fighting and drinking companions, but the conversation is a bit limited sometimes. Anyway, I need to appear before my parents before they decide to write to me in Asperilla. Or worse—visit me!'

Halfway through the meal, Randa broached the subject of his lifestyle and ventured her suggestion. 'Sandron, you know you want excitement, but said the army was not for you? You also said you liked leading, but that it would take too long to get to such a position in the army.'

Sandron looked at her, head on one side and a quizzical look in his eyes. 'What are you getting at Randa? If you've something to say, come out with it. It's not like you to beat about the bush.'

'In those days when we were children, learning from Snagtooth, we learned the history of Grosmer, and also some of the wider histories of Vimar, or at least the northern parts north of the Inner Sea.' She looked at Fero apologetically. 'Not much was, or is, known about the lands south of the Inner Sea, especially beyond the Great Desert. At least, not the histories of those lands. Anyway, Sandron,' turning back to the bandit leader, 'We learned that in the past there were mercenary bands who hired themselves out to whoever would pay them.'

'Ye-es,' said Sandron slowly. 'That was at the time before the kingdom was united. Where are you going with this, Randa?'

'There was one band, if I remember correctly, made up mainly of people like you. Youngest sons, or occasionally, disgraced nobility, who chose the life rather than exile or jail.'

'The Red Hawks. I remember,' Sandron put in, 'but I don't se–'

Randa held up her hand. 'Let me finish, please, Sandron. I know there's no war now, nor are there any city-states, at least not in Grosmer, fighting each other. However, on our travels, we've seen more than normal activity of evil races. We were captured by hobgoblins, remember. The elves are stopping everyone entering their lands because of activities of strange beasts and the like. Some unusual wolves attacked us just before reaching Roffley. My father sent us on this quest because of some information he got from a friend. (Remember Danu of Bluehaven? Not given to flights of fancy, I think). I have a bad feeling something is going to happen soon and we may need some help from the army. Why don't you re-form the Red Hawks?'

There was a pause as Sandron looked at her in amazement. Then he seemed to regain his powers of speech and replied, 'What? Me?'

'Yes! You!'

Davrael then spoke. 'This helmet is shape of Hawk,' he pointed out. 'I believe in the gods, and although they not get involved with what we do, I think they give us push in right way to go. I think they give us helmet, or perhaps help us find it, and they bring us to you, as idea this is what you should do. I give this to you, Sandron, as leader of new Red Hawks.' He held the helmet out as he spoke these last words.

'I can't take it from you, Davrael,' replied Sandron quietly. 'It's a very generous offer you're making, but the helm is yours. You braved great dangers, for what purpose I know not, but this helm was one of your rewards.'

'Oh, tush!' replied Kimi. 'He's never been happy with that thing on his head. Makes him hot, he says. Take it, Sandron, please, so I'll not have to put up with his complaints.'

They all laughed at Kimi's words, but Sandron reached out and gently took the helmet from Davrael's outstretched hand.

'Thank you. You are most generous.'

Then Muldee, who had been unusually quiet in the camp said, 'It's magic, you know. It will give you extra protection, and also help you see farther.'

The others looked at him in surprise.

'You never said you knew what it did, Muldee,' complained Carthinal. 'I know you said it was magic, but that's all you told us.'

'Took me time to study it. Magic detection's easy. Identification takes longer, and then you never asked.'

'If we didn't know you could do it, why would we ask?' pointed out Asphodel logically.

'I never thought of that.' The little creature looked abashed. He cocked his head to one side. 'Do you want me to tell you about the other things?'

'Yes, please,' said Randa. 'Start with the Sword.'

The dragonet closed his eyes and thought. 'I remember now. It will warn you of danger. That tingling feeling you get is the warning, Randa.'

'Now he tells me, when we've been caught twice!' said the girl, rolling her eyes heavenward.

'It also has a Special Purpose,' went on the dragonet, ignoring her. The others could hear the capitals in his voice. 'Someone made it especially to help maintain the Balance between good and evil in the world. Hence the name, Equilibrium. It'll help to overcome evil if that is what is required, but also, if the Balance has swung the other way, it will work for evil against good.'

'I don't like the sound of that,' Asphodel said, looking concerned, and glanced with some anxiety at the Sword.

'I wouldn't worry at the moment, Aspholessaria,' said Muldee. 'Have you noticed too much good in the world recently?'

'No-o,' she replied, slowly, 'There always seems to be more evil. Even amongst those who profess to be good.'

Sandron looked at her puzzled. 'How does that idea work, then?'

She went on to tell him of her experiences in the temple in Hambara. How she was forbidden to heal a man judged by the Great Father of Hambara to be evil, and how the Most High of Sylissa had decreed that they should try to eradicate evil completely. This, he conceded might mean the destruction of some humans, elves, dwarves and other sentient races.

'It was a similar story in Bluehaven,' she continued. 'That was why Mother Caldo sent me to Hambara. I disobeyed an instruction not to help the family of a local thug. They weren't to blame, though, and there were little children involved.' She looked down at her hands as she spoke. 'And now I don't suppose I'll ever rise far in the service of Sylissa, cast out as I am.'

Sandron looked at her with sympathy. 'Asphodel,' he said softly, placing a hand on her arm, 'You're a good and true cleric of your goddess. It's she who'll decide who rises in her service, surely, not mortals, whoever they are, Great Father, Most High or whoever.'

Asphodel brightened slightly at his words. 'Yes, I suppose you're right,' she smiled. 'Thank you for reminding me. While we are here, do you have any people who need healing, or otherwise tending?'

Sandron thanked her and said he would be grateful if she would look at one or two of his people who had wounds. Not all were from bandit activities he hastened to point out. One man cut himself while skinning game, and the wound did not seem to want to heal. There were the usual injuries sustained by the children and one pregnant mother whose baby was due any day. It pleased Asphodel to help, although she was not sure why she needed to look at the pregnant woman, as there did not seem to be any complications. However, she agreed if only to set Sandron's mind at rest. She wondered if the child were his since he seemed so concerned, but she pushed the thought away. It was none of her business.

Asphodel spent the morning in healing duties, which she enjoyed immensely. She gave advice as to how to treat simple wounds to prevent infection, and on hygiene, which seemed to be sadly lacking in the camp. After a tiring morning, she sat down gratefully for her mid-day meal in Sandron's tent.

'We thank you for your hospitality, Sandron,' Carthinal said after the meal, 'but we must leave first thing tomorrow morning. We've been gone too long as it is.'

'Thank you for your company. I think that capturing you was one of the gods little "pushes", Davrael, and I will look into forming that mercenary group as you suggested, Randa. It would be exciting, and as my own boss, I could fight with the men and also wouldn't have to obey stupid orders that I disagree with.'

They had to make one other farewell, though. Muldee decided he would like to experience a different type of life, and so elected to stay with Sandron. He would accompany the young man to his home, and pose as a rare purchase Sandron had made in Asperilla. Randa pointed out that if he wished to experience luxury, he could come home with her to the Palace in Hambara, but the little creature said that it was not the luxury that attracted him, but the experience of building up a mercenary troop, and possibly fighting with it. He had also discovered a latent, telepathic ability in Sandron, similar to that of Thadora, and so he would be able to converse with him without people knowing he could speak whenever it was necessary. Thadora hugged the dragonet until he protested she was going to break his wings. They each took their farewells, Thadora with tears running down her face.

'Don't worry, Red Cub,' Muldee reassured her. 'Now I know your mind's signature, I can always find you. I'll come and see you in this Hambara place, but I won't stay there. I've decided I don't much like cities.' He turned to Asphodel. 'Except your capital, Aspholessaria. That I did like. Very much.'

So the next morning, after breaking their fast with Sandron, the company were led back to the road and headed off northward in the direction of Berandore.

Chapter 22
Home

They had a pleasant journey along the road to Berandore. The Mountains of Doom rose majestically to their right all the way, and the road followed the valley of the river Kromb. This river rose in the mountains, and flowed from North to South, following the border between Erian and Grosmer, until it emptied into the Inner Sea at Sendolina, the seat of Sandron's father. The weather, too, was pleasant. The sun shone warmly on their backs as they walked, and the nights were mild. The mountains to the east looked kindly, for once, and it they all found it difficult to believe they had nearly died in blizzards in their midst only a few short months ago. A few, fluffy, white clouds occasionally obscured the highest peaks but otherwise, the sky was a brilliant blue, and the visibility amazing.

Birds sang in the trees and they occasionally disturbed a squirrel or rabbit. Asphodel had become quite accomplished with her sling in their travels, and she brought down some game for meals, as did the others. Randa, too, had learned new skills. She now cooked quite well, and could gut fish and prepare birds and small mammals for the spit as well as any of them. She had also learned the names and uses of some of the culinary herbs and fungi they used and enjoyed going to search for them. Kimi, too, had become quite proficient in the use of the two knives Davrael bought her before they set out on their long journey. They were all very, much fitter than when they left, although they had considered themselves pretty fit when they left Hambara at the end of Khaldar.

One day there was a light shower. It did not worry the Wolves, though. They thought it pleasant and as Fero pointed out, there was the need for rain as well as sunshine if things were to grow well. The rain made the Kromb swell slightly. It must have been harder higher up in the mountains. The sound of it as it gurgled its way along, bouncing over the stones in its bed sounded soothing, and it seemed as though it were chuckling to itself. The sound soon put them in high spirits. Eventually, after nine days of this, they reached Berandore.

Berandore nestled in the hills below the Mountains of Doom. It was a border town, and as so many such towns are, it had high walls and a strong castle. Grosmer had not always enjoyed peace with its neighbours and towns such as Berandore and Meridore had their fair share of raids from neighbouring Erian in past times. It was situated in a loop of the river Kromb. The river ran deep here and had carved itself a valley with steep walls. The town had grown up to the west of this valley, using the steep cliff as a fortification. The river ran along the base of the cliff and curved round three sides of the town. The castle perched at the top of the cliff, its walls seeming to grow out of the rock itself. Curtain walls surrounded the town to the west of the castle, and none of the buildings had spilled outside, unlike many other towns, including Hambara itself. It had a dour and solemn look.

'It looks none too inviting,' pointed out Kimi.

'I think that's rather the idea,' replied Randa. 'It's supposed to put off and repel any invaders.'

Only one gate led into the town and as the road that they were following approached closer to the gate it swung round to the west to join the road from Roffley. No roads led north or east from here. The Mountains of Doom swung westward just to the north of the town making passage difficult in that direction, and there were no passes to the east. Travellers wanting to enter Erian had to pass through Meridore, not Berandore. People travelling to Pelimor usually took a more northerly route through the town of Frind. There was, of course, the pass the Wolves had taken over the mountains, but most people considered it too difficult and impossible for freight.

As they entered the town, along with rumbling wagons and farmers with a variety of goods, they noticed a carnival feel to the air and realised tomorrow would be the Summer Solstice, a day dedicated to Candello, the god of the sea and the weather. Although this god was particularly beloved by fishermen, farmers, anyone else who depended on the weather also worshipped him, hence the influx of people to the town from the outlying villages.

'I hope we can get a room,' worried Carthinal. 'I'd not realised it was the end of Zoldar already.'

'Summer tomorrer,' pointed out Thadora, needlessly.

'How long should it take to get back to Hambara?' asked Kimi, her geography of the land of Grosmer being far from perfect.

They were just passing through the gate and the guard stopped them, so she did not get an immediate answer to her question. The guard asked a few questions before allowing them in.

'Just routine,' he told them. 'We've never become lax here like in other parts of the country. Can't be too careful right on the border like. You never know but what the neighbours might take it into their heads to do something silly. Like invade.' and he laughed at the idea. 'There's things in them mountains too as 'ud like to get in here and make a bit of a mess, given the chance. Trolls, hobgoblins, ogres, yeti and the like. There're bands of orcs, too, I've heard tell, though I ain't seen none myself.'

Thadora was just about to say the yeti were not a threat when Carthinal caught her eye and she quickly shut her mouth.

The guard went on, not noticing anything. 'You seem to be fine. Magnificent Sword you have there, miss. Don't suppose you'd like to sell it? No! Didn't think you would.' He answered his own question. 'Likes of me couldn't afford a sword like that, anyway. Not on my wages!' he grumbled to himself about the low pay of guards as he waved them through. 'Enjoy your stay. Happy Solstice and may Candello bless you all.'

'And the same to you,' they replied, 'May you have a good summer.'

They found an inn. Not one of the better ones, it being in the poorest quarter of the town, but the beds seemed clean, and although there was no bathhouse, the landlady told them they could have hot water to wash. They decided not to eat in the inn, but to try to find somewhere where they would get a reasonable meal since they now had gold from their "Singing Wolves" escapade. They had a discussion as to whether to stay for the festival of the Solstice the following day, but eventually they agreed they should really be on their way.

Early the next morning, the second hour after sunrise saw a small band of travellers leaving through the gates against the traffic arriving for the festivities. They were, it has to be admitted, a little disappointed to miss it, but all knew they had been away too long. Randa especially wanted to put an end to her father's worries. She knew he would have sent men out looking for her as soon as he realised she had not gone to her mother's family in Frind as she had told him, and by now would be certain she was dead. This thought made her sad, as she loved her father, and did not wish him to be unhappy. She knew how he missed her mother, even after all these years, and that he had relied on her more than many fathers rely on their daughters and so they left with the early-morning mist still clinging to the ground.

The companions had an uneventful journey to Roffley. They met with a few other travellers on the way, and stayed at two inns en route. They covered the distance uneventfully and found themselves entering Roffley in the early afternoon of Candar ten. They made their way straight to the inn where Mandreena and Fat Ander, her father, greeted them very warmly. Mandreena was very excited, as she was to be married later that summer to the young man she was seeing at the equinox. She took Thadora away to regale her with all the details of the wedding preparations. Fat Ander then became apologetic.

'It's your horses, Miss,' he said to Randa.

'What's happened?' she asked anxiously, thinking all kinds of things that could happen to a couple of horses. They were both, valuable animals, Storm being of the highest bloodstock in Grosmer and Moonbeam a Plains horse.

'Oh, they are in good health, Miss,' said Fat Ander, seeing the look of anxiety that crossed her face. 'You see, I put your mare in with my mare, and the stallion in a separate field.' He paused before continuing. 'You see, first my mare, then yours came into season. I thought I had put your stallion far enough away, but he can jump very well can't he? He cleared the fences and got in with them. Well, you know how he is at the best of times, Miss. Difficult isn't in it. There was absolutely no way we could get him away from those mares. So...so they will both have foals next spring. I'm so sorry. A stallion like that should not be bred to any old mare. His foals will be valuable, and my mare is of no breeding whatsoever.'

Randa burst out laughing, much to Fat Ander's surprise.

'You're not mad, then?' he asked.

'No! I should have thought of that myself,' Randa told him.

'So should we,' Davrael put in.

'But my mare will have a foal by a valuable stallion! I could no way afford such stud fees you know.'

'Take the foal as a gift from me,' Randa told him. 'Storm had his fun. As to Moonbeam, well she's a mare of the Plains and her foal will be worth quite a bit, I suspect, especially when it's known it's from Storm. No. You've done a good job there, Ander. How much do we owe you for their keep?'

'I couldn't consider taking payment, Miss. I'll have the foal and that'll more than compensate for any losses I incurred looking after them.'

Eventually, at Randa's insistence, they managed to persuade Fat Ander to take some money as a token gesture and so everyone was happy.

The next morning, Randa, Kimi and Davrael went to the field on the outskirts of the town, where the horses were grazing. Moonbeam and Storm were there in a field together with another mare and a gelding, both bays. Randa climbed up onto the gate and whistled a three-tone whistle. Storm, who was grazing at the far side of the field, lifted his head, ears pricked, and then trotted meekly to the gate. He saw Randa and whickered in pleasure.

'Well, he's remembered his whistle,' Randa said, pleased. 'I wondered if he'd forget.'

The girl had begged some of last autumn's now wizened apples for the horse. As soon as he reached the gate, Randa climbed into the field and the horse nuzzled her clothing looking for the treat he knew she would bring for him. She fed him one of the apples and then turned to ask for the bridle from Davrael, who held it out to her. While her back was turned, the black stallion butted her with his head in affection, nearly knocking her over. She turned and scolded him affectionately. If it is possible for a horse to look chastened, Storm did so. He hung his head and looked at her from out of his big, brown eyes as though to say, 'I didn't mean it. I only wanted to say I'm pleased to see you.'

She retrieved the bridle and slipped it over his head. Not having had any restrictions for several months, the stallion objected at first, but Randa eventually got the bridle fixed and led him from the field. Kimi in the meantime went in and easily caught the mare, and they led the two animals back to the inn yard where they begged grooming materials from the inn's stable boy.

'I'm sorry he looks such a state, Miss,' apologised the boy. 'No one could get near him to groom him. He's been well fed, though, and looked after as well as we could, not being able to go too close; you understand.'

Randa reassured him she knew exactly what her horse was like with strangers, and set about giving him a vigorous brushing to remove the dried mud and loose hairs. Kimi did the same with Moonbeam, but the mare had been groomed, so her job did not seem so arduous. The two girls then examined the animals thoroughly, helped by Davrael, and declared them to be in excellent condition, and fit to travel back to Hambara.

While this was going on with the horses, Thadora spent time with Mandreena. The innkeeper's daughter talked about her forthcoming marriage and insisted on regaling the other girl with all the details of the event planned, as well as singing the praises of her husband to be. She extracted a promise from Thadora to come to her wedding on the Festival of Bramardar, the goddess of marriage and the family. This festival happened on the first day of winter, the winter solstice, and so six months ahead. Mandreena and Allvid, her fiancé, wanted to have it in the summer, but they were overruled by both sets of parents as weddings held on the Winter Solstice were considered to be especially lucky, being blessed by Bramara herself.

The rest of the group had been shopping for supplies for the journey back and were now sitting in the inn, having a well-needed drink.

'It's a bit like the beginning,' mused Basalt. 'The four of us sitting, drinking in an inn.'

'A lot has happened since then, as well as a lot of time having passed,' Asphodel pointed out.

'We hardly knew each other then and didn't know the others at all. Or how important we'd become to each other,' Carthinal said.

Fero looked towards the door leading to the stable yard, and Asphodel looked at Carthinal at these words. Basalt noticed these glances and wondered again what fate held in store for the four.

On a warm and sunny day, the guard at the Doom Gates at Hambara saw a group of people approaching late one afternoon. There were eight of them and two horses. He screwed up his eyes to try to see more clearly. (He was a little short-sighted). That black horse looked very much like Lady Randa's black, but it couldn't be. The Lady Randa had been missing since before the Spring Equinox, and the Duke had reluctantly given up hope she would be found alive and had in the last week declared she must now be considered as dead. The town had gone into mourning, not so much for love of Lady Randa, who everyone knew as a difficult girl and something of a snob, but for respect and love of the Duke.

A ceremony of remembrance was going to be held in two days at the Temple of Kalhera, the goddess of death and the underworld, to pray for Randa's soul. Since her disappearance, the Duke had rarely been seen in the town and planned to leave for his estate in the country just as soon as the ceremonies were over. His brother's son would run the day to day ducal affairs in Hambara while the Duke was away. Rumours said he did not plan to return, and that his nephew would, in everything but name, be the Duke.

The group came nearer. The guard called his superior officer from the guardhouse.

'What now?' grumbled the man. When the guard told him about the horse, he sighed and said, 'The Lady Randa isn't the only person in Grosmer to have a black horse, you know. Anyway, Lady Randa wouldn't be walking her horse when she could ride him. Walking's beneath her. Or should I say "was" since she's obviously dead by now. You called me away from a card game for this, and I looked like winning for once. Just get on with it. You'll never get promotion if you call me out for every little thing.'

The sergeant stretched, and as he entered the guardhouse he glanced at the group, He paused, and looked again. The horse did have a look of Lady Randa's Storm. He could not say what it was about the animal, but it definitely looked like Storm. And as for the person leading him... The sun caught long, blonde hair, making it shine like silver. Who were the people she was with? She walked next to a tall, dark man dressed all in black. He looked menacing, but she seemed to be at ease in his presence. Then there were the others, a couple of barbarians from over the Western Mountains. '*Call themselves Horselords,*' he reminded himself. The other four were just as strange a group. A tall mage, a black-haired elf wearing a white tabard over chain mail denoting a cleric of Sylissa, a fierce looking dwarf and another girl, with red hair. No. It could not possibly be. Not with such a group of ne'er-do-wells, and looking so relaxed in their company.

It was, however. The Wolves agreed to allow Randa to speak to the guard at the gate, as that is what the guard would expect, and she did so now.

'I'm Lady Randa. Please let us pass with all speed. We need to get to the Palace to see my father.'

'My Lady!' Both guards saluted smartly.

The sergeant stood back, saying, 'We'll get you an escort, My Lady. There are all sorts of people in the streets. It's not safe for you to be abroad without a guard.'

'Thank you, Sergeant...?'

'Gamillo, My Lady.'

'Sergeant Gamillo, I don't think that will be necessary.' As the sergeant opened his mouth to protest, she went on. 'My friends and I have been on a very long and dangerous journey. My friends are all the protection I need if any is required here in Hambara. I doubt there will be worse dangers than those we've passed through to get back here.'

The sergeant looked nonplussed.

'Of course, My Lady. Should we send word ahead of you to the Duke?'

'No. That won't be necessary. Please stand aside and let us pass now.'

The amazed sergeant and guard stood to one side and saluted again as the little band passed by.

'Well, Serge, What do you make of that?' the guard said to his superior.

'I don't know. I really don't know. She seemed different somehow, but I've no doubt it was the Lady Randa. No one else has hair like that. And those eyes. They seemed to look right through me.'

As they approached the Palace gatehouse, Randa told the others she thought it would be a good idea if she went in to see her father alone at first, and they come afterwards. This they readily agreed to, none of them looking forward to the Duke's ire at them allowing his beloved Randa to accompany them on a dangerous mission and readily agreed to put off the moment, even if only for a few minutes.

Randa rode Storm into the stable yard, leaving her companions at the gatehouse. The stable boys rushed out on hearing hooves and then slid to a standstill as they recognised Randa and Storm. They could hardly manage to speak to her, so surprised were they. They eventually managed to welcome her back and took Storm away to his stall to groom and feed him. Randa surprised the two boys by accompanying them and insisting on unsaddling the horse herself. The head groom came into the stables and welcomed her back. If it surprised him to see the haughty, young lady unsaddling her own horse and reaching for the grooming tackle, then sending the stable boys away, he was too polite to mention it. He greeted her as though she had just been out on one of her normal rides.

The horse seen to and settled, Randa approached the doors of the house with some trepidation. She had decided to enter through the main doors and had circled the house to the front. She climbed the steps slowly. Once at the door, she took the massive knocker in her hand. She held on to it for a few seconds, and then, taking her courage in her hands, knocked on the door. She heard the sound of feet and then the door opened and she saw Daramissillo. The elf's face showed amazement when he saw Randa standing there, but he quickly regained his composure and spoke to her as though she had just returned from one of her habitual rides.

'My Lady.' He bowed to her. 'It's good to see you back.'

'Hello, Daramissillo,' Randa greeted him as she handed him her helm and shook her hair free of its confines. 'It's good to be back, too.'

The elf looked at her with some distaste as he took in her dishevelled appearance.

'I will call for one of the maids to run you a bath, My Lady. You can get bathed and changed. I will go and inform the Duke of your arrival.'

'No, Dara,' To his surprise, she referred to him by the diminutive she had used when as a small child he had carried her on his shoulders and played with her.

'*That was before she became so haughty,*' he thought. He caught himself in time to hear her next words.

'I'll see my father first. I owe him that much, having been gone for four months.'

'With all respect, My Lady,' Daramissillo said, 'I feel he should be prepared for this. He's given you up for dead, you know, and has gone into mourning.'

The Duke's voice, coming from just outside his office, interrupted the discussion.

'Daramissillo, I thought I heard the door, and then you talking to someone. We're not expecting anyone, are we?'

Footsteps sounded and the Duke appeared from the side of the grand staircase. He saw Randa, and gasped, reaching out to the wall for support. His face displayed a gamut of emotions. First, there was surprise, then disbelief, followed in quick succession by delight and finally anger. However, delight won the day over anger, and Duke Rollo ran across the hall to his errant daughter and swept her up in his arms in a great bear hug, swinging her round as though she were still five-years-old. When he put her down, he held her away from him and gazed at her.

'Randa! Randa! Randa!' he seemed unable to say anything else at first then he looked her up and down and an expression of distaste for her dirty condition crossed his face.

'Go and get cleaned up, girl. You look like a Wanderer. No, on second thoughts, that is unfair to the Wanderers. They are clean even if they have no settled home. You look like someone who's been sleeping rough for weeks. Then come down and tell me where you've been, and more importantly, why.'

'No, I won't get changed yet,' the girl told him, 'and as to where I've been, wait until the others arrive.'

'Others? What others?' Rollo asked his daughter. Then turning to Daramissillo, he said, 'Go and tell the cook that Lady Randa is home and that she has some friends with her. We'll eat in the small dining-room. She'll need to prepare a meal for...' He stopped, realising that he had no idea how many would be coming. He turned to Randa questioningly.

'There are seven more and they'll be here in about half an hour. I told them to wait at the gatehouse for an hour. I cantered

Storm down the drive so that made up some time, but then I saw to him first and gave him some food and a quick brushing. That would add time, so I think they'll be half an hour. Tell cook there will be nine of us, including my father and myself.' she said, turning to Daramissillo, who affected a bow and left in the direction of the kitchens.

'Then you'll have time to change, my dear,' the Duke pointed out.

'No. That wouldn't be fair to my friends. They're just as dirty and weathered as I am. Changing would make me different. Turn me into the Duke's Daughter, the Duchess-in-Waiting instead of the friend and companion of the last four months.'

Rollo took Randa's arm and led her to his study.

'Come and tell me where you've been, then.'

Again, the girl refused.

'The story isn't just mine,' said the girl. 'You must wait and contain your questions until the others get here.'

Duke Rollo had to contain his curiosity. With some difficulty, it has to be admitted. As he waited with his daughter, he found that his relief and pleasure at having her back began to give way to anger. The fact she had gone off on some jaunt without a word, disappeared for four months, and now the fact that she would not tell him anything until these mysterious "friends" arrived.

'Randa, you are, and have been, most irresponsible and inconsiderate in what you've done. I was worried sick. For four months I had hardly any sleep, worrying about you. Every time a letter arrived I thought it would be a ransom note. You lied to me that you were going north to stay with your mother's parents in Frind, but when I heard you'd not arrived, after a month, I began to worry. I looked in your room. None of your clothes had been taken, just your mail and helmet and a sword from the armoury. Oh, and your horse, of course. The guard said they saw you leaving by the Water Gate and told me you'd said you were going to catch up with the caravan that had left earlier in the day, heading north to Frind, but when we questioned the leader, he knew nothing of you.'

The duke paced up and down the room. He paused and looked at his daughter.

'I should punish you severely for this. I've had men out looking everywhere, from the Mountains of Doom to the Western Mountains, and the Inner Sea to the Roof of the World. I've had posters up in every town, village and hamlet in the land. Now, you refuse to tell me where you've been until some group of so-called friends arrives.'

'Father, you're ranting,' Randa surprised herself as to how little she feared her father's anger. As a child, she had easily been reduced to tears, although his angry outbursts at her were rare. Now, though, she felt only a slight guilt for the anguish she had put him through. She wished she had been able to spare him that, but he would have forbidden her from going, and she knew she had to go. She turned to him.

'I am not a child, you know. I can no longer be punished for misdeeds. I'm nearly nineteen-years-old. Many girls of my age are married with children.'

Her father turned from looking out of the window.

'And whose fault is that, lady?' he demanded. 'There are any number of young men, aye, and older ones, too, who would marry you tomorrow, but you are so fussy. None of the ones I've suggested meet with your approval. I should just do as other fathers do and tell you whom you'll marry, and you'll obey. Yes, many girls of your age are indeed married with children and have been since they were sixteen and officially adults. Some even married at fourteen or fifteen and have two or three children...'

Just then, a knock came at the door.

'Come in,' called Rollo.

Daramissillo entered ,a look of distaste on his face.

'There are seven...' he paused and cleared his throat. 'People here to see you, Your Grace. They say they are Her Ladyship's companions. A rather unpleasant and dangerous looking group if I may be so bold as to say so, sir. Should I call the guard before letting them in?'

Before the Duke had a chance to reply, Randa said, 'No, Daramissillo. That won't be necessary. I can promise you they won't do any harm.'

The elf glanced at Rollo for confirmation. Rollo gave a brief nod and turned once more to contemplate the gardens. Daramissillo bowed and left to show the rest of the Wolves into Rollo's study.

Rollo turned from the window to observe these "friends" of Randa. He saw a group of ne'er-do-wells, just as unkempt as his daughter, and all carrying weapons and wearing armour, which, unlike the people, were beautifully kept. He reconsidered calling for the guard and raised his hand to ring the bell on his desk when he recognised the one person with no weapons in sight wearing the red robes of a newly, promoted mage.

'By all that's holy!' he exclaimed. 'Carthinal! I didn't recognise you. And Fero, Basalt and Asphodel. I'm sorry my welcome was somewhat muted. I'd almost forgotten about your mission in my anxiety for Randa. Whatever was she doing with you, and how did you get past the gatehouse with all your weapons?'

'We sort of threatened him a bit,' grinned Basalt. 'He was being very difficult. We told him we'd maybe kill him just a little if he insisted we leave our weapons there.'

'Papa, don't be angry with Carthinal, please. I gave him and his friends no choice. I decided I wanted to go with them. I've been wrapped in cotton wool all my life. Oh, you allowed me to learn to fight when I asked, and let me go hunting and many other things only a son would normally learn, but I knew I'd never have the chance to actually use these skills. You were merely indulging what you thought would be a passing fancy, but I needed to prove to myself that I could survive outside these walls and your watchfulness.' She put on a smile, went over and hugged her father. 'Say you're not still angry, Papa, please. We got what we went for, you know.'

Rollo had put his arm around his daughter and had just started to tell her they were all forgiven when the import of her last words struck him.

He turned her to face him, and said, 'You've got the Sword? Why didn't you say so? For that alone, you are all forgiven.' He turned back to Carthinal. 'Who's carrying it? May I have it please?'

'Your daughter has it, Your Grace,' replied the half-elf.

'Come on, Randa. Don't play games with me. You've got the Sword, so let me have it. We need to find a champion to use it. Danu was certain it was going to be needed, and I'm becoming more convinced he may be right. We're living in strange times.'

Randa took the Sword from its scabbard at her hip and held it up for her father to see. He gasped at its beauty. It seemed almost to shine with an inner light.

'This is it, Father. Equilibrium is its name, but I think you'll find you can't use it. In fact, I don't believe you will be able to take it from me,' With that, she lowered the blade's point to the ground.

Rollo looked puzzled.

'That sounded like a threat, Randa,' he said quietly to his daughter. 'I can't believe you are so greedy for this Sword that you'd threaten your own father.'

Randa laughed.

'Oh, Papa, I wasn't threatening you. The Sword has a mind of its own, of sorts, and chooses its wielder. It chose me, and won't let anyone else handle it.'

'Don't talk nonsense, child,' snapped the Duke. 'Whoever heard of a Sword being able to choose its wielder.'

Carthinal then rose to Randa's defence.

'It's true, Your Grace,' he said quietly. 'We all tried to take the Sword, and only Randa could pick it up. Others have tried to take it, too, on our journey, and all failed. I know it's hard to credit, but it's true.'

The rest of the Wolves murmured in agreement.

'Here, father. Take it and see for yourself. Maybe then you'll believe.' And Randa held the Sword out to her father, hilt first.

The Duke looked at the Sword, then at his daughter, and finally at the group standing in his study.

'It won't kill you, Papa. At least, it hasn't done so yet, just given warnings.'

The Duke slowly moved his hand towards the Sword, and, making up his mind, grasped the hilt firmly. Then he gave a yelp of pain and dropped the Sword, looking at first his hand, then down at the Sword lying at his feet.

'It had thorns. I saw them and felt them. Where are they now?'

Randa calmly bent and picked up the Sword. She felt no effect. She put it back into the scabbard.

'So you see, father, I'm the Swordbearer. There's no choice.'

She sat down on one of the chairs by the fireplace. There was no fire as it was a warm evening. 'I didn't ask for this. In fact, I'm not sure I actually want it. I just wanted an adventure, then I'd have chosen one of the young men you've suggested, and got married and lived like a normal, young woman. However, things have changed. I'm the Swordbearer. Whatever plans you have for the Sword, must of necessity, include me.'

Now Duke Rollo sat down. He sank into his chair behind the desk and put his head in his hands. After a few minutes, he looked up. He regained his composure and turned to the others saying:

'This needs some thought, so we'll leave it for the time being. I know four of you, but the other three I've not had the pleasure of meeting. Perhaps you would introduce them to me, Carthinal?'

Carthinal bowed to the Duke, and firstly introduced Davrael and Kimi, who although they did not bow as such, inclined their heads as a mark of respect, and then turned to Thadora. She lurked at the back of the group and had her hood pulled up so her face was in shadow. She was not happy in this house. She was a child of the Warren and a thief. The Duke represented the ultimate authority of the Law in Hambara. She certainly did not want his attention drawn to her, or to be in a position where she may be recognised again. She would have to continue with her life as a thief after they left here, as she had no other skills. No, she did not want to be recognised. She did not, however, allow for the Duke's authority in his own house. When Carthinal turned to her, he hissed under his breath.

'Remove your hood, Thadora. Show some manners to the Duke.'

The girl shook her head, so the half-elf pulled it from her head himself, rather impatiently, saying, 'This "shy" young person is Thadora. She was invaluable in helping us to remove the traps placed in the tomb and in keeping up our spirits.'

Thadora bowed to the Duke, so she did not notice the expression pass over his face. It was one of incredulity, but Carthinal did not miss it nor did Basalt.

The Duke then spoke to Thadora.

'Who are you, girl?'

'Just a poor girl from th' Warren, Yer Grace,' replied the young thief.

'Are your parents alive?'

'I never knew me father, Your Grace.'

The man's face became pensive.

'And your mother? Who is she? What is her name?'

Thadora did not reply.

'Come on, girl. Surely you know your mother's name!'

'I'd rather not tell yer, Sir,if yer don't mind. I 'ave pers'nal reasons fer that.'

The Duke was no fool. He quickly realised that Thadora must have run away and was afraid of being returned to her mother.

'How old are you?' he asked gently, as though Thadora were a frightened animal that he was trying to calm.

'Sixteen, Sir.'

'Then you are a woman, and capable of controlling your own destiny. No one can tell you what to do anymore. You obviously don't want your mother to know where you are. Did she mistreat you?'

'Oh, no, Sir, Your Grace, I mean,' the girl replied. 'She were a good mother. Allus did 'er best fer me.'

'Then I don't understand.'

'She said she were goin' ter send me ter Madame Dopari's.' Thadora suddenly realised how she had been cleverly led into her confession, and smiled.

'You got me there, Your Grace, Sir,' she said, looking up at him. 'Very clever. Caught me off me guard.'

The Duke found himself looking into the greenest eyes he had ever seen, except on one other person. That convinced him.

'I would like you to come with me to see something,' he told the girl. 'You others can come too if you wish,' he added, seeing the girl's look of reticence. Without waiting to see if anyone followed them, he took Thadora's elbow and guided her out of the room.

'What's going on?' Fero whispered to Randa as they followed her father and Thadora.

Randa shrugged. 'No idea!' she replied.

They followed the Duke and Thadora up the stairs and then turned left to a door. The Duke opened it and they found themselves in a long gallery. There were windows on the right, overlooking the gardens and the small park beyond. The surrounding wall could just be seen in the distance through the trees. It was not the view the Duke wanted them, or at least Thadora, to see. He turned to them. 'This is the Formal Dining Room,' he said, rather superfluously, as a long table ran down the centre of the room surrounded by chairs and a sideboard at the end. On the wall, opposite the windows, stood a large fireplace and a number of portraits. It was to these portraits that Duke Rollo drew their attention.

'There are portraits here of recent members of the family,' he said. 'The older ancestral portraits are in a gallery in the east wing. This room has been little used since the death of my beloved wife. I've not had the heart for large parties. However, let's look at these portraits.'

'What are you getting at, Papa?' Randa asked him. 'I'm sure they aren't really interested in family portraits.'

'You've not been in here much, have you Randa, or you may have noticed what I have.'

'Now,' went on Rollo, 'this is my father and next to him is my mother.'

They could see where the Duke got his looks. Hanging before them they saw a man in his prime, looking much as Rollo did now, but with brown hair, and sporting a moustache, and striking blue eyes. Next to him hung the portrait of a rather plain woman, but with very, blonde hair.

'Randa and I both inherited my mother's hair and my father's eyes,' pointed out the Duke. Over the fireplace is my portrait.'

There was a gap next to it, and Rollo explained.

I took the portrait of my wife down to my study. You saw it there, I believe.'

They all nodded.

'Now, at the far end are my grandparents. This is Grandfather.' A stern man gazed down at them with the same, blue eyes as previously. 'The eyes are the same, you'll notice. A feature of most of my family. Now this...,' and he paused. 'This is my grandmother, and what we came to see.'

Thadora looked up and gasped. There, looking down at her, she saw her own face as it might be in ten years time. The portrait showed an attractive woman with unruly, red curls and laughing, green eyes. There was the slightly, upturned nose, sprinkled with freckles. There was the smile on the generous mouth.

'I don't understand,' she said, turning to Rollo. 'She might be me in the future.'

'Come down and allow me to explain,' said Rollo as he led the way back to the study. 'Or would you prefer to get clean first?'

'I think explanations first, father,' said Randa.

They found themselves once more in the Duke's study. He called for extra seating and wine and then began to talk.

'This is embarrassing for me to explain in front of you, Randa. The reasons will become apparent as I go on, but you must know. After you were born and your mother died, I thought I, too, would die. I lost all interest in life. But life does go on, and I'd you to consider. Many people advised me to remarry, but I couldn't face the idea of another woman living in this house as mistress in place of your mother. It seemed a betrayal of all she meant to me. But time passes, and although I could never have put anyone else in the place of my dearest Fenissa, I felt the need of female company on occasion, so I started to visit Madame Dopari's establishment from time to time.'

Randa looked at her father. 'Visited a brothel? Oh, father! How could you?'

'I said it was embarrassing, Randa dear. Anyway, one girl there took my eye. A pretty, little thing. All eyes. She was also kind and understanding. She never knew who I was, though. I always went in disguise, and at night. No one knew I went there. I think Daramissillo may have suspected, but he's too polite to say anything to anyone. It wouldn't have done for the Duke to be known to be consorting with prostitutes, although many nobles visited that establishment, and still do. To the household, I went on night walks, as I couldn't sleep. Then, one night, I went to visit my little courtesan only to be told she had left. I stopped going then but did wonder what had happened to her. I decided another man had taken her away to be his mistress and set her up in a house somewhere. It would have been about seventeen years ago. I now have a different idea. I think she became pregnant and had to leave the brothel. I think she was your mother, Thadora, and that you are my child.'

With this dramatic statement, he stopped. No one spoke.

Then Thadora said in a whisper, 'Sir, me Ma's name's Nandala.'

'Nandala. Nandala. That's it! That was her name! Where is she now, girl?'

'Promise me yer won't let 'er send me ter that place?' pleaded Thadora.

'Of course I won't. If my suspicions are correct and your mother is, in fact, the Nandala I knew, you are my daughter. I would definitely not allow my daughter, illegitimate or not, to become a whore.'

'Not even if that's what 'er mother is?'

'Not even then. Not even if my daughter's a thief, or rather if a thief is my daughter,' he added with a smile.

Thadora then told Rollo where he could find her mother and he dispatched a guardsman to bring her to the Palace. In the meantime, he called for Daramissillo to show the others where they could bathe and get cleaned up in time for the evening meal.

Chapter 23
Nandala

The young guardsman who had been detailed to go to the Warren to find the prostitute known as Nandala did not relish his job. The Warren was known for its hatred of anyone and anything smacking of authority. To say it was a lawless place was untrue, for it had its own laws and rules, but they were not the same as those of the rest of society. There were guilds and societies here, as in the rest of the city, which protected those such as assassins, beggars, thieves and many others, and gave an invaluable service to those with "hot" goods to get rid of. Here was poverty in the extreme.

The place was, as its name implied, a warren of small streets and back alleys. Only someone born in the Warren could ever say they truly knew where they were all the time. And the smells. The sewers ran under the Warren, as they did all the rest of the city, but the inhabitants could not afford the fee that was charged to be connected. The waste was usually dumped straight into the streets, where open ditches ran down the middle. People threw garbage into odd corners, or often not in corners at all. The noise also assaulted one. The city was a noisy environment anyway, but here the people seemed to make more noise than anywhere else, as though noise were an important factor in affirming they were alive. They shouted to each other across streets, children ran laughing, shouting and screaming, babies cried endlessly as they were usually hungry. Dogs barked at everything and there were rats, mice and other pests seemingly with little fear. The only things that seemed to be quiet in this place were the cats.

The young corporal was afraid. He grew up in a village under the jurisdiction of the Dukedom of Hambara, and, since joining the militia, had never ventured this far into the Warren. Everyone who came to Hambara went to see the notorious place, but few went far, and fewer ever returned for a second visit. Brallo was no different. Eyes watched him, seen, and unseen as he passed farther into the slums. He was sure he was being followed, and he kept stopping to look behind him.

Eventually, to his relief, he came to the alley he was looking for. It was narrow, and looked dark even in the full light of day, and as it was a warm day, it stank more than usual. He looked round again before entering the alley. He saw nothing unusual, but his skin crawled, and the hairs on the back of his neck were standing up. He drew his sword and turning his back on the road, but ready to wheel round at the slightest, unusual sound, Brallo entered the alley.

He counted four doors down on his left, and at the fifth he paused. This was where he had been told to go. He sheathed his sword and was about to knock when the door opened and a man came out. He was a large, burly man with a bushy, black beard. He turned to someone inside saying:

'Same time again next week then. Don't forget to keep the slot for me. I need your services.'

He turned to leave and nearly walked into Brallo.

'Sorry, mate,' he said. Then he grinned a knowing grin. 'Good choice yer've made. She's one o' th' best. Used t' work for Madame Dopari they say, and I can believe it. Left because she got pregnant and refused ter get rid o' th' brat. Stupid cow!

Could 'a' lived a life o' luxury at that place, and mebbe even got tekken away by some lord an' med 'is mistress, but no, she 'ad a conscience an' 'ad th' brat, so now she's 'ere in th' Warren, servin' folks like me. Stupid cow.' he muttered again as he disappeared down the alley.

Brallo looked through the door the man had left open for him. The room was shabbily furnished with just a table, two chairs and a cupboard, but it was clean, and although it had an earth floor, it was strewn with fresh rushes, which were mixed with herbs to help overcome the ubiquitous smells coming in through the door. He saw a woman of perhaps forty, lacing her blouse. She had once been beautiful, he thought. She still had something about her. Her hair was black with not a sign of grey, but that meant nothing. Many women dyed their hair as the grey began to show, and he supposed it was even more important for a woman of her profession. He could not see much more as she was turning away from him. He coughed and she turned back abruptly.

'Hello, dear,' she said, fixing a smile on her face, which he noticed was still pretty, even if there were wrinkles in the corners of her large eyes and around her mouth. 'You're in luck. I have a spare half-hour. Follow me to the bedroom. It will cost you between 10 royals and 2 crowns, depending on what you want.'

Her speech was more refined than the common folk who lived in the Warren, giving credence to the fact that she maybe had once been at Madame Dopari's Emporium.

She turned and walked away. He noted the deliberately provocative way she moved her hips as she crossed the room. He was tempted, truly tempted. He had never been with a whore and wondered what it would be like. If this one had in fact been one of Madame Dopari's girls, then she would have been trained in many different ways to give a man the most pleasure, and he certainly could not afford the courtesans at Madame Dopari's

Emporium on his pay. He quickly quashed those thoughts and his temptations and called to her now disappearing figure.

'No. I'm not here for that.'

She turned at that and he saw her professional expression fade and one of anxiety replace it.

'It's not Thadda, is it?'

'Who?'

'Thadora, my daughter. She's been missing for some time.'

'I really don't know what it is. I was just sent here to find you,' he replied. 'You are Nandala?'

'Yes. I'm Nandala. Why do you want to know?'

'I need to be sure I've got the right woman. I have to take you somewhere. Someone wants to see you.'

'Who are you?' asked Nandala. 'Why should I trust you? Who wants to see me?'

The woman was obviously suspicious, and Brallo could not blame her. A strange, young man dressed as a corporal of the guard comes into her house and asks her to come with him with no explanation. He would be suspicious, too, if it happened to him. He tried to set her mind at rest.

'Look, Nandala. I know it seems strange, but I don't know who wants to see you. You're right to be suspicious, too. However, I am a genuine corporal in the guard. Here're my papers to prove it.' He handed her some papers. She barely glanced at them.

'Forgeries exist,' was her reply. 'Good forgeries. Anyone can get papers.'

'Oh!' The wind was completely taken out of Brallo's sails. He did not know what to say to convince this woman he was genuine. He was also surprised at her obvious ability to read, so he just said:

'I know it's difficult for me to prove to you who I am if you won't accept my papers. You'll just have to trust me. I really don't have any idea who wants to see you. I'm just doing a job.'

Curiosity was beginning to overcome suspicion in Nandala. She decided to risk going with this young man.

He seemed genuine to her, so she said, 'May I take someone with me? For security that is.'

'My orders said nothing about bringing you on your own. Who'd you like to bring?'

'I'll ask my neighbour. He works at night so is at home now. He's quite friendly, and not too big,' she added as Brallo looked anxious at the thought of a large man from the Warren accompanying them. He agreed and went with Nandala to the next house where the man had a room.

'I'm lucky round here,' Nandala said as they waited for a reply at the door. 'I've got a whole floor to myself. Three rooms. Thadda had one of them before she ran away.' A sadness crossed her face as she mentioned her daughter. 'I wish I knew why she went.'

'Have you no idea where she could be?' asked Brallo. He was beginning to feel sorry for this woman.

'For some time she was living in the Warren on the streets, that I do know because money appeared every so often on the table, but no one ever saw her coming in, and no one seemed to see her about the streets, either. Then, about four months ago, the money stopped. I tried to find her from the very beginning, but it's too easy to disappear in the Warren. I'm so worried. Something must have happened to her. She wouldn't have stopped leaving money just like that.'

Just then, the neighbour, a burglar in fact, hence Nandala's comment about him working at night, came to the door, and agreed, if reluctantly, to go with them just to ensure the veracity of Brallo's mission, and Nandala's safety, so the three of them set off out of the Warren.

They entered the barracks of the guard shortly afterwards. This did not make Nandala any happier at coming with the corporal. She looked around anxiously, and her companion, the burglar looked as though he was about to bolt.

'Ah! Brallo. I see you've found the woman. Who's this with you too?' A tall captain came out from a side room, went up to Nandala, and offered his hand for her to shake.

She did so nervously, and said, 'This is my neighbour, sir. I was worried about coming with your young corporal so he came to ensure my safety. You can't be too careful in the Warren. Why do you want me, sir? I've not done anything. Is it to do with my daughter, Thadora?'

The captain turned to the burglar.

'Now you know there's no trick, you may go if you wish. Nandala will not come to any harm. You have my word on that.'

He had hardly got the words out of his mouth before the burglar fled the guardhouse. The captain smiled to himself, then he dismissed Brallo.

'Now, Nandala. You've not done anything wrong, nor do we know anything about a girl called Thadora. Someone wants to see you. Someone who's very important. I'm to take you to the meeting this afternoon. Have you eaten yet? No? Then we must rectify that. Sit down, please.' He indicated a chair at a table in the middle of the room.

He pulled the chair back as though she were a great lady. Her training at Madame Dopari's immediately came to the fore. The girls had learned to behave with courtesy and thoughtfulness, so she inclined her head and thanked the captain with a dignity that belied her shabby but provocative dress.

A meal was brought, and Nandala and the captain ate. Nandala had not eaten so good a meal for many years. The earnings of a common whore do not run to much food when the rent had been paid. Meat was a rare luxury, and here was some succulent pork, along with fresh bread and steamed vegetables. Afterwards, the captain, who told her his name was Horaic, offered fruit and cheese. When she had eaten her fill, he called for his horse and ordered it to be saddled with a pillion.

'I don't expect you've ridden? You will be safe on a pillion. Just hold tightly to my belt if you're nervous.'

She was. Very nervous. Not of the horse and riding, but where she was being taken and why. A young guard lifted her onto the pillion behind Captain Horaic, and he set off at a gentle walk at first, then as he felt her grip lessen, he kicked his horse into a trot. They passed onto Western Street and trotted along towards the very centre of the city. The mage tower in its grounds rose up, and she made a sign against magic as they passed. Like many another citizen of Hambara, she did not fully trust those who used magic. She could see the magnificent roofs of the temples behind and around the tower. Some were domes, some spires. Some had several spires and a few had high towers. Some had been roofed in copper which had turned a greenish colour over the years, yet others showed red or grey, even the yellow of gold, depending on the roofing material and wealth of the said temple. It did not seem wrong to Nandala that so much wealth was lavished on the temples, while many were living in abject poverty. They were there to honour the gods, and the gods were known to be fickle if one did not treat them in the right way, or at least so the priests said.

Eventually, they came to the gates of the Palace. Nandala was amazed to find they were trotting towards these gates, which were opened by an old, retired soldier. He saluted the captain smartly as he reined in to speak to the man.

'Here's my sword,' Captain Horaic said. 'I know the Duke doesn't like weapons brought into the Palace.'

'Tell that t' th' group what came yesterday,' grumbled the old man, 'Dangerous lot. Threatened me and then left fer th' Palace fully armed they did.'

'Did the Duke arrest them?' asked Horaic.

'No. Dunno what 'e's doin', but 'e kept some of 'em there at th' Palace. They came wi' 'Er Ladyship. Kidnapped 'er if yer ask me, and then came for their ransom.'

'And he let them go?' Horaic was both surprised and incensed. 'Dangerous criminals allowed to go free?'

'Aye. Dwarf was th' worst. Growled at me an' 'eld 'is axe at me throat if I didn't as like let 'im keep 'is weapons. Th' mage scared me, too. Only dressed as a probationer, but looked as if 'e'd turn me into summat nasty given 'alf a chance. Dunna trust them mages.'

'Very strange goings on,' replied Horaic. 'Don't like the sound of that at all. More criminals loose in the city, and dangerous ones at that. as if we've not got enough of our own.'

With that, he turned his horse and trotted off down the drive. When they came to the house, he turned to the left and went round the back to the stable yard where he dismounted and then lifted Nandala down. She was relieved to feel solid ground beneath her feet again. She felt as though she was going to fall off all the way.

'Come this way,' said Horaic, taking her arm and guiding her towards a door in the side of the house.

The door opened onto a huge room filled with people. It was obviously the kitchen. There were three, large tables down the centre of the room where a number of people prepared meat and vegetables, and on one, a man was assembling a dessert from pastries and cream, stacking them carefully into a beautiful design and piping cream in intricate whorls over it. On the opposite wall were a number of large ovens, all with their separate fires to heat them, and there was a spit over a great, inglenook fireplace to the left where a whole pig was roasting. The smell was mouth watering, and although she had only eaten about an hour previously, Nandala found herself getting hungry again. On either side of the door, were two large cupboards and two windows, and set in the fourth wall were two doors and a large dresser with drawers and cupboards. In the far right-hand corner of the room was a door leading to the main part of the house. The place seemed at first to be totally disorganised with people shouting and talking, but it soon became apparent that there were orders being given and obeyed with alacrity. A tall elf appeared from one of the two doors leading out of the room. He spotted the pair and came over.

'There you are, Horaic. I see you found her. I hope you didn't have many problems.'

'Hello, Daramissillo. Still as efficient as ever, I see,' It seemed the pair knew each other well. In fact, they were great friends and often saw one another when they were both off duty together, which was not as often as they would have liked.

'Follow me. Nandala, isn't it?'

Nandala nodded. She was a bit overwhelmed and rather nervous. As soon as she realised she was on her way to the Duke's residence she really thought that for some reason she was in great trouble. Why would she have caught the notice of the Duke or one of his household? Horaic noted her discomfort, and reached out and squeezed her arm.

'Don't worry, Nandala. You've not done anything wrong. All will be made clear shortly, I'm sure. Right, Daramissillo?'

Daramissillo smiled at his friend and the smile made him seem more approachable and less the efficient man who ran the Duke's household with a rod of iron.

'Yes, Horaic,' He turned again to Nandala with a smile on his handsome face. 'I don't mean to make you nervous. It's just the way I behave at work. One has to keep these people at it or they'll shirk their duties. I can't afford to be too nice. Please, follow me.'

With that, he led the way to the door in the corner of the room and led the way through it, followed by Nandala, feeling very shabby.

The door opened onto a short corridor down which Daramissillo led her, then they passed through another door onto a beautiful quadrangle. This open space in the centre of the Palace had a fountain in the centre, playing into a square pool, which reflected the contours of the building around it. There were paths passing among flowerbeds with a multitude of coloured flowers blooming in them, and there were some bushes cut into the shapes of animals and birds. To Nandala, it seemed an enchanting space, especially as it was in the heart of the house.

Daramissillo led the woman to a door in the opposite side of the quadrangle, so they had to pass the fountain and Nandala caught a glimpse of fish swimming around in the depths. Passing through the door, Nandala found herself in a large hall. It was magnificent. She had thought Madame Dopari's Emporium magnificent, but this room spelled out wealth and taste, whereas Madame's was only wealth, with little taste. There was a staircase leading up in the centre of the room, and the passage emerged next to it. On the opposite wall were two huge doors, obviously the main entrance to the house. Two doors stood on either wall and there were plinths with urns and vases as well as a bust or two. The floor was cream marble, as were the stairs, and they had a wrought iron handrail, which was gilded in places. The floor had a golden carpet running the length of it to take some of the chill off the marble floor.

As she moved farther into the room, she saw another passage on the opposite side of the stairs. Then, she noticed the people. There were two of them, both, young girls, but so different. They were arranging flowers in one of the urns. At least one was, the other was holding the flowers and passing them as required. The girl holding the flowers was obviously a servant of some kind. She was wearing a blue dress with a spotless, white apron. Her hair was brown, a kind of nondescript colour and she could have been pretty but for her long nose, and in comparison with the girl arranging the flowers. Nandala stared at the girl.

She had long, fair hair, almost silver in colour, fastened back by a clasp, but otherwise loose, and she was wearing a deep blue gown with a fitted waist and a low-cut neckline. She was intent on arranging the flowers just so and she had an expression of deep concentration on her face. And what a face. Nandala had never seen such beauty nor such a flawless complexion. Then the beautiful girl saw them and spoke to the elf.

'Ah! Daramissillo. I take it this is Nandala?' She came towards them wiping her hands on her dress, careless of the expensive cloth.

'Yes, Your Ladyship. I'm taking her to the Duke now.'

Nandala swept into a curtsey she had learned in her youth as a courtesan with Madame Dopari. She remained so until Lady Randa told her to rise. Her heart was beating so hard she thought it would leap right out of her chest, and she was sure all three people in the hall could hear it. The Duke? Was she to be taken to the Duke? Why? She was not dressed to meet the Duke. She thought she was going to pass out. Her throat was dry and her palms were sweating. She heard Lady Randa's voice in the distance.

'You can go back to your duties, Daramissillo. I'll take Nandala to my father.'

At the back of her mind, Nandala remembered hearing that Lady Randa was missing and had been presumed dead. This must surely be a dream, then. There was no way the Duke of Hambara, the richest and most powerful man in the country after King Gerim, would want to see her, Nandala, a common whore from the poorest area of the city.

Believing this, she followed Lady Randa down the passage on the opposite side of the staircase to a door, where Lady Randa knocked and then entered. Lady Randa spoke to someone inside and then she stood aside for Nandala to enter.

Nandala entered the Duke's study with her eyes lowered, and curtseyed to the man she saw through her eyelashes. He was seated behind his desk, but that was all she was aware of. She heard a movement and then felt herself being raised to her feet.

'Yes, you are indeed Nandala. Somewhat older, but then so am I, but I'd have recognised you anywhere. Those big eyes of yours are unmistakable.'

That voice. Her memory flew back through the years. It was at Madame Dopari's that she last heard it. It was her regular and favourite client; the man who had told her to call him Perro. She looked up into a pair of blue eyes and immediately recognised him.

"Why is he here in the Ducal Palace?" she wondered, then decided he must work for the Duke.

Her eyes must have betrayed the fact that she recognised him and he smiled.

'Perro!' she exclaimed. 'What are you doing here in the Palace? Do you work here?'

"Perro" smiled. 'You could say that,' he replied. 'I often think I work harder than anyone else here.'

'Do you know why the Duke wants to see me?' she asked. 'Or is it the Duke who wants to see me? Or could it be you?'

'Yes, to both questions,' replied Rollo, relishing her confusion.

He would have to disillusion her in a minute, but he was enjoying his few moments of informality with her. It took him back to the days when she was a courtesan and he had booked a double session so they could talk as well. He had enjoyed talking to Nandala. She was intelligent and had a sharp wit. He sighed. She was showing her hard life. The woman was all skin and bone, but the beauty she had in her youth still showed through. "*With good food and rest she will once again be a handsome woman,*" he thought.

Suddenly, Nandala realised something. The girl who showed them in had called this man "father." Maybe she was mistaken in thinking that she was Lady Randa. Maybe, she was the daughter of a highly placed servant, this man, Perro. Then, she realised with a suddenly, racing heart that Daramissillo referred to her as "Your Ladyship." Then, if this man were her father, he must be… her mouth dried as realisation dawned. She once more swept into a curtsey.

'Your Grace,' she said, 'Please, forgive my presumption in speaking to you so familiarly. I thought you were someone else.'

'I am someone else, Nandala,' came the reply from above her head, 'And I am who you think I am. I am "Perro". I gave a false name when I visited Madame's all those years ago. It wouldn't have done for the Duke of Hambara to be seen consorting with courtesans, would it? Now get up and come and sit down in one of these chairs so we can talk properly.'

Nandala did as the Duke told her, although she felt uncomfortable in the presence of the most powerful man in the city. In spite of what he said to the contrary, this was not Perro, whom she had known in the past. The Duke was talking again. He was telling her something important. She listened. He told her he believed her daughter, her little Thadda, was, in fact, his daughter.

'Your Grace,' ventured Nandala, 'With all due respect, Thadda could be yours, but she could equally be the daughter of any one of dozens of men. What makes you think she's yours?'

'Come with me,' he said in reply, and he took her to the Formal Dining Room and showed her the portrait he had shown to Thadora.

'That is why I think; no, why I know she's my daughter.' He pulled one of the dining chairs out and sat down on it.

He looked up at Nandala. 'Before I send for your daughter, I want to ask your permission to acknowledge her as my own.'

'Thadora? You know where she is?' Then Nandala remembered herself and the Duke's last remark. 'Your Grace,' she said, casting her eyes downwards. 'You're the Duke. You don't need my permission to acknowledge Thadora or to do anything.'

'Yes, I do, Nandala. Firstly, you've brought her up and undergone many hardships to do so. Legally, I may not have to ask you before acknowledging her, but morally, I feel I do. Secondly, I want to adopt her and for that, I do legally need your consent.'

Nandala's legs suddenly felt weak. The Duke pulled a chair out and helped her to sit. He sat back in the other chair and turned to face her.

'You can think about it, Nandala, if you wish. I don't want to rush you.'

'No, Your Grace,' she replied, 'If you wish to both acknowledge and adopt her, you may do so. She'll never have the opportunity to do much with her life in the Warren, except perhaps to become a better thief than she is now. But as she's now past her sixteenth birthday, you'll have to ask her what she thinks.'

The Duke rose. 'Thank you, Nan,' he said. 'And now, I'll send for our daughter and you two can be reunited.'

With that, Duke Rollo went to the door and called for Daramissillo to go and find Thadora and to bring her to the green drawing room.

They went back down the stairs and this time, the Duke took her into a room off the main hall on the right, opposite the doors to the great library where Basalt, Carthinal and Randa had worked four long months ago. It was a reception room and was comfortably furnished. A window overlooked the drive, and another, with large patio doors opened out to the west and overlooked the garden. These windows were open, and a terrace could be seen with a balustrade. The room was furnished in shades of green and was very restful. The fireplace on the wall opposite the smaller window had a magnificent array of flowers.

Rollo noticed Nandala looking at them and said, 'My daughter, Randa does all the flowers in the Palace. It's a gift she has and she enjoys it.'

'They're beautiful, Your Grace,' replied Nandala.

'Yes. They are all grown here at the Palace. Now, please, take a seat and I'll tell Daramissillo to go and ask Thadora to come here. I'll leave you both alone for a while, then I'll return to discuss our plans.'

With that, the Duke left, and Nandala wandered around the room. There was beautiful porcelain ware on the mantelpiece and on a side table. The floor was covered with magnificent rugs over shiny wood. The chairs were soft looking, but Nandala felt too shabby to sit down. Surely, her clothes would dirty the fabric. Just then, she heard the door open softly and she turned. There, framed in the entrance to the room, was Thadora. She had not seen the girl for four years, since she was twelve, and she scarcely recognised her. She was a young woman now, but there was no mistaking that red hair with its unruly curls that had been the despair of her mother. The two stood and looked at each other for a minute, not knowing what to say. Then Thadora suddenly rushed forward and they were hugging each other. Both of them had tears streaming down their faces, and Nandala was grateful for Rollo's foresight in allowing them this time alone.

'Ma! I've missed yer so much,' cried Thadora.

'And I've missed you. Oh, Thadda. The Duke's told me why you left. Did you really think I'd send you to Madame Dopari's if you'd told me you didn't want to go? It seemed the best option for a girl in your position, but I'd never make you do anything like that if you were set against it.'

They talked about their problems and about the intervening four years. Thadora told her mother about going with Carthinal and the formation of Wolf, their capture by hobgoblins and the encounter with the undead guardians of the Tomb. They were deep in conversation, sitting close on a sofa holding hands when the Duke came in.

He sat down in a chair by the fireplace and said, 'I've ordered tea to be brought. Now, I think we've some business to discuss.'

It was decided that Duke Rollo would both acknowledge Thadora as his daughter, and formally adopt her to legitimise her. There was some heated discussion as to what her mother was to do. Rollo wanted Nandala to live in the Palace, but this Nandala refused. She was proud of her independence and wanted to keep it. She told Rollo she would accept a position in his household, but that was not satisfactory to the Duke. He could not have the mother of his daughter working as a servant in his household. It would not be seemly, and would make Thadora's role very ambiguous. Eventually, not without some argument, Nandala agreed to live in a house provided by Rollo. He would provide a small income for her, too. This she was reluctant to accept at first until Thadora pointed out to her that she could hardly carry on working in her previous profession while living in the Duke's house. She also pointed out that Rollo owed her mother many years of back money for her, Thadora's, keep, and anyway, the Duke could afford it. Nandala reluctantly agreed to this, and so Rollo went to arrange for the purchase of a house in the affluent, merchant district. He also spoke to Daramissillo and told him to engage a reliable servant and cook for Nandala's house. He did not press any more servants on her, although he privately thought that she really should have at least one more girl and a butler. He knew she would be appalled. Perhaps in the future?

With the discussions finished, the adoption and acknowledgement of Thadora was begun.Nandala remained at the Palace until her own home was ready.

Chapter 24
Yssa

Carthinal decided to stay in the Mage Tower while he remained in Hambara. His plans from here on were non-existent. He supposed he would have to go to Bluehaven soon to look through Mabryl's belongings and sort out whatever needed doing, but after that, he had no idea what he was going to do. He decided he may as well remain here in Hambara for a while until he had decided. Mabryl's affairs had waited for over four months now, so a bit longer would not do any harm. Besides, he was looking forward to seeing Yssa again.

With these thoughts, he walked the short distance from the Palace to the Tower. He was dressed in clean, new robes, his others having been thrown away as too dirty to even consider washing. He had a good dinner the night before at the Palace and had slept in a warm, soft bed in a luxurious room, all to himself. The others were assigned rooms, too, in the east wing of the house. Each of them, except for Davrael and Kimi of course, had their own room and took advantage of the luxury of hot baths and clean clothes.

Carthinal wondered if Fero had slept alone, or if Randa had found her way to his bed, then he shook himself. It was none of his business what the pair did, especially now that their mission had been successfully completed, but a faint worry still nagged at him. They were both his friends, and he could see disaster ahead for them. Fero was a man of the wilderness who hated to be bottled up in towns, while Randa was a sophisticated heiress, well used to living in the cities of the country, and mixing with nobility and royalty. She was also the heir to the dukedom and would one day be running it. He sighed again as he approached the gates of the Tower.

As he entered the Tower, the feeling of disorientation he always felt when entering the building again beset him. Surely it was bigger inside? How it had been accomplished was beyond him. One day he would pace it out to find out for sure. He decided to go up to see if Yssa were in her rooms first of all, and then see if he could find Tomac and Emmienne, who had been his companions as apprentices of Mabryl. He was striding over to the staircase when he was hailed from across the Hall.

'Carthinal. It is you! We thought that you were dead. You've been gone four months, Yssa says.'

Carthinal turned and saw a young man dressed in tawny robes, the like of which he had so recently worn. He had a mop of unruly, black hair and mischievous, brown eyes. A broad grin appeared on Carthinal's face.

'Tomac! I was going to come to try to find you as soon as I'd seen Yssa. How do you like it here?'

'It's wonderful, Carthinal,' replied the boy, his eyes shining. 'You look thin, though. And that red doesn't suit you, you know. Clashes something shocking with your hair. You'd best hurry and get through your probation so you can wear a different colour.'

Carthinal gave a mock groan and threw a playful punch at the boy.

'Not you, too!' he said. 'So many people tell me that. I may refuse promotion just to spite them all, and you, too.'

Tomac grinned. 'Well, it's true!' the boy responded. 'I'm working in the library today with Emm. She'll be glad to see you back. I reckon she fancies you, Carthinal. Been really worried since you disappeared. Anyway, Yssa's in her room, I think. At least, she was a few minutes ago when she sent me here to find out about some new spells she wants me to learn. See you later.'

The boy turned and continued in the direction of the library, whistling as he went, while Carthinal made his way over to the stairs leading to the rooms Yssa inhabited. He took them at a bound and soon found himself at the door to Yssa's suite of rooms. He knocked on the door.

'Come in!' came Yssa's voice, and Carthinal opened the door. As soon as she looked up, from her work at her table by the window, Yssa got to her feet and embraced Carthinal, elven style with two kisses on either cheek.

'Carthinal,' she said, smiling. 'We all thought you'd been killed, and the rest of your group, too. What took you so long?'

'Oh, this and that,' replied the half-elf, looking at her.

'You look thin,' Yssa said. 'You need feeding up. Where are you staying?'

'I stayed last night at the Palace, but I thought I may stay here in the Tower for a while until I decide what to do from now on.'

'Were you successful in your quest?' She filled a kettle and put it on the hearth to make tea.

'We found the Sword and brought it back, yes.'

'But?' Yssa read Carthinal's tone.

'It seems the Sword chooses its wielder and will allow no one else to touch it.' He paused. 'The wielder is Randa.'

Yssa looked up from her task.

'No! Rollo won't take kindly to that. What's going to happen?'

Carthinal shrugged. 'Not my problem,' he said. 'I did what I was asked to do and brought it back. It's up to others now to decide how it's to be used.'

'But Rollo…he won't allow Randa to be exposed to danger. She can't wield the Sword in anger. Anyway, what was Randa doing there?'

Yssa made tea, and they sat drinking it while the morning passed and Carthinal told the whole story.

At the end, Yssa said thoughtfully, 'So, Randa is going to have to go into battle if that's what's needed, is she? I hope it doesn't come to that, but there seems to be a lot of activity amongst the races like orcs, trolls and hobgoblins. And, what were those wolves you told me about? Super-intelligent, dire wolves you said. I don't like it, Carthinal. There's trouble coming.'

Emmienne came into the room just then and greeted Carthinal. Tomac had told her he was back, and she had come straight up as soon as she heard. Carthinal was pleased to see the girl. Emmienne was seventeen and was nearing her Tests.

'Emm,' Carthinal greeted her warmly, 'Good to see you again. I hope you like it here.'

'Like it? Oh, Carthinal, it's the best. The city is so exciting and being in the Tower with all these mages, well, it's something else!' She turned to Yssa. 'Are you coming down to the Dining Room for lunch or should I ask Tomac to bring you something up here?'

Yssa's face clouded for a second, then she said, 'Ask Tomac, please, and then leave us. I've something to discuss with Carthinal.'

The girl turned and left the room. Carthinal turned to Yssa with a quizzical look, but she was busying herself with clearing a space on the table for them to eat. Carthinal watched her. She was a beautiful woman, but if he was not much mistaken, she had put on some weight since he left. Not much, but she seemed a little plumper. He supposed it was because she had been engrossed in her translations of the books of magic that he and Basalt had found in the secret room in the Palace, and had neglected to exercise to compensate for such a sedentary lifestyle.

Shortly, Tomac brought some lunch for them. Yssa tucked in with relish, eating more than Carthinal remembered her doing before. He was compelled to make a comment.

'Yssa, I know it's none of my business, but you seem to be getting quite plump. This sedentary lifestyle of translating old books of magic is not suiting you. You should take more exercise.'

To his surprise, Yssa looked embarrassed.

'That's the business I wanted to talk to you about, Carthinal,' she replied, looking away from him into the fire grate.

'What? You putting on weight, translating old books of magic, or you not taking enough exercise?' he teased.

She looked at him. 'I couldn't decide either when or how to tell you, Carthinal,' she said, turning to look at him again, 'but now seems to be the moment.'

The half-elf looked puzzled.

'Tell me what, Yssa?' he queried.

'Don't be angry, Carthinal,' she went on. 'It wasn't intentional, I assure you.'

'Yssa!' Carthinal said, 'Stop being obtuse. Tell me what it is.'

'I'm pregnant, Carthinal,' she blurted out. 'I'm not getting fat, at least not with overeating or lack of exercise. I'm carrying your child.'

Carthinal stared at her for several seconds, then he rose, and went over to the window. He did not speak but stood staring out over the grounds. Yssa remained where she was, head bowed, and her golden hair obscuring her features. Then, Carthinal turned and walked slowly over to her. He placed his finger under her chin and raised her head so she was looking at him.

'It takes two to create a child,' he said gently. 'If I'm angry with you, I must be equally angry with myself, but I can't bring myself to regret our liaison. It was good, Yssa. If a child is the result, then so be it, but it's as much my child as yours, and I'm as much to blame.'

'I was responsible for taking the herbs to ensure no pregnancy ensued,' she responded. 'I was so excited about the books you and Basalt found that I completely forgot.'

'When will the child be born?' was the next question.

'Sometime in the second sixday of Pardar,' Yssa replied. 'That's four months from now.'

'And you told me afterwards there were no strings attached to our relationship,' he responded.

He remained kneeling looking into her face. What he was seeing was not golden hair and blue eyes, but black hair and grey eyes, but he dared not let that show in his face. Asphodel was now totally beyond his reach. But she was even before this happened, he told himself.

'That was true then, and it's true now,' lied Yssa. 'No strings I said, and no strings I meant. I don't go back on what I said. I only told you of this because I felt it would be unfair if you didn't know. Rollo agreed with me, that he would like to know if a woman were pregnant with his child.'

'Ironic, that,' muttered Carthinal to himself.

'What was that?' Yssa asked.

'The Duke saying he'd like to know if a woman was having his child. Our little thief, Thadora, who accompanied us on our quest, turns out to be Duke Rollo's daughter, conceived by one of Madame Dopari's girls. He only found out because she looks so like his grandmother. Does this mean the Duke knows, then?'

'That I'm pregnant? Yes. That you're the father? No.'

'I suppose everyone in the Tower knows about the pregnancy at least. It'll be hard to conceal it from now on anyway.'

'For the moment, only Magister Robiam knows. I felt I had to tell him as the Chief Mage, and I told Emmienne and Tomac, too, but no one knows it's your child, and need never know, either.'

'What happens now then?'

'I get larger for the next four months, and then the child is born. I'll stay here in the Tower and continue with my work afterwards. There's always someone free to look after a child. I may go to my parents for the last days of my pregnancy and have the baby there. I haven't decided. Mother will be shocked at first, but she'll come round when she sees her first grandchild.'

Carthinal went back to the window and was silent for a time, watching the sun shining on the water of the Blue Lake in the distance.

He suddenly turned. 'Yssa, I was an orphan, and I know something of what life is like for a child without two loving parents. I can't pretend this isn't a shock to me, but I also know what shame there is in elf society to bearing a child whilst unmarried. You will be looked down on by all and sundry. That your parents are standing by you is wonderful. I don't want my child to be born a bastard and have that burden to bear all through its life.' He took a deep breath. 'Yssa. I'm asking you to marry me and legitimise our child.'

Yssa stared at the man by the window. The sun was too bright and she could not make out his features. Knowing Carthinal, he had probably worked that out before he spoke. At his words, her stomach turned over. Against all the odds, and against her better judgement she had fallen for this man. She had no illusions that the feeling was mutual, though. That he liked her, she was sure, and he respected her as a mage. The friendship between them was good. Would marriage spoil that? That he found her physically attractive, too, was without question; but what if sometime in the future he fell in love with someone else? To elves marriage was sacred. It was blessed by Bramara, goddess of marriage and the family, and was generally considered indissoluble. On the other hand, the child would undoubtedly suffer in the Elven Homelands and from elves here in Grosmer if it were born out of wedlock. She did not know what to say, so she remained silent. After a few minutes, Carthinal spoke again.

'Yssa?' he walked over to her and sat down beside her. 'Yssa?'

He lifted her head again. Tears were coursing down her cheeks. He gently wiped them away with his thumb.

'Yssa. Please don't cry. My offer was made genuinely, not as a rash thought. Maybe, we are not in love, but, we are good friends and,' here he smiled, 'you are a beautiful woman and the sex is good. Don't answer me right away if you want to think about it, but don't leave it too long. We've only got four months, remember.'

Yssa then made up her mind. Carthinal did not know of her love for him, and she did not want him to, either. It would only add another complication to an already complex situation.

She turned to the half-elf and replied, 'If you are absolutely sure you know what you are doing, Carthinal, then I accept, but first, what will happen if you fall in love with someone else after we're married?'

Carthinal looked into the distance, thinking of Asphodel. She was the only one he would ever love he knew, and she was far beyond him. He would never be able to marry her.

'I will not fall in love with anyone else in the future,' he replied honestly and bent to kiss Yssa, now his betrothed, on her lips.

Epilogue

Four sixdays later found the Wolves getting dressed in preparation for the wedding of Carthinal and Yssa. Tradition stated that both groom and bride have two attendants. Carthinal had asked Basalt and Fero to attend him, while Yssa had asked Randa and Thadora. She had not known the young thief before her adoption by Rollo but had since met her and liked her. She considered asking Emmienne, but decided that asking her apprentice was not a good idea, so had asked Thadora, as Rollo's other daughter. Thadora was thrilled at attending Yssa. She had never been to a proper wedding before and was most excited. In the Warren, formal marriage was a rare occurrence; most people just decided to make a home together if they were in love.

Yssa was staying at the Palace for the last few days before her wedding. Her parents arrived four days previously, and at Rollo's insistence agreed to stay in the Palace. He would not countenance them staying at an inn, even the Golden Dragon. Yssa's mother, Glissimillaria, was as beautiful as her daughter. She shared the golden hair and blue eyes with her. As is the case with elves, she looked as young as her daughter. Elves have a long life span and age very slowly. An elf is not considered old until well past 600 years, and there have been cases of elves living for 1,000 years, although these are few. Yssa's father was called Porishillarrisimar and was a handsome elf, with brown hair and grey eyes, which were crinkled at the corners with his constant smile.

Glissimillaria was less than pleased at her daughter's condition but was somewhat mollified that a wedding was to take place after all. That Carthinal was "half-human", as she put it, did not please her, but at least he was doing the honourable thing and marrying her daughter. She was not pleased either that her grandchild would not have "pure" blood, but have some human blood running in its veins. She was, however, prepared to make the best of things, and after a long talk with Carthinal, she was won over by his charm and charisma and from then on began talking of him with pride as her son-in-law.

The day before the wedding, Fero and Basalt stayed in the Tower. Carthinal had to get permission for these two non-mages to stay there, but Yssa had enough influence to persuade the council to allow it "just this once."

On the day of the wedding, Carthinal woke early. They were not due at the Temple of Bramara until five hours after dawn, but Carthinal woke with the sunrise. He rose and wandered outside into the gardens. Already, it was warm. In fact, it had been a rather, sultry night. The sun had just risen and the birds were singing their morning song. He wandered to the summerhouse. Here, in the cold of last winter, his child was conceived. He sat down on one of the benches and thought over the last year. One year ago, he was a carefree youth, getting excited about going to Hambara just before the New Year to take his Tests. Now, here he was, about to get married. His old friend and mentor was dead. He had new friends to whom he had pledged an oath. He had been captured, escaped and captured again. He had even had a brief foray into show business. He had talked to and travelled in the company of a dragonet. He smiled at the thought of Muldee trying to drown them in the lake and Basalt's indignation. He counted amongst his friends a thief from the Warren (albeit now the acknowledged second daughter of the Duke) and a Duke's heir. The Duke, himself, had asked to be called Rollo and not Your Grace. Now, here he was, about to tie himself to a woman he did not love, although he was very fond of her, and to become a father. The woman he did love was out of his reach. Suddenly, he was aware of someone coming. He looked up. It was Basalt.

'There you are. Thought you'd got cold feet and run away,' said the dwarf.

'No, my friend. Just thinking about how my life has changed in the last twelve months.'

The dwarf sat down opposite Carthinal.

'It all changed with that flood, you know. We'd probably never have met if it weren't for that. Did you ever wonder if the gods had a hand in that? If we'd not met, then Wolf wouldn't exist and the conditions for retrieving the Sword couldn't have been met.'

'I wondered about that, but it was a bit harsh, wasn't it?' replied Carthinal. 'So many lost their lives, and others, their livelihood. Anyway, the gods don't directly interfere in the affairs of Vimar, or so we've been told.'

A clock in the town began to chime. It was the second hour.

'Come on, Carthinal. You must eat, then get ready to go to the Temple. It wouldn't do for you to arrive late.'

The pair then made their way to the Tower and preparations for the wedding.

In the Palace, all was chaos. The two Bridal Attendants were busy dressing and trying to organise Yssa at the same time. The Duke was panicking about the carriages, while Yssa's mother was driving everyone mad trying to help to get her daughter prepared. Eventually, her husband came and took her away, with a wink at Thadora, saying he was having some trouble with his necktie and would she please tie it for him.

Eventually, all was ready. Rollo and Glissimillaria climbed into the first carriage and set off for the Temple. With her mother out of the way, Yssa seemed calmer. Porishillarrisimar was waiting at the bottom of the great staircase when the second carriage that was to take him, his daughter and her attendants to the Temple. Yssa appeared at the top of the stairs and instinctively paused for effect. She began a slow walk down. Porishillarrisimar looked at his daughter and thought he would burst from pride. She was dressed in a silvery dress with a long train. Her arms were bare, but she was wearing a pair of long elbow-length gloves in the same silvery fabric. As she moved, the fabric of the dress seemed to change colour as it caught the light. Her golden hair was caught up in a spray of silver flowers and then flowed around her shoulders. She looked to be a gold and silver goddess. Behind her, holding up her train, were Randa and Thadora. Randa looked as beautiful as Yssa. She was wearing a gold dress with similar gloves and golden flowers in her hair. With her silvery hair, she looked like a negative image of the bride, all gold and silver. Thadora was more colourful. The gold and silver look was not possible for her with her red hair, so she had chosen a white dress with copper-coloured gloves and a copper-coloured sash. Her hair, which had grown quite long during their journeying, was tied back with a copper coloured ribbon. Yssa and Randa glided down the stairs, but Thadora had not yet managed to come to terms with the wearing of dresses. At least not negotiating stairs in them. She looked less than graceful, and just as she neared the bottom, she tripped, threatening to bring Randa down with her.

'Walk with smaller steps,' her new sister suggested as she put out a hand to catch her.

The four climbed into the carriage, pulled by four horses, two greys, and two golden palominos, to continue the gold and silver theme, and the carriage itself was decked with more gold and silver flowers. The ride to the Temple was not long, but it took them down streets lined with people who waved and cheered. They had heard that Randa had returned, and wished to welcome her back and that a wedding of one of the mages who was a friend of the Duke was to take place at the Palace. They were in the mood for celebration.

Eventually, the wedding party arrived at the Temple. The music was playing as they formed themselves for their entry. First, Yssa and her father, followed by Randa and Thadora holding up Yssa's train. There were gasps of wonder as the little procession made its way down the long aisle towards the altar where a dove would be sacrificed later in the ceremony to ensure Bramara's blessing of many children and a happy, family life ahead. There was Carthinal with Basalt and Fero. Yssa looked at her husband-to-be and thought how wonderful he looked. He was wearing his auburn hair tied back and his deep, blue eyes gazed at her with admiration as she walked slowly towards him on her father's arm. He was wearing a blue tunic that almost matched his eyes, over a white shirt and blue trousers. Fero was in his customary black, and Basalt had chosen to wear a bottle-green tunic and trousers and a white shirt.

By the time she had taken all this in, Yssa was at Carthinal's side. Her father handed her to the half-elf, with a whispered, 'Take care of her, son. She's our only child.'

Vows were exchanged and then the dove was sacrificed to the goddess and it was all over. Only then could the couple begin to look around them. They walked slowly back towards the large doors followed by Fero and Randa, then Thadora and Basalt smiling at the people gathered there. As well as Rollo and Yssa's parents, there were the rest of the Wolves. Carthinal smiled at Davrael, Kimi and Asphodel. Some of the mages were there, and to Carthinal's surprise, he saw Magister Robiam. Tomac was there, grinning all over his face and standing next to a slightly more subdued Emmienne. There were more faces Carthinal did not recognise, then to his surprise, he saw Sandron with two other young men and an older couple.

'*His parents and brothers I expect,*' he thought.

As they got through the door, there was a flurry of wings that revealed itself to be none other than Muldee who landed on Carthinal's shoulder saying, 'They wouldn't let me go in to see you get married. Sandron said I'd cause a disturbance. As if!'

'I take it this is Muldee,' said Yssa. She turned to the little creature perched now on Thadora's shoulder.

'I'm very pleased to meet you, Muldee. Will you accompany us to the Palace for something to eat?'

'She's got good manners, at least,' the dragonet observed. He said to Carthinal, 'I approve of her.'

The young mage turned, laughing.

'I'm so glad, Muldee. I don't know what I'd have done if you hadn't.'

'Is he being sarcastic?' asked Muldee to the air.

The wedding party left the Temple and only a few people were still waiting around by the temple. Basalt noticed Asphodel was still standing at the top of the steps of the Temple and he got out of the carriage he was sharing with Fero, Randa, and Thadora telling them to wait for a minute. He climbed the steps again towards the great doors and stopped by Asphodel. She was looking along the road in the direction the carriage carrying Carthinal and Yssa had gone.

'Don't upset yourself, lassie,' he said. He noticed two tears escape from her eyes.

'It's a mess, truly a mess. I know you love him, and I think he loves you, although he's hard to read when he wants to be, and for some reason, he doesn't want anyone to know. But he's honourable, whatever else he is, and he felt he had to do this. I know your dreams are shattered and your heart broken, but it will mend. Truly. There will be scars, but you will heal. Believe me, Asphodel, if I could do anything I would, but what's done is done and there's no going back.'

The elf looked at the dwarf.

'Thank you, Basalt, for being so kind, and understanding.' She dried her eyes on the handkerchief he gave her. 'Now let's go. We've a wedding feast to attend.

The End of Part 1
of
The Wolves of Vimar

Appendix 1
Time on Vimar

From early times, it was known that the planet Vimar took almost exactly three hundred and sixty days to travel around its sun, the people divided this into twelve months of thirty days each. This number, and the three hundred and sixty days in the year meant that the number six took on a significance, and so they further divided each month into five 'weeks' of six days each. This was called a 'sixday'.

The months were unrelated to moon phases as the planet has two moons, Lyndor and Ullin, each with a different cycle, but the study of the moon phases became important as they were believed to indicate something of the future, both for individuals and the world as a whole.

The year was deemed to begin at the Vernal Equinox when life was beginning to spring anew, and each of the twelve months was named after one of the gods of Vimar. (See Appendix 2) the first month of the year, Grilldar, was called after the god Grillon, god of nature. The months are as follows:

Spring
Grilldar	Grillon	Nature
Kassidar	Kassilla	All
Zoldar	Zol	Knowledge

Summer
Candar	Candello	Weather and Sea
Sylissdar	Sylissa	Life and Healing
Allandrindar	Allandrina	Deceit and Persuasion

Autumn
Pardar	Parador	Agriculture
Rothdar	Roth	Mining and Metalworking
Bardar	Barnat	War

Winter
Bramadar	Bramara	Marriage and the family
Majordar	Majora	Magic
Khaldar	Kalhera	Death and the Underworld

Days used to begin at dawn whatever the season or place in the world, but eventually it was seen fit to begin them at the time of dawn at the Vernal Equinox in all parts of the world, which was the equivalent of 6 am on Earth. Each day was about the same length as that of Earth, and because of the importance of the number six and its multiples, each day was divided, as on Earth, into twenty four hours and hours into sixty minutes. Seconds were not usually considered on the planet as timing to that accuracy was neither needed nor, for most people, possible. Thus the second hour of the day would be equivalent to 8 am on Earth. Noon on Earth corresponds to the sixth hour on Vimar etc.

Appendix 2
Religion on Vimar

The Gods

First there was nothing. The One saw in His mind a new Universe, so He created Kassilla to create and oversee this new universe. He then departed. So Kassilla created the universe and then Vimar for her to live on. It was a truly beautiful world with a great variety of land and water, but Kassilla was alone. So she created Zol to be her companion and consort. Between them, they made the race of Elves to serve them. The elves were very long-lived and so had low fertility, as new individuals were not required as replacements very often. Kassilla and Zol made them mortal so they would not think they were like the gods.

Kassilla then created four more gods to make a holy number six. She created Allandrina, Barnat, Roth and Grillon. Then Kassilla and Zol began to have children of their own, and so they created the dryads, nymphs and satyrs to help them to look after their world. Their children spread through the world and created and moulded things to their own liking. There were six in all—Bramara, Parador, Majora, Candello and the twins, Kalhera and Sylissa. Each took a particular thing as their own jurisdiction.

The elves, thought Barnat, the god of war, were becoming too proud, and so he created humans with much shorter lifespans.

Roth thought he would like to find and use the minerals under the mountains and so he created the dwarves as a race of small but tough and strong people to mine them. The gnomes evolved almost on their own from the dwarves, and no one is absolutely sure where the races such as trolls, hobgoblins and orcs came from. Some suspicion fell onto Zol as the god of neutrality who would have to try to redress the Balance, but some thought it maybe one of the gods who had embraced evil, such as Allandrina, Ellindran or Nello in order to have their own followers.

Allandrina the goddess of deceit, subverted some of the humans to her own devices, and even some dwarves and elves fell under her sway, aided by Barnat, and war entered the world.

Eventually, the gods found their world becoming more and more populated by the humans who bred quickly, so they created another world on a different plane of the universe and they withdrew from Vimar. Kassilla laid down that they should not interfere directly in the lives of the people on the planet. They could only suggest courses of action by indirect means such as dreams, and she stipulated that the balance between good and evil must be retained. So the gods watched the lives of the many peoples on Vimar. Sometimes Kassilla's rules were broken, and one god or another interfered directly, but these violations were few and far between.

The Priesthood

Each priesthood had its own colour, worn by all clerics of the god. Sashes of different colours denoted the different ranks of priests. Thus Asphodel begins by wearing a scarlet sash to denote that she is only a novice, but when she advances to Curate, she wears a lilac sash.

Each Church was ruled by one cleric, known as the Most High. His word was law, and all must obey his dictates, something that Asphodel found difficult on occasion. Below him were a number of different ranks. The individual temples in the larger cities were ruled by a person known as the Great Father or Great Mother, and they had absolute authority over the clerics in their jurisdiction. In the smaller towns, the highest ranked cleric was considered to be in charge and was called 'father' or 'mother', regardless of their rank. Mother Caldo in Bluehaven was a case in point. She was a Deacon, but as the highest-ranking cleric was called Mother Caldo.

The Most High was elected by his peers. That is, by Great Fathers and Great Mothers of his or her particular religion. The post was for life and could not be resigned no matter what. (This had led to the mysterious death of some Most Highs in the past.)

Advancement in the churches had to be vouchsafed by a higher-ranking cleric by that cleric overseeing the work of the candidate. A candidate was forbidden to work at a higher rank unless this procedure had been gone through. Thus Asphodel's concern that she would remain forever a curate due to her actions in the Temple.

When performing magic, clerics were granted their powers by their god. They prayed for the ability to channel the power to perform the task in hand, and it was or was not granted by the god. However, clerics needed to gain experience in handling the simpler tasks before the god would grant them the power to perform much more difficult miracles. Less experienced clerics could not handle the rigours of the higher magic, as it would have destroyed them until they were of sufficient experience to be able to channel the huge amounts of the god's essence required.

Appendix 3
Magic on Vimar

Mages used the mana that covered the world to perform their magic. Some people seemed to be able to absorb this arcane form of energy and use it to perform spells, and these were the people who became mages. However, unless tutored, this could be dangerous, as the results were unpredictable. Even the practitioners themselves may not know they were actually bending the mana to their will without training.

The mages built towers in several of the major towns of the world and these towers were where the young apprentices came to be tested, as Carthinal did, to make sure they were equipped to continue in their advancement. A Magister elected from the ranks of other magisters by the magisters themselves ruled each tower. The post was for a period of six years. Every year, there was a conference of the ruling Magisters from the towers.

Advancement after the apprentice tests was untested. Things were very informal in the Towers and by the time Carthinal took his tests, ranking of mages had long been abandoned as being too divisive and hierarchical and mages could wear any colour they wished once their probation was over. The only ranks that were kept were those of mage, arch-mage and magister. To end a mages probation before the year was up was the only thing that required any overseeing. All that entailed was for a full mage to tell the magister of the tower that he or she felt that the probationer had gained enough experience to become a full mage.

When spells were performed, a mage needed to shape the mana within him to the shape of the spell. This was done by visualising the outcome, and then, by means of words and gestures, force the mana to obey. Mages as they advance, can gather more mana within themselves, and even some very exceptional mages can gather it from the surroundings, especially in particular places, called nodes, where mana seemed to gather. It was not understood fully how or why mana should gather at particular points in the world, but one theory was that it flowed, something like rivers or winds, and these places were where one or more 'river' joined.

Mana could be intensified or collected by certain crystals. Quartz was very good at collecting mana and was often used to recharge magical items such as Carthinal's staff, which he inherited from Mabryl.

Young mages were very limited in their spell usage. They could gather insufficient mana to perform many or complex spells, and even if they could, the more difficult spells were beyond their learning. A bit like trying to teach a child calculus before it had mastered simple arithmetic.

Mages were knowledgeable about the moons and other planets too. They were the astronomers and astrologers of the planet. They paid particular attention to the phases and alignments of the moons, as they were considered to be particularly influential on the life of the planet. At birth, almost every child had his or her destiny read by a mage, and the positions and phases of the moons were considered to be most important.

The magic itself was divided into five disciplines. These were:

Energy. Spells of this kind controlled or summoned such things as fire, cold, electricity etc. They were among the first spells learned as they seemed to be easier than the others.

Mind. These spells worked on the mind of others and spells of charm or friendship were in this group, as well as all illusion spells and spells creating fear.

Physical. Physical spells worked to bring alterations to the physical world. They include all spells of summoning.

Time. This group contains all spells of foretelling and scrying.

Spirit. Spirit spells include all spells that affect magic and all spells dealing with other planes of existence.

There was also thought to have been another discipline that had been lost in the Forbidding when the practice of magic was proscribed, but its existence had never been proved.

Appendix 4
Languages

The language spoken by most of the characters in this story is Grosmerian. However some of the characters met speak other languages. The neighbouring lands of Erian and Perimor have their own languages as have the Horselords over the Western Mountains. Fero speaks his own language of Beridonese, but since there is no one else to speak it to, it does not figure in this narrative.

The elves speak their own language. It is a very beautiful, liquid language with no harsh sounds and many sibilants. Few who are not of elven heritage can speak it. Pronunciation is as follows:

ll sounds as ly, like the Spanish ll.

r is slightly rolled and rr strongly rolled.

b is pronounced softly as is d and g.

f is always unvoiced.

o is always 'oh' and u always 'you'.

j and k do not exist in the language.

Diphthongs are always sounded as separate letters. E.g. 'io' is pronounced as 'ee-oh'.

Construction is similar to Latin, with the verb at the end of the sentence and adjectives and adverbs following the word they govern.

Nouns form the plural by adding 'er' and the female gender by adding 'i'.

e.g. tree   pressil(singular)   pressiller(plural)
elf(male)   Eldiss(singular)   Eldisser(plural)
elf(female) Eldissi(singular)   Eldissier(plural)

Verbs are regular, and there is only one conjugation.

Dwarvish is a much harsher language, and its construction is much more similar to English. Word order is similar to English, but adjectives generally follow the noun. Pronunciation is simple. All sounds are hard. Ch is pronounced as Welsh or German. K is very hard, and r is sounded at the back of the throat similar to French.

Definite articles do not exist. Indefinite article singular does not exist, only the plural, 'plo', meaning 'some'.

There are 3 conjugations of verbs.

Plurals are formed buy adding -ghi to nouns.

Gender is non-existent. Everything is masculine.

A bit about V.M.Sang

She was born in the north west of England in a town called Northwich, which is between Manchester and Chester.

She was educated at Northwich Grammar School for Girls, which was a selective school. It has now become a comprehensive school and takes in all ability levels and both sexes. From there she went to Elizabeth Gaskell College in Manchester to do teacher training where she studied Science as a main subject and Maths and English as subsidiary.

After finishing her training she taught in several places, beginning in Salford, near Manchester, then she taught in Lancashire, Hampshire (south of England) and Croydon (a London borough)

She is married with 2 children, a girl and a boy, and 3 grandchildren, 2 boys and a girl. She likes to spend time with them as they are great fun. Her other interests are a variety of crafts (cross-stitch, card making, tatting, crochet, knitting etc) and painting as well as writing. She also enjoys gardening and walking, cycling and kayaking.

She is now retired from teaching and lives in East Sussex with her husband.

Find out more about The Wolves of Vimar and V.M.Sang by visiting her website
http://vmsang.moonfruit.com/
or her blog
http://aspholessaria.blogspot.co.uk/
or
http://aspholessaria.wordpress.com/.

I would be very grateful if you could take the time to post a review of *The Wolf Pack*. It does not need to be a long essay, just what you liked or did not like about the book. Thank you.

Reviews are very important for authors and readers alike as they help the readers to discover new writers and books they too might like.

Lightning Source UK Ltd.
Milton Keynes UK
UKHW021925091120
373110UK00003B/67